DAWN

DEAN MCLAUGHLIN

FIVE STAR

An imprint of Thomson Gale, a part of The Thomson Corporation

Detroit • New York • San Francisco • New Haven, Conn. • Waterville, Maine • London

LIBRARY OF CONGRESS CATALOGING-IN-PUBLICATION DATA

McLaughlin, Dean, 1931–
   Dawn / by Dean McLaughlin. — 1st ed.
     p. cm.
   ISBN 1-59414-350-1 (alk. paper)
   I. Title.
PS3563.A31794D39 2006
813'.6—dc22   2006023361

U.S. Hardcover:
ISBN 13: 978-1-59414-350-2
ISBN 10: 1-59414-350-1

First Edition. First Printing: December 2006.

Published in 2006 in conjunction with Tekno Books and Ed Gorman.

Printed in the United States of America on permanent paper
10 9 8 7 6 5 4 3 2 1

COPYRIGHTS AND ACKNOWLEDGMENTS

For

Mikolaj Kopernik	Ralph Waldo Emerson
Galileo Galilei	John W. Campbell
Johannes Kepler	Isaac Asimov
Isaac Newton	Howard DeVore

—who pointed the way.

AUTHOR'S NOTE

This is a work of fiction. With the exception of Isak, a variant of Isaac Asimov's name for which he generously gave permission, the names of all the characters within are my invention. Should any resemble the name of a real person, it's pure accident and without intent on my part. Similarly, no character, Isak included, is meant to represent any real person, living or dead. Any resemblance will exist only in the mind of someone with a more powerful imagination than my own.

—DMcL

A man of antiquity sailing a boat, quite content and enjoying the ingenious comfort of the contrivance. The ancients represent the scene accordingly. And now: What a modern man experiences as he walks across the deck of a steamer: 1. his own movement, 2. the movement of the ship which may be in the opposite direction, 3. the direction and velocity of the current, 4. the rotation of the earth, 5. its orbit, 6. the orbits of the moons and the planets around it. Result: an interplay of movements in the universe, at their center the "I" on the ship

—*Paul Klee*

"Would our gods desert us?"

Isak kept hands clasped behind him where only the Audience Chamber's deaf-mute doorkeepers could see how his fingers strained at each other. To the Council of Brothers he let himself give no sign of his unease. He'd spoken truth and only truth, he told himself; therefore he should fear nothing. These men—who of all who served the gods most wise—would surely know truth when it was told to them.

Yet he had seen them scowl as he spoke, this Council of Brothers, and also had seen one drop his doubled chin onto his paunch and doze, while another stared gap-mouthed and vacant at the high mullioned window across from him. Perhaps that one heard what Isak said, though he had never looked his way; but had those others? Did they understand how he had come to

11

his strange knowledge?

They were not as he'd imagined: ancient men, all of them, their faces jowled and seamed. The table at which they sat, six on a side, had once been black marble polished to a glossy sheen; now it was dull and scarred. The man nearest him on the right had crooked yellow teeth, the one on his left had none at all. At the far end, hands clasped over a grotesquely bloated belly, slouched Sedmon, Brother of All. Only a single curl of grey hair showed under the up-tilted brim of his plain priest's tricorn. He was too distant for expressions to be clear on that almost fleshless face, but Isak had seen the same wary look in the eyes of trapped voloo ao, frightened and in pain, they sought escape from a menace they did not comprehend.

Isak shifted his weight from one foot to the other.

"Well?" It was the same one who had spoken before, the one midway down the table on the left. A puckered scar traced a ragged signature above his eye. A dark gap showed where one of his fangteeth had been. Isak flinched as if stung. He'd hoped the question had been rhetorical.

He found his tongue. "I do not claim to know what the gods would do," he said, doing his best to keep the tremor out of his voice, "nor what they would not do. As you must know, I am only a scribe, not worth the honor of standing in your presence. But I come to you by referral of the hierophant in whose shrine I serve. I have told you my studies have given me knowledge that our world shall suffer a time of darkness. Knowing that, should I tell no man?"

"You claim to have no understanding of our gods," said Balchin, the Legate Priest who stood behind Sedmon's right shoulder. Above him, a sunburst had been incised and gilded in the grey, speckled granite of the wall. Like an eye, it seemed to watch. The priest's voice carried challenge. "Yet you say," he went on, "that all shall leave our sky. So! Your own tongue betrays your true belief."

The reference to his tongue gave Isak a quick chill. "No! That is not the way of it," he protested. "I plead you to understand. I say nothing of their purpose. I say only that if they do not break the pattern of their motions across our sky, within the limits of how I have come to understand that pattern, they will permit to happen this one thing."

Isak saw scowls and frowns. He saw two heads lean close together to exchange a muttered comment. One Brother lifted a hand to the base of his throat, to touch the torque of his office as if to be sure it was still there. The Legate Priest bent down to speak and then to listen to the Brother who sat by Sedmon's left hand. His eyes stayed on Isak as if watching the bones inside his flesh.

"This prophecy," A precise, insinuous voice from midway down the table; a purse-mouthed man whose tricorn with a red cockade was pushed back to expose a naked, scaly scalp on which blue veins traced twisted courses. "This prophecy—did it come in a dream? A vision? Did it come unbidden to your tongue?"

Asked with a different inflection, those questions might have been a sign of sympathy, an attempt to understand. But asked thus, in sarcastic challenge, it gave Isak the feeling he had somehow, all unknowing, done a terrible offense. Only knowing he had not kept Isak from retreating to the door, recanting all he'd said, and taking flight. But he had spoken truth, and he served the gods. Somewhere he found the strength to speak again.

"None of those, respected Brother. Given the knowledge with which I began, and with the wit to think about what will come as consequence, any man would foresee what I have foreseen. It is no more miraculous than arithmetic."

"No inspiration whatsoever?" Now it was pure disbelief.

"None, good Brother." He felt as if, with that admission, he had lost his last hope of convincing them. He swallowed; it did nothing to relax the clenched hurt in his throat. "Is it so terrible," he asked, "to seek a better understanding of the gods? Must it be only what comes unsought to our minds?"

"How else can we be sure it comes from our gods?" Balchin demanded. Stentorian, his voice filled the Audience Chamber like the stroke of a deep-throated bell. His jowls burned crimson.

"Can there be no other way of knowing?" Isak wondered.

Sedmon laid a hand flat on the table. It was all dry skin, grey bones. "It is we who ask questions, scribe."

Was that his error? "I am sorry, respected Brother," Isak said quickly. His lips felt numb. Did they not know truth when it was spoken? "I did not mean . . ."

Balchin drew himself to his full height. His body seemed to swell inside his vestment. The jeweled scapulum of his torque rose against his chest as if afloat on air. "What you meant means less than nothing," he said.

"Enough," Sedmon said. He lifted a hand. His voice had been soft, almost a whisper, but it brought instant stillness. He glanced around. "Dissent?"

"None." A Brother brushed at food stains on his vestment's brocade. Another scratched his armpit and turned grey brows to the table's head. "No reason I can think, to hear more such preposterous babble."

The one who had stared through the window while Isak explained his discoveries stirred himself. "Aye. Enough." With folded arms he slouched down. His torque was almost buried in the globe of fat under his jaw. His gaze went again to the realm of the gods.

Isak felt cold sweat trickle from under his arms. On either side of the Chamber, higher than the top of his head, open windows pierced the stone walls. Behind the Brother who had just spoken, one of the gods—it would be Blazing Alpher, Isak thought—cast his light on the floor, while Actinic Gamow, now standing high, shone on the sills of the western side. How could they watch, Isak wondered, and permit such things to happen?

Silent as ever, the gods did not explain.

"We thank you, scribe, for entertaining us with your strange . . ." Sedmon paused, then twisted the word. ". . . your prophecy. Go. Your hierophant waits." His eyes were set deep in his skull. Dark, tiny eyes. Lifting his fist, he opened it and with the open hand made a formal warding gesture. "Submit yourself to his guidance. Pray that our gods shall be merciful."

One of the doorkeepers came up behind and took Isak's arm.

"I give thanks to my Brothers," Isak said. His voice trembled and his knees were not steady. "For hearing me." With his free hand he touched his forehead above the left eye. The doorkeeper led him away.

It does not pay a prophet to be too specific.

—*L. Sprague de Camp*

The doorkeeper thrust Isak out into the access hall and, retreating back into the Audience Chamber, hurled the door shut with a force that sent thunder to the top of the Temple's tower and down to its foot. By then Artaneel had risen from the bench. His sandals whispered on the stones. Taller than Isak, he peered down at Isak's face with eyes that were not as good as they had been once. Nevertheless, they saw enough. With a grimace of distaste and a heavy sigh, but not a word, he led Isak away.

The stone stairs downward had been hollow-scalloped by millions of feet and great reaches of time. Small apertures gave illumination from outside, but much of the descent was in dim light. Several times Isak had to slow his pace and pick his way. Artaneel clung to his sleeve. When the stairway's spiral took it down within the Temple's body, only burnished metal reflectors that splashed pale light from higher up against the walls made it possible to see at all. He wondered how it would be when the darkness came. Like blindness, he thought with a catch in his breath, and he thought of the massive panic such a blindness, suddenly suffered by all, would cause. People had to be told it would happen, had to know it was a thing they need not fear. His mouth was dry as a desert stone.

The stairway came down into a cramped, barren gallery which gave entrance through a narrow doorway into the Temple's great hall. All the shutters were open and the hall was full of light and the gods' glory. Gold fittings gleamed. Jewels glittered. Fine carpets seemed to glow with inner flame. Isak found that he could breathe again.

There they had to pause while a troupe of pilgrims filed past into the hall, softly singing as they strode a hymn of honor to the gods. By their garb they had come a long way. Their capes and cross-gartered leggings were of a style Isak had not seen since his wanderings took him into the watershed of the East Sea.

Not many came from so far at this season, for it meant a crossing of the Middle Mountains before the storms ended, and the desert after the heat began. It meant also a similar ordeal for the return. Only great dedication or terrible need could have caused them to undertake such a journey. The skin of their faces had a too-smooth look, like hide stretched over the mouth of a drum. It told of privations along the way.

But now their faces wore expressions of pride. They had come to the Temple. One of them limped. Another hobbled on a crutch; his foot was withered and his leg oddly bent. An acolyte struck a gong and brasses brayed a fanfare. Their hymn rose exultant, filling the cavernous space. For a moment Isak watched as they advanced down the nave and hoped for their sake that the gods would give their mission more success than he himself had been allowed. His tongue tasted metal and dust. At last Artaneel touched his arm. Their way was open now.

They stepped out into the light of the gods. Isak looked skyward. There Blazing Alpher stood high in the east; Actinic Gamow, having passed his zenith point, was already descending to westward. All as he'd known they would be. More difficult to find was the Pale One, but at last he found her among the clouds that clustered low above the grey, dark, humpbacked shapes of the Defender Mountains. White like a cloud herself, only her perfect roundness and the faint stripes across her face gave her away.

Only when he was sure the gods were where he had expected did he look out across the square. It was a broad expanse of fitted stones where nothing grew except the Obelisk's tall spire: the Obelisk that was, so the priests claimed, the center of the world. In truth, Isak knew it was not, though if he were asked where it truly was he could not have said. That thing no man knew. Even from this distance and from this low angle, curved lines and marker spots of other-colored stones made reading how its shadows lay almost effortless to a knowing eye—its Alpher shadow moderately long and pointing northwest, its Gamow shadow at medium length and aimed aslant across the square, northeast toward the threshold of the Great East Road. Yes, exactly as they should with the Pale One newly aloft.

"As you expected?" Artaneel asked.

It brought him back. "The gods?" He nodded toward the Obelisk. "Yes," he said. "The Brothers . . . ?" His voice broke. It was like pain. "I do not understand them."

A breeze touched his tunic as they started down the steps. It was dry and tasted of sand. Through the braided rope of his sandals he felt the scatter of grit on the stone treads. It had been dry all summer. There was talk that the barley crop had failed except in fields near the river, and that other crops had yielded less than their normal abundance. Down in the city the merchants had begun to ask more for even the most plentiful foods. There was grumbling, and some were openly asking how the gods could permit it to happen. Isak, whose wanderings had taken him to places of far worse famine, and who had heard tales of still other places and times, had no answer for them. None he could trust. Possibly it was merely that it made no difference to the gods—a fearful thought; his mind cringed from it. But he could think of no more sophisticated reason.

He told himself it was his own deficiency; that the gods did what they did for reasons of their own, which men could not hope to understand. But that, too, left him dissatisfied. He let the question be asked. He said nothing.

"Did I not warn you, Isak?" his hierophant asked. "Did I not say they would be skeptical?"

The stones of the square were well laid, affording a level pavement to their feet. They set off toward where the Great Way entered, off-center, beside the massive stone bulk of the Archives. A file of petitioners in tradesmen's smocks, flanked by an amply robed priest and a bell-shaking acolyte, came toward them on an opposite course. Near the Obelisk another priest paced the stones. A gaggle of off-duty acolytes, their cloak-clasps loosed, drifted toward the gate on the square's western side; beyond the wall the tiled roof of their refectory burned under Alpher's strong light.

"I disbelieved it myself," Isak said, "when I saw how the paths would come together. And it is such a strange thing to happen. But they would not even think about it. They thought it was not possible. As if it could not happen if they did not believe."

"It is said they know our gods," Artaneel reminded him.

Isak trudged across the stones. Feet and time had worn them smooth. Where the tip of the Obelisk's Alpher shadow came down, a Guards' candidate lay face down, naked, arms out-sprawled while a mumbling, wall-eyed priest inflicted scars of honor under and between his shoulder blades with a black glass shard. Clutching the stones, flinching at each stroke of the cutting edge, still he uttered no sound. His back was a mass of graven flesh. Blood trickled on the stones. Isak's own back felt each gash as the priest inflicted it. Impassive, a file of Guards looked on.

Dumb, obedient to his hierophant's nudge, Isak detoured around. They passed through the shadow and he felt for a moment the relative coolness of its shade. Gamow's light, though, stayed on them. The priest who had been pacing near the Obelisk strolled off toward the looming facade of priests' apartments that bounded the square's east flank. Artaneel's sandals briskly slapped the stones as he walked.

"You did poorly," he said. "Isak, you did poorly."

"I know, respected hierophant," Isak said. "But should I not have tried to tell them?"

Another small procession emerged from the Great Way. Stout and sour-faced, a bridesmarket matron conducted her charges with a stern eye and frequent behests that they comport themselves more ladylike. The girls, in fine long skirts and shawls and lace caps on their heads, skipped along and babbled effervescently among themselves. Their maiden's chains clinked like tiny bells.

At sight of them, Isak's stride faltered. For them this was the most exciting time of their lives; within a few passings, their suitors would contest for them at the auctions, and they would have the delicate and careful pleasure of deciding which swain's bride-price they would accept. A happy time, Isak thought, for young girls, and for young men who had the wealth, the household, and the presence to hope their offers might be welcome. For himself, who now could hope for none of that . . .

"I had hoped they would be wise," Isak said. "They are said to be wise. They are said to know truth when it is told to them."

Artaneel said nothing. He stalked across the stones with his mouth compressed. He did not look in Isak's direction.

From the point where the Great Way entered the square, traffic diverged. Most, both priest and citizen, were going to the Temple, but some turned to enter the Archives and others toward the priests' apartments. One compact group, outfitted for travel, orox-mounted and leading bulky-laden drome, aimed directly for the corner of the Temple where the West Road began. Almost without knowing, Isak gave them the wayfarer's sign. They returned it. He felt a touch of envy for them; even the road could be thought of as one's own place—a place with as much honor as any other—for those who journeyed endlessly. Their world, though, had no place for a scribe. Looking back over his shoulder, Isak watched them go.

Artaneel had to nudge him, had to break the thread of his thoughts and turn him to the path of the Great Way. It extended before them, straight and broad and—each fifty paces—watched by statues. Tricorned priests, most of them, facing each other across the pavement. Seated, most of them, with lens and mirror in hand or in their laps; a few stood in postures of succor, beneficence, or instruction. They seemed to guard the high walls at their backs; walls beyond which nothing could be seen but an occasional frond or slope of roof-tile. As if it was a different world on the other side; but only the highest priests would know the truth of that. Isak wondered, not for the first time, what truth was. Somewhere, he thought he heard a girl's pure laugh.

"Did you think they would reward you?" Artaneel asked. His voice stung.

"I had hoped at least they would honor me," Isak said. He still couldn't understand. He had brought them a foretelling of terrible importance, yet they had not welcomed it. Was it possible they did not welcome truth?

The Great Way stretched on. They paced its length, Isak in his bewilderment, Artaneel in his chilly rage. At last they passed under the gateway arch; on either side Guards lounged, two on each side, swords in scabbard and pikes within easy reach. One gnawed a sausage. They watched the passersby with the dull neutrality of idle men.

From the plaza outside the gate they could see the city. The smoke of many fires filled the valley with haze and shadows. The river curved through the mass of crowded buildings like a silvered path for giants. Barges, sailcraft, and skiffs dotted its surface. Piers jutted like snaggled teeth. On either shore, warehouses, fitters' yards, livestock pens, and wagon docks squeezed side-by-side like voles at a desert seep, while farther from the river crack-like clefts of narrow streets twisted through the throng of tenements, shops, and the massive, hulking shapes of the guildhalls. It was said there were places down there that the light of the gods never touched; Isak thought it very likely. Only the awnings of market squares and the green of the public baths' garden gave color to the jumbled mass. Grey plumes of smoke trailed slowly windward. So many places. Each was someone's own.

"If they had given me honor, my skills would have been proved," Isak said. "I could achieve a place that was my own."

"Humph," Artaneel said.

Isak gave the city one more wistful gaze. Above the tenements, the villas of gentry—those of wealth or privilege, or both—clung to the slopes. Up from the valley floor they lifted, stairstep and terrace, irregular reach upon reach, in zigzag upward quest. Like aspiration. And on the far side's crest, glowering over all below from its narrow headland, the old dark castle whose ruined wall, deeply broached in a dozen places, dribbled its rubble down the face of the cliff below its footings. Citadel Lagash. Isak thought of shattered hope.

They did not linger. From the plaza two streets led down; one eastward, one west, each trailing across the face of the slope until turned back by the deep, empty void of a ravine. The westward one, the Avenue of the Acolytes, was the one less traveled, for it did not lead toward the city's central parts and was the sharper descent, but it was not as far that way to the Shrine of the Narrow Streets District. As hierophant, Artaneel had to be at his shrine in time for the observances of the 'Twinned Ones' rising, and for Gamow's set. Isak wanted to be there also, to mark those moments on his charts. In spite of disappointment, his research should go on. As soon as they were under the brow of the bluff, the villas began.

"When you came to me," Artaneel said, "I told you that to go with it to the Brothers would not be wise. You know as well as I the peril in which a prophet stands. You insisted."

"I thought they would want to know," Isak said. "I thought it was important they should know. And it was only a foretelling."

"And when they summoned you, I warned you they would see it as a prophecy. I offered you protection. Offered, even, to tell them it was all a mistake. Still you insisted."

"I thought, if I could explain to them, they would see that I spoke truth," Isak said. "Even if they hadn't before."

"If you thought that, you are a brash young fool. To say that our gods dance a pattern that is known and changeless implies things which are heretical. Your foretelling may be proved correct or wrong—I do not know—but I know this: the Brothers would not hear with open ears a prophecy attained by no more revelation than the plodding step-by-step by which you say it came. Events so radical should come with portents of commensurate power."

"But I told them truth," Isak protested.

"When you speak of our gods, it is the Brothers who decide what is truth," Artaneel said, and with a slash of his hand dismissed the argument that quivered on Isak's tongue. "I've done all I could to protect you. I've even let them know the foretellings you've produced for me have been uncommonly reliable. But I can do no more, and they will do what they will do. The only sign of hope I see is that they permitted you to leave their presence. Putative prophets have been known to enter their chamber and not be seen ever again. Feeding the eels, no doubt."

Now they walked between high walls again; gated walls on the street's uphill side, over which the roofs of villas could be glimpsed, while on the downhill side the walls were blank-faced bastions. The homes they guarded stood too low on the slope to be seen, and their street gates would be on the next level down. Filth littered the stones; there had been no rain for more than twenty passings. Insects were a squirming skin on the choicer bits.

Climbing toward them, a four-drome team strained against the weight of a wagon loaded high with wine casks. The ratchets were set on all six of its wheels. In arrhythmic spasms they whacked and clicked while the wheel rims scraped on stone and the dromes' paws scrabbled for purchase among the cobbles. Isak backed against a villa's wall to avoid the snapping jaws of the leftlead drome. Beside him, Artaneel did the same. The drover beat his goad against the wagon's side.

"Ho, good hierophant," he called, leaning down. "Already the leaves be full on the vines. How promises the vintage?"

Artaneel's jaw lifted. "You have asked at your shrine?"

The drover waved his goad. "Aye. And gave offering."

"Beyond your tithe?"

"Aye. Half again my tithe."

"Yet you must ask?"

"They have been known to mislead, good hierophant," said the drover. He touched his brow. "Seeing you come from the Temple, I had thought, perhaps . . ."

"From," Artaneel stressed. "Not of. As for the foretelling, you were told what our gods would have you know."

"You want to know if the wine will be good?" Isak asked. "That, and whether the harvest will be plentiful or slack, and when it will come. And what the storms will do."

"You expect more of our gods than they will give," Artaneel said.

"They will give some storms," Isak said. "I cannot say where they will fall, but there should be only a few."

"As few as the last growing time?" the drover asked.

"Possibly a few more," Isak said. "More like the time before that." Artaneel's hand clamped on his arm, but he paid no attention. "As for the season, it will soon turn cool. Rain will fall on the vineyards. The grapes will ripen slowly and the harvest will come late. I know you do not welcome this—" He could see it on the man's face. "—but I tell you truth. That is what the gods will send."

It was hard to look up at that man's scowl, that man with the goad in his hand. But he had spoken truth, unwelcome though it was. He should fear nothing.

"You be not a priest," the man said, narrowly peering. "How can you be saying what the gods will send?"

Artaneel's hand on his arm was urgent now, but he did not move. Nor heed. "I tell you what I know," Isak said. He nodded to his hierophant. "He has never known me to read them false."

The peering eyes turned to Artaneel.

"His foretellings go beyond the sanctions of the Temple," Artaneel said. "His methods do not conform to doctrine. But . . ." He paused, but honesty compelled him to go on. "Where I have had occasion to review his foretellings, I have discovered no fault."

The drover's glance returned to Isak. His face wore a new look. "A prophet?" he wondered, cautious, but with a touch of awe.

"No," Isak said. "They are only foretellings. I am not a prophet."

"And you have said enough," Artaneel said. "Come. Already we are late. You—" To the drover. "Go again to your shrine. Give offering again. Thank our gods for the knowledge they have given."

"Even though the shrine priests told otherwise?"

"They serve our gods," Artaneel said. "As do you and I, and—yes!—this boy. Gods whose signs and ways are often beyond understanding. Isak, come."

They edged past the wagon's big wheels while the drover shouted at his drome and applied his goad to the midbody haunch of the one nearest. The beasts snarled annoyance and pawed the stones. The wagon creaked, lurched, began again its jolting uphill progress. Isak cringed from the rear wheel as it moved past him.

"Should I have said nothing?" he asked as they continued on. "Clearly the knowledge had value for him."

"You should have left it for the priests of his shrine to decide what he should be told," Artaneel said. "They had their reasons."

"Their own reasons," Isak said "No one knows what reasons the gods have."

"It is not needed to know our gods' reasons, to serve them," Artaneel said.

"Do I not serve them also?" Isak wondered.

Artaneel glared but said nothing.

"It appeared to me," Isak said to his hierophant's surly quiet, "the priests of his shrine must have seen advantage for themselves in falsely telling him. As you must know, it is a thing that happens, and it is the only reason I can think of."

"Something about the wine," Artaneel said. "Very possibly. Nevertheless, by speaking you cast doubt on all the Temple. Gave weight to the most subversive whisperings, of which there are many. You would put in danger the entire structure of—"

"Should I permit to stand a thing that is not true?" Isak asked.

Artaneel uttered an exasperated snarl. "You are a puzzle to me, Isak. In some ways so perceptive. In others, an innocent boy."

Isak struggled to understand. "Because I thought the Brothers would be wise? Should I have thought otherwise?"

"Men have had their tongues split for asking such questions. Be warned."

"Do they fear the truth, that they are not?" Isak asked.

"Enough," Artaneel said. The firmness in his voice forbade another word. "Isak, it is only this: they are men not thinking of our gods in the way you have taken to think of them. As I took pains to warn you. Nor will they adopt your way of thinking, merely to accommodate you. To explain your prophecy—your foretelling, that is—in terms of your own way of thinking, not theirs, and expecting to convince them by that method is folly of the highest order."

"I could explain to them no other way, good hierophant. Should I have been less than truthful to the Council of Brothers?"

"You twist what I say," Artaneel snapped. "I say only, you expected too much of them."

"But if they were wise . . ." Isak began, but saw the look on his hierophant's face. "Have my foretellings ever led you false?"

"That has nothing to do with it," Artaneel said. "I must admit, I do not myself grasp how you come to know how the gods shall stand in our sky. Nor has it concerned me to know. Scribe's work. But now that I am caused to think on it, I see that I should have been more thoughtful. I should have realized that, to do what you were doing, you had to be dabbling at prophecy, regardless of what you said you were doing."

"But I am not a prophet," Isak said. "I am only a scribe who has come upon a method to anticipate how the gods will share our sky. Anyone, properly informed, could have thought of it and—knowing the method—anyone would come to the same findings as I. Should I claim mystery where there is none? Is it not enough of a marvel, merely to have that knowledge?"

A gate opened in the wall a few paces ahead of them. A woman in servant's smock and leggings bustled out. She glanced their way, but dumped her jar of slops on the cobbles without a pause and disappeared back inside. They barely missed being splashed. Wrinkling his nose, Artaneel stepped around the mess.

"It does not matter what you call yourself," he said. "The Brothers see it as prophecy. No—" He corrected himself. "They see it as an *attempt* at prophecy. Had you the wit to be facile in explaining to them, perhaps they would have believed. But you were not."

"When it happens, they will know I offered truthful guidance," Isak said. "It will be a frightening time for people if they have not been forewarned, but—" He shrugged, and scuffed the stones. "I have done what I could. And it shall pass, and nothing will be changed. I—" Slowly he had realized that, in his disappointment, he had been graceless to this man who, for all his scolding, had tried to shield him from harm. "I hope your efforts for me will not bring their displeasure on you."

Descending steeply, the street doubled back from the edge of a ravine to begin another traverse. The cobbles were almost like stair steps. Artaneel reached out. "Steady me, lad." Isak took his hand and helped him pick his way down. Beyond the turn, the way leveled. Here the villas were smaller. Flakes crumbled from the stone of the walls on either side. Artaneel took back his hand.

"Their displeasure will not touch me," he said. "I am expected to report all prophets that come to me. In their view, that is what I have done. From the beginning, the hazard has been only yours."

Mention of hazard turned Isak's thought inward again. He trudged on in silence. Here the cobbles were strewn with more garbage than among the higher villas. It was necessary to be careful where they set their feet.

"But they will wait until after the overtaking, won't they?" he said suddenly, speaking even as the thought came. "And then they would know."

"If they thought it possible your prophecy had a crumb of truth," Artaneel said. "Otherwise, why should they?"

"But in the *Annals of Prophecy*, every time there was doubt, that is how it was done."

Artaneel snorted. "Children's tales." The toe of his slipper sent a salt roast's rind skittering over the stones. "Is that your true belief, Isak? Truly?"

"Is it not true?"

"Once I believed it," Artaneel said. "Now . . . now I have come to suspect such tales are told to encourage a prophet to reveal himself." His hand sliced the air. "Have you thought? In all the *Annals*, there is no account of a prophet who was wrong."

"But I am not wrong," Isak said. "In all my studies I have not found one occasion when—"

He broke off at the scuffle of paws behind them—looked back in time to see an acolyte with flying cloak astride a piebald hund pelting down toward them. The beast's speed and near-ness magnified its apparent size; it seemed to fill the street. Thrusting Artaneel against the wall on the street's downslope side, Isak flattened himself alongside. On his shoulders he felt the breath of the beast's passing. When he looked again, he caught only a glimpse as steed and rider disappeared around the next switchback's turn. Flurries of scavenger bats burst skyward from the lower streets, marking their progress.

"They do not often show such haste," he said, still shaken.

Artaneel stepped away from the wall. "A fact you might wisely contemplate," he said. He found a clean stone with enough of an edge to scrape his sandals, removing the worst of the mess he'd stepped in while getting out of the hund's way. "We do not, of course, know the nature of his errand. But he came from the direction of the Temple, and now he is ahead of us in the direction we are going. Do you know of any other matter that presently occupies the attention of the Brothers?"

"There could be many things we have no knowledge of," Isak said. Unexpectedly, the hierophant had begun to walk again; Isak had to scramble to catch up. "Many things. Have we reason to believe his haste was in the service of the Brothers? It could be an entirely personal errand. Or some priest's."

"While he wears that crested cap?" Artaneel demanded. "And that hund wore Temple livery?"

"It has been known to happen," Isak said.

Artaneel's response was to stop and turn to face him. "And you would take that risk? Isak, though I may earn the Brothers' censure, for your welfare I would suggest you turn back—take some other course. Even . . . those travelers we passed might let you join them. Then you would be safe. Whereas—"

"But if I flee they would have reason to think I had doubt of my foretelling," Isak said. "Then, even when the darkness has come as I told them it would, they would not see my right to honor, nor the merit of my understanding of the gods."

Artaneel snorted. "Small benefit for you, if by then you are feeding the eels."

"Surely they would wait." Almost painfully, Isak wanted to believe.

"Gamble your life as you wish," Artaneel said. "I have given my advice."

"Have you less . . . less respect for them than I?" Isak wondered.

For a moment, the hierophant's face wore a closed, sullen look. Warily he looked around. They were almost alone on this part of the street and none of those who shared it were near. Nevertheless, when he spoke, it was with careful words.

"I have known them longer than you, Isak, and more closely. They are men like other men. Like all men, they have failings."

Less sure of himself than he wanted to be, Isak moved his weight from one foot to the other. But it was purposeless to stand there, going neither uphill nor down. He took a tentative step. Then another. Downhill.

For a distance they walked in silence, around one turn, down the length of the next traverse, and around the turn at its end. Through that silence Isak's discomfort grew. He had made the proper choice. He was sure of it. Yet still he felt doubts. As they descended, his doubts deepened.

"Do you think I have not been wise?" he ventured finally.

Here the street had widened and become more populous. Servants in household liveries came and went on their masters' errands. Merchants' wagons stacked with goods labored up the slope while attendant hawkers pounded blank-paneled gates, shouting their wares, or haggled at opened gates with those inside. A beggar with a dirty rag across his face felt along the wall crying alms, rattling his bowl. A few bareheaded acolytes strolled carelessly with the human tide. A gentleman's carriage passed them, city-bound, two matched-pace drome at its hitch and four footmen in crimson-trimmed black tunics ahead to clear a path. A curtained palanquin followed, borne by four stolid, barefooted porters who, with no choice in the matter, trod onward regardless of the filth that lay thick on the stones. Gorged bats hopped from under their feet, hopped back to feed when they had gone on.

"I am divided," Artaneel said. Isak hardly heard him above the noises of the crowd; had to walk close with his ear turned to hear at all. "You have served me usefully. Your foretellings have brought me stature in my service, and might have brought me more had I dared place greater reliance on them. Yet this prophecy of darkness has seemed from the beginning too preposterous for any clear thinking man to consider. No. In this, from the moment you spoke to me of it, I must say you have been terribly unwise."

"Should I have done . . . done nothing?" Isak asked. "Told no one? To know that such a thing will happen and not speak? Not to anyone? Could you, if it was you who had foreseen?"

Artaneel shook his head. "I do not know," he said. "I have foreseen no such happening. I do not believe it possible. You asked if you have been unwise, and I have told you. If no one believes it will happen, have you done any useful thing by speaking?"

"But the truth will come, and then they will know," Isak insisted. "It will happen. I promise it."

"And by then, if you persist in your unwisdom, the eels shall have eaten," Artaneel snapped. "I advised you and warned you. Now, do you see . . . ?" He pointed.

Far down the street, at the end where it turned back on itself, a squad of Guards toiled upward around the turn. Traffic parted around them as a stream might break around a stone.

"I would suggest you decide what you should do," Artaneel

31

said, "before the choice is taken from you."

"They might have nothing to do with me," Isak said. It felt unlikely, though.

"A risk you could take," Artaneel said.

They were midway along the length of the traverse. On either side, the walls blocked view of all but sky. On the uphill side, the arched gateways all were shut, the stout carved doors as blank as sightless eyes. Across the street, the walls were feature-less except for the scratched scrawls and crude drawings left by generation after generation of vandals. On both sides, ugly barbs capped the walls, unspoken warning to intruders.

Isak looked back the way they'd come. Around the turn another file of Guards advanced downslope at measured pace. Citizens dodged from their path. Gamow's light flashed from the tips of their pikestaffs. Their helmet crests were bobbing poufs of color, gold and green and indigo. Swords in scabbards bumped their thighs.

"They might have nothing to do with each other," Isak said, but even as he spoke he doubted. His glance went to Alpher, now almost at his highest, and Gamow, now significantly to the west. The Pale One, still low, was hidden by a shoulder of the bluff above. "The Guards at the Temple should be changing soon."

"If that were their mission, they would walk the Way of Priests," Artaneel said. Isak nodded. He had known that. But he didn't want to believe.

Again Isak searched his surroundings for escape. Both ends of the street were now sealed. The Guards advanced. The crowds, so thick only moments before, had suddenly vanished. He looked again at the walls, but they were all too high to climb and those serrate crests were like knives. There were places where the wall around one villa did not quite join with the wall around the next, but nowhere was the gap so much as a hand's span wide. He put a hand against a gate and pushed, but it held firm, barred from the other side.

He could do nothing but walk on, his hierophant beside him. He tested the next gate, but it yielded no more than the first. The gap between that villa's wall and the one beyond was wide enough to wedge his arm into, but no more.

The Guards from below continued upward. The ones from above continued down. As they came near, the ones from below spread out from their straggled file to form a line that blocked the street. Glancing back, Isak saw the ones from above doing the same. His last hope and his last doubt died.

The corporal in command of the squad coming up from the city leaned an ear to the priest who trotted at his elbow. The priest gesticulated and, between deep gasps for breath, talked animatedly. He pointed at Isak and, a moment later, pointed again. Isak knew him: Plomme—Old Plomme was how the acolytes at the Narrow Streets Shrine spoke of him—past middle-age and plump, rheumy-eyed and still hopeful for advancement despite ample evidence he lacked the competence even for the post he held, that of Artaneel's second deputy.

Isak pretended not to notice him. With the last few others in the trap he moved to slip through the line of Guards. Crossed pikes barred his way.

"Those two?" the corporal asked Old Plomme.

"What? Oh yes. Yes. Definitely." Plomme bowed affably. "Oh my, yes."

The corporal advanced, a thumb snubbed on his buckler's waist strap, a handsbreadth from the hilt of his sword. His glance fixed Isak, then Artaneel. "You will come with us," he said, firm as stone.

Artaneel spread his hands. "For what offense?"

"I did not ask," the corporal said. His eyes were like pebbles. "I never ask."

Artaneel turned to Plomme. "My Brother," he pleaded.

"Why, on yourself you have brought this thing," Plomme said. He doffed his tricorn, held it to his chest with both hands. He sounded astonished. "Had you remembered to serve our gods, as I . . ."

"But . . ."

"They say you have judged a prophet before he was judged," Plomme said. "Credulously, you listened."

"I?" Artaneel spoke appalled. "I?"

"I only repeat what has been said," Plomme said.

"You will come with us," the corporal said again.

Artaneel touched his throat, aghast. "I? I?" Still not able to believe. Then, "No-o-o-o!"

He flung himself against the corporal, sending him against his nearest man. As they staggered, Artaneel broke through the gap in the line and fled down the street, shawl fluttering behind him.

Isak saw a Guard turn, notch a throwing stick to his pike, take stance, and heave. The pike lanced through the air, a long hissing shaft, and struck between the hierophant's shoulder blades. Artaneel's stride faltered. His hands clutched the metal spearhead that had burst from his breast. His legs buckled. He sprawled headlong on the stones. A second pike clattered down beyond his outflung arm.

It was over between one eye-blink and the next. Isak felt a terrible silence. Down the street as far as he could see, people crowded against the walls; the street itself was empty. Artaneel lay convulsing, lost tricorn beside his hand, brow pillowed on a rotting melon husk. Red blood oozed on the stones.

Isak hesitated no longer. He wrenched the pike out of the hands of the nearest Guard, who had been making ready to hurl it. Holding it awkwardly, close below the tip, he jammed its butt into the man's face. Changing his grip as he ran, he ran along the line of Guards toward the wall across the street, knocking aside pike butts and spearheads with the shaft. As the men farther along dropped their pikes and reached for swords, he veered away. A thrown pike hissed beside his ear. As he neared the high wall, still gripping his pike near its tip, he turned its butt downward. The wall bore a badly done picture chipped into the plaster, probably obscene if he could have taken the time to look at it; also the scrawl, "Our priests and their gods, who be ever with us." A fragment of his mind wondered, some learned person?

As the pike's butt struck at the foot of the wall, he leaped. He hadn't done it since he was a boy, didn't know if he still had the knack. Still gripping the pike, he twisted his body upward as the pike's rigid shaft and his own momentum also swung him upward, upward toward the wall's saw-toothed crest. Up and over. Another thrown pike whisked past under him.

He hadn't known how far he'd fall. Until now it hadn't seemed important. Now he fell. It seemed to take a very long time.

He came down in a thorn bush. In a garden. A young woman rose from her loom with a startled cry. Thorns plucked at his tunic and leggings as he struggled out of the shrub. Some of the scratches on his wrists and ankles were deep enough to bleed. The woman fled to the house. Her upper body was bare; her belly, under the loose muslin skirt, was swollen with child. A pike's shaft stood before him, its point driven into the turf at his feet.

He grabbed the shaft, pulled it free, and turned to look back at the wall. It was twice as high on this side. Had he known he'd fall so far, he'd never have dared. Looking up, he saw a Guard, balance momentarily on the wall's narrow top, straddling the barb between his feet. The Guard raised his sword and, with an animal yell, leaped.

Without thought, Isak raised the pike's point to defend himself. It was enough. The point entered the Guard's body under the edge of his buckler, burst out behind his shoulder. His yell became a strangled, shuddering gasp. He slid down the shaft like a bead on a string. Isak's grip was knocked aside. The Guard's sword clanked on the fountain's rim. He fell to the turf and writhed, blood bursting out around the shaft, legs jerking mindlessly, teeth bared in a grimace of ultimate pain. Isak retrieved the pike. Blood smeared his hands. Standing over his kill, he looked up.

The head and shoulders of another Guard showed above the barbs. Black brows under a tarnished, dented helm; edge of a dirty sweatband glimpsed between. For a long, still moment, Isak looked up into those eyes.

Then the Guard turned his head and shouted something to men out of sight on his side of the wall. His shoulders moved in a vigorous go-around motion. He dropped out of sight.

Isak whirled. He was alone in the garden with the dozen-colored flowers and the thorn bushes, the quietly spouting fountain, the now-abandoned loom. And, at his feet, the dead Guard. He dropped the pike and picked up the sword. The Guards would be coming around to the gate. He had to get out to the street and away before they reached it.

A gateless doorway led into the house. It was the only way. Sword in hand, Isak trotted around the fountain and along the flagstone walk. The woman had gone that way, but he'd seen no one else. And, though he knew almost nothing of how it should be used, a sword was in his hand. Three steps ran up from the walk to the portico; he cleared them in a stride. Two more took him within.

It was a kitchen. A fire-blackened oven squatted in the farthest corner like a watch beast's hutch. Above an ash-strewn hearth a black pot hung at the end of a chain. Knife-scored, a cut of heart-meat lay on the stoneboard to drain. Ahead of him another doorway led deeper inside.

He stepped through. It was a larger room, opening out on both sides of the doorway. Long, narrow openings high under the eaves let in the gods' light, and more came through the doorway beyond, through which Isak glimpsed a colonnade, an atrium lush with ferns, and a pool. But it was a soft light, there in that room, and for a moment while his eyes adjusted, he was half-blind. He looked to one side—saw the outlines of a leather couch, a low table, an open-fronted cabinet with jars on its shelves. On the wall, recognizable even in its sheath and in spite of the poor light, the graceful curve of a Tokku sword; his glance flashed over it, but there could be no mistake. He knew what it was. He stopped as if his feet were noosed in a trap. A Tokku sword in some man's house? An ordinary house? What sort of household could this be?

For an instant he was tempted to take it in place of the sword he held; but it was a treasure; probably useless as a weapon; and no time to waste.

He began to turn the other way—saw movement from the side of his eyes—turned more quickly then, raising his sword, and saw the woman, saw her arm come down and something white in her hand. Something hard struck the side of his head. Light exploded in his eyes. After that, for a long time, nothing.

On a clear starry night near the beginning of the survey we all lay wrapped in our blankets gazing at the sky. The men, a little distance from me, were arguing and eventually appealed to me to arbitrate. Three of them contended that our journey across the lake from Kalokol, a distance of twenty-four miles, had brought us significantly closer to the edge of the earth, while the fourth maintained that it was still a long way off.

—Alistair Graham

He woke to dim light, silence, and a head full of sharp pain. He moved and discovered the hard, uneven surface under him. His hand found the lump above his ear and a sore spot that hurt like a flame when he touched its stickiness. He tried to rise. A hand pushed him down.

"Mind y'r head, lad, else ye'll klonk it again."

He opened his eyes. It had been good advice. So close he could reach up and touch them, thick rafters of old wood supported a ceiling of stone slabs. He turned his head, seeking the source of the light and the voice. A grey-bearded man in servant's tunic sat beside a stinking oil lamp. His head almost touched one of the rafter beams.

"I'd suggest ye lie quiet, lad, and—if ye must—talk soft," the man said. "Ye'll notice ye be not trussed. 'Twas the young mistress' thought ye'd not mind these accommodations overmuch, considering the Guards be seeking to have conversation with ye, they in unfriendly mood. Aye, and besides, ye with a Guard's blood on thy shirt."

It was more information than Isak could make sense of; his head hurt even more than he'd first thought. He put a hand to the sore spot again. "What . . . ?" It was as much of a question as he could put together.

"Aye," the old man said. He chuckled. "A gentle girl she be; but ye should know to knock upon the gate. 'Tis more polite. Bashed a fine pot, she did, and now—it be her way—speaks hope thy head shall have proved more durable."

He hesitated, and when he spoke again his tone had changed. " 'Twould gratify us all. She be having much sufficient sorrow for one small girl."

Again Isak tried to rise. He had to find out more. The old

man put a hand on his shoulder. "Patience, lad. Time enough when fewer Guards infest the neighborhood. Aye, and when thy head be less rattled. For the now, ye're safe, which is more than ye was. 'Til the master's settled his mind about ye—aye, and those he talks to—'tis better ye're told not much."

It didn't satisfy, but as a prisoner he couldn't demand to be told more. "At least," Isak said, "may I see where I am?"

The old man cocked his head, gestured permissively. "But mind the rafters."

Cautiously, Isak rose on an elbow. The lumpy surface under him, he found, was a pile of muslin-wrapped bundles stacked neatly against one wall. As for the chamber itself, it was narrow and only a stride or two longer than the length of his body. He'd seen acolytes' study cells that were bigger, and his booth at the Narrow Streets shrine had been almost as large. The lamp that gave their only light perched on a corner of a massive leather-strapped chest that blocked one end. The servant sat on a smaller chest in front of it. The rest of the opposite wall was clear and had been cut, apparently, from layered stone. So had the other walls, what he could see of them. Thick timbers which looked very old supported the roof beams. The floor was pounded earth.

Behind him, the chamber narrowed to the width of a man's shoulders and closed down to half a man's height. At the end of a short tunnel three stones, one large with two smaller resting on it, blocked the passage.

That told him where he was. Every villa had such a place: a secret vault where heirlooms and treasure could be hidden from pillagers, thieves, and tithe collectors. Some had several. It also confirmed what the old man had said; for his own reasons the villa's owner was keeping him safe. But also, it would seem, captive.

It was less than he wanted to know, but more than he'd

known. And it gave a thread of hope. He lay back on the improvised couch. "Could you put out the lamp?" he asked.

The servant started to move. A careful look came to his eyes. But then he grinned as understanding came. "Hurts thy eyes? I'll shield it for ye." Twisting around, he reached for the lamp.

"No," Isak said. "I want to know what it is like to have no light."

The careful look came back. "Ye daft? If it be seeing nought ye're wanting, 'tis enough to shut the eyes. Seek ye to evade even such of the gods as watches through a lamp's fire?"

"I'd like to know," Isak said. He couldn't explain it more clearly than that. "I don't think closing the eyes is exactly the same."

The servant snorted. "Huh! And why, now, should I satisfy ye?"

Isak hadn't thought about that. "I was hoping you might want to know, too."

"And why should I that?"

"It would be useful to know," Isak said. "A time is coming when none of the gods will give us their light. I think it might be worth knowing what to expect."

"The mistress klonked ye too hard, lad. Ye're daft. Daft as a minedigger."

"It's true. I know it," Isak insisted.

The servant chuckled. "Aye. And then the world shall be tipping up on edge and such of us as lack strong grip shall slide off."

The man was no more able to understand than the Brothers had been. Well, he should have expected no more. "It makes no difference if you don't believe," Isak said. "It will happen. And I would like to know what it will be like. That is why I have asked."

"It be a morbid curiosity ye indulge, lad."

"Perhaps," Isak admitted. "I have noticed many people are

not curious about our world. How is it possible not to be curious? I think I must be different from them." He shrugged. "I suppose they must think I am the one who is strange."

The old man touched a finger to the side of his nose. "Indeed, lad. All of that."

"Nevertheless," Isak said, "I hoped you might be curious."

"That I be not," the old man said. He leaned back, hands on knees. "But now, the young mistress has said ye be a guest, and in this house a guest's pleasure be indulged if it be not too exotic. Strange be what ye ask, but not a difficult thing to grant. And while we're blind ye'll not embarrass the house by such adventures as to wander off? 'Twould stand a blot against our hospitality, that, and perhaps attract some less than welcome notice from the Guards."

"If I am hidden from the Guards, why should I want to leave?" Isak asked.

"We've got thy honor?"

"More than my honor," Isak said. "I am in your debt."

A smile gleamed through the white beard. "Aye." He patted his belly. " 'Tis odd entertainment ye request, lad, but never be it said this house would disappoint a guest."

As he spoke, he reached behind him to pluck the lamp's wick from the lip of its vessel. He snubbed it on the floor between his sandals. For an instant a red spark persisted. Then it, too, died.

"Do it satisfy, lad?"

"I don't know," Isak said. It was strange, this darkness—a darkness such as only the buried dead might know. He closed his eyes and opened them again. It was as if he hadn't. Strange. He could hold a hand in front of his face. He could know it was there as surely as his tongue knew the location of his teeth, but his eyes saw nothing. Not so much as a shadow. Black wrapped in blackness.

"Ye been seen enough?"

"No," Isak said. "I want to think about this."

They'd be terrified, he thought, breathless. People would be terrified if a darkness such as this broke upon them without foreknowledge. Even knowing there was nothing strange about the black he was in, he could feel the desolation, the forsaken emptiness of being removed from the sight of the gods. He wanted to reach out, find them, call them back. He didn't know how. They were gone, gone beyond reach of his hand, beyond the farthest extreme his fingertip could strain to touch. But it wasn't real. He knew he could end it: he had only to speak and the old man would spark the lamp again. The darkness would go.

That made it possible to bear. Those frightened people would need to know: that the gods and the benevolence of their light would return; that the darkness would be for only a small breath of time.

He put out a hand. The thick wood beams that supported the ceiling were where they had been. The stone wall beside him was unchanged. The coarse-woven sacks and whatever they contained still formed the couch on which he lay. In the air he breathed, the taint of the snuffed lamp was a biting stench. His nostrils burned. His eyes stung. Though they did not see, they could still feel pain.

So the world existed even when the gods did not watch. He wondered if that meant the world existed independently of the gods or whether it meant only that they knew of it even when they did not watch and it continued to exist by that frail thread. He had no way to know which possibility was true. He wondered if . . .

"Now, lad?" the servant persisted. "Ye've been enough indulged. It be unnatural."

"I'd like to think a little more," Isak said. It wasn't possible to grasp the whole experience in a moment. Unnatural? The servant had used the word, but it implied some things were natural and some were not. Did that not mean all possible things were natural?

"Ye tricked me, lad," the old man accused. "Blind as ye've made me, and me without a coal to spark our lamp, to gain again the gods' attention be outside my power."

"I hadn't thought of that," Isak said. "Really I hadn't." Was it possible there were things beyond the power of the gods?

"Now ye and I be trapped in this dark, deprived as mine diggers. Ye swear ye did not scheme it?"

"How could I know? You have no flint? No tinder? I never imagined it would be like this."

"Nor I, lad. Ye say a time like this be coming for the world?"

"It will be much like this," Isak said. The old man made a sound like a shudder. "It won't be for long," Isak said. "Less than he passing of a single god."

"Long enough, that be."

"But you'll know it's coming, now," Isak said. "You know it's nothing to fear."

"Still I dislike it, lad. It be unnatural."

That word again. "Can a thing that happens not be natural?" Isak asked. Could the gods intervene, he wondered, and by their powers cause an unnatural thing? Did the gods have such power?

Could . . . ?

"Tease me not with riddles, lad. What's natural be natural. Strange things as ye talk of, can such be natural?"

"I don't know," Isak said. "I'm wondering."

"I've no answers for ye, lad."

"I have none for myself," Isak said, and fell silent. It was hard to focus his thoughts. There were so many questions, and he could answer none of them.

For us like any other fugitive,
Like the numberless flowers that cannot number
And all the beasts that need not remember,
It is today in which we live.

—W. H. Auden

A long time passed. It seemed a long time. He grew accustomed to the dark—even found it, in a perverse way, restful. There were fewer distractions now that the old man was quiet. It let him think. The only troublesome part was that he couldn't write down all the questions that took shape in his thoughts. He would have to remember them.

How long he waited in that dark, sometimes talking with the old man, sometimes silent, he never afterwards found out. It ended with the scrape of stone on stone, the intrusion of faint light from the entranceway, and a woman's voice.

"Hobur? What happened to the lamp? Are you all right?"

"Aye," the old man said, rising. Hunched over to save his head from the ceiling beams, he approached the entrance. "To quench it he inveigled me, but we be not harmed."

"And our guest? Is he all right?"

The old man was now in the entrance, kneeling. His body blocked most of the light. "Aye. Wakeful," he said. "Seems to talk sense if ye think not too sharp on what he be saying. A strange one, be him."

"I didn't hurt him, did I?" Anxious.

That brought a chuckle. "Not the strangeness of an addled skull, lass. Be sure of that. More like . . ." He left it hanging for the space of a breath. Two breaths. "More like a boy knowing more than be good for him."

"Perhaps I should see him myself."

"It be not necessary."

"Hobur." Scolding. "I'll decide that. Here. Take the lamp." A pause. The quality of the light changed. Brightened. "Help me up, Hobur," she said. Then, complaining, "It didn't used to be this hard."

The lamp shifted from one position to another. It made odd shadows. " 'Tis thy affliction, lass. Patience. Soon be done with. Take my hand."

Light and shadow flashed wildly on the walls. Sounds of strained muscles given voice, a scuff of feet. "Mind thy head, lass. 'Tis not a place for walking tall."

They came into the chamber, Hobur leading with the lamp, the woman following. Both walked in a crouch, though the woman, being much the shorter, did not have to bend as much as the servant. It was the same woman, though now a shawl covered her breasts. She was small and she might have been slim but for the coming child that bloated her. And, seeing her now in less hasty circumstances, Isak saw that she was very young.

"May I look at your head?"

Isak raised up on an elbow, turning his head so she could see where she'd struck. "Hobur, I need the lamp."

Hobur brought it closer. Her fingers probed Isak's hair around the wound. "Who are you?"

"I was a scribe who served Artaneel, hierophant of the Narrow Streets Shrine," Isak said. He could not look at her as he spoke; she was still exploring his injuries. "Now . . . he's dead, now. My name is Isak."

"I'm Kalynn," she said. "And you are a guest in the house of Palovar." She touched the sore spot, so sore it made him suck his breath. "I didn't mean to hurt you," she said.

"Giving me to the Guards would have hurt more," Isak said. "I should thank you."

"We might yet do that," she said. She let him lie back. "You wear the Temple's trappings, but you fled the Guards. And killed one. They said you are a false prophet. Is that why they wanted you?"

"It's not a prophecy," Isak said. "I produced a foretelling that a time will come when no god's light will shine on us. I tried to bring it to the Brothers, but they would not believe. I think they sent the Guards to take me. They . . . while they were killing my hierophant, I escaped. You know the rest."

She frowned. "But always there is at least one god in our sky." she said. "How . . . ?"

"Actinic Gamow shall overtake the Pale One," Isak said. "He will pass behind her. She will block his light. No other god will stand in our sky when it happens. So, for a time, there will be darkness."

Her frown was still there. "Can such things happen?"

"It shall," Isak said.

"And that would be terrible?" she wondered. "I have stood in the light of the gods. It is no blessing. Would it matter if the gods do not watch for a while?"

"Do you know what darkness is?" Isak asked. "I—"

"Mistress! Do not listen to him," Hobur warned. "He will trick ye."

"Please," Isak said quickly. "I mean no deception. I was going to say only that darkness is—" He didn't have the words. "It is very strange, and I had thought the Brothers should know. But I think even they were made fearful by the thought of it. So . . . here I am, your captive instead of theirs. Perhaps I deceive myself, but I think I need to fear you less."

Grave-eyed, she studied him. Her face wore a blend of thoughts and feelings more difficult to read than an apprentice scribe's first scrawl—or a scholar scribe's most learned treatise.

"If it were only what I wanted, I could say you are safe with us," she said at last, carefully. "But it's not that simple. The Temple has no friends in this house. I think it's all right to tell you that much. But . . ." Her hands gestured emptily. "I don't know what we can do with you. I don't know what we should. My father will decide; he and his friends."

While she spoke, he had watched her face. What he noticed were the grey eyes, the curve of brows and rounded chin, the broad mouth that—smiling—would have glowed with warmth. Her hair was yellow. The lamp's light caught a few stray strands and turned them into threads of gold.

"We left your sword outside the gate," she said. "It fooled them. They thought you'd escaped down into the city. We let them look through the house. We even let them see our other vaults. We've got . . . well, never mind how many. And they cleaned up most of the mess you left, though I don't think we'll ever get all the blood off our fountain. We'll have to keep you hidden—they still might come back—but right now you're safe. At least until father decides what to do about you."

"Palovar," Isak said. "Is that your father's name?"

She nodded. "He's the one who will decide. I wish it wasn't all so complicated."

Her talk of decisions made him uneasy, but it was out of his hands. He lifted a hand, let it fall. What happened would happen. "I have no other place to go," he said.

"I hoped you wouldn't mind," she said. "It's just that we don't know what to do. You came so suddenly." She started to turn toward the entranceway. "We know almost nothing about you."

"But you're willing to learn?" he asked hopefully.

For a moment amusement transformed her face. As he'd thought, she was beautiful when she smiled. She touched his shoulder—just her fingertips, quickly, and away again. "You must be hungry. I'll send something down."

He hadn't thought of it. It was low in the priority of his concerns, but she was right. He knew as soon as she spoke. "I would like that," he said.

"We're terrible hosts. Really we are," she said.

"You didn't know I was coming," Isak said. He'd hoped to make her smile again, but she only made a face at him. Then she was gone.

In a constant environment the great majority of the individuals of a species are very precisely fitted to their habitat, and almost any change from the typical will be a disadvantage.

—*S. A. Barnett*

It was a long wait. Isak asked to have the lamp snuffed again, but Hobur refused with a growl. When the food came it was cold meat and warm apo cakes and a jar of wine. Enough for both of them, but Hobur ate only a little. He sat on the small chest with the big chest at his back. The lamp, perched on its corner of the big chest, burned brightly behind his ear. Indisposed to talk, he sat with his hands on his knees and looked straight ahead down the length of their chamber. Isak had little to do but think.

He asked for a waxboard and writing tools. Hobur leaned back, gazing at the ceiling beams. A scowl squeezed his brows. He handed Isak the board their meat had come on.

"Perhaps enough grease be there to serve thy need. It be as near to what ye ask as this house holds." Having spoken, he resumed his silence.

The board was dark and the grease a thin film on its grain-ribbed surface. Nibbling a fingernail to the proper edge, Isak made a few experimental scratches. Had it been a waxboard, and had he been in his own booth, he'd have handed it back to the apprentice. Here and now, though, it was an improvisation he could only make the best of. With the heel of his hand, he rubbed it smooth, paused to collect his thoughts, and began carefully to put down all he could remember of how it had been to be in darkness. More and more as he scratched the board, he realized what a strange experience it had been. He filled two columns with careful notation, began a third.

He was still at work, about to begin another column, when the grinding sound of stone on stone announced another visitor. Hobur rose, gave Isak a scowl that told him to stay where he was, and disappeared into the entranceway. More stones moved, voices sounded, then Hobur returned. Another man followed.

There was nothing subservient, though, in the way this man moved. Less tall than his servant, the newcomer was thick of body, heavy of limb. His hunched-over gait gave an emphasized view of the almost hairless top of his head and the gone-to-grey dark hair of the tonsure that rimmed it. He wore the doublet and breeks of a prosperous townsman, though nothing of it betrayed the nature of his trade. Isak felt the scrutiny of his eyes.

"My daughter tells an interesting tale," the man said. So this was Palovar, his host and gaoler. Isak waited.

"Unfortunately," Palovar went on, "she knows only part of it, and what she knows is not enough to make judgments on. So . . ." He planted himself on the chest Hobur had used. "How did you come here?"

Hobur had been hovering over the chest. He scuttled to a corner near the entranceway and crouched there.

"I think they would have killed me," Isak said. Not until he spoke did he realize it wasn't the way to begin—that it would make no sense to the man. He made the thumb-smudge gesture only scribes ever learned and only few others ever learned to recognize; rub it out and begin again. Palovar nodded as if seeing a surmise confirmed.

"I am a scribe," Isak began again, and told his story. It was long in the telling. As he talked, he watched the scowls and narrowing eyes and quirking corners of the mouth of the man he was telling it to. He saw the expressions of a man who didn't understand and was skeptical of what he was told. Time and again Isak paused in his narrative to explain one point or another. There was much that needed explaining. Sometimes he knew that he failed. "When I woke, my head was hurting," he concluded. "And your man was watching me."

"More to be sure you weren't seriously hurt than as a guard," said Palovar. He spoke absently, as if his thoughts had turned elsewhere. His thumb scratched his jawline through the greying beard. "You've told me much I must think about." Again, a long, paused silence. "My daughter is impulsive and frequently too kind for her own good. It might have been wiser to give you to the Guards, or let you escape to the street. Then we'd not be involved. Now, though . . ."

He got up slowly, careful of his head. "For now, you'll stay here. Not very gracious quarters, but the best we can offer under the circumstances. You understand, I suppose."

Isak didn't. Not entirely; only that Palovar was reserving final judgment of him. He waited. Again he felt the scrutiny of that man's eyes.

"Do you doubt me?" Isak asked. "You could go up on the street behind your garden. I think you would find some blood on the cobbles."

Palovar nodded absently. "I've seen the blood on my fountain, and my daughter saw that Guard die. That part I do not question. But now my house has given you protection when you might have been given to the Guards. That complicates matters. We must decide what to do with you."

"I did not ask her to hide me," Isak said. Anxiously he

gestured his innocence.

"So I understand," his host said with a wry chuckle, then added soberly, "That doesn't change your situation. Nor mine."

"You could let me go," Isak said. "Put me out in the street and you'd be done with me."

Again, a preoccupied nod. "Almost right. But if, then, the Guards took you, they might learn my house had hidden you."

"I would not tell them," Isak said. "I promise you I would not."

"Willingly, perhaps not. But they have been known to use . . . call it persuasion. No. Our choices are, first, we could keep you prisoner indefinitely. There would be risks in that, but that is one choice. Or we could accept that all you have told me is true and let you go, taking with you the knowledge that my house is not unfriendly to those who are themselves not friendly with the Temple, which we would prefer the Temple did not learn. Or we could . . ." Pause. ". . . dispose of you in a way that will not leave us exposed to those hazards."

"Kill me, you mean." He could speak of it with objective calm, as if it were a stranger they spoke of. But something inside him shrank to the size of a pebble.

"Or cut your tongue." Palovar looked thoughtful a moment. "But you're a scribe, you say, and you talk like one. Perhaps take off your writing hand also. And, yes, your eyes."

"The other fate would be more kind," Isak said quietly.

Palovar grimaced with distaste. "For now, you'll stay here," he said. "Until we decide."

Isak nodded, as if resigned to accept what he could not change. To himself he resolved to watch for opportunities, and take what chances might come. He'd be a fool to do anything less. He might as well have let the Guards take him.

"I have done my best to tell you only truth," he said.

"We'll investigate that," Palovar said. "Such as we're able.

Understand, it's not as if we want to do you harm." He started to turn away, but paused with a sudden thought. He turned back. "Even when you say the gods will abandon us?"

"It will happen," Isak said. "I know it as surely as one can be of anything in this world."

For answer he was given a dark scowl. "Although that is the most preposterous thing you've said?"

"Do you know with the same sureness it will not happen?" Isak asked. "Do you know a proof why it is not possible?"

The scowl did not change. "I've learned not to bicker with scholars. It is useless, and brings me not a whit closer to truth."

"I must admit there is wisdom in that," Isak said.

That brought a bark of laughter. "Common sense." Decisively, but mindful of his head, Palovar stood up. "I may come again. I may not." With a gesture he instructed Hobur to go ahead of him. In the entranceway's throat he paused.

"I can promise you nothing. The safety of myself and my household is not the only aspect of the matter we must think about. But I will say—my daughter wants you to know—the . . . ah, third choice I mentioned, though it would be the simplest and would assure us the greatest protection, is the one I find least attractive. My daughter feels . . . well, responsible for you. As if she has not had troubles enough! Aye, and much unhappiness. But should you try to escape . . ." His hand chopped down.

Wherever I found a living creature,
there I found the will to power.

—Friedrich Nietzsche

For a while after they left him he scratched at the board. Remarkable how much he could write about darkness. He considered snuffing the lamp again, to refresh his perceptions, but decided not. There'd been the problem when Hobur wanted to light it again. Meanwhile, he was finding the board a poor writing surface. The grease was uneven in thickness, and he had to take care how he held it, for even the lightest touch in the wrong place would obliterate what he'd written. It was easier to make corrections, though, than in wax; he'd have to remember that. Too soon, his notes filled the board.

He explored his little prison. The entrance tunnel was blocked at its far end by a clutch of large stones wedged together from the outside. They fitted tightly and the few chinks that remained were filled with mortar, giving the appearance, even from the inside, of a solid wall. The floor sloped gently downward away from the entrance. From behind the stacked chests at the other end, a drainage hole watched like a dark, hidden eye. The floor itself was pounded earth, scuffed and uneven. At one time it might have been oiled, but that would have been long ago. The chests were padlocked and wax-sealed, their seams caulked with bitumen. Knotted thongs secured the sacks and bundles, their ends also fixed in wax. Gaps at sack mouth and bundle edge gave glimpses of treasure within: polished wood medallions from the river's high reaches, nuggets of raw turquoise from the Mountains at the Edge of the World, faience coins from the Valley Between the Two Deserts, and a glimpse of rainbow opal which could only have come from a wasteland plateau near the shores of the South Ocean. Through the opening where a bundle's wrap didn't quite come together, he saw a tapestry woven of threads so fine they gleamed with a coppery sheen.

He was investigating the slabs of stone above the ceiling beams when Kalynn came again. Almost certainly, if there was to be a way out of this prison it would be upwards, for beyond doubt the vault was underground. One by one he was testing them, hoping to find one that could be shifted, however slightly, when he heard her take the first stone from the entranceway.

"Isak?" she called.

He crawled into the entranceway and helped her remove the rest of the stones. She was bringing more food, which surprised him because he hadn't thought so much time had passed. She handed up a plate of meat pastries, still warm from the oven, and a bowl of porridge so hot the earthen bowl burned his fingers through the folded cloth she'd wrapped around it. Also a small jar of wine. Behind her, as he took the dishes, he glimpsed a chamber not much different from the one he occupied. Yes, it made sense to conceal the entrance to a hiding place inside another hideaway. As he turned to take his food into his quarters, she set a foot on one of the stones and reached both hands up to him.

"Help me up," she said.

Wordless, he looked at her.

"I want to talk to you," she said. "While you're eating. And I'm supposed to take the dishes back. They're afraid you might try to use them to dig your way out. Do you mind if I watch you eat?"

He helped her up. She wasn't heavy, nor did she lack strength. Her pregnancy made her awkward. They bumped and tangled clumsily in the narrow opening. She laughed at their confusion.

She showed him how to hold the porridge bowl—just with the fingertips up close to the rim where it wasn't as warm, and with the cloth double-folded. She carried it, following him into the chamber. She took the armchair he'd contrived out of bundles, leaving the bowl beside the chest that had been Hobur's seat.

"I played here when I was little," she said. She leaned back against the wall. "Before my head bumped the ceiling. It was my favorite place."

Isak sat with the plate of cakes on his lap. "Did you ever have your lamp go out?"

She tipped her head back and closed her eyes. "A few times. The first time it frightened me. But there was always a little light coming from outside. I never closed myself in like you were. Hobur's still complaining about that. The gods always knew I was here. Sometimes I'd put it out on purpose."

The cakes were tough-crusted, soft and moist inside. The wine was plain. Her talk seemed to need no responses beyond an occasional nod to let her know he still heard. He ate and listened to her voice.

"I think father wants to believe you," she said. "It's just that he's afraid of being wrong. He could lose everything he has. They might kill him—might kill all of us. He's trying to find out if you're telling the truth. He's sent the servants out to ask questions. And some of his friends. All but Hobur. Oh, and Bellreo. He's our gatekeeper. Hobur's just outside the vault. He's being silly. He didn't want me to come in here. He's afraid you'll do something to dishonor me, which—" She glanced down at herself, her swollen body. "—under the circumstances, is sort of ridiculous. Do you really think the sky will turn black? Father says it's the most preposterous thing he ever heard."

It seemed to call for a reply; Isak swallowed the mouthful he was working on. "I have tried to speak only truth," he said. "It's not easy to be sure. But all our sky's light must come from the gods, for the color and strength of it changes according to the gods that are above us at the moment. And you must have seen how almost black it becomes when it is heavy with clouds. So I think if all the gods are gone from our sky, there will be no light. That would be blackness, would it not?"

"I don't know," Kalynn said. She appeared to consider the

question. "I haven't thought about such things. But it sounds so strange."

"It may never have happened before," Isak said. "It may never happen again. When I try to extend my calculations too far, the errors accumulate. They become too large and I can be sure of nothing. I would think it should have happened before; I would believe the conditions would repeat, but it would have been long ago, before records were kept, before we knew the gods, and no one remembers."

"Oh," she said, and was quiet a moment. "Hobur was right. You're strange. But interesting. And . . . and what I really wanted to say, I don't know what father's going to do about you, and maybe it's his friends—he doesn't tell me much about his friends—who'll decide what to do. But I don't want anything bad to happen because of something I've done." Her fingers twined around each other. "I don't want them to hurt you. I want you to know that."

It was her innocent sincerity that caught him. He wanted to tell her it would be all right, but he knew he could promise no such thing. "What happens, the gods will let happen," he said.

Easy words to speak, but the thought was growing in him that the gods did not care what happened. Not to him or any man. "I have been taught it is absurd to think because you played a role, you have a guilt for all that happens after. As well to say the river flows because it wants to fill the emptiness where you dipped a pot of water from it."

She tilted her head as if to listen to an inner voice. Her mouth shaped tentatively to speak, but Hobur's voice from the entranceway interrupted.

"Mistress! Someone pounds our gate!"

"Oh." Quickly she was on her feet. For an anxious moment, before he could utter a warning, Isak was afraid she would strike her head, but with an easy movement he could never analyze she avoided all the beams.

"I have to go," she said. "If it's the Guards and they want to search again, they'll know I'm in the house, and if they don't see me they'll want to search until they find me. And we don't . . ."

Isak's glance went to the food. He'd hardly started to eat, and he didn't know how long it would be before she came again. "Oh, go ahead and eat," she said. Her hand fluttered. "If we're going to keep you here, the least we can do is not let you starve. Do you think father will let me keep you? I never had a pet before."

"Mistress!" Hobur called urgently. With a backward, glance, she scuttled into the entranceway. Hobur's hands came in sight to help her down. Her face reappeared in the opening for just a moment before the stones chocked into place. "I still want to talk with you," she said. Then the way out was blocked again. The place seemed much emptier, more silent, with her gone.

If the Lord Almighty had consulted me before embarking upon creation, I should have recommended something simpler.
        —Alfonso X (of Castile and Leon) "The Wise"

He was still eating, though, when the stones were again taken out. Palovar was first to come through the entranceway. The two who followed could have been anyone, wrapped as they were in voluminous muslin robes which got in their way as they climbed into the opening and came, crouch-bodied, through the tunnel. The first one growled curses; the one behind him was silent. Across their faces they wore masking scarves. Also cowls over their heads like desert venturers. Isak had only a glimpse of their eyes.

"You will forgive the masks," Palovar said. "They do not wish you to know them, nor to recognize them later."

Isak nodded. It was a reasonable precaution. Presumably they were some of Palovar's mysterious friends.

The first of the newcomers paused where the entranceway widened, blocking the man behind him. He was the taller of the two. His eyes scanned around. "Where can we sit?" he asked. It was a voice that carried the tones of command.

Palovar moved quickly to pull down bundles from the pile against the wall. Isak rose to help, but was waved back. "Until we know more, you'll stay there."

"Father?" Kalynn spoke from behind the second masked man. "Would it be all right if I listen? I could just sit here and be quiet."

"The less she knows of our activities—" the tall one began. Her father lifted a bundle, paused, leaned back to ease its weight. He half-turned.

"Some she knows," he said. "She's known from the beginning. Do you think—" His voice took a sarcastic tone. "—you think she has a cause to love the priests?"

"Women have been known to be strange in such matters," the tall one said.

"Well, I don't," Kalynn said. "I didn't before, and I certainly haven't had any reason to change."

"More to the point," Palovar said, "we're not here to talk of what we've done or hope to do. We're here because you want to question this fellow yourselves. Do you plan to tell him more than my daughter has already known?"

"Please," Kalynn said. "It's only that he tells of such a strange thing. I want to hear how he explains it to you. Eb—"

"No names!" the tall man thundered.

She swallowed the rest of the name, corrected herself. "Your man has the learning to judge his telling, and I think—I would hope—he will tell you how such a strange thing could happen. It is so hard to believe, but he sounds so sure."

"As to that," the one identified as Eb growled with a glance toward Isak, "I say it's not possible. What I seek to know is what delusion lets him think we might take his prophecy seriously."

"Please, may I hear him?" Kalynn asked.

"It would do no harm, my lord," her father said.

His Lordship gave consent with a wave of his hand, as if it had never mattered. Palovar completed his task with the bundles. "Your place is ready, my lord," he said, sidling away from the settee he'd contrived. "I should ask your pardon; usually this house does not have guests in these quarters."

"Indeed," His Lordship said. He sat down, paused stiffly, then shifted his weight and shifted it again. Finally he slouched, every line of his posture giving evidence of dissatisfaction with the comfort provided. Eb scrambled down to sit cross-legged by his feet. Palovar took the place that had been Kalynn's and, before that, Isak's.

"Very well then," said His Lordship. He faced Isak directly, but even so Isak could see only those watchful eyes. "We have been told your story, but we would ask to hear it from your own tongue."

"Of course," Isak said. Hardly knowing he did so, he touched his brow, then told his tale.

It seemed less difficult to tell, this time. Less had to be explained. More could be left out. His listeners nodded as he spoke, recognizing a narrative they had heard before. Through it all Eb sat with his head turned aside, eyes on the floor, while His Lordship watched intently, sometimes narrowing his gaze. Once or twice Isak's glance found Kalynn in the entranceway. She smiled encouragement.

Then it was done. Eb raised his head. "My lord?" he said with a glance over his shoulder.

"Proceed," His Lordship said.

Eb turned to Isak. "You claim to be a scribe. How did you learn the craft?"

"My teacher was Lurgien, in the village Remoss. I do not think you would know either."

"I do not. He was your father?"

"No," Isak said. "My father was a sea hunter. One voyage his boat did not come back. I was still young. I had no harpoon, and felt no calling to the sea. My mother lacked resources to provide for me; I was all she had that was worth selling. Lurgien bought me for apprentice."

"Hmm," Eb said. "And the village? Its fame has not reached me."

"I would be surprised if it had," Isak said. "It is small. When I kept the records there, it numbered eighty-six households. Its Temple was only one man, Lurgien, who served his gods both as priest and scribe. He was old. His eyes were not good. He taught me, that my eyes could see for him."

"Still you have not told me where," Eb said.

"I had not thought—" Isak began, but broke off as Eb's brow tilted upward. "In the province Periphal, where the Lesser River divides among marshlands to enter the sea. Remoss stands on the south bank of the second-from-the-north branch, which is known there as Haven Passage because of the shelter it gives from storms. It did not shelter my father."

"Thank you," Eb said in a tone that contained scant gratitude. "You come from far."

The remark had the sound of a question. "Lurgien was old, as I have said," Isak explained. "When he died, my bond was severed. Until a new priest came from Taramuth, I did his work. Already I had been doing it for almost two overtakings; Lurgien was not able. The new priest was young. He did not need my help. By then I was nearly grown, and I had no close kin living.

I journeyed seeking a place that had use for my skills. In the end, I came to Center and took service at the Shrine of the Narrow Streets District. The rest I have told you."

Eb rubbed his masking scarf against his jaw. "It could be as he tells it," he told his lord. "In the distant provinces, especially the poorer ones, fosterlings have thus been used. The scribes that come of such a teaching are an indifferent lot—less skilled, as a rule, than the product of a scholarium. But some are competent enough."

His Lordship grumped a skeptical noise. "Do you believe him?"

"I neither believe nor disbelieve, my lord," Eb said. "All he has said does not conflict with facts we know, which means only that he knows those facts also. Only his prophecy stands as a thing of strangeness. And, as you know, my lord, prophecy is a thing men may fruitlessly argue. Only the gods know the truth of prophecy, until it pleases them to give us the event. Or give it not."

"I do not claim a prophecy," Isak said. "Only a foretelling."

"Such things as you foretell, it makes no difference," said His Lordship. "I call it prophecy."

"Explain it to us," Eb said.

"The Council of Brothers, when I told them, did not understand," Isak said. "Can I hope that you will comprehend, when they did not?"

"Perhaps we are not so much in awe of accepted beliefs," His Lordship said. "Perhaps we stand to lose less if they are shown false. Do your best."

Isak closed his eyes. He took a deep breath. "I must begin with basic things," he said, and sought in his mind a point where he could start. "One of my duties at each shrine I have served has been to keep record of the courses of the gods across our sky, for it is how they share our sky that gives foreknowledge of the tides, the depth and span of seasons, the flow of the Great Rivers; all the things that touch and shape our lives. At least, so we are taught. At first, I sensed no order to their coming or departure. Neither did I think it strange. I saw no reason why there should be order, and did not think about it. After all, the gods are gods. But then—it was while I was still bound to Lurgien—I began to feel there was a pattern. There were . . . oh, many things that said to me the gods cross our sky according to a plan."

"A delusion that afflicts many young scribes," Eb said. "Sometimes I think the gods amuse themselves by deceiving them to that foolishness."

"Do you say there is no plan?" Isak asked. He hadn't meant it to sound like a challenge, but even to his own ears it had that sound.

"None of those hatchlings has found one," Eb said. "They produce schemes which seem to fit what is observed, but before a single round of overtakings is complete, we find the gods have gone their own way. It is not in human powers to describe the way of the gods."

"Yes," Isak said. "At first I made the same mistakes. But when I found the gods would not hold to the pattern I thought I had found, I did not let myself be discouraged. I felt still there was a pattern, though perhaps one more complex than I had believed. I searched records going back through many rounds of overtaking. It was difficult. Some were badly kept. Others, I think, were not correct. And they had been kept for purposes different from mine. I can understand why all the others gave up, or did not try."

"Do I infer," Eb asked, "you claim that you have found a pattern? One that none before you found?"

"I believe that I have," Isak said.

Eb studied him. "My lord," he said at last, turning to the

man behind him, "this hatchling is a charlatan who thinks he speaks to fools."

"He's not." It came quickly, an impulse. Kalynn's voice.

"Be quiet, daughter," said her father.

His Lordship placed a hand on Eb's shoulder, light but firm. "Let us not judge too hastily," he said. He pointed to Isak. "You, hatchling. Will you tell us your secret?"

Isak swallowed. The chamber had become unaccountably cold, and he was terribly aware they were not in the presence of the gods. "I should want to," he said. He tried to speak with a boldness he did not feel. "I would be judged by that which can be tested by things outside of us, instead of being measured against what is presently believed."

"Do not tell us how to make our judgments," His Lordship warned.

"No one who taught at my scholarium would have said that," Eb said. "That much, he tells truth."

"Would the Brothers seek his death for that?" His Lordship asked.

"For that alone, I think not," Eb said. "Joined to other things he's said, perhaps. Especially his presumptions on the gods."

"So perhaps all his tale is true," His Lordship mused.

"I did not say that, my lord."

Again His Lordship touched Eb's shoulder, holding him quiet. "Very well, hatchling. Explain your thinking."

It was this man he had to convince. Isak saw it with a sick feeling of hopelessness. The man knew nothing of a scribe's methods, nothing of how knowledge could be gleaned from the endless tabulations of the gods' flight across the sky. Well, he could only do his best.

Damn the Solar System. Bad light; planets too distant; pestered with comets; feeble contrivance; could make a better myself.

—*Francis Lord Jeffery*

"I would begin with how we measure time," Isak said. He watched His Lordship for the first signs of incomprehension as he talked; it would be hard with only the man's eyes and hands in sight, and only his hands not in shadow. "We have the passing, which is the duration of a god's flight across our sky, and we have the anti-passage, which we have always taken to be a similar length, and which is the time between the moment when a god has gone under the world to westward until he has reappeared in the east. Those are for short durations. For long durations we have the overtaking, which is measured from the time when one of the other gods has moved past Blazing Alpher in our sky, through the round of seasons until, having outdistanced Blazing Alpher and for a time not shared our sky with him at all, he rises in the east before Alpher has gone down in the west and, passing after passing, has narrowed the space between them until at last he overtakes him again. Of course there are also the lesser 'takings, which do not involve Alpher, and those of the Pale One, which are more numerous and also different from those of any other, but—"

He saw the restless clench of His Lordship's fingers, and noticed a space on His Lordship's right index finger which had the pallid look of a scar; a place where a ring was normally worn but where none was now. It told much; very few would publicly make claim to noble ancestry. Isak thought of the castle across the river with its ruined wall, and wondered.

"But they would needlessly complicate the present discourse," Isak said. "I—"

"Yet, hatchling, you complicate it yourself," His Lordship said. "You have told us nothing we did not learn as children."

"Not yet," Isak said. "I—"

"My lord," Eb said, "it shall be his own tongue that betrays him. Let him speak."

"In discourse of this kind," Isak said, though his fear was very real, "one begins with what is known by all and not disputed, does one not?"

"True," Eb said, annoyed. "Proceed."

Isak touched his brow. He hoped they would be patient. They had so far to go. "Thank you," he said. He took a deep breath and plunged on. "I should mention also that both a god's passings and his 'takings will overlap with those of the others by awkwardly proportioned fractions that continuously change. And each of a god's passings is separated from the ones before and after by an interval—the anti-passage—which is difficult to measure by ordinary methods, so neither is very useful for exactly measuring long reaches of time. And that, I would tell you, is what has been needed to understand the pattern of how the gods share our sky. Further, I have discovered that these measures are misleading, for although they are very similar, neither the passing nor the overtaking of one god is exactly equal to that of another. Even if you consider those of only one god, a particular passing or 'taking will not be equal to the one before or the one that comes next. The same is also true for the anti-passage, nor are a god's passing and subsequent anti-passage as similar in duration as we have thought. Therefore, for the purpose of discovering a pattern, those methods of measuring time are useless."

Eb humphed. "No one has ever claimed that any of those were equal."

"I know," Isak said. "But neither has anyone given much thought to the fact they are not."

"So? Does it matter?" Eb demanded. "They're sufficiently similar that it makes no difference. We're able to arrange our affairs by those measures to the satisfaction of all. What more is needed?"

"Isn't it good to know they are not true measures?" Isak asked. "Would you accept, buying cloth, less than the length and width agreed upon? Or wine, a cask of unspecified size?"

"Eggs and melons I buy that way," Eb said. "A particular passing or 'taking is the same for everyone."

His Lordship's brow began to shape a scowl. "I will admit," Isak said, "for ordinary purposes the differences I discovered are not important. But to understand the pattern of the gods— their flights across our sky—then they become significant."

Again Eb snorted. "If there are differences—and, mind, I say *if*—how did you find them?"

Inwardly, Isak sighed. This was a part he couldn't hope to explain to His Lordship. He might not even be able to convince Eb he spoke truth. It depended on—

"Do you know of the discoveries at the Scholarium of Filorna, of the remarkable properties of a weight that swings on the end of a cord?—that neither the size of the weight nor the width of its swing is important? That only the string's length affects the duration of its course from one extreme to the other?"

"I had heard of it," Eb said, but the words had scorn in them. "An intriguing bit of lore, if true, but useless. Or do you claim the gods are similarly attached to strings?"

"I do not claim to know the nature of the gods," Isak said. "No more than any man. But I must say it is not useless knowledge. This characteristic of the pendulum makes it possible to construct a machine to measure time, independent of the passings of the gods."

"Only if true," Eb said.

Isak appealed directly to His Lordship. "Your . . ." How to address this man, to whom he owed nothing but who might order his death, was difficult. "Your Presence, I have myself experimented with these artifacts. I tell you, the discovery is true."

His Lordship leaned down beside Eb's ear. "Have you . . . ?"

"Of course not," Eb said. "Until this charlatan invoked their claim to justify his own—which he has not yet done—it would have been a waste of effort."

"I shall have to ask you, now, to do it," His Lordship said. "Though it sounds suspiciously of magic."

"Perhaps some influence of the gods, not previously known?" Isak suggested.

"Umm," Eb muttered, displeased but reluctant to argue.

"Well, hatchling?" His Lordship prompted.

Isak swallowed again. "Your Presence, given a machine to measure time, it is possible to gauge the passings of the gods against a scale that is apart from them, which therefore provides a true measure. It was lack of such a measure that prevented a pattern from being discovered long ago."

"So you would claim no revelation? No special favor of the gods?"

"None," Isak admitted.

"And any man could come to your findings?"

"If they were sufficiently curious, and willing to do the work," Isak said.

It seemed to trouble His Lordship. "No favor at all?"

"Your Presence," Isak said, "I am sorry. In all of this, I have not felt the touch of the gods."

"Then can you say why you are alone in your discovery?"

"I do not claim to be alone," Isak said. "I do not know of others, but I do not say they do not exist."

"You see how clever he is in argument, my lord," Eb said. "We shall not find truth by discourse with him."

"Nor in blind disbelief, either," said Isak quickly. "Your Presence I do not ask you to believe me, but only to hold back judgment until your man has done his investigations. If he is truthful, I have nothing to fear."

"Fear nothing, then," His Lordship said, "so long as you can say the same for yourself."

"Enough," Eb said, raising a hand. "In time, we'll know who speaks truth. Now, do I think right, that you base your prophecy on this pattern you claim to have found?"

"Any man, knowing the pattern, could foresee it," Isak said.

"You say this, even knowing that always at least one of the gods stands in our sky? That they have watched since the time of the first men?"

"I know that," Isak said. "But also I know—the pattern tells me—when the moment comes, Actinic Gamow shall stand alone up there, and he shall pass behind the Pale One. For a time, she will block his sight."

"Ah," said Eb. He leaned back, looking upward. "And that is it? That is the whole of it?"

"It will be a time of darkness," Isak said. "Yes."

Eb still was not satisfied. He still had questions. He wanted to know why Isak thought the Pale One would pass in front of Gamow rather than behind, and whether it would make a difference, for the Pale One gave the appearance of a cloud, and a thin one at that, and it was well known the whole sky could be masked with cloud without blinding the sight of the gods.

Isak nodded; they were reasonable objections. He had pondered them himself. What had settled his mind, he explained, was the record he found in the Archives from Kagglan, a village far southward, on the shore of the South Ocean, of a time when Alpher overtook the Pale One, passed behind her and watched the world, as it were, over her shoulder. The scribe's telling, which even on parchment shrieked of fear, told how Alpher had appeared to have had a bite taken from him, and his heat was less, his light was strange, and the fear had been great that Alpher was destroyed; but when next they rose in the east Alpher had moved ahead of the Pale One and was restored to his full, blistering roundness. He had suffered no harm. At the same time, a village not quite so far south, though a great distance eastward, had reported the event as an almost normal overtaking, but one in which the edges of the two discs appeared actually to touch. The priest of that village had sent to inquire what such a happening could portend.

From those records, Isak said, he drew two conclusions: that the Pale One's body was a solid thing through which a god's light did not shine, and that the Pale One's course of flight lay much nearer the world than Alpher's.

Eb had trouble understanding the second point. "Look at me," Isak said. He held up a hand at arm's length in front of his face. "Lean aside, either way, and look at me again. Do you see? When you look from the side, you can see my face. When you look directly, my hand is in the way. Now . . ." He brought his hand closer until the palm touched his nose. "Now, no matter how far you lean, my hand blocks your view. Therefore, I conclude the Pale One is much closer to our world than Blazing Alpher. It is a thing you learn, watching boats on the river."

"Perhaps," Eb snapped. He seemed annoyed. "But is she nearer than Actinic Gamow? That, after all, is what your prophecy must have."

"It is only a foretelling," Isak reminded him.

Eb's hand chopped air with a force that would have cracked stone. "Call it what you will. You cannot speak of one god, then say the same is true of another unless you have proof."

He was right, of course. Isak nodded. "I have studied the Pale One's aspect through many configurations. Once it is known that she is not a wraith, but solid, and that Alpher is more distant, it is not difficult to understand her shifts of hue. It is most apparent when Red Bethe or the Twinned Ones let her share their sky. Then—it seems a paradox, but I am sure it is not—the face she turns to us is most pale. Almost white, and the streaks across her face are hard to see. That is specially true when all the red ones stand close to her, except you may notice her edge on the side toward a red one has the color of blood mixed with water that her whole face shows at other times. When the red ones are farther apart from her, more of her face is reddened. I have watched the play of color on her face, and I have come to believe she is a sphere, and that she is nearer to our world than any of the gods; that when the red ones all stand close to her and only her edges show redness, it is because their light falls mainly on the side of her that is turned away from us."

Eb held up a fist to the lamp's light. He studied it, shifting his head to look at it from one angle, then another.

"Ummm . . ." he grumbled. He had grasped the idea, but he did not like it. "And Gamow?"

"His sight is not as brilliant as Alpher's, nor as easily distinguished," Isak said. "But in certain advantageous configurations I have seen the edge of his light on the Pale One's rim. It could be none other's. So I am certain that, when the moment comes, the Pale One shall mask our world from his sight."

Eb cocked his head. "And you say the Pale One is solid," he mused. "Solid things have weight. Can you explain what prevents her from falling out of our sky?"

"I do not know," Isak admitted. "Perhaps the gods ordain that she does not."

It brought a harsh bark of laughter. "Very well," His Lordship said. "You—" His hand touched Eb's shoulder. "—you shall investigate these things he has claimed."

"I intend to, my lord," Eb said. "If only for my own satisfaction. For now I will say only that he is a very clever young man. Never before have I been told so many preposterous things I could not instantly disprove."

"If I were clever," Isak said, "would the Brothers not have believed me?"

"Perhaps they did," His Lordship said, "but feared you."

"What had they to fear?" Isak wondered.

"I have another question," Eb said. "You say you believe the Pale One is shaped like a ball, and that you have seen the light of the gods illuminate a portion of her face while shining mainly on the side of her that is turned from us. If that is true, it should be possible to measure the angle from which the gods' light shines on her, and from any shadow post you could measure the angle from which that same god's light comes to us at that same moment. From that information you should be able to determine that god's distance from us."

"In comparative terms," Isak said cautiously. "His apparent distance, at least. Theoretically, at least, it is possible."

"Have you made such calculations?"

Was it a trap? Isak wondered. Certainly it was a subject about which there was much argument and many conflicting opinions. But his only hope of safety lay in speaking truth. "I made an attempt," he admitted. "You must understand, to measure the fall of light on the Pale One's body is difficult. I could not do it with great accuracy. And even a small difference in the measurements would cause a large difference in the numbers produced."

"But you attempted it. What did you find?"

"The numbers were so large I could not believe them," Isak said. "Thousands of times the distance between us and the Pale One. Many thousands, and for some of the gods it was millions."

"Not infinite?" Eb asked. It was what most men believed; those who thought about it.

"I would have felt less disbelief if it were," Isak said. "At least that would be consistent with them being gods, but that is not what my calculations produced. Perhaps it is among their powers—did you think their powers are limited to those we have perceived?—to give the appearance of holding whatever distance they wish; certainly, if those distances were real, it would be cause for us to feel awe. There is not so much distance in the world."

"Faugh," Eb snorted. Even the set of his shoulders seemed a sneer. "And you say that for each the distance is different?"

Unhappily, Isak nodded. It was contrary to common belief and possibly to common sense as well. But that was what his calculations had found. "As I have said. I put no faith in it. It is only the appearance that they give. But I must say also I repeated my measurements many times, and while my calculations from each set of measurements did not produce exactly the same result each time, for each of the gods except Red Bethe the distance was always so close to the same number that small errors in my measurement would account for the discrepancy. And for Red Bethe, whose distance I must admit was never the same twice, I discovered it was different each time in a way that was consistent with the change he displays in his apparent size and warmth and brightness."

He paused for breath. "I do not know how much of what I found is truth, nor how much is only appearance. Nor, for that matter, do I know how much I may have erred because the gods are gods and therefore beyond our understanding. But I know that not all my measurements could have been incorrect, nor could I find any flaw in my calculations. Therefore I must say that, though I cannot believe the numbers, the appearance of distance they have given is a true appearance. I did not imagine it."

"And your assumptions?" Eb demanded. "You did not question them?"

"I did, learned one. I did," Isak said quickly. "Did I not say I put no faith in the numbers? I have not been able to find my error, but could any man if the gods would deceive him?"

"And yet you feel no doubt that you have discovered a way to predict how they will share our sky?" Eb asked. His bony finger skewered air. "If they have deceived you in the matter of distance, why not also in that?"

"That I can directly observe," Isak said. "I have done it since I was a boy. In that the gods cannot deceive. Perhaps I should say also I would not have looked into the records from Kagglan, had not the pattern shown me it was there that the Pale One most recently might have been seen to pass across a part of Blazing Alpher's face." He hesitated. "Such things do happen. Kagglan was only the most recent time. There have been times—they are in the Archives—that Alpher has passed completely behind the Pale One's body, and sight of him was completely lost."

"And was there darkness then? Would not such an event be remembered?"

"Other gods stood in the sky," Isak said. "They watched while he could not. Have you noticed? Alpher never stands alone in our sky. Always at least one other is with him."

Eb's head came up. For a moment he was wordless.

"Is that true?" His Lordship asked.

Eb clamped a hand on his knee. Almost imperceptibly it trembled. "My lord, I can think of no occasion when it was not true." The words came tart and angry. "I shall investigate."

"I think also," Isak ventured, "Kagglan must be several leagues farther south than has been thought. I had expected they would have been seen barely to touch."

His Lordship bent close to Eb's ear. "That distance. How well is it known?"

"A distance such as that is a guess," Eb said in an edged voice. "A measure of the provisions a caravan must take to journey there; the straightness of the road, the difficulties on the way."

"Could he have known that?" His Lordship asked.

"It is well known, my lord," Eb said. "The strange thing is that he would claim to have a different way to measure."

"But If the Pale One is nearer than Blazing Alpher, it is obvious," Isak said quickly.

"To you, perhaps," Eb said.

"Enough," His Lordship said. He spoke to Eb. "He has told you more than you need to discover if he speaks truth, or whether—as you say—he is a charlatan. You shall do that." His glance returned to Isak. "You, hatchling. One final question. Tell us when this darkness shall come."

"If it ever does," Eb grumbled.

His Lordship thumped Eb's shoulder with a hard, stiff finger. "Hatchling?" he commanded.

Isak hesitated only a moment. It was a temptation that His Lordship might be more persuaded if he gave it in the vague phrasing common to prophets. But it would have been less than full truth, and his greatest hope lay in being different from any prophet ever known.

"Between that time and now," he said, "Actinic Gamow will overtake the Pale One only once. When that happens, Red Bethe will stand low in the west at the moment Gamow is abreast of her centerpoint, and the space between them will be less than the breadth of your thumb held at arm's length. The time after that, when he overtakes her, he will pass behind her. She will block his sight, and Bethe shall have gone below the horizon before that moment, nor shall any other god stand aloft. There will be a great darkness."

"So you say, hatchling. And before that moment, how long do we have?"

It seemed a question to which he'd given the answer already.

"Why, the interval between one 'taking of the Pale One by Actinic Gamow is always the same to the limits of my power to measure," he said. "It is . . . oh." He'd been thinking of his own scheme of measurement, not the ways of common usage.

"How long in words that I know?" His Lordship said.

"It is not easy to convert to ordinary units," Isak said. "As I have told you, the ordinary units do not indicate equal durations. But, as nearly as I can, I would say the time between one 'taking of the Pale One by Actinic Gamow and the next would be forty-two and four-fifth's of Blazing Alpher's passings. Sometimes it is a little more, sometimes less."

"And the time between now and the next overtaking?" His Lordship asked.

"Why, that would be . . ." Isak began, and stopped. "Your Presence, I cannot answer that. I do not know how long I have been in this hiding place, so I do not know the moment I should measure from."

His Lordship looked back over his shoulder. "Mistress Kalynn?"

"I do not know, my lord," she said. "When he came, I did not note how the gods were standing. I was thinking about other things." She raised her voice. "I'm sorry, Isak."

Isak's gesture said it didn't matter. "What I need to know is how the gods stand now. If you could tell me . . ."

"Did you note?" His Lordship asked Eb.

"I had no reason to, my lord."

"Nor I," said Palovar.

"Please." Kalynn's voice. "I could find out."

"Do that," His Lordship commanded.

Isak glimpsed her as she moved back into the entranceway. "I need to know which gods stand aloft," he called after her. "And what parts of the sky they hold. Read the shadow post."

She paused, half-turned. "The shadow post?"

"In the garden," he said. "I want to know how the shadows lie around it."

She fluttered her hands. "Why, as the gods cast them, no different from ever. What more . . . ?"

The idea that meaning could be found in the fall of those shadows was strange to her. He shrugged. It would have helped, but he could do without. "Tell me how they stand," he said. "But the Pale One. I must know about the Pale One."

"What should I ask?" she wondered.

"I must know how she stands, the same as for the other gods," Isak said.

"Oh." She backed into the entranceway. "Is she a god? She is oo difforont from tho othoro."

"Enough," His Lordship said and slapped his knee. "Make your inquiries and come back."

"I'm sorry, my lord," she said meekly. And, "I'll try, Isak," she called. Then, half hidden in shadow, she was at the opening and talking to someone outside. Impatiently, His Lordship shifted his weight. "Knowing that," he said to Isak, "you can tell us how long?"

Was it so strange? "Certainly, my lord," Isak said. "If the Pale One is aloft, I need only to know how the gods stand relevant to her. If she is not, I will know which gods she does not stand among, and from that it should be possible to estimate when she will rise and how the gods will stand at that time. Although," he added, "if I must estimate, I cannot hope to be as accurate."

They waited. Isak felt the glower of their gaze. No words came, and time's passage could be measured only by the beating of his heart.

At last she returned. Her father made room for her to pass and she came on as far as she could. She knelt behind His Lordship, so close she could breathe on that one's shoulder. "Isak, Hobur says Red Bethe stands low in the east with Bright

Dalton above him, very close. He believes it is the Twinned Ones whose light comes from the west. He can see no others."

Isak nodded. "Yes. It would be the Twins." But then he frowned. He scratched some marks on the hard earth at his feet. It was difficult to keep track of all the facts at once. "And the Pale One? Is she . . . ?"

"He did not speak of her," Kalynn said.

"But there are clouds? You said he was not sure it was the Twinned Ones."

"Yes," Kalynn said. "There are clouds halfway up the sky. They cover all the west and part of the south. I'm sorry, Isak."

"You've done as much as you could," Isak said. And to His Lordship, "I believe the Pale One is behind those clouds, or else only lately gone down. If I knew her height, I could say with more certainty, but I believe Actinic Gamow will overtake her in no more than twenty-seven of his passings, nor less than twenty-three."

"That's not very exact," His Lordship said.

"Any man could make a guess such as that," Eb said. "It is easily within the limits of short term variation."

"I made no special claims," Isak said. "But I did not know how long I have been here; for part of that time I was not conscious. It could have been less than a passing. It could have been five."

"Or more than five," Eb said. And over his shoulder, "My lord, he is guessing."

"It could not have been more than five," Isak said. "I would have felt more hunger. My throat would have been dry."

His Lordship spoke to Kalynn. "You've said nothing to him about the time he's been here?"

"Not that I can remember, my lord."

"And your servant? Might he have said . . . ?"

"I do not know, my lord. We did not know it would be

important. Should I ask?"

His Lordship was gesturing the question aside when Hobur spoke from the entranceway. "Mistress. The clouds be lifted from the world's edge. The Pale One be up there, but soon to complete her passing."

"You see?" Kalynn urged. "Oh, thank you, Hobur. Thank you."

Isak had half-risen. "Have the Twinned Ones overtaken her?"

"Aye, those two be standing below her, lad," Hobur said. "Though she yet nip their heels. I'd not gamble it be fully done."

"If not, it will be very soon," Isak said. He knew now where he was in time. "Before they go under the world."

"You know that?" His Lordship demanded.

Isak nodded. "As surely as I knew she would be in our sky when I learned Blazing Alpher was not. At least—" He had to speak truth. "—I thought it likely."

His Lordship turned to Eb. "Could you have been so sure?"

"A conjurer's trick, my lord," Eb replied with a belittling wave of the hand.

"Conjurer's tricks done with the gods?" His Lordship demanded. His glance went from his man to Isak, then back. "What other powers might one have, who could do that?"

"The power to confound with a glib tongue, my lord," Eb said. "Were my life at stake, I too would clutch at chance and do my utmost to deceive. I must advise, my lord, apply great caution in your dealings with this wretch."

"I have never thought otherwise," His Lordship said. He twisted around, rising, careful of his head under the ceiling beams. To Palovar he said, "My scribe will have much scratching and thought to consume him. Myself also. But you judged right: we may have use of him."

"My lord," Palovar said, touching his brow, "it was my daughter who suggested . . ."

But His Lordship was not listening. He gave Eb a nod that sent him scuttling into the entranceway. Turning again, he studied Isak for a long silent moment before he, too, turned to go.

Kalynn edged into the space they had vacated. She reached for the bowl and the serving board. "It's gone cold," she said. She meant the food. He'd forgotten all about it. "I'll get you more."

He caught her wrist before she could touch the board. She tried to pull away and he could see the alarm on her face. "Please," he said, feeling hurt that he had frightened her, and carefully turned the board so the light would let her see his marks. He heard the sharp catch of her breath.

"I think I could get some waxboards," she said. "Would you like that?"

"Could you?" he said.

She looked down at the bowl in her hands. "I could try."

He nodded assent. "But if they must come from outside, be careful. No one must see them. They would mean you have a scribe inside."

"Oh, that's right," she said, touching her cheek. It was something she hadn't thought of. "We'll be careful."

For a long moment, then, she studied him closely. She touched his arm. "I never met anyone like you," she said, awe in her tone. Quickly, then, she backed away, turned. "Are you really a prophet?"

But before he could blurt an answer, she was gone.

Much may be made of a Scotchman if he be caught young.

—Samuel Johnson

She returned with a generous chunk of roast sliced on a board, boiled yams, a jar of wine. Threads of steam drifted up from the meat and the yams. Silent, she watched while he ate. Finally, softly, she asked a question. Then another. After that one, more. They were casual questions, sparked by random curiosity more than any need to know. Having never herself gone more than a few leagues beyond the city's edge, she asked about his wanderings, the towns and villages he'd known, the mountains, the Great Desert—of the delta village where he was born, where he had lived his first twelve rounds of 'taking.

It took a while to tell. He told how he had left it on a skin trader's barge; how a caravan crossing mountains and tundra had left him in a village so far to the north that for a whole season almost the only god to hold the sky was Actinic Gamow, but Gamow watched all the time, dipping close to the ice-choked sea in the north, circling high to southward. Though giving light, he yielded little warmth. Sometimes the Pale One shared his sky. She gave no warmth, either. When at last Blazing Alpher peered above the southern horizon, showing only an edge of his disc, the people celebrated.

From there he had drifted southward. For a time he served a grain buyer in a town where the Temple priests saw portents of a bountiful harvest. Watching how the gods shared the sky, Isak felt doubts; Red Bethe had been slow to depart from Alpher's sky, that spring, and as the season advanced the shadows Bethe laid became longer and longer while Alpher's grew short. He warned his employer, who laughed.

As the time of harvest came near, the heat instead of waning deepened. The wind burned hot. Crops withered. Dust storms blackened the sky, concealing that land from the sight of the gods. When the second storm came, the people killed the priests who had given false counsel. When the third storm came, people began to leave, still wondering why the gods had closed their eyes to them.

Isak joined the exodus. He saw deserts and a vast arid gorge with a river twisting through its depths. Mountains where deep snow lay in cold white brilliance under the gods' chill gaze and all the higher peaks were forever shrouded in cloud. Once, after a particularly grueling trek, he was so exhausted that he lay down on the turf beside a stream and actually slept—a sleep so deep that he knew nothing, and which lasted almost the full duration of Bright Dalton's passing. It was a thing which had happened to him only two other times in his life. He wondered if sleep was possibly something like death; if it was, he did not like it.

For a full round of 'takings he lived in Filorna, having found his way there in the hope that at the Master Scholarium he could receive more thorough instruction at his craft. Many times when he had sought employment he had seen the frown when he admitted his indifferent schooling, and seen the frowns darken to scowls when, pressed but speaking only truth, he was compelled to explain that, though no scholarium had endorsed his proficiency, his skill was equal to that of any youth who came from those schools. At Filorna, though, he was disappointed; the Scholarium's syndics judged him half taught and therefore unteachable. But they did not disallow him from the library, said to be the best in the world, and some few of the junior scholars were willing to converse with him. In time, he came to know several well, was welcome in their quarters; sometimes, even, he found himself participating in their discussions almost as an equal. Proud as boys, they showed him their discoveries. Once, asking a question, he realized it was something they had never wondered about; he saw them glance at each other, saw them look at him, then, with a different look in their eyes. It was the most exciting time of his life, filled with the euphoria of new things learned.

Through that time, he supported himself at scribe's work for several small merchants. None of them, alone, could have mustered even a scant scribe's pay, nor had they, individually, that much need for one. Combined, they provided sufficient work to justify a meager wage. He would have taken his pay in bread crusts, ditch water, and bones if it would have let him stay in Filorna, but such a time could not last. The syndics became aware of his continued presence, and thought him a disturbing influence on the placid function of their school. In that they were wrong; long before he came, the younger men had been adventuring into far realms of discovery. He was little more than a watcher beside the flame.

Nevertheless, he was suddenly barred from the library, from the quadrangle, and from the private quarters. Soon after, the merchants—some of whom depended heavily on the school for their business—discharged him. Nor could he find others who would give him work or wage.

So he became a wanderer again, but with a difference. Before, it had been the aimless travels of one who went where the caravan track might lead; now he journeyed in search of knowledge. He went south—as far south as a caravan would take him in trade for his labor along the way. In the villages where they paused he visited the Temples, spoke with the scribes. More times than not, they let him search their records. What he found seemed to confirm his expectations; for already he believed he had glimpsed the pattern by which the gods apportioned the sky.

From the town where the caravan left him, the river Leeth coursed west through a gorge in the Stone Mountains. Isak found passage on a trader's flatboat. He swung the long, heavy sweep which steered the awkward, fragile craft while around him the water roared and burst into fountains of spray. Once, thrown overboard, he came near to drowning. It was far different from the smooth, deep-running water he had known as a boy.

Beyond the mountains, the river curved north. They came to towns, sometimes on one shore, sometimes the other. There they paused. The trader conducted his business and Isak went to the Temples. Also, as they traveled, he made notes of his own: how in each successive passing the gods shared the sky; what gods stood aloft, and what part of the firmament each one held, and also where they stood when the next came above the horizon; similarly how each stood as each in turn descended from sight in the west. It was not possible, aboard a wallowing water craft, to carefully measure the length and compass-point of each god's shadow at such moments, but except when the river was at its most tumultuous he was most times able to make rough measurements of the angles between those shadows.

The trader watched him with dour skepticism—thought him unbalanced—but said nothing. Isak compared his notes with Temple records in the towns. All facts fit the pattern.

Though it curved and twisted a thousand times, the river kept its northward trend. Isak could see it in his notes and his calculations. At last, it joined the Great Western River under high, frowning bluffs. Isak had never seen a city so large as the one that crowded those shores. There the trader beached his craft for the last time, to market his accumulated wares and let the boat be salvaged for its timber.

Borne down now by a clumsy bundle of waxboard notes, for he could afford neither parchment nor ink, Isak continued where the river's course led, sometimes on foot, sometimes aboard such boats as kindly would take him for a reach or two, to come at last to the Center of the World where the Temple stood. There in its Archives would rest the final evidence, the proof that would affirm or refute his surmise. And there he had found it.

Eating and, at the same time, talking made both a slow process. Before he was done the meat was cold and the wine had warmed. He hardly noticed either. He noticed only that Kalynn listened with eyes half closed. It seemed a long time after he stopped talking before she opened them.

"But you're hardly older than I am," she said.

"I was born in a different place," Isak said. "And to a different station in life."

"I've always wished I could see other places. You—you've seen the whole world."

"Only part of it," Isak said. "If I can accept what I found in the Archives, I have seen not a tenth of it. And all my life I have wanted a home that was mine."

"But to have seen all those places!"

"Even the river trader had a home where he went between journeys," Isak said. "To be a wayfarer is a . . . a very desolate way to live."

She began to gather up the utensils. "I shouldn't have stayed so long," she said, not looking at him. "Father will be angry if he finds out. Hobur probably already is." Clutching the dishes awkwardly, she made to rise.

Isak took back the serving board. He could use it for note-making. "I should not have talked so much," he said.

"I wanted you to," she said. For just a moment she looked at him, honest-eyed. She touched his hand. "You're nice to listen to."

By then she was on her feet. Between the ceiling beams she could stand almost straight. "I'll bring the waxboards as soon as I can. Maybe I can get some parchment, too. I think father has some at the trading yard. Would you like . . . ?"

Even better than waxboards. "I would need ink and brushes

also. But yes, I would like parchment very much."

"I'll try," she said.

He helped her climb down into the outer chamber, aware of Hobur's suspicious eye watching him, and handed down the utensils one by one. Again she tried to stack them, failed, and let Hobur take part of the load. For the space of half a breath he wondered whether, if he leaped out now, he might escape them before they could put their encumbrance aside. But he knew nothing of what lay outside this outer chamber; couldn't see, even, where its exit was. And, oddly, to make such an attempt would have felt like a betrayal. She had said she would bring him parchment. While he hesitated, the moment passed.

Though she was looking up at him, she could see none of his thoughts. She arched an eyebrow at him and gave him a sidelong smile which he didn't quite know the meaning of. Then she was turning away and Hobur, his burden set down on a dust-filmed chest, was advancing to lift the first stone into place. He found himself hoping she would come back soon.

Everyone must do his own believing, as he will have to do his own dying.

—Martin Luther

In the time that followed, she came often and stayed long. She brought his meals, and she sat on the floor near his feet and asked him questions. As she had promised, she brought waxboards and, later, parchment, ink, and writing tools. Sometimes, when the conversation flagged, she sat quiet and watched him work, or left him for a while to think, to calculate, to ponder.

But for much of the time she was there, and he came to accept her quiet presence. He taught her to read a shadow post's

85

castings and after that, each time she came, she told him how the shadows lay. At first there was some confusion because the artisan who, long ago, emplaced the post had laid the marker tiles according to a decorative scheme of his own instead of where they should have gone, but once the trouble's cause was known it became no more work than a few quick scratches to know exactly how the gods shared the sky. From that he could measure the passage of time.

He showed her how the sounds of her name, spoken, were marked on a waxboard. She tried to imitate the scratches, clumsily at first, but then with growing skill. He had always been told that women lacked the intellect to learn a scribe's craft. Now he saw that, like so many other things commonly believed, it was not true. He taught her how to record a shadow post's castings. After that, she brought him the readings freshly scratched on a board. He was surprised and pleased how quickly she learned.

During that time, Palovar did not come, nor did His Lordship, nor Eb; only Kalynn. Sometimes he glimpsed Hobur glowering in the outer chamber, but that was the only other face he saw. After the first few visits, she began to bring her own meals. Though Palovar sometimes came home at Alpher-rise and setting, she explained, just as often he ate with his men. She thought it foolish for her to eat alone while Isak also ate by himself; for his part, Isak was glad for her company. When she was with him, he could almost forget his circumstances.

Almost.

"They're still trying to find you," she told him one time as she settled herself. She'd brought a set of tasko pieces and a playing board. She placed a lance-piece to begin the game. "We found out they've told the streetwardens all over Center to watch for you, and what you look like, and to ask if you've been seen. They stopped a caravan halfway across the desert to search it for you. They've searched boats on the river and all the towns from here to the mountains. And there've been acolytes going all around wanting to look at everyone's scribes and asking questions and saying if an out of work scribe comes, to lock him up and call the Guards. They'll pay a half thousand goldmarks to anyone that catches you. Are you really worth that much?"

She'd started the game; it made him the defender. He set a lance-piece of his own on his side of the midline, toe to toe with hers. "I could not have earned so much in all my life."

Another lance-piece in hand, she looked up from the board. "Is a scribe's pay that scant?"

"For one who did not learn his craft at a scholarium," Isak said.

She'd been tempted to play her second piece in the same square as her first, but now she placed it in the adjoining square. "But your death would be worth that much?"

Reaching for another lance-piece of his own, he paused. "Did they say they want me dead?"

"They haven't said it, but they do, don't they?"

It seemed likely. He set his piece toe to the midline, two squares to the right of his first. "If they have offered that price, that is what they think it worth." His eyes scanned the board but hardly saw. His thoughts were not on the game. "It is true, they have such wealth. To them it would be a pittance, but even so I cannot think why they would offer so much."

"You don't?" She added a sword-piece to the square held by her second lance. "I think I do."

It looked as if she might attack through the gap in his line. He added a sword piece between his two lancers, but this time one square back from the midline. "I do not understand how they think in the Temple," he said.

"But it's obvious," she said. Carefully she chose another sword-piece from her dwindling rank of uncommitted pieces.

"You've said that a darkness is coming. That the gods will close their eyes to us. I don't care what you call it, it's a prophecy and you're its prophet. And that's how the Temple must think of you. And—have you thought?—if that darkness comes . . ."

She placed her sword-piece on the other side of her first lance. She could begin her attack now, as soon as she had positioned her crown. "If it comes—don't you see what it will mean?"

"When it comes," Isak corrected. He put a sword-piece on the board opposite her latest addition, one square back from the midline.

"All right; when it comes." To her it was an unimportant quibble. "Do you see?"

"Must it mean something?" Isak asked. "Can't it be just something that happens?"

"Doesn't everything the gods do have meaning?"

He studied the board, trying with half his mind to think what her strategy would be, and with the rest how to answer her question. "I know only that for many things we do not know the meaning. Even the most wise in the Temple can only guess and pretend."

Her fingers found her crown-piece, though he was sure she had not sought it with her eyes. She added it to the board directly behind her attack line in the row of squares against the edge of the board. "Don't you mean almost always?" she asked.

To put his own crown-piece on the board was obligatory. He placed it to his right in the edge square, second row from the back. "Perhaps," he admitted.

"And if it was sent by the gods, what would the darkness mean?" She advanced her first sword-piece diagonally across the midline into the square held by his number two lance.

He wasn't surprised. She'd declared her intention to attack when she put her crown-piece on the board. Now he studied the pattern of pieces and tried to guess her plan. "It would seem a sign of their displeasure," he said. That much was obvious, so obvious it hardly needed to be mentioned.

"Exactly," Kalynn said. "So when you say the gods will send darkness, you are saying they are displeased. It's still your move."

He'd finally decided, rather than commit any of the pieces he had already in position, to add a sword piece against the midline, in the square between his two lance-pieces. But part of his mind still gnawed at the other question. "When the gods show displeasure, people usually blame the priests," he said, putting the swords in place. "The priests would have us believe they speak for the gods, and also to the gods in our behalf. If the gods are displeased, it would appear the priests have in some way failed."

It was her turn to study the board. "So? You still don't see it?"

He frowned and shook his head. "They believe I do not speak truth. So does it matter what I say?"

She added a lance piece on her side of the midline, immediately across from the square where her sword-piece had his lance engaged. "I know they don't believe you," she said. "But you are speaking as a prophet speaks, and what you were saying—maybe not directly, but it's what you implied—was that the gods are displeased with those who stand high in the Temple, who claim to serve them, but who everyone knows do not. So of course they would want to stop you from telling anyone else. And what better way than to say you're a false prophet and cut your tongue?"

He had the feeling of having glimpsed truth without truly comprehending what he saw. There was the sound of sense to what she said. But if she was even partly right, she had to have an understanding of the Temple and the Temple's minions far better than his own. How could a sheltered girl know so much, he wondered, when he had himself worked among priests and the servants of priests all his life and had thought he knew them, but knew now that he did not?

"I said nothing about the Temple," he said. "I spoke only of what the gods would do. I did not claim to know why."

She gestured at the board. He had forgotten the game again.

He advanced his number one sword into the square where his lance-piece stood, engaged by her sword. "Kill," he announced formally, and took her sword-piece from the board. Then, the kill having won him another move, he advanced the sword-piece across the midline to engage the lance-piece waiting there. It brought a momentary twist of pain to the corner of her mouth. He told himself it was only a game, but he wished he could have made her smile instead.

"What matters is what they thought you were saying," she said. "That's why they want you dead." As she spoke, she placed a sword-piece behind the lance he'd engaged. "Oh, you're too quick for me, Isak."

He'd advanced his lance piece across the midline to join his sword, killing her lance. Now he considered his next move. "And you?" he asked. "What do you think I was saying?"

She, too, was studying the board. "Why, I think if you had meant what they thought, you would have said it plainly. I don't think anyone knows what the gods want, or why they do things. Maybe they do things for reasons that have nothing to do with us."

He'd considered attacking her backup sword, but her lance in the square beside the one he'd taken was in position to come to its defense. Instead, he advanced his sword diagonally into the square beside her sword and behind her lance. Nothing now stood between his piece and her crown. "The priests would say you were wrong," he said. "But if you asked they could not tell you how they knew. Myself . . . I must say I know very little about the gods."

Touching a thumb to her lower lip, she took another lance-piece from her reserve and, after a hesitation, placed it in the square ahead of her crown. "They'd say they know because they know the gods," she said, looking directly at him. "But that's silly. The only way they could know what the gods want, or think, or feel would be if the gods told them. But if the gods tell them things, they'd know you never left this house, so you must be still inside. Because the gods watch. They watch all of us, all the time. But the priests don't know where you are. Father had some men he knows up the river at Where They Fought and another at Deep Crossing—local merchants he trades with—had them tell the Guards a scribe that looks like you asked them for work. It's too soon to be sure, but we think it's fooled them. But if the gods could tell them things, they'd know it wasn't true. They wouldn't be looking all over for you. They'd be taking this house apart a stone at a time."

Abstractedly, Isak nodded. Without direct knowledge, she had deduced a truth. For all the Temple's pretensions, the gods did not communicate. All that was known of the gods was inferred, argued out, guessed at, or merely believed. And yet . . . and yet . . .

He advanced his lance-piece to join his sword, consolidating his hold on the square. "The Temple does not know much about the gods," he said. "Every local Temple has its records. The priests do not lie when they say they know the significance of how the gods share our sky. But why the gods do those things, or what they think, or what they want of us—those are things we do not know. Any man who claims to know, that man does not speak truth."

"Would you say, then, all prophets are false?" she asked, and added another lance-piece to the protection of her crown, this one toe to toe with his sword. She challenged him with her eyes.

"I have not claimed to be a prophet," he said. For the moment his attack was stalled, as he'd known it would be. He would have to bring more pieces into action. He studied the board.

"But you are, Isak," she said. "Whether you want to be one or not. The Temple's said you are."

"A false one," Isak said, still pondering the game.

"That's what the Temple says. But people don't always believe the Temple. Not any more." For a moment she looked about to laugh with delight. "That's another thing father and . . . and his friends are doing. They're going to have men talking about your prophecy—telling other people, as if they'd heard it somewhere. And travelers. And boatmen—especially boatmen, because they go up and down the river, and they could have heard it anywhere. And . . ."

Talking about it animated her. He let her talk on and on, and thought about the game until, his strategy decided, he positioned a new sword-piece against the midline, toe-to-toe with her number one sword. "Why?" he asked.

"Don't you want people to know? Wasn't that why . . . ?"

"It is what I had sought to have done," Isak said, "though I would have had the Temple proclaim it. But I am wondering why your father—the men he is involved with—why they would take the risk of telling such a thing when the Temple has said it is false? Are they so anxious that people should be told? Do they . . . ?"

A new thought came. "Does it mean your father—his friends—now believe I have given them truth?"

She sighed. "It's not that simple," she said, and for a while she pondered the board. At last she added a lance to back up her number one sword. "They don't tell me everything. But I think they're doing it because it's a way of saying the gods are not well served by those who now hold power in the Temple—a way that will make a strong impression on a lot of people. It doesn't make any difference if they believe you or not."

Isak nodded. It made a narrow kind of sense, but it left him troubled. These were men who cared for nothing but their own goals. They did not care about truth. They were indifferent toward serving the gods. He advanced his second line sword to the midline, into the square held by his number one lance. He did not like to think of his foretelling being used by men to further goals of their own, even though it might be what the gods wanted.

But that he could not know. Not he nor any man. He tried to think what he would want, were he a god, but no answer came. He did not know, even, if—given the power—he would take one man from those who ruled the Temple, or all, or none. Could any man claim to know how the gods should be served?

"It's your turn," she said. It brought him back to the game. He hadn't noticed she had moved.

The game. He added another sword-piece to the board. The game. That was a world he could understand. It functioned by a simple set of rules. It had no mysteries.

The sword of the Japanese samurai was a triumph of the metalsmith's art. It should be stressed, though, that it was art, not science; those who worked the metal had only the most superficial understanding of what their rituals accomplished. They knew those procedures would create an amazingly useful piece of steel. Little more.

Modern, civilized commentators (momentarily forgetful of

napalm, hydrogen warheads, and zyklon B) may think it barbaric that such artistry and, yes, reverence, should be devoted to the manufacture of a tool good only to kill with, but in those times, in that place, a man who expressed such sentiments would himself have been considered odd. It was a civilized instrument. It gave clean death.

—Benjamin Dana

Another time, over a serving board of pickled eel and greens, he asked about the tokku sword. Escape was still a thing to think about; His Lordship might decide to keep him alive, but it seemed unwise to let his life turn on that man's whim. It needed careful thought, though. Should he try and fail, his life would not be worth as much as a desert stone. His experience with swords was meager, but to have a sword such as that might, even so, be all the difference. Tales of feats done with those blades were still told in taverns and around desert cookfires, as if their metal held a power greater than—and apart from—the men who wielded them.

But first he had to know if it was still a living blade. He had seen only two before in his life, both Temple prizes. One was snapped close to the hilt. Both wore crusts of corrosion.

At first, when he spoke of it, she frowned. She tilted her head and peered at him. It took him a moment to realize she didn't know what he was talking about.

"In the room where you . . ." He touched his head. The wound was almost healed.

"Oh," she said. "First Palovar's tokku."

It was his turn to frown while he groped to understand her nuance.

"Tokku," she repeated. "That's Old Tongue for sword. I only know a little Old Tongue, but that's one word I know. So I don't think of it as a sword. It's not a sword. It's a tokku."

94

He nodded. He understood now. "It's your father's?"

"Now it is," she said. Her hands made small motions, as if she was trying to say more than her words communicated. "It was First Palovar's when the Temple came. He held station in the household of the Duke Lagash—he who was then the Duke. It was given him by the Duke himself. When the Temple came, he helped defend the castle, and when it was taken he escaped and found a place to hide. And he kept his tokku. You probably don't understand, but it was important for a man to keep his tokku. They had a saying: *'Tokku ha, it gotch.' 'In my hand or my belly!'* First Palovar kept his tokku. Not many did. And you've heard what the Temple did to the smiths who made them. Nobody knows how to make them any more."

Isak knew what was done to the smiths. He could almost feel the blades on his body. "And ever since, your house has intrigued against the Temple?" It was hard to believe. So many generations?

The shake of her head was quick. "That's something recent. Oh, there were a lot of other houses that felt the same way. But as for hoping to do anything, it's only been the last few rounds of 'taking that we've . . . and mostly it's been only talk. We haven't the strength to do it by ourselves. We'll have to win a lot of common folk to our side. That's why . . ."

She broke off. She made a fluttery gesture. "We think your prophecy might help us."

He could have argued. His foretelling said nothing of what the gods expected of men. But he had told her that—told her, it seemed, a thousand times. Meanwhile, he wanted to know more about the sword.

"The sword," he said. "The . . . the tokku. Your family kept it because you hope to . . . to use it?"

"A tokku is power in the hand of he who holds it," Kalynn said. "If the chance comes, yes, of course it will be used."

"After so long? The others I have seen had no edge, and one was broken."

"Temple relics?" she asked, and smiled when he nodded. "Yes. Those are the ones they show, because they seem to confirm the Temple's power. But those of us who kept our tokku . . . Almost every 'taking, as far back as I can remember, father has taken it down and seen that its edge is true, and held it in the light of the gods whose overtaking it was. He showed me its grain because that is the mark of a true tokku, and because he is proud of it, and because he has no son; it is like the grain of fine timber. And he would polish it with oil and put it in its scabbard and hang it back on the wall. Even before we began to work with others, he said the time will come when it shall make priests' blood spill. I hope it, does,"

There was fire in the way she said that. He paused in his eating to look at her. She was not a different person. She was the same person he had thought he had begun to know, and even now he thought he knew her—knew her better, now, than before this moment.

"You hate the priests," he said.

"If they had done to you . . ." she began, but broke off and looked away. And when she looked at him again, her mouth wore a wry half-smile. Forced, but still a smile. "When they wanted to search the house we had to take it down and hide it."

Yes, had the Guards seen it, they would have pressed their search until they found him. And the Temple would have taken it, broken it. Another prize.

"You killed one of them," she said. "Not a priest, but at least one of those who serve the priests. That's almost as good."

"I felt no pleasure in it," Isak said uncomfortably. "It's still hidden?"

"They might want to search again," she said.

He couldn't ask where it was; to do so would betray his interest. So much for using it to help him escape. He pushed the serving board toward her. "You're not eating."

"I guess I'm not hungry," she said. She looked down at her swollen lap. "I'm sorry, Isak. I think too much about . . ." She shrugged. "Things." She looked up. "I'm not very good company."

"I have no other," he said. He set the board aside and reached for the waxboard she'd brought. Best to draw her mind from such thoughts. He motioned her to come around beside him. "Now, here is how we correct the lie of shadows at your post. We have determined, first, that the vector of true north turns six radiants westward from the vector given by the marker tiles. Therefore, to know the true standing of the gods, we must subtract that number from . . ."

She knew, he was sure, why he had changed the subject. She watched the marks he scratched on the board. Her golden head leaned close to his arm, almost touching. He was conscious of the warmth of her, and her closeness. Conscious, too, of the child in her body. With a deep ache part of him wished it could be his. But of course that was not possible. He tried to put it out of his mind but it stayed with him like the sound of a lute behind a singer's voice as he went on with her lesson.

Above all things, two forces shape our lives: what we believe about the nature of our world, and the intractable nature of our world as it truly is.

—Benjamin Dana

She said, finally, that she had to go. He wondered, had his tongue let slip too much of what was in his thoughts? But, well, he could not object.

She did not come back for a long time.

At first he didn't notice. He had his notes to study, to amend and think about, and new thoughts he'd only now thought of to put on waxboards and ponder; and other things he'd already pondered should be put on parchment. By now he had the beginnings of a treatise, an exploration into what was truly known about the gods and how they related to the known world. It was very hard to keep his thoughts clear and he lost track of the passage of time. But after a long time he became aware that a long time had passed and Kalynn had not come.

He broke off his work. He crawled into the entranceway and put his ear to the chinks between the stones. No sounds came. He sought a crack of light, but found none. Placing his hands on the stones, one by one, he tried to move them. They held as firm as if one with the earth.

He hesitated then, not sure what he should do. Perhaps a more forceful effort would dislodge them; but, though he had glimpsed the chamber outside, he had no knowledge of anything beyond. And, knowing the penalty for failure, he was not yet prepared to take the risk of breaking out. He retreated to his quarters and tried to resume his work. She'd left him a small jar of wine and a brick of cheese. He nibbled the cheese and sipped the wine and thought how his universe had narrowed to this tiny cell. All that he knew of things beyond its walls had to be brought to him. He could not confirm its truth by his own observation. The whole world could have ceased to exist and he would not know it. Perhaps even the gods were gone.

It was an absurd thought, but though he tried he could not contrive a way to prove it wrong. He sat with a clean waxboard on his knees and searched his mind. Several times he touched his fingernail to the shiny, slick surface, as if about to begin, but each time he paused and, after a moment, withdrew. Finally, he put the blank board aside and took up again the one he had been working on. He found, now, that his thoughts on that question came easily, smoothly, and with a clarity he had not felt before.

He was no closer to knowing what the gods were. Most likely he would never know. But he did know how they shared the sky and the sequential process by which they changed that sharing. Knowing that, and separating that from all else men thought they knew of the gods, he found it was no more difficult to describe their motions than it would have been to describe the workings of an elaborate machine. He was still at work, scratching marks on the board as fast as his finger could move, when at last Kalynn returned.

When the first stone was taken from the entranceway, he put the board aside and scrambled into the tunnel. While one part of him was careful to notice how the stones locked together, another felt the gladness of relief that she was all right. He'd been afraid, though he could not have explained what of.

"I'm back," she said.

He helped her climb up. "I had begun to wonder . . ." he said. He hadn't meant to say it. It came from his tongue without thought.

"I had to go talk to some people," she said. "And the midwife. I wanted to talk to a midwife, because . . . well, I'm sort of afraid and I don't . . ."

She saw the look on his face, his involuntary glance to her swollen belly. "Oh, not for a long time yet." Belittling. "I think not until after the darkness. I hope not. She said I shouldn't get excited, or try to do too much, or . . . oh, a lot of things. If you hadn't told me about the gods—about the darkness—I think I'd be terrified when it happens, and that wouldn't be good. So even if you haven't helped anyone else, you've helped me. I want you to know that. And all I've done is hit you on the head and put you in this hole."

"Could I have found a better place to hide?" he asked.

Hobur handed up the basket she'd brought. "Have care, young mistress," he said, and touched his temples before bending to lift the stones into place.

Isak took the basket and, made clumsy by its bulk and the cramped space, worked his way back into the chamber. Once there, Kalynn unpacked their meal; fresh yellowbuds still in the husk, water nuts, a melon so perfectly ripe her knife sliced through it at a stroke, a jar of wine. She plucked a yellowbud from its husk and offered it to him. He matched her gesture. "You must be starved," she said.

As they ate, he noticed she had put the knife down where, if he wanted, he could snatch it up. Held against her throat, it could win his freedom.

It tempted him, but he let it lie. Looking deep into himself, he knew he could not put a blade to her no matter how desperate he might be. He sensed she knew that.

She poured the last of the wine into his mug and, looking straight into his eyes, picked up the knife and dropped it in the basket behind her. "They wanted me to test you," she said, turning back to him. "I told them we could trust you. They weren't sure. Now . . ."

She broke off. He saw her lips move, though he heard no words. Thank you, he thought she was saying. Or something private, to herself. He couldn't be sure. But then she was looking straight at him again.

"Isak, how do you feel about the Temple?"

The question came unexpected. He had to pause, to think how he should answer. "I have been trying to decide," he said at last.

"They want to kill you," she said. "You know that."

He nodded. "That does not mean they are evil men. Perhaps it is what the gods would have happen."

"Do you believe that? Would you let them kill you?"

"I would prefer to live," he admitted. "I do not know what the gods want. Perhaps they enjoy to watch, to see how we play the game. Can anything happen that the gods do not want?"

She bent to clear away the melon rinds, the other leavings of their meal. When she turned again to him, her shoulders were set. "The priests say they serve the gods, that all they do is for that purpose. I say they lie."

He frowned. In spite of all that had happened, all he had seen and learned, he could not bring himself to accept that. The Temple served the gods, who were the life of all men. To speak as she had spoken was to speak against the gods. Could anyone serve the gods and still say such things?

She guessed his mind. "We have no argument with the gods," she said. "They are . . . well, the gods. But the priests . . . they claim to read portents, tell us what the gods intend, and claim we benefit from their foretellings. For that we give them tithe and privilege. But they're not satisfied with that. They mislead us, lie to us, and say it was the gods, for reasons only the gods can know and which no man can understand, while they—the priests!—see their own holdings prosper at our cost. Did you even know a thin priest?"

Isak thought of Lurgien, gaunt with age, seamed jowls and sunken eyes. "Once," he said.

"Once!" She seized it like a prize. "Once!"

He hadn't meant it as an argument. "I do not say that no priests are corrupt," he said. "I know that some are. But I have known others who were decent, honorable men. And it is true that portents can be seen and understood, though I must also say that often they are difficult to read, and the foretellings are not always certain."

Her tongue had been poised to resume the attack, but instead she only looked at him. She might have studied an intricate carving with that sort of look. "It's something you know," she said at last.

"It is part of a Temple scribe's craft," he said. "We keep record of how the gods share our sky. We search old records for previous times they took a similar configuration and search out the happenings that followed. From what we have found, the priests prepare a foretelling. But often we will find that similar sharings of our sky were followed by events that were very different. I do not know if the gods deliberately deceive, or whether it is only that we fail to understand them."

"Isak," she said, intently frowning, "are you saying that anyone could do what the priests do?"

He spread his hands. "Only the Temples have the records."

"And it gives them power." She slapped a hand on the floor. "Power to do as they want, take what they want, gather wealth to themselves and leave none for others."

"Some of them," Isak admitted. "They are men, no different from other men."

"And the higher they stand in the Temple, the more self-serving."

Of that realm, he had no certain knowledge. He said as much with a wordless gesture.

"Do you doubt?" she asked.

"I do not know," he said. "I know that you hate them."

"Do you think I shouldn't?"

Struck by her vehemence, he could only draw back. "My lady, I do not know. Have you a reason?"

For a moment she was very still. "You didn't know? You didn't even suspect?"

Dumbly, he shook his head. "My lady . . ." he began, and found that his confusion let him say no more.

A moment longer she looked into his face. "You have never spoken anything but truth to me," she said. She spoke as if from a great distance. "I . . ."

Abruptly she held out her arm—pulled back her shawl to show the bare wrist. "You see that I wear no man's cuff. You did not wonder?"

"My lady, I . . ." In his circumstance he had not had the right to raise such questions. And . . . "What use would it have been to wonder? I could see you have a child, and I could see that you do not admit to being owned. Should I have thought you were so careless as to have had an accident at the baths?"

"They do happen," Kalynn said. "It isn't always a matter of letting it happen."

He nodded. "But that is not why you will have a child." She had implied as much by her words; he had never thought it likely. "My lady, the happenings of a person's life are even less knowable than the gods. I could invent a thousand conjectures which would do you honor, and there might be yet another thousand that I do not have the wit to make. Any might be true."

"And another thousand that would do me no honor at all?" she suggested. She said it lightly, but she rested her chin on a fist, challenging.

Isak pretended he had not heard. "I have made no judgment," he said. "I do not know enough."

She looked away.

"Have I said words that hurt?" he wondered aloud. "I did not mean . . ."

"Isak. Please. I know you're trying to be kind. That is what hurts, because there were others who were not. I would . . . after the next harvest, I would have gone to the auction. I was eager for it. There were—" She closed her eyes. "— oh, several young men who would have entered bids for me, any of whom I would have welcomed whether they offered much or little. But, since . . ." Her hand touched the bulge of her pregnancy. ". . .

they have turned their interests elsewhere. The best I could hope, now, would be to find place as a secondary woman to a rich man whose principal woman is barren, perhaps to be discarded once I have produced an heir. I think I will ask father not to offer me."

"If their interest waned, I think they must never have valued you," Isak said.

She was slow to reply. "I'd like to believe that." She looked straight at him. "Would you have turned away?"

For a moment his thoughts were stuttering confusion. The idea was completely new, nor did he know enough to guide him to an honest reply. "How can I say?" he managed at last. "I, who have never owned a spare farthing, who did not know you before I became your captive? None of it could have happened."

She smiled a sad, quiet smile. "And if you had a farthing now?"

He found that more than anything else he did not want to hurt her. "I think you would be worth far more." He could say that in honest truth. "But I have no farthing, and small hope I ever shall."

Again she looked away, again with that sad smile. "You're being kind," he said. "It wasn't fair to ask. I . . . ." She reached out. Fingertips brushed his arm. "Others have not been kind." Her posture changed then, and her eyes became direct. "But I was going to give you truth. I have no way to prove what I say; I can only ask you to believe. It was a priest who put the child in me." Her eyes faltered. "I don't really know. It may have been several priests."

I think the gods, if gods there be, would like to be consulted
before a thing is done in their name.

—Benjamin Dana

She told it all then.

It had been warm in spite of the season and she had gone to the
baths. She had passed through the waterfall curtain from the
thermal pool and, still tingling from the cold water's shock, had
turned to follow the concourse toward the courtyard when the
priest stopped her. She had hardly noticed his approach; her at-
tention had been taken by the wealth of honor scars on the
muscular back of a Guard—with such scars, even naked he
could be mistaken for nothing else—who strode ahead of her.
The sight woke troublesome feelings, feelings she did not
understand. For a moment she did not breathe.

The priest had been coming the other way. His body still
reeked of the masseuse's unguents and his belly wobbled gelidly.
He was ugly flesh, white as an unfrocked gavial and fat as a
filled oil bladder, so she was hardly aware of him until, as he
was about to pass, he put out an arm to block her. His soft
hand cupped her shoulder. She gave a startled cry but the Guard
did not turn. Why should he?

"I saw the torque at his throat, so I knew he was a priest,"
she said. "Just as he must have seen the maiden's chain at my
waist."

She did not understand what was happening. She was a little
afraid, though she knew someone was sure to come in a mo-
ment. In a stern voice the priest demanded her name and her
household's name. That made her even more afraid, for when
one was naked in the baths she left identity with her clothes in
the entrance hall. But he was a priest, and if she understood his
torque's designs and decorations, a priest of high station. She

105

did not dare defy him. She blurted her name, but then her voice failed out of fear. He repeated his demand, her household's name. His hand tightened on her shoulder. Trying to avoid his eyes and the sight of those dewlapped jowls, she looked down and saw unequivocal evidence of the nature of his interest. She twisted out of his grasp, ducked under his arm, and fled.

He did not follow, and she thought the matter ended. In the courtyard she emerged into the sight of the gods. Their warmth bathed away a chill she had not known she felt. She looked up, gave them honor and gratitude. They were all in the sky, all but Actinic Gamow. In the west, about to go down, the Twinned Ones hovered above the horizon's dark haze, while ascending the eastward sky, forming a canted triangle, Blazing Alpher and Red Bethe stood very close now to their overtaking, with Bright Dalton to southward, soon to overtake both, trailing less than a hand's span behind. Standing north of them and following all, the Pale One floated white, ghost cold, like a perfectly round, hard-edged cloud. Such a clustering of the gods was not common, and was almost certainly portentous, though she could not have guessed what of. In her present mood she found it disquieting.

She took a leather pallet and spread it on the lawn, and let the gods warm her body. Previous basking, both there and in the garden at home, had already stained her a smooth honey brown, which she took as a sign of special favor of the gods. Memory of the priest began to fade.

For a while she lay there, turning now and again so that the gods could examine all of her, taking pleasure from the warm intensity of their regard. As always, Alpher blazed too bright to look at. She reached up a hand to mask his sight and sought Red Bethe in the sky beside him. Even unschooled in the finer points of god watching it took her only a moment to find him. He stood north and slightly east of Alpher's disc, not more than a finger-joint's length away. He was at his smallest, a tiny, round fleck, shining like a ruby heated to brilliance. After only an instant she had to look away. That their overtaking was very near she had known. The city was full of preparations for the festival, though she had given it scant thought herself. It was a thing the Temple did. Perhaps it had already begun, although she hadn't heard the Temple's gong.

After a while she joined a game of tag—a team of girls against a team of boys. When a boy held the sponge, she ran to escape him, dodging around the other boys who tried to block her; when a girl had the sponge, she moved to block escaping boys so the girl with the sponge could mark them. Kalynn took her own turns with the sponge and shouted with delight when she made a score. There was much laughter, good-natured taunts, more than a few tangled sprawls. Her body acquired a dozen different colored blotches. Half a hundred. So did all the others. When it ended she never knew how long it had gone on. Returning to the baths, she washed off the stains, the sweat, and the grime in a tepid cascade.

The way the game had ended had made her uneasy. A boy and two girls had fallen in a complicated tangle which their efforts to sort out only made more complicated. At first it was comic, cause for laughter from both onlookers and the persons involved. Then the girl on the bottom gave a cry of alarm and it was instantly apparent that the boy had lost control of himself. Hastily, two other boys moved in to break them apart. No real harm was done; the girl quickly regained her composure and the boy was horribly embarrassed. After that, no one had wanted to continue the game.

In the cascade, thinking about it while the water splashed against her body, Kalynn remembered the priest. What had happened in the game hadn't been all that uncommon. At one time or another in the course of it almost all the boys had shown

107

signs of similar arousal; it was a commonplace of bath-garden games, more a cause for amusement than scandal. It was just that this time, accidentally, it had gone beyond fun. What bothered her was that she couldn't forgive the boy and yet think ill of the priest. The impulse he had shown had been natural and ordinary.

But he had touched her, and he had demanded her name and the name of her household. It wasn't right to ask someone's identity in the baths. Even a priest should not have asked. It disturbed her that he had.

She swam briefly in a scent-giving pool, then dried herself before the thundering flames of the furnace room and stepped out into the entrance hall clean and new, though still uneasy in her mind. She was taking her clothes from the shelf when the Guards—clothed Guards—came upon her and clamped hands on her arms.

Startled, she tried to pull away, but they did not let her. They turned her around whether she wanted or not. She looked up into the face of a Guards Captain.

"You should be proud," he said. "The gods have chosen you." Beyond his shoulder, across the hall through a swirl of moving people, she saw the priest. The same one, though now he was clothed in his robes. Fine robes they were. She felt his eyes on her body.

Frightened now, she tried again to break away, but still they held her. Her clothes were on the floor, tangling her feet. She hardly noticed.

"You will come," the Captain said.

Naked as she was, they took her out into the street. They lifted her into a wagon and bound her to a post that was wrapped with garlands and stood in the center of the wagon bed like a ship's mast. A flowered crown was placed on her head. The scent of flowers dizzied her. The Guards made her drink *from a bowl. It was a cool fluid, thin as whey, but it burned her throat and became a core of heat deep inside her. The drome were goaded. The procession began.*

Acolytes flanked the wagon on either side, endlessly chanting. Another acolyte came behind, striking the gong that hung from the wagon's tailsprit, waiting each time for the last dull vibration to die before he struck again.

Ahead walked the priest, in his hand a staff that carried a carved, gilded sunburst on its head. With staff and open palm he gestured flamboyantly to the people in the street who paused to watch them pass. A squad of Guards followed, bright fluttering banners tied to their pikes. Then came the wagon, its drover a hunchbacked dwarf who stood on the seat, capering and waving his goad to the crowds who seemed to have gathered from nowhere. Desperately Kalynn tried to tear herself free. She was naked outside the baths. Her mind was a chaos of terror and shame. But the thongs were tough and tightly knotted. Nor could she find voice.

Slowly, the procession ascended the streets of the city. Flowers and green leaves were thrown into the wagon, and handfuls of barley and rye. Something strange began to happen inside her; the hot glow within seemed gradually to expand, to fill her, as if Blazing Alpher's brilliance shone from her innermost core while she herself was far away and all that was happening happened only to her body. The procession twisted from street to street. Flowers covered her feet, collected into a mound almost to her knees. Behind the wagon, now, a crowd followed. Some held aloft boughs of new growth. Others bore the tools of a trade. Children rode shoulders, chattering excitedly, waving hands in the air. The wagon bumped over the cobbles. Its wheel rims scraped and rasped. Joints creaked. The gong sang. The acolytes' chant droned on and on.

The procession came onto the Avenue of Priests, but altered neither pace nor ceremony. Step by step, stage-by-stage, it ascended the high bluff's wall toward the height where the Temple waited. The drome hissed frustration as their paws fought for purchase on the smooth stones. Acolytes leaned against the wagon's thwarts, urging it upward. The cadence of their chant never faltered.

She looked skyward, where the gods watched. They could hardly dazzle her more. In a remote, dissociated way, she knew what was happening. She had known—perhaps she had always known—a woman was brought to the Temple as part of the observance of the Time of Overtaking. She'd never concerned herself with such events—never wondered where the woman came from, who she was, how chosen. Neither did she know what was done with her. It had never seemed important; nor had she, now, the will to do more than let it happen.

"It is done differently in different places," Isak told her. "In Remoss it was the same woman for many rounds, and then it was her firstborn daughter. And I saw a town where all the young women met in secret and chose one from among themselves. They thought it was a privilege. In Filorna, it is the winner of a game."

"And in those other places," Kalynn asked, "what is done to them?"

"That is also different," Isak said. But he was almost sure, now, what must have happened to Kalynn. He felt a need to give her understanding of the reason for it. "The overtaking comes always between the time of harvest and the time of planting, just as the season of most growth comes when so many do not stand together in our sky. The ceremony is to honor the gods for the bounty of the round of seasons ended, and to seek their favor in the round to come. It is no small thing."

He saw the frown begin between her brows and hurried on. "You know—I am sure you must know—how different a round may be from the one before and the one that follows; that in one an enterprise may prosper, but in the next, in spite of equal skill and effort, it may utterly fail. I have myself seen pastures turn to barren earth, crops dead for lack of rain, and mud where a river had filled its banks only the round before. I have seen boats come back to shore with their catch baskets empty, voyage after voyage, and storms that came suddenly from beyond our world's edge, from which no boat ever returned. My father sailed on one of those. I was myself with a caravan trapped in mountains under rains that seemed would never end. No man has control of such forces. Only the gods can do such things."

She did not speak at once, and when she spoke, she spoke as if from far away. "And for that I was given a child I did not seek, by a man I would never have let touch my hand."

He'd never thought of it from that point of view, but as she spoke he understood it clearly. Still . . .

"I have been told of a town where the woman's belly is cut open, and all that is in it they scatter on the fields. Of course she does not live."

He thought, telling her that, she would see that worse could have happened, but he spoke without watching her face. When he looked, he wished he had not spoken.

"And that is done as honor to the gods?"

"That is what they believe, those who do it. At least, that is what they would say."

"And what was done to me, that also was done to honor the gods?"

"That is what they would have said," Isak said, feeling very uncomfortable now. She'd made him think about it, and his thoughts were disquieting. "I must admit I do not know of any time that doing such things has changed the prospect foretold by how the gods were standing in our sky, so I would hesitate to say that they speak truth. I . . ."

He broke off and picked up a waxboard. He scratched a hasty note and laid it aside. "I will have to think about that," he said, still drawn into himself, thinking, trying to find the shape of his thought. "If it is true the gods share our sky according to a systematic pattern, however complex, and if it is true that how they share our sky foretells how an enterprise will prosper against the variations of the seasons, then it must follow that there is a pattern, also, to the variability of the seasons. I would have to search in the Archives to be sure, but . . ."

She touched his hand. "Isak, if that is true, what they did to me was . . . useless."

The same thought had come to Isak. He nodded. "Yes, that would be true," he admitted

"I've tried to talk to Father about it," she said. "He wouldn't listen. I . . ." She looked down at her hands. Her fingers struggled with each other.

"If you want to tell it," he said. He made his voice as gentle as he could. "If you feel you must. It's not a thing I have a right to ask."

"But you do," she said.

He looked at her, not understanding.

"You said I was worth at least a farthing," she said, as if that explained everything. In a strange way it did; at the same time, it explained nothing.

The procession topped the final slope, turned, and trod the Great Way. Ahead the Temple yawned. She should have felt afraid, but it was not like that. It was as if she only watched, was not involved. Musics—perhaps they'd always been there— appeared, the thud of drum joining the beat of the gong, brasses erupting to a fanfare, the reedy keen of bagpipes. The Temple loomed nearer, then nearer still. The acolytes' chant and the beat of drums advanced their tempo, blended with the fanfare into a throbbing crescendo that went on and on, rising and rising until it was the only sensation she could still perceive. Then it ended.

Surrounded by the sudden quiet, the wagon had stopped close beside the Obelisk in the broad expanse of the great square. With a swirl of vestments, the acolytes spread from the wagon and, augmented by more who appeared as if sprouted from between the cobbles, formed a circle around the wagon, the Obelisk, and the shadows it cast across the stones. Linking their arms, they held the gathering crowd from invading that zone. Kalynn felt the thong at her throat come loose, and then her waist, and then the one that bound her knees. Her wrists were set free. Hands took her arms and guided her down off the wagon. Her feet scattered flowers as she moved. The hard, god-heated stones seared her unprotected soles.

She was brought to the place where the shadows thrown by Blazing Alpher and Red Bethe lay, one within the other (so the overtaking had begun!); to the place where Bethe's deeper darkness ended and only the red-tinted shadow of Alpher reached beyond. They turned her to face the Obelisk, a tall black column against the blue sky. In that shadow, she felt suddenly cold.

A lesser priest advanced and draped a garland on her shoulders. She felt a tug at her maiden's chain, heard it snap. It rattled on the stones. But for her dazzled distantness, she would have screamed. Somewhere a voice was speaking Old Tongue. Hands took her right arm; something closed around her wrist like an animal's jaw. Other things, softer, were pressed against her palms and her fingers were made to close and hold them: a clutch of winter blossoms and a sheaf of yarrow, and on her wrist a jeweled, gold cuff, as if she were a bride. Emeralds, opals, and jade gleamed in Bethe's saffron blaze. Rubies flashed with inner fire.

The bowl was put to her lips again and she was made to drink. The fire of it traced a scar down her throat and pooled, a *knot of flame, in the center of her body. Perhaps she swayed.*

The priest approached. The same priest; she knew that face. He bent, scooped up her maiden's chain and faced her, cascading it from hand to hand. His jowls wore a self-pleased look. Abruptly, without a glance to see if one was there to take it, he passed the chain to an acolyte. He lifted his hands under her breasts, as if to test their weight. His thumbs stroked the smooth, soft skin. His pleased look deepened.

Turning then, he raised his arms—outward at first, and the crowd's babble stilled. Then upward, open-palmed, toward the gods. He spoke an invocation. It was in Old Tongue; Kalynn did not know the words. The acolytes, all of them, wherever they stood, voiced a reply. Another bold toned call. Again the acolytes responded, then broke into a chorus of parts; one cluster, then another, uttering their litanies and, in their turn, falling silent. The voice leapt across the open space from group to group like a bounding ball, at first with a ponderous rhythm, but relentlessly quickening—becoming faster than her dazed attention could follow, then faster yet, and faster, becoming a resonant cacophony that yammered through her being endlessly. A drum took the rhythm, beginning softly, then more loudly. Another joined, and another. Brasses glazed the air. Chimes clanged.

Acolytes turned her around, urged her forward. Her body obeyed; she had no will to do otherwise. Perhaps the priest followed; she did not know. She walked the path of Alpher's shadow; a lesser priest touched her shoulder each time she began to stray from it—followed it all the way to its end. Touches at her shoulder turned her now—turned her toward the Temple.

A way opened for her through the throng. In moments it was carpeted with flowers and fern fronds. They were cool and soft after the hard, warm stones.

Into the Temple through the high central arch. Down the nave of the great hall through dim light to the transept. All the great hall's shutters were closed; she could see almost nothing. They stopped her before the High Altar. Deep shadows bloomed around her, dark as deep water, and still the din of drums and flutes and bells and, loud, the chanting voices. A blaze of light shone down on her, warm on her brow, her shoulders, her breasts. An oval pool of brightness surrounded her feet on the smooth stone floor. It dazzled her downcast eyes. The smoky sweetness of incense filled the air she breathed.

"There are mirrors on the Temple's roof," Isak said. "They can be turned to reflect a god's light down into the hall, no matter where he may stand in the sky."

"I didn't know that," Kalynn said. "I didn't know where it came from. I thought it was the gods."

At the time, she hadn't wondered. It was all experience. Things felt and seen. To have questioned any part would have been beyond the strength of her will. She had no will. A lesser priest brought the bowl again. He raised it to her lips. Again she drank. The heat glowed through her body. She felt as if the light around her shone from that inner flame, like fire shining through glass.

The chant slowed, became again a perceptible rhythm reinforced by the march of the drums. The horns and chimes fell silent. Four senior priests took station around her, facing inward from the edges of the pool of light. She was induced to turn, to face them one by one, and as she paused before each one, that one advanced a step and touched her shoulder with a talisman; the coiled, stuffed skin of an eel, a wine sack, an ungulate's plump egg pouch, a wand of gold. Beyond the pool of light, as she turned, she could see only shapes and shadows, the massive roof timbers, stone arches, and a bright patch where the entrance arch gave a glimpse of the sky. Again she went around the circle, to be touched again with talismans; a water tuber, a skein of gossamer yarn, a leviathan's tusk gnarled and brown with age, and a cluster of agate berries the sight of which, even in her dreamlike state, made her breath catch. But even then she did not have the will to resist when, after touching the cluster to her shoulder, the priest plucked one of the berries and placed it in her mouth. Its skin broke. Her mouth was filled with sweetness.

This time, as she turned again to face the altar, she was stopped. Again she was given the bowl. Again she drank. Behind her the chant exploded to a crescendo of pure sound.

Something made her look up. Standing beside the altar, benignly smiling on her, stood the priest, the same priest, the one who had chosen her. For a moment their eyes met. Peripherally, she saw his hand move.

The light around her narrowed, blinked out Darkness wrapped around her like a cloth. Before she could move or think or even draw breath, hard hands took hold of her. Thrust forward, her feet gone from under her, she would have fallen. There was a scuff of sandals, a rustle of robes. Half-carried, half-dragged, they took her away. A latch snapped. Ahead a curtain was flung aside and she was in a passageway with walls of dressed stone. Small lamps in niches gave dim light. Flanking her on either side, two senior priests hustled her along. She stumbled, could not find her balance. The quiet gloom was cold on her nakedness.

"I have seen it done several times," Isak said. "In several places. There is a frame between the mirror and the skylight, and when it is turned it closes like a scissors except that blades come together from six sides instead of only two. The shaft of light you were standing in becomes thinner and thinner and then it is gone. And then they take you away, and then the frame is opened again, and it would seem to all who watched that the gods whose light it was had plucked you from the Temple."

"But that's not true," Kalynn said. "I was still in the Temple. If they serve the gods, why would they contrive a deception like that? And . . ."

Isak shrugged. He could give no explanation beyond things he'd already said.

She had very little more to tell, or possibly she remembered less than had happened, for by that time her awareness had become like a tiny spark that floated in the air far behind her.

After a long journey—it seemed long—through passageways and stairways and, thick, squeak-hinged doors, she was in a chamber where again the light of the gods shone—muted now, as if through gauzy curtains. And there they left her on a soft leather couch, bathed in that light, and there the priest came to her while her self watched as if from a distance, unable to do more than watch and feel. He laid his weight on her body. His torque bruised her cheek and his body smelled of sweat and scented oils; and his body invaded her body in the way that a man did his woman, and though the part of her that watched knew she was not his, her body yielded and received him.

And received him.

And received him.

When it was done, the priest went away. A lesser priest came with the bowl, and two acolytes who bathed her, a task they performed with the detachment of butchers handling meat. When the light in the chamber changed its tone, as if a god had gone below the horizon or another had risen, the priest came again. Or perhaps it was another priest. She was too far away, then, to know faces. Her body accepted him. The light changed again, and again he came, and again she watched while her body was used.

Again and again, that was the way of it, the light changing and the priest coming to her and the hard edge of his torque cutting welts in her cheek, her throat, the side of her jaw, forcing tears to her eyes. Again and again he used her body and went away until the next time the light changed. She never knew if it was one man or many. Only one face stayed in her mind but there could have been others. Many others.

When they were done with her, they wrapped her in an acolyte's robe and put her in a curtained carriage. Then—she never remembered how—she found herself outside the gate of her father's house. The overtaking was done; Red Bethe's shadows edged Blazing Alpher's on the right hand side as the two began to separate. It seemed a long time she leaned against the gate's hard panes before she thought to lift the knocker bar. Old Bellreo peered through the spy box, quickly unbarred the gate, and shouted to the house. Hobur came and carried her inside. The jeweled cuff was still on her wrist; her broken maiden's chain was clutched in her hand.

"So now I wear neither," she said. "If I believed it was the god who put a child in me, I'd proudly wear a cuff. But it wasn't the gods. It was the priests, and they are only common men."

"A priest would say he acted for the gods," Isak said. "That the gods acted through him."

She looked directly into his eyes. "Do *you* think that?"

Isak pondered long before he gave reply. "No, I do not," he admitted. "I think once I would have, but now I do not know a reason why I should. Like yourself, I must question whether—as they claim—they serve the gods. Would the gods send a darkness, if all was right with how they serve?"

"You know they wouldn't," she said.

He hesitated. "No," he said. "I do not know that. I do not know why the gods do what they do. I do not know what they want. That they affect the world we live in, no one doubts, but why . . . ? I believe no man can know, that those who say they know do not speak truth."

She brushed a strand of hair back from her face, tossed her head. "Then you would say the priests—the one who used me—that they used me because it suited them. They acted for themselves, and only for themselves. They did not serve the gods."

Isak could not face the direct look of her eyes. He looked down at his hands. "Admitting that I could be wrong, I would have to say that is a logical derivative of what I believe. But I must also say I do not know the gods."

She studied him a moment longer. Subtly her gaze softened then, and the faint touch of a smile warmed her mouth. He could not guess what she was thinking. Then the moment was gone, and her posture had nothing but the hardness of bones.

"Isak, I want to see their power broken," she said. Her teeth flashed. Her chin lifted. "So does Father, for that reason and for other reasons. So do his friends, though I'm not so silly as to think their reasons have anything to do with me."

As she spoke, her eyes seemed to watch something behind his right shoulder. The illusion was so strong Isak had to reject the impulse to turn, to see what was there. He knew there was nothing.

"Do you still think I'm worth a farthing?" she asked.

It took him by surprise. "More than that," he blurted, even before he thought.

"And . . . and if you had a farthing . . . ?" She spoke with aching hope.

He didn't know how to answer. "How can I say?" he asked. Though his thoughts stuttered, the words came easy to his tongue. "Does it matter? That an ill-schooled scribe, a wanderer without wealth or station, known to have spoken heresies, whom the Guards would kill on sight, and whom the Temple's enemies might kill for lack of knowing what else to do with him—that he might think you worth a farthing at bride auction? Do you think so little of yourself?"

"And you?" she countered, whip quick. "Is that all you think of yourself?" She did not wait for a reply. Reaching out, she touched his knee. Her hand paused there. "Isak, if you had a farthing, it would be your whole wealth. So it would mean more to me than any fraction of a rich man's horde. That is what I was asking." She took her hand back. She looked away. "Perhaps I was silly to ask."

It was his turn to reach out. He touched her forehead, made her look at him. "No. Not silly, or foolish, or thoughtless," he said. She was such a baffling mixture of softness and iron. "If there was a thing I could do that would heal the harm that has been done you, I would do it. If I had a farthing, and if it were enough to win your nod at the auctions, I would be in truth the equal of a man of great wealth."

"I think you just did," she murmured, so soft he wasn't sure, at first, what he'd heard.

He frowned. "Did what?"

Her shoulders flexed uneasily, but her voice was calm. "Healed me," she said simply. "Won me."

He was slow to understand. Then, understanding, he discovered his mind was divided equally between excitement and doubts. "But I do not have a farthing," he said. He had to speak truth. "And small hope I ever shall. I may not even live."

She shrugged. "We'll just have to do something about that," she said, as if it was the easiest thing in the world.

Today, when astronomical discoveries pour in at a stunning rate from our telescopes and space probes, it is easy to forget that one of the greatest astronomical advances was something seen only in mind's eye, quite independent of observations.

—*Owen Gingerich*

Later, when she had gone and he could think more calmly, he saw it was a hopeless dream, the sort of fantasy a marketplace storyteller might invent to coax a few coins from his listeners. Real life did not happen like that. Too many improbable things would have to happen; to begin with, he would have to stay alive.

She returned after a while, bringing hot food. Again there was the business at the entranceway, helping her to climb up, then taking the serving board from Hobur, and then the bowls and jars. Through it all she hardly spoke, but her hand seemed to linger on his arm; she bumped against him almost playfully; and the way she looked at him was, at the same time, both disquieting and pleasant.

Back in their chamber again she busied herself arranging the board and the bowls and filling their mugs from one of the jars. Now, though she spoke while she worked, it was only to tell him she hadn't been able to read the shadow post. Thick clouds filled the sky from one horizon to the other, she said, and a cold, thin rain was drizzling down. He nodded at the news; it affected nothing. Time would pass at the same pace as if the sky was clear and the gods looked down.

She lifted the cloth from the board, revealing a stuffed roast sandlapper. Working deftly, she scored the glazed skin with a knife and poured a steaming sauce over it from one of the bowls. Another bowl contained brookweed hearts in thin broth. There were prawn nuggets baked to a flawless white, and kyrt bean pods showing pale yellow where the flame had burst them. She broke a scrap of bread from a loaf still redolent from the oven and offered it, host to guest. Almost without thought, he took it and, tearing off a shred of his own, gave it to her in return. She accepted it, hesitated, smiled a shy smile, and put it in her mouth. Only then did he remember it was by that gesture that the bargain at brides' auction was sealed. He felt her grave eyes on him.

It seemed the wrong moment to talk about realities.

"Isak," she said, "I want to know how you do it—how you foretell the gods. Is it something you can teach?"

With his wine mug halfway to his lips, he paused. He had taught her the rudiments of writing and reading, and some of the simpler manipulations that could be done with numbers. She'd been an able student, at least the equal of a scholarium novice. To bring her into understanding of the gods as he had come to understand them would be severalfold more difficult, but there was nothing intrinsically beyond her ability.

"You are the first to ever ask," he said, and set his mug down.

"Would you?" she asked. "Please?"

"I would like to," he heard himself saying. "I think the gods would want me to. No one else has thought it possible to know."

She sliced a joint from the sandlapper and passed it to him. "And the gods? They would not be unwilling to give a woman their signs?"

A wisp of steam trailed from the piece of meat in his hand. "The only sign they give is how their shadows fall," he said. "That sign they give to everyone. From that it is only a matter of calculation. I have not yet shown you how fractions are treated, and there will be the special considerations that result from dealing with cycles, but except for those you know all the parts of the process. The only other thing you must learn is the relationships you will be dealing with. I see no reason you cannot learn any of those things."

She had cut a joint for herself and had bitten a mouthful off the bone. Slowly, thoughtfully, she chewed and swallowed. "And when I have learned these things, I will know how the gods will share our sky from one passing to the next? And in a hundred passings? A thousand?"

"You will know how to evoke that knowledge," Isak said. "Yes."

"And there is nothing magical about it? No ritual? They do not speak to you in a secret voice?"

He shook his head. "It is only a matter of knowing their paths and their pace. The rest is nothing but arithmetic."

Her eyes watched him. "That's strange," she said in a far away voice. "So very strange."

He finished the last of his meat. She cut him a piece of the flank. "Sometimes I wonder if the gods are anything like we believe them to be," he said. "So many things we have always believed, I have discovered they are not true."

"Is anything really true?" she asked, all innocence.

For a moment it seemed a nonsense question. But then Isak saw the deeper implications of it, and the words he had been about to speak vanished from his tongue. He wondered if she realized the profundity of what she had asked. He found his voice, but now he had no words. "My lady, I do not know," he said at last.

Moreover, the recent measurements suggest that the neighborhood of our galaxy may not be a representative sample of the universe. If true, this observation implies that cosmology has its own "Catch 22"—whereas the vicinity of our galaxy may not be typical of the universe, only that region can be studied accurately.

—Beverly Karplus Hartline

He delayed the start of her lesson as long as he could. All the while they ate, talking casually between mouthfuls, he had thought about what she needed to know. Perhaps it would have been enough to make a chart of the measures and their rates of change, and then to have shown her the arithmetic he used to construct a foretelling; but that was a poor way to learn. True understanding was more profound than numbers, more marvelous than a cast of shadows. He wanted to wake that vision in her.

Besides, he might not live to tell it to another person.

So much he would have to explain, such a vastness, and the poetry was not in him. So many things he felt inadequate to tell, and felt also the terrible void between what he knew, or thought he knew, and what still lay beyond the reach of his understanding. The smoke of the lamp made his eyes hurt. He closed them and spoke to the darkness in which he could see more clearly than in the light of the gods.

"I do not know how to begin," he confessed. "Once before I tried. I did not do it well. It is hard to hold so much clear in the mind, like water in the hand." He squeezed his eyes against the pain.

"Try again," Kalynn said. Her voice was calm. She understood. He took a breath, thought back, searched memory for what had gone wrong that other time.

Artaneel had found him on the roof of the shrine, sitting on the warm tiles, knees hugged to his body as if he was cold.

"Isak!" His voice broke the peace of that place. "At once! I need you."

Hardly more than a murmur in the wind, it reached into his trance, if trance it was. More nearly it was a looking inward, seeing within a cosmic expanse which frightened and filled him with wonder. He could hardly breathe.

"Isak!" The sound of his name struck like a pebble.

"*Darkness,*" *Isak whispered.* "*Darkness.*"

Then part of him was in the real world again. He blinked against the brightness of the gods' light. Had his eyes been shut?

"*Darkness,*" *he said, looking up as Artaneel's shadow fell across him.*

"*Don't babble like an addled boy.*" *Artaneel's sandals scuffed the litter of bat droppings on the tiles.* "*How long have you been hiding up here?*"

Still in two worlds at once, Isak shook his head. "*Not long.*" *He let go of his knees.* "*We must tell them. Darkness. I came up here to take a measure. I had to be sure. And . . .*"

"*I told you, quit your babble.*" *No more patience than a thunderstorm.* "*Pay attention. A caravan master comes with the intent to try for Hrodah. Yes! Now, with Alpher casting shorter shadows with each passing. He asks what prospect. Your foretelling. He must have it immediately.*"

Even when Alpher held low to the south it was a fearful road. Isak cringed as he remembered that flame-dry heat when he had walked it, the white bones and dead shrubs around a red crusted seep that tasted of iron and gall. "*The gods will burn every shred from his bones.*"

But then a thought came. "*No!*" *Excitement exploded within him.* "*There is a way. Tell him . . . say to him . . .*" *He knelt to retrieve the waxboard on the tiles beside him, rubbed it smooth with the heel of his hand, took stylus from the thong around his neck. Still on his knees he sketched a few quick marks, a pause, then several more.*

"*Yes.*" *Now it was clear in his mind.* "*Tell him it is the part where the road must cross between the two lines of mountains and the valley between is all salt and sand and broken black stones. If he has ever gone that road he will know that part. While Alpher stands high the wells are not likely to have water,*" *nor most of the seeps, and the way is too long for a caravan to carry its water."*

"Children are born knowing that," Artaneel said. "He asks a foretelling, not trivial facts."

Isak looked down at the marks on his board and almost wept. Did not the hierophant understand that problems could not be solved until they were stated clearly? "I did not mean to mock, honored one. I am saying, if he wants to make that crossing he must do it another way."

"How else?" Scorn oozed from the words. "It is the only road."

"He must do three things which he may think strange." Anxiety made him speak fast, blind to Artaneel's darkening scowl. Gone from his thoughts was all knowledge of the darkness, though he knew it would come as surely as he knew his name.

"He must stop every time Blazing Alpher comes into our sky," he said, "From when he stands a fist's width above the eastern ridge until a standing man casts a shadow three times his height. That is when the heat will be worst. His men must put up their tents for shade and share it with the animals. If they try to travel while Alpher stands high, thirst will kill them."

"They will die unless they make the crossing as fast as they can," Artaneel said.

"As I have said, it will not seem reasonable. Wait, there is more." Momentum carried him on. "When he begins the part from the rest camp at Last Water, for every three beasts that carry goods he must have one with a load of waterskins. Full ones. And when he has stopped the second time to rest while Alpher stands high he must send back all the animals he does not need to carry the water that is left. Before they go, the ones he sends back should drink their fill, men and animals both.

Without more, they should be able to get back to Last Water all right."

"Leaving the ones on the road marooned?"

"No," Isak said. "That is the most important part. The others must go on. When they have made three more stops, they will have water left for only one more, and the distance left for them to go will be almost four. At that point, they must send ahead all the animals whose water loads have been used and all the men not needed for the animals that are left. They must take all the empty waterskins with them and one full skin for each two beasts."

He took a breath, saw Artaneel gather self to quash the flood of words, and with his voice forced him to keep his silence. "When they reach the freshwater seep at the narrow end of the lake called Dying River," he said, "they must fill all their skins and return to meet the rest of the caravan which, by that time, will have used all the water they had left. Do you see? That way it can be done."

Artaneel gazed out across the river toward the heights beyond, to where the temple hunched small with distance and the obelisk in silhouette was like a single thorn against the sky. For a long time he was silent, so long that Isak had to let his breath out, take it in, and let it out again. In that silence he remembered. "There is another thing I must tell you," he said. "Darkness."

Artaneel turned, his mouth pinched to a tight, bloodless wound. "All this you have seen by how the gods stand it our sky?"

"I have seen the darkness, yes," Isak said. *Did he mean something else?*

"Talk sense or say nothing. What darkness?" Artaneel waved a long fingered hand; the light of the gods was all around them. "Hear me, Isak. What you have said is no part of our task. We have been asked a foretelling, nothing more. Instead you spout a *piece of folly he will not understand and will not be so stupid as to try. Should he be so big a fool, when his caravan has come to grief before his eyes, it will be our gods who have betrayed him. Our gods and we ourselves."*

Thus struck, Isak could only clutch the waxboard against his smock as if such a fragile thing could protect him. He felt Alpher's blaze against his cheek. Warm wind fingered his hair. "It can be done," he said. "It is possible he could lose a few animals, more likely drome than orox, but the crossing can be made if he has the . . . the wisdom to try a new way to do things. In Hrodah he will earn a fortune with his goods. He will be grateful to us and to our gods. Ask him for a double tithe."

"You, a barefoot scribe without household or sense, you presume our gods speak with your tongue?"

"I believe I can say how they will stand in our sky," Isak said as meekly as he could. "But that is not what . . ."

"And I have heard more than I need," Artaneel said. "This caravan master, I will have to tell him our gods would watch displeased should he attempt the journey. That, at least, will be safe. When I have done with him, and that will not take long, attend me in my loft. We must talk."

"Yes. I must tell you about the darkness," Isak said, but Artaneel was already striding off across the tiles. He gave no sign of having heard.

"He did not believe I knew that road," he told Kalynn. "He did not believe I knew how much water a man must have, how much an orox must have, how much a drome. The rest was only arithmetic, but he would not think about it. I do not know what he did think about. Never did I understand him."

"Not just arithmetic," Kalynn said. "It's . . . well, a different way of looking at things. It's knowing what you can do. What's possible." She looked at him. "Isn't it? But that's not what you were going to tell me about."

"No," Isak admitted. He felt awkward in the face of her . . . was it praise? "But I think the idea I had came out of the . . . the pattern I have found in how the gods share our sky—that Red Bethe turns around and goes back, and then goes forward again. It is a similar pattern. If I had not thought of one, I do not think I would have thought of the other."

Kalynn's gaze never left him as he spoke, head tilted a little to one side as if to see him better, hear him better. "Turns around? Goes back? Isak, what are you talking about?"

He was not telling it well. Not well enough. "I should not have mentioned that yet," Isak said. "I will come to it later."

When he had stepped into the loft, full of unease and shapeless apprehension, he clutched three waxboards to his chest as if they were his only possessions. Between two of the boards the pale yellow edge of parchment showed. That Artaneel would resume the scolding already begun he did not doubt. The unfairness of it hurt. Artaneel should have been excited as he had been. Great honor could have been won for the gods. Even after much hard thought he could not understand why the hierophant had been displeased.

Just inside the doorway Isak stopped. Artaneel turned from the slotted rack that held the permanent baked clay records of times before when the gods had stood in configurations similar to how they stood now. Guiltily Isak remembered that he should have brought up another group from storage, and taken back the ones no longer relevant. Doubtless he would be tasked for that lapse also; but there had been so much else on his mind.

Alpher's blaze through the high west window cascaded down the steep slanted front of the rack like melted glaze. From the east window, splayed, came the weaker beams of Gold Ephron and Embrous Zwicky, the Twinned Ones, to lie within a handsbreadth either side of Artaneel's sandals. The waxboard in his left hand he put down on the study table with a clack that spoke of undiminished ire.

"You told me to come," Isak said.

"I did," Artaneel replied. "Half a passing ago I told you. Now mark where Blazing Alpher stands. I said nothing about coming when you found it convenient. I expected you long ago."

"I had to complete my measurings, honored one," Isak said. "And I had to go down to my cubicle for these—" He nodded to his waxboards, one of which was now slipping loose from his grasp. "... and I thought it well to advance my calculations to incorporate the new measures—is that not among my duties?— and when I came you were not here. I thought you might still be speaking with the merchant. At times you have ..."

"Enough." Artaneel's hand chopped down. Isak flinched and the waxboard slipped and clattered on the floor. As he tried to catch it, another slipped. He went to his knees to collect them.

"Isak," Artaneel said, "your foremost duty is to attend me and to supply whatever service I require. Without dispute and without introduction of matters which are extraneous. In short, to make my own tasks simpler, not more difficult. That parchment! Have a care!"

With the waxboards more or less under control, Isak was struggling to rise without losing them again. The parchment, not a quality grade and neither fine grained nor fresh, now showed itself bent double between the boards. "It is a salvage scrap I have been using. Nothing of value," he explained. He found a clear space on the study table and unburdened himself. "May I?" Then he turned. "Have I not done much for which you have been pleased to take honor?"

"Only because of that have I tolerated your ... your unorthodox approach to things. When I discovered you were anticipating how our gods would stand, I very nearly discharged you. Only the quality of your other work ..."

"It has been at the core of all I have done," Isak heard himself say. *He hadn't known he would say it. Terribly aware he had said more than was wise, he found he could not stop.* "If I know how the gods will share our sky ten passings from now, or twenty—I can do it for more than a hundred now, and make it very close for half a thousand—knowing how they will stand, I can make a foretelling more true and for a longer time than we could do ever before. Does that not have value?"

Abstractedly, Artaneel had taken a waxboard from the ledge above his writing desk; a recent reading of the shadows by the look of it, though Isak could see no mark to indicate when it was taken. Now Artaneel thrust it into the sorting box so forcefully a cloud of dust spilled upward into Blazing Alpher's light. "You claim a power no man has. Our gods are the gods!"

"Have not my foretellings been dependable? Have they not been true?"

"You have made a streak of lucky guesses, nothing more," *Artaneel said and, when Isak drew a breath to reply, waved him silent.* "Enough of that. Isak, I have required you to present yourself because it is quite apparent that you do not understand some very important aspects of our work. It is time—past time!—you were told."

"When Lurgien was into his slow death, I did almost the whole work of our shrine," *Isak said.* "Could there be a thing I did not learn?"

"A tiny husting in the marshes? Far from Center? I think it likely," *Artaneel said.* "Listen with care. As you know, it is from how the gods stand in our sky, the splay and the reach of their shadows, that we can infer the quality of seasons to come: their wetness, warmth or chill, and duration. This we are able to do because of the lifetimes of records the Temple has kept, which tell us how the seasons were each time before when the gods have stood as they stand."

"I think I have always known that," Isak said. "And also that each time it is not exactly the way we expected. And that the season will be different from one place to another, though how our gods stand for a passing is almost the same configuration everywhere."

"Yes. Yes." Impatiently Artaneel waved him silent. "That is not my point. Hear me and think. When we speak a foretelling, we believe the gods speak with our tongues. And all men must have our foretellings; no man's life is not touched. It follows, then, that we must risk no error. To guide a man false, in his eyes it would be our gods who misled. We dare not speak a foretelling to which any but the traditional methods have been applied. Too much hazard entails. The whole Temple trembles at the thought."

"Most of what he said was true," Isak told Kalynn. "A farmer must know what to plant, and when, and whether he should graze his animals or slaughter them. A merchant needs to know the value of his wares, which is different according to the season because each thing has its own time when people want it, and when the supplies are abundant or poor. The traders—they want to know when the roads can be traveled, and when the rivers will be placid, and when they will flow strong and evil. Sea hunters will ask about storms, and also when the Big Ones will migrate past their piece of shore. For all their livelihoods depend on knowing. Sometimes it is their lives. Told false, how after that could they honor the gods?"

"I know about the merchants," Kalynn said. "The rest I have not thought about." She thought now. "But you said most."

"The rest that he said, I think he believed it was true," Isak said. "I think once I would have believed also. Now . . . ." Why did his throat hurt so much? "Is it not possible that even the little we know about our gods is not truth? That there is much we will never know, but that by careful study and thought we could see a little more than we have seen? Could we not know more, and more clearly, than we have always known?"

He had asked Artaneel the same question, there in the hierophant's god-warmed loft, and very distantly had felt a fear that the gods might burn him down to scattered bones. But they did not; their light changed not by so much as a pulsebeat. Artaneel's answer, when it came, was in almost the same words as Kalynn's, though from his tongue they came with very different meaning.

"I will not argue that," he said. "It makes no difference. In this it is what men believe that matters." He vented a scornful snort. "I am telling you, Isak, restrict yourself to the tested ways. No others can be counted on. To do otherwise, you court destruction of the world we know. Who knows what horrors might follow?"

Isak thought of one that would come by no man's doing and which no man could forestall. Yet was it a thing to be feared? Were not all the works of the gods essentially benign? He thought of storms and drought. Was it not enough that a man should bend like a shrub in the wind? If he was wise enough to know which way to bend? And which way was that?

"I have watched the gods," a voice said. It was his own, forced from his body by a power of which he was not aware. "Honored one, I have studied how they share our sky and I have thought with . . . with terrible care. I have found a pattern by which their configurations change. It lets me calculate how they will stand ten, fifty, and a hundred passings ahead. I have done it many times, and the only time I was wrong it was an error in my calculations, not the pattern. If I can do that, should I not use the knowledge? Would it not be disrespectful of the gods if I did not?"

Artaneel pounced like a raptor bat. "You admit that you

miscalculated." As if that was all he had heard.

"Let me explain it to you," Isak said. "Please."

"*Definitely* you should explain." Artaneel's smile was a grim, almost evil thing. "Somewhere in that thicket of absurdity will be the thorns to prick it like a bubble. No man understands the gods."

So he had begun. His hands shook a little as he arranged his waxboards and his bit of parchment side by side on the writing desk. He could hardly breathe. Knowing how strange the things he must say would sound, knowing Artaneel would refuse all such thoughts, he nearly lost heart. Yet, having gone so far, he could not quit the road. Not to go on to the very last stride would be to let the darkness fall upon the world with all men but himself unprepared.

"First I must ask you to set aside everything we have always believed about our gods and our world," he began. "Understand that I do not say those things are false. Only the gods know that. All I know is that, thinking about our world, I have noticed things which I find simpler to describe as parts of a pattern which is different from what we were taught."

"You admit it is imaginary? A fabrication?"

"It is consistent with all I have seen and measured," Isak said. "Applying it, I have anticipated how the gods will stand. It has never led me false. Whether it is truth or not, I make no claim. It could be only an appearance the gods have chosen to hold, for reasons we can never know."

Artaneel barked a laugh. "Clever!" But he was not pleased. "Proceed."

Nothing would persuade him. Isak forced himself to take a breath, to hold it while he sought for words. "Let us begin with a basic thing. Our world." Artaneel blinked and scowled; Isak hurried on. "We think it lies under our feet and we stand on it upright. It is a slab, we think, like . . . like, well . . ." He pointed to the study table. *"If we think about it at all, we think it floats in the salt ocean like a carpet of pond greens. How far down it goes, and how far out the ocean reaches are things we do not even ask, nor do we wonder what lies beyond."*

"And you, a callow scribe, you dare to ask?"

"It may be true," Isak said. "All of it. But I will have to say I have doubts. I have noticed too many things not consistent with that view."

"Such as?"

He had known the question would come. Nevertheless he had not been prepared for its sharpness. Ruefully, now, he knew he should have been. "Does stone float in water? Does soil?"

"Of course not," Artaneel said, then lapsed to a silence that declared more forcefully than words that he expected more. His eyes watched like polished stones.

"And in my wanderings I discovered a curious thing," Isak plunged on, headlong now. "In the north the gods cast longer shadows than here, and farther south their shadows are even less long. In some places near the South Ocean, some of them, their shadows sometimes lie on the south side of the post."

"That last has been noticed." Artaneel's voice was dry as parchment ash. "The rest . . . it is well known that the gods cast shadows of different lengths, and that from one passing to the next each god's shadow will change length—or not, by their caprice. No one who serves the gods could be ignorant of that. You magnify the commonplace to the imaginary."

"No," Isak said. "I mean all places at the same time."

"What? Nonsense. Do you claim to have been everywhere at once?"

"I copied the records, the places I had been. I had begun to suspect . . ." But he was getting ahead of himself. "I copied the records for a twenty-passings period, all the places I could. The same period each place. It was not easy to sort out. In some

places the records were poorly kept. Very poorly. I could not always be sure which passings had been which. And of course, some places, clouds prevented our gods from giving shadows some of the time, and the passage of time without a record of their shadows was not always mentioned. The people who kept those records may not even have thought that, were it not for the clouds, there would have been shadows. The point is not obvious until you think about it."

Stepping within reach, Artaneel poked Isak's breastbone with a long finger hard as a lance point. "How can you know there would be shadows?"

"Clouds are not everywhere at once," Isak said. "And to make the task less difficult I took records from the time of overtaking three rounds ago, when—so the records here at Center would have it—there were clouds part of the time. The overtaking progressed at the same pace here as other places. Everywhere the clouds were not, there were shadows, and where the clouds were—where such mention was noted—the light had the same quality as if the proper gods stood in our sky. Therefore I believe the gods stand in our sky even when they do not see us. Certainly there is light, and from where could we have it if not the gods?"

"From our sky! Even when only one god watches, shadows are not black. Therefore . . ."

It was a question that had been settled long ago. Did Artaneel not know? "Honored one, it is dispersed light. Surely you have noticed dust motes in the air, and other things around us reflect light also. Some scholars think perhaps air scatters light the same as water does. It would explain some strange things I have seen myself when I crossed a desert once. Perhaps the wind moves light as easily as it moves grains of sand—easier; light does not weigh nearly as much. But all the time we know light has the strength and color of whichever gods stand in our sky at that time."

Glowering, Artaneel said nothing.

Almost without breath, hastily, Isak went on. "And by using the records from an overtaking I was able to tabulate the sky positions of the gods—how they stood as seen from many places at the same time. I could infer when there were clouds because the way the gods stood was consistent with there being periods when no shadow records were taken, and otherwise it would not be possible to account for the differences between one place and another. And when I studied the tables I had made and thought about what they showed, I . . ."

"Enough!" Artaneel decided. "From all this manipulation, what did you conclude?"

"I believe our world has a rounded shape," Isak said, "and turns with a steady movement to face the gods who stand in the sky around our world and move only slowly among themselves."

"He was impatient when I explained that I knew the relative south or north positions of the towns by the shortness or length of Bright Dalton's shadow," Isak told Kalynn. "He said I was proving a thing by an argument that included the thing itself. I reminded him that Bright Dalton's shadows have not been known to change their length as measured at any one place in all the sixteen lifetimes records have been kept. It made him angry. He did not let me explain that I had traveled between those towns and knew in a general way which direction I had gone, and how far. I had made an effort to know."

"Wasn't he right?" Kalynn asked. "I mean, if you assumed the shadows were telling you where the towns were, you couldn't turn around and say the shadows proved the same thing."

"I did not," Isak said. "I had established the north and south of the towns by my own travels. What Bright Dalton's shadow did was to give me a measure, one that was not made inexact by the difficulties of the road. From that I could then confirm the regularity of the other gods, and then an even more curious thing. He would not let me tell him about that."

"I am not he," she said. "Tell me."

"That village in the north where I lived for a while," Isak said. "I told you about it. There Actinic Gamow never left our sky. His path was a circle curving down close to the icefields in the north, rising higher as he came around to the south. It was very strange. Bright Dalton and the Twinned Ones were never seen at all. I wondered how that was possible."

"The gods can do what they want, can they not?"

"I do not know. Can they appear one way in one place, and a different way in all other places? All at the same time? Because that is what I would have to believe. Near that village, they gave the appearance I have said. For the same time farther south I found records that said Gamow had passed almost all the way around our sky, only going below the horizon when he stood far north, while at the same time Blazing Alpher made his passing in a short arc far to the south. As I came southward, the records were more ordinary. No one who had not been north would have thought them remarkable."

"But to go from that to say our world is . . . like a ball?"

"Rounded, at least," Isak said. "And turning. I am not sure. It may not be truth. I know that. But it accounts for most of how the gods appear to move as they cross our sky, and when I have removed that appearance from consideration the other part of their motions becomes clear."

Artaneel's hand had clawed air. "And what," he had demanded, "if that is just how things are? Meaningless!"

"Even if it is not," Isak said, "it would be a useful simplification. If thinking that thought makes me able to calculate things no one could calculate before, and I find that what I calculate is always borne out, does it matter if the thought describes a real thing? Does it matter if it does not?"

"It is not truth! It is a lie about our gods! Most vile!"
"How do we know?" Isak asked.

"I will show you," he told Kalynn. The bowl she had brought greens in was large and had a rounded bottom. Turning it over and with a dab of sweet glaze from the meat he stuck a bone splinter erect on the shoulder of its curve.

"Think of this as our world," he said, touching the bowl. "And this—" He pointed to the bone. "—is a shadow post. That—" He nodded to the lamp on its perch near his left shoulder. "Imagine that is Gamow. Now . . ."

He put a hand inside the bowl, balancing it on a fingertip. He held it up, made it spin. "Watch the shadow. Do you see?"

Her face was very close to his. As the bowl turned the bone's shadow swung around like a finger tracing a circle on the surface of the bowl. Gravely she watched, then lifted her eyes to look into his.

"But does it have to be that way?" she asked. "Couldn't it be Gamow who goes around?"

"That is possible," Isak admitted. He put the bowl down. "It could be either way. But our world would still have to have a rounded shape or his shadow would not do what it does other places. Here . . ."

He retrieved the bowl and fastened another bone splinter on its side, farther down, less than a thumb's length from the rim. He held it up again and off to his right so Kalynn could see its illuminated side. "Watch," he said.

Now when he spun the bowl the bit of bone on its upper curve whirled its shadow around as before, circle after circle; the other, down near the rim, as it came around threw its shadow horizontally, quickly sweeping downward, then upward until it was nearly horizontal again just before the splinter passed around to the shadowed side of the bowl.

"You see?" Isak said. "Both observations from a single cause."

"Isak, it's a . . . a wonder. How did you think of it?"

"I do not remember. All at once I knew. It was like someone had taught me, and I wondered why I did not understand before."

"The gods . . . ?"

He shook his head. "Were it the gods, I would not have doubts. Then I would know it was truth and not only a . . . a convenience."

"But if the gods didn't want you to be sure . . ."

"Then they could do their will and I would never know. But why would they do that? They are the gods, who do not need tricks to make us feel awe. We already know their power."

She leaned forward, touched the bowl, made it turn slowly on his fingertip while she watched the changing fall of the shadows.

"It only turns one way?"

"As far back as the records reach, the gods have risen in the east and crossed our sky to the west," Isak said. "Yes. One way only. And, so far as I have been able to measure, at a constant speed."

"And we would be . . ." She touched the bowl down close to the rim. ". . . *here?*"

"If it is true our world is shaped like that, yes. Somewhere in that zone."

She looked straight at him with the beginnings of a frown. "Then why don't we fall off?"

"Why do we not fall off?" Artaneel had objected.

Isak gave the only answer he could. "I do not know. I have thought about it. Must I say again that what I suggest could be only a geometrical convenience? But if it is truth, is it not possible that the direction we think of as downward is not everywhere vertical to the slab on which we stand? That actu-

ally it is inward toward the center of a ball? Is one belief more absurd than the other?"

"Downward is down!" Artaneel declared.

"How would we know the difference?" Isak asked. "Our world is too large for us to have all of it in sight at the same time. Even from the highest mountain you cannot see it all. The curve I am thinking of would be too slight for us to see. All we have is the evidence of how long a shadow the gods cast in one place compared to another. Should we not trust what they tell us?"

"You try to complicate the obvious!"

"Is the obvious always truth?" Isak asked. "I have tried to put all I have seen into one understanding. If that disagrees with the obvious, then I see no choice but to set the obvious aside. I try to remember that what I have constructed may not be truth, either. Perhaps nothing is truth. But have you thought . . . have you noticed how a drop of water on a glazed pot collects itself together like a bubble? Is it not possible a similar force might be at work in larger realms?"

"Were that true, why does not the river roll itself up into a ball and roll downstream instead of flow?"

"I do not know," Isak admitted. "Perhaps the force of our world is stronger on it than the strength of the water alone. Perhaps in the river the water shapes itself into millions of balls each smaller than a grain of sand and so slippery and deformable that they slide over each other like melted wax."

"You say perhaps. You do not know. Remember, Isak, it is our world we are speaking of. Our world, which is real and cannot be changed from one shape to another no matter what the strength of your tongue. Take care, or they will slice it like a scrap of meat."

"Either way, it would make no difference," Isak told Kalynn. "We could live our lives and never know what was truth. I do not say I know the truth. I do not know if there *is* a truth."

Kalynn frowned. She turned the bowl and watched again how the shadows swung around their tiny posts; how, depending where she held the bowl relative to the lamp, one or both of the shadows were swallowed by the greater shadow of the bowl's body.

"If we were very small," Isak said, "and standing on the surface of the bowl, what we would see when its turning carried us around into the shadow . . . what we would think we saw . . . would be that god going down from our sky to the horizon. Then below the horizon. In the west."

"But if it is not like that . . ." Kalynn said.

"Truth or not, illusion or real, by reserving judgment and accepting the idea as if it was real, I was able to sort out the other parts. Once I could set aside their apparent motion across our sky, it was not difficult at all."

"But our gods do move across our sky," Artaneel had protested. "You have seen with your own eyes."

"That is their apparent motion," Isak told Kalynn. "Whether it is real or not does not matter. They all move at essentially the same pace. When that is subtracted from the observations, what is left is how they move in relation to each other, without regard to us and our world."

"But how can we do it?" Kalynn wondered. "Not all the gods stand in our sky at the same time. Never. If they all move around against our sky, wouldn't there be times when they were all on one side of our world, and none on the other? That doesn't happen. Always at least one is watching."

"Our sky surrounds our world," Isak said. "At least that is how I have come to think of it. Our world turns to look up at one part, then another, around and around." Impulsively he reached for the bowl; he would show her. She held it back from

142

him, spun it herself, and smiled saucily at him over the compass-sweeping shadows.

"Like that?" She nodded in the direction of the lamp, then looked the other way. "Like that?"

"There should be another lamp over there," Isak said, "or we would see only darkness. But I was saying, if I assume one of our gods does not move—it does not matter which, but after several trials I found Bright Dalton appears to move almost not at all—it becomes possible to measure how each of the other gods moves in relation to him. By studying the records for a long period—several rounds—it is possible to learn if the rate of movement stays the same or whether over time it changes. And . . . this is the thing that surprised me . . . for Red Bethe there are changes in the direction he moves. When I discovered that I almost gave up. I did not think I could anticipate when he would change. But then I noticed that it only happened when he stood in the part of our sky on the other side of our world from Blazing Alpher. I do not know why that is."

"And why should we?" Artaneel had demanded. "Our gods do not need to explain themselves. To us or anyone!"

"Does that mean we should not try to understand them?" Isak asked. "That we should not want to? How can we serve, if we do not understand?"

Kalynn set the bowl on the floor. Taking the lamp from its ledge and kneeling, she held it over the bowl, moving it off to one side; then, thoughtfully, around to the other. "I think I could find another lamp. Would it help?"

"Only a little," Isak said. "I think you have caught the important idea. Always at least one god stands in the part of our sky that our part of the world is turned toward. Often it is several. That is because some of them move hardly at all."

"And I suppose," Artaneel had said, sarcasm thick on his tongue, "you also say our sky is different from what we have thought."

"About our sky—its nature—I am not sure," he told Kalynn. "Sometimes I think it is a bubble with our world and all our gods inside it. But sometimes I wonder if it might be just an emptiness that reaches out forever, the way most of us think the ocean does, those who think about it at all. Either way it is hard to think about. If it goes on forever, I wonder what forever is. If it is a bubble, I wonder what lies beyond."
"Would it change anything?"
He shook his head. "But I would like to know."

Artaneel had pounced. "How can you claim you understand our gods if you do not know that?"
"Many things I do not understand about our gods," Isak said. "All I am sure of is how they appear to move in our sky."

"So?" Kalynn asked. "How do they move?"
He took a breath to speak, and stopped. "There is one other thing," he said, feeling foolish to have forgotten it. "How far they stand from our world. Some are farther than others. I do not have numbers. Once I tried to calculate from things I could measure, but the numbers that came I could not believe. I must have done something wrong."

"They stand against our sky, all of them," Artaneel had said. "How far? That is a thing they will never let us know. They are as far from us as they want to be. As near!"
"Do we know that?" Isak had asked. "How do we know? Have they told you? To me they have never spoken. I do not think they ever will."
"Yet you claim to know them better than we, who have

marked their passings for a thousand rounds?"

"Would you not say it is a different thing, to watch, than to think about what one has seen?" Isak asked.

"Thought is pointless. Our gods are the gods. They show to us the face they would. Never shall they let us see them as in truth they are!"

"Yet we do watch and, some of us, try to understand," Isak said. The ache to know was a heartsick pain at the core of his being. Why should the gods make themselves so hard to know? "Would we honor them less if we knew more?"

He said the same to Kalynn. He did not tell her the epithets with which Artaneel had replied.

"So?" she asked. "How do they stand?" She reached for her waxboard.

How much to tell her? How quickly? He took a breath. One step at a time, he thought. One step at a time.

"The Pale One stands nearest our world," he began, and waited while she marked it on her board. "Her path is a circle around our world which is almost in the same direction as our world turns. I say almost because the plane of her circle is tilted a little so that sometimes she appears to stand farther to the north than other times. It is that which will cause the darkness to happen."

"Such a small thing?" She made a note on her board. "But if that has been happening since . . . since forever, how can it do something different now?"

"It is a thing of no consequence," Artaneel had declared, and when Isak tried to show him the waxboard chart he had made, had waved it away. "She throws no shadow."

"She does," Isak said, though he had never thought of it that way before. "It just has never touched our world before."

"This is the first number you must know," he told Kalynn. "She completes a circle around our world every forty-two and four-fifth's of Bright Dalton's passings. The exact fraction is a little more, but for short durations it is not enough to make a difference."

She repeated it as she marked it on her board, then remained head down in thought, stylus poised. "Wait," she said, and looked at him. "Are you saying she is a god? Like the others?"

He looked back at her, waited. He wanted to know what she would think next.

"But she does not give light," she said. "And her face . . . we see streaks across her face, and oval shapes that move across, and . . . did you not say there was a time near the South Ocean when Blazing Alpher made an overtaking with her and passed partly behind her, and she blocked some of his light? As if her body was something solid?"

"I did find such a telling in the Archive," Isak said. "I do not know if it was true."

She laid her waxboard aside. Kneeling in front of the inverted bowl, she enclosed it between her hands. "And you say our world has a rounded shape, and we know it is solid; and we know the Pale One is round and we have a reason to think she might be solid, too. Could . . . could she be a world like ours? Not a god at all?"

"I would like to know," Isak said. "Possibly she is both. I do not know the true nature of our gods. Just because they warm us and give light does not mean their bodies are not solid. A burning shrub root is solid and does both. So many things I do not know."

For a moment then she seemed completely wordless, looking into his eyes as if to see the person within. "Then do you say the gods are worlds? They also?"

"It is possible," Isak said with care. "I do not know."

"As big as ours?" she asked.

She waited; the knowledge was not in him. Together, separately, in their tiny chamber, they contemplated a terrible, vast cosmic all.

At last she sat back. She took up her waxboard again. "And Bright Dalton?" As if not so much as an instant had passed. "He does not move at all?"

"I assume he does not," Isak said. "It is possible he moves a little, though I have found no evidence. He is the anchor point against which I measure movement by the others. But I believe, no matter what else is truth or not truth, he is one of the distant ones, the ones who stand farther from our world."

She made a mark. "Who is nearer?"

"Of those who give light, Blazing Alpher is the nearest," Isak said. He felt a great relief to be speaking a thing he could be sure about, even though at once he must go on with things that might be wildest fancy. "Like the Pale One, he circles our world at a regular pace, completing a round every three hundred seventy-nine and one-eighth of Bright Dalton's passings, which is the same duration as between his overtakings by Bright Dalton who, as I have said, does not appear to move. Make note of that; with each passing Alpher advances his position in our sky—in a direction reverse to the turning of our world—one part in three hundred seventy-nine and one-eighth of a circle."

Kalynn wrote it on her board and scowled at it. "Such a strange number," she said slowly. "One would think the gods would have numbers that mean something."

Isak had been troubled by the same thought. "Perhaps to them it does. Or possibly the gods measure time in different units. They have not told me. Now, I have said Blazing Alpher moves in a circle around our world, but it is possible . . ." And here the doubts began again. ". . . possible that our world circles him. From here on our world it would look the same either way.

147

It could be a little of both. I find it less complicated to say he goes around us, but I make no claim it could be truth."

"And the Pale One? It is the same with her?" Kalynn asked.

He was pleased she had caught that. Even after he had sensed the ambiguity about Alpher, it had been almost a hundred passings before he realized the Pale One's true motion was equally unclear.

"It is very confusing," he said. "So long as I hold to one assumption and ignore the other it gives no trouble. I try not to think about it, but I know I will have to think about it more."

She made another mark. "And the others? Is it different with them?"

"For Red Bethe it is almost the same." He closed his eyes, the better to see with his mind. "He goes around our world, or our world goes around him, but either way I am sure that neither he nor our world stands at the center of the circle. I am not even sure it is a circle. Perhaps you have noticed—many have, and in the Temple it is common knowledge—that when he does not share our sky with Blazing Alpher he appears as a small disc, so small the nail of your little finger at arm's length would more than cover him, but that when he comes around to overtake Alpher he has become smaller and smaller until at the time of overtaking he is diminished to a spark no larger than Actinic Gamow or the Twinned Ones."

He saw her frown and paused to let her think. He might have to repeat this part, which even he had trouble grasping. But for now, with awkward discomfort, he went on. "I know I have used the wrong words to say what happens—what I think happens—but I do not know the right words. What I believe is that when he stands in our sky without Alpher he stands nearer our world than when they are in the same sky together. He appears larger because he is less far away. I think also that at his overtaking of Alpher he stands even farther from our world than does

Alpher. It is hard to be sure, but I have seen records that . . . they are not clear, but they suggest that sometimes at Overtaking he passes behind Alpher rather than above or below. Certainly, sometimes he completely disappears in Alpher's blaze, and if his apparent path is a circle around our sky, as I believe, then in the course of some overtakings we should expect him to pass either behind or in front of him. Were he in front, it should be possible to glimpse him, but on those occasions I have searched the Archives carefully. There has been no mention."

"Is it possible he passes through?" Kalynn asked. Her hand went to the lamp. Her little finger flicked quickly through the flame. "Like this?"

"I do not . . ." His breath caught, but she wiggled the finger at him and grinned, unhurt; and it was a possibility he hadn't considered. "I will have to think. If their bodies are solid—if Alpher's is—I do not see how. And if he does, and keeps his form, his size, his color . . . I do not know how. I will have to think."

"Absurdity!" Artaneel's voice had been nearly a screech. "No man dares look our gods in the eye. Our gods would blind! Red Bethe goes around. It is well known our gods do not touch."

"It is said in the writings," Isak admitted. "That is not the same as knowing. And we know that the Pale One . . ."

"The Pale One is different. As for Red Bethe, you make too much of too little. He changes his size. What we see is what is. Our gods do not lie!"

"How would we know?" Isak asked.

"Might it be," Kalynn asked, "that Blazing Alpher goes around our world and that Red Bethe goes around both of us? With Alpher at the middle of his circle?"

"I do not know." So many things he did not know! It was hard to think about all the actions at once. He thought about complicated machines, wheels turning wheels that turned wheels; levers and pulleys and cranking rods. Could it be something like that, unseen, which caused the gods to move?

"I have no reason to think that either stands at the center," he said. "All I know is that they go around. They might not be circles, either; it is only simpler to think of then that way." Then he went on. "Red Bethe is the strange one. It is not only that he seems to change his size and brightness. When he appears smaller I think his heat is less, as if our world stood farther from his fire. And the rate of his going around our sky is not steady. What I do not understand is that he seems to move most slowly when I think he is standing nearest, which is not what I would expect. When a thing is close, it should appear to move fast; when it is far away, more slowly, though actually it is the same speed."

He paused. This was the difficult part. "And . . . and when he stands in the part of our sky on the other side of our world from Alpher, he seems to stop and for a few passings then he goes the other way, then stops again and resumes his usual course. He is the only one who does that, and always deep summer comes when he does. I do not know why, or whether it means more than only that those things happen. Sometimes I think the gods do things for reasons that have nothing to do with us, reasons we will never know, and it is only happenstance that they touch our lives."

He stopped, knowing how such thoughts must shock; but she looked up from her board. "Why should they care about us? They are the gods." Then quickly she looked down again as if she, also, had dared too much. Frowning, she studied the marks she had made. "When I am walking in the street," she said, "and I pass someone going the same way, if I look back he seems to be going backward away from me. But neither of us has changed our pace or the direction we were going. Could that have something to do with how he moves? How it looks like he moves?"

"It might. It might not." He had struggled with the idea himself, long before, and come to no answer. "You are speaking of motion in a straight line, but since we know—well, think—Red Bethe goes around our sky his course must be bent or curved. I am not sure what difference that makes. If I walk in a circle and you walk in a circle outside mine, even if we walk at the same pace, you would seem to lag behind me because you have farther to go. But I believe also that Red Bethe stands nearer our world some of the time and farther away at other times, and it is when he is nearest that he appears to go the other way. Do you see why I am confused?"

"You are confused because you think you know our gods, and you do not!" Artaneel had raged.

"I do not know how far away from our world they stand," Isak said. "If I could measure, I would know many other things. I am still trying to think of a way."

"They are all the same distance," Artaneel declared. "Against the bubble of our sky! To speak of distance with the names of our gods still in your mouth is nonsense. Neither near nor far! It is not a distance. A presence they are! A presence!"

Isak could not refute him; it was possible he spoke truth. How hard it was to argue, being unsure, against a man who knew he was right. "I have no evidence of that," he said, knowing how lame it must sound. He braced himself for the tirade Artaneel was visibly gathering himself to hurl. It was not fair.

"I can express how he moves with arithmetic," Isak told Kalynn, "but it is complicated. When you have learned more about what can be done with numbers I will show you. Now, to mention it is enough. We must remember, also, it may not describe a real thing. It could be only the way things appear from where we stand."

She stopped him with a raised finger. "Do I understand this right? That every time he goes around our sky there is a place where he stops and goes back—as if to pick up something he dropped?—and then he goes on?"

He had left something out. "That is not quite right," he said. "It is not one place. It is not even one part of our sky. And it happens every time Alpher goes around. Bethe does not move as fast. While he goes around once, Alpher has gone around almost nine and two-thirds times. That number is not exact, but it is good enough until I have told you more about fractions. Also I think the exact difference changes a little from one time to the next. Sometimes, when he changes direction, it complicates the measuring."

As he spoke, Kalynn smudged a thumb across her waxboard as if she had been correcting notes all her life. Hard to believe he had shown her that economical trick only a few . . . how long had he been prisoned here?

"And the other gods?" she asked. "How long for them?" She waited, stylus poised.

"The others do not go around," he said. "For the most part they seem to hold their places against our sky. Almost as if they were fastened to a solid thing."

"Almost?" Quick as ever.

"I think there is a little movement," he said, hating that he had to be so unsure. "For Bright Dalton, of course, I cannot know because it is by his position that I measure the movement of the others. For Gold Ephron and Embrous Zwicky it is obvious. They circle around each other like dancers and the distance between them changes all the time. But they stay in the same part of our sky and they never touch. If I could draw a circle up there they would never go outside of it. A small circle. Possibly in time the circle would show movement, but it must be very slow."

"*Slow?*" *Artaneel had raged. "They race each other across our sky. One takes the lead, then the other, and their paths cross. We see it happen.*"

"*Do we truly understand what we see?*" *Isak asked, knowing how futile it was to ask, but knowing also he must speak in spite of it. "When we stand on a boat in the river, is it our boat that moves or does the shore?*"

"*The boat! The river! Of course it is the boat.*"

"*How do we know?*" *Isak persisted. "How can we be sure?*"

"*Poppycock! Poppycock and sophistry! Watch.*"

With absurdly high steps, Artaneel turned and turned again, all the way around until he faced Isak again. "Now, did you see the walls go around, as I did? Did our whole world turn because I changed how I put my feet? Give me no more of this foolishness."

"*To your eyes, did it not look that way?*" *Isak asked. "Does it make a difference if you say it one way or the other?*"

"*And our gods?*" *Outraged now. "Did they go around? Do you say that I command our gods?*"

"*Do you know that you do not?*" *Isak blurted, so quick he did not know the thought before it leaped from his tongue. Appalled, yet oddly fearless—could it be the gods had spoken with his voice? No; how could they have?—he waited breathless for god or man to strike him down.*

"That leaves Actinic Gamow," Kalynn said. "What does he do?"

"He moves," Isak said. He had not felt ready to explain this part but, having gone so far, he plunged ahead. "It is not very much, and at first I did not notice because the direction of his notion is different from the others. All the others. Those who move, the greater part of their motion is in the same direction as our world turns. His motion . . ."

"Across our sky!" Artaneel had yelled. "Like all the others! Across our sky! All of them!"

"His motion has been mostly southward," Isak said. "It is very slow. In a lifetime it is less than the Pale One's width."

"If he is farther away, couldn't it really be a lot more?" Kalynn asked.

How could she think of things that quick? "It would have to be," Isak said. "I do not know how far he is, so I do not know the true distance he moves. It is the same for all our gods. But yes; it must be more. His apparent notion, now, that is what matters, and that is so little that except for one thing it would make no difference. To say how our gods will stand from one passing to another—one round to the next—I can say he will not change his place. There will be only his apparent motion from the turning of our world."

She made a mark on her board, but then looked up. "There's an exception?" Then, suddenly understanding, "The Darkness?"

So quick. So very quick. And it had taken him so long to see it. "Yes. The Darkness," he said. "When he overtakes the Pale One, not the next time but the time after that, the Pale One will be standing so high from the south that she will pass in front of him. I am saying it poorly, I know. The apparent motion will be that he goes behind the Pale One. If I am right about the turning of our world, the true motion will be that the Pale One passes in front of him while he moves hardly at all."

"Across our sky!" Artaneel had raved.

"By itself that would not mean darkness," Isak said. "But it will happen at a time when no other god stands in our sky.

There will be none to give us light. As simple as that."

"It will not happen," Artaneel had said. "Close they may pass, but the Pale one will let him go by. This has been seen before. Even if she did not, he would shine through. Like a cloud she is, not a stone."

Isak knew she would block Gamow's sight. He knew also that Artaneel would never admit it. Not until it happened. "The Brothers must be told," he said.

"There is nothing to tell them. It will not happen."

"Do you know it will not?" Isak asked. "Are you sure? And if it does, will you say that I told you and you did nothing?"

"It will not happen!" Artaneel insisted, so loud that Isak thought it would echo. He waited for silence to return.

"If I must," he said then, "I will go to the Temple myself. I have that right."

"That would be folly, Isak. You know—you must know!— what they do to those who claim prophecy. When they are kind, the death is quick."

"But this is not prophecy. Only a foretelling."

"That is not how they will see it. Call it what you please; they will say it is prophecy."

"That would not be truth," Isak said.

"Truth is what the Brothers say it is."

"It is no different from the foretellings I have made for you. Have I ever led you wrong?"

"That has nothing to do with it."

"When it comes—the darkness—they will know I gave truth."

"By then they will have your tongue in two parts."

"But people must know. Everyone. They will think the gods have quit their watch, that they will never give their light again. We must tell them the darkness will be only for a little time or they will . . . I do not know what they will do. To be . . . to be

without our gods would be a terrible thing."

"And you, without your tongue," Artaneel said. "Isak, I want to hear no more of this. Even if you are right it is dangerous talk. Dangerous to the Temple, to our Brothers, to me, this shrine, and to yourself. It directly puts to question all that we know is true. It affronts our gods."

"But if my foretelling is truth, how could the gods be offended?"

"Exactly."

"I could not answer that," he told Kalynn. "Is it possible the gods do not value truth?"

"Is there a reason they should?"

It was a troubling thought, yet his own tongue had sent it forth. That she could calmly accept it when he could not himself feel comfortable with it made him pause. He looked at her in wonder. Could she know things about the gods which he did not? The eyes that looked into his seemed untroubled by the terrible thought they shared. What were the gods, he wondered. What were they really?

"I know of none," he said. He could only give truth. "Either way. I know almost nothing about the gods."

He had pleaded with Artaneel. "You would not have to tell them I speak truth. Even I am not sure of that."

"Hmph!"

"If you would say that the gods have never strayed from my foretellings, regardless how Red Bethe might race or lag, and that now I have a foretelling that speaks of fearful things, would you be saying anything that was not truth?"

Artaneel waved a hand as if to fend a nagging insect. "It is they who decide what is truth, not you or I."

"The gods?"

"Our Brothers. They decide."

"Well," said Isak, amazed to hear it come from his own tongue, "should we not let them?"

The lamp's flame fluttered as if touched by a breath of air. The reek of its smoke sharpened. His throat ached; how long had he been talking? "I had thought they would be wise men," he said. "Learned and thoughtful and . . . and open to possibilities no one has thought of before. But they . . . they . . ." It hurt too much to say more.

Kalynn touched has hand. Two fingertips were all, but it was enough to stop his breath. Why, he wondered.

"You don't have to tell me the rest," she said, "I know what sort of men they are. All they understand is power." Her hand lingered; then, as if suddenly aware of the intimacy, she drew it back.

He felt bereft. Did she see that? She smiled a nice, shy smile. Had he dared, he would have reached to her and . . . he did not know what he would have done. Was this what it was like to have been touched by the gods? Was it possible, after all, that there was something in the Overtaking rite which had put their power into her?

"You . . ."

Afterwards he never remembered what words were lost from his tongue. In the entranceway stones gritted weightily against stones. The lamp's flame shivered.

"There you are, daughter." Palovar's voice thundered in the cramped space. "Things are happening now. Bring him out."

Kalynn twisted around, so quickly Isak expected to hear the crack of bones. "Will he be all right?"

"That depends," Palovar said. The entranceway's darkness concealed him. Isak would have liked to see his face. "If he is sensible, no harm from us."

She held very still. "Father, I want to know."

"And I have said . . ." He stopped. The silence stretched

long. "Darkness have it! Come out, daughter. We must talk."

"I don't want him hurt."

"Daughter!" His tone said more than the word. "Come."

Something in her bearing said she would not go, but then the resolve faded out of her. She turned back to Isak. "I have to." But, reluctant still, she stayed where she was. "I want to know the rest of it. You'll teach me? Promise?"

"I do not know if I will live," he said. "How can I promise?"

She looked straight at him, chin up just a little. "Maybe I'm the one who decides."

He knew she wasn't. He felt helpless, powerless, unable to speak.

She flashed him a smile. "Promise?"

How could he refuse her anything she asked when she smiled? Mute, feeling a desperate need to empty his throat, he bobbed his head.

"Daughterrr!" Both warning and threat.

"I'm coming." Over her shoulder. And to Isak, very soft, fierce, "I won't let them hurt you."

It would be wonderful to believe her, but to hope for so much was beyond hope. Neither could he tell her that. With empty hands, wordless, he said to her things his tongue was not able.

He watched her go, bent only slightly at first but then, as the entranceway closed down on her, down almost to her hands and knees. Now that her body did not block the lamp's light he could see past her all the way to its end. At the portal, carefully, she sought a foothold outside. Unseen hands assisted her. Once more she looked back, face framed in the opening. "Promise?"

Before he could answer, before words could come, she was gone.

Crafty men condemn studies; simple men admire them; and wise men use them.

—Francis Bacon

He waited long. She did not come.

Solitude was a thing he had known, in one sense or another, most of his life. Idleness, though, he could not endure. He held a waxboard close to the lamp's prow until the wax softened. He rubbed it smooth, his hands doing automatically what they had done so many times it was as if they had always known how.

The problem of how the world moved still bothered him. Taken into its parts it was simple enough. The world spun around and around like a top, and possibly—keeping to the analogy—possibly it wobbled like a top about to fall. That would account for most of the length-of-shadow changes. If it were suggested that the gods who moved around the firmament moved also northward and southward in the course of their rounds, most of the remaining change could be explained. The similarity between the duration of the shadow cycles and the duration between Alpher's Gamow-overtakings could be dismissed as an interesting coincidence. But that analysis could not explain why the change of shadow-lengths for Gamow and Dalton, who seemed fixed to the firmament, was different one from the other. There seemed no geometry by which the world's spin or wobble, or any combination of the two, could account for that difference. Again he reviewed the possible configurations. One by one he had to reject them. They did not fit the patterns he had found. They were not, therefore, satisfactory descriptions of how the world and its surroundings were arranged.

He was still at work, still pondering, when Hobur again removed the stones. Isak put the waxboard aside and started to rise, to go help Kalynn up, but it was Hobur's face that appeared in the opening.

"You be told to come out," the old man said.

For a blank moment, Isak didn't understand. On hands and knees he paused. Only slowly did the significance come to him. "What will they do?" he asked, not moving.

"Old Hobur hears only what the master do want him to be hearing," Hobur said. "If more be wanted, ye must seek it of another tongue. Be you coming?"

It was hardly a matter of choice. In the outer chamber Hobur had set one of the stones against the wall, but even so it was a long step down. Hobur steadied him until he found his footing. When one of the stones slipped in Hobur's hands as he was lifting it, Isak caught it before it fell and helped the old man raise it the rest of the way. It fitted solidly into the wall. Hobur turned. "Be thanked, lad. These hands . . ."

He held them out. Isak saw the awkward twist of the fingers. He could almost feel the old man's pain. He looked away—looked at the wall. Where the stones had fitted now looked like every other part of the wall. If he hadn't known, he could not have said where the way into his hiding place was concealed.

Hobur nodded him to proceed and retrieved the lamp, which was their only light. They threaded their way across the chamber on a narrow zigzag path between high-piled bales, chests, jumbled bundles, and lidded wicker baskets whose open weave gave glimpse of scroll ends and parchment sheet edges. He paused and fingertipped the dust on a hamper top, and tried to guess if the records it held went back only a few rounds, or if they covered lifetimes. He wondered if, allowed to study them, he would find relationships between their accounting and the way the gods had shared the sky, and whether those relationships would match the Temple's list of auguries.

Hobur thumped his shoulder. "They be waiting, lad."

At the far wall their path ended with no apparent way to go

further. Hobur nudged Isak aside, set down the lamp, and knelt before an unblocked section of the wall. He groped down close to the floor. A section of the wall hinged upward. A stick dangled by a thong from a corner. Hobur used it to prop the panel open. With a nod, no words, he told Isak to go through.

They came out into yet another storage room. Isak had a vision of an endless series of such chambers, one after another, through which he would pick his way until he died of age, but then Hobur came through with the lamp and he could see more than shapes in the darkness. Old furniture crowded against the wall through which they had come; a scarred bench had been their step down to the floor. Hobur closed the panel and heaved a bundled rug onto the bench. Scooping up a handful of dust, he covered all trace of their passage, then scrubbed his grimy hand on the front of his smock. With his other hand, he turned Isak's attention to the flight of steps that mounted the wall at one end of the chamber, almost hidden in the gloom. "Upward, lad."

Hobur stayed close behind, his lamp casting wild, erratic shadows. A glow of stronger light, muted, beckoned like a promise from above. The steps were stone, scalloped by use and gritty underfoot. Where the two walls met, the stairway entered a tunnel. The light strengthened. Isak looked up, saw the skylight high overhead, and the shadow-cloaked roof beams.

A few more steps and his head came level with the floor. On his left a wall ascended, blank and plain, all the way to the skylight. Ahead, another wall blocked the way; that one would have been featureless too, but for the ragged scar where the stucco had cracked off. The bricks within were lumpy, earth colored, many sizes. To his right the floor sprawled out. A carriage wheel with a splintered spoke leaned against the wall. The clean-swept, hard-packed earth bore the imprint of sandals and drome paws and wheel rims. One of the people waiting was

Kalynn, which raised his hopes, though she was primly clad now as if for the street, her shawl tucked into the waistband of her ankle skirt. The other was Palovar. Between them a barrel stood on end, its upper end open, the staves splayed like the shards of a flower beginning to blossom. Beyond them, like a frame to their tableau, a pair of coach-sized solid doors admitted a sliver of the gods' light through the crack where they joined. Angling to the right across the open floor, Alpher's ray was like a streak of gold. Another ray, red-tinged along one edge, lay leftward; that would be Ephron and Zwicky, standing now so that their rays, like their shadows, merged.

He did not realize he had paused until Hobur's hand at the small of his back urged him on. He looked to Kalynn. "What . . . ?"

Palovar gestured him silent. Kalynn moved as if to take a step toward him, but hesitated. Isak stopped again at the top of the stairs. Hobur was still behind him, but that wasn't a way out, anyhow. Nor did he know if he needed to escape. "I don't . . ."

Palovar advanced, but stopped beyond arm's reach. "Not the ordinary way a guest leaves." He nodded to the barrel. "Nevertheless . . ."

Isak followed his nod with more than mild unease. Inside the barrel he would be helpless. His eyes went to Kalynn. There was much he wanted to say to her, much he wanted to ask, but he could speak none of it. He could only touch his brow. "I did not come in the ordinary way. Now, I will be permitted to go?"

"Not exactly," Palovar said.

"Isak, it's all right," Kalynn said. And to her father, "Please, let me speak." Then she was standing so close that, had he dared, he could have put his arms around her.

"It's just we can't risk them seeing you come out of our gate," she said. "The streetwardens . . . we know they have been told to watch, and there's so many of them." Isak nodded. It made sense.

"You'll be some bad wine going back to a merchant of equally bad character, along with footmen enough to enforce our complaint," she said.

"But then I'll be let go?" Isak asked. The thought came, then, that once free he would have no place to go. Such freedom lacked attractiveness.

"Not exactly," Palovar said, the same words as before. He came to stand beside Kalynn, his arm possessively around her shoulders. "She has convinced my friends you might be useful to them."

The word made Isak turn his head. "Useful?"

"I speak carelessly," Palovar said. "They will explain. Considering that the Temple would have your tongue, I think you'll not object."

"Would I have a choice?" Isak asked.

"Discuss it with them." Palovar nodded again to the barrel. "They're waiting."

"I still want you to teach me, Isak," Kalynn said.

"You are with them in this?" Isak asked.

She looked down. It made him notice again the bulge the child made in her body. A priest's child. "I know what they hope, what they plan. I have talked with them." Then her chin came up. "They might have killed you."

Hobur helped him climb into the barrel and began to close it around him. Hugging his knees, he looked up into Kalynn's face. "As you see, I am not in control, not even of myself."

She leaned closer, though not so near as to interfere with Hobur's work. "Isak, have you thought? Isn't it possible, when you say how the gods will move, actually it could be you who decides how they will move?"

In another context, from someone else, he would have

laughed; but she meant it seriously. "No," he protested earnestly. "It is not that way at all. I . . ."

"Mind thy noggin, lad," said Hobur. Hardly waiting for the warning to be heard, he brought the barrelhead down—snapped it into the notches on the inner faces of the staves. The last two hoops scraped wood and with a few hard strokes were hammered tight. Quickly it was done. A crack between two staves let in a scrap of light, but Isak couldn't turn his head enough to see.

"Can you hear me, Isak?" Kalynn's voice; a tapping on the wood above his head.

"I hear," he said. His voice made a hard echo in the cramped space.

"Try not to make noise. They'll let you out as soon as they can. And Isak—"

A long quiet.

"Yes?" he asked.

"When you can—if you can—please, come back. Teach me."

"Daughter, enough," said her father in tones that forbade her to speak more. And, "Hobur, see if the wagon has come. Our friends will be waiting."

Then what is the answer?—Not to be deluded by dreams.

To know that great civilizations have broken down into violence, and their tyrants come, many times before.

When open violence appears, to avoid it with honor or choose the least ugly faction; these evils are essential.

To keep one's own integrity, be merciful and uncorrupted and not wish for evil; and not be duped

By dreams of universal justice or happiness. These dreams

will not be fulfilled.

—*Robinson Jeffers*

The wagon rattled as its wheels bumped over the street's uneven stones. Very quickly under Alpher's blaze, the barrel's interior turned warm. Soon it was like the steaming pool's chamber at the baths. Isak's body turned greasy with sweat. For a while, grimly, he endured.

The barrel had been skillfully chocked and lashed; held tight, it thumped and shuddered with the hammering jolt of the wheels. Downslope they clattered, the drome's paws sprawling and slipping on the cobbles, the drover and his helper straining at the levers that forced brake blocks against the wheels, spitting curses at the beasts and vehicle parts with impartial fervor. Downward and downward, past the voices of street children, the shout of a melon pedlar, the huffy complaint of a drome toiling upward. Drovers yelled. Hard tires scraped the stones. Once Isak heard the measured tread of a file of Guards. He held his breath until the rhythm of their cleated shoes faded away.

The slope leveled out. There came a subtle change in the scrape of wheel rims on the stones. The wagon's pace slowed, and there was the cacophony of many voices, near and distant, mingled. Sometimes the wagon paused and drovers shouted insults at each other and at their beasts. Gradually, Isak became aware of the fetor of the lower town. The cart lurched one way, then another, turned and turned and turned again, and Isak thought of how the lower town's narrow alleys branched and twisted and crossed at a thousand different angles, never any two the same. He thought of the high, looming tenements of the poor, the taverns and cribs, the necessity shops, charm dealers, and money changers, the vacant faces of homeless men, the calculating eyes of masterless women. Anything could be hidden in that maze. Only when he caught the river's special stench did he have so much as a hint where they were taking him.

It was only a hint, though. The riverfront curved from above the Stranding Bar's lagoon to the marsh below the Widow's Quay where ancient shacks crouched on stilts above the reeking mud. When the wagon stopped at last, it could have been anywhere.

Men vaulted into the wagon, freed the barrel of its lashings, kicked the chocks aside. Grunting, they wrestled the barrel down a plank ramp, across a reach of gritty, hard, rutted ground, and up another. Isak had to brace against the barrel's sides to keep from being tumbled. Far off, men shouted. Water washed against pilings. Close by, drome hissed. Oron growled. There was the sneer of a hinge. Hollow boards drummed; the barrel thumped against a padded obstacle. Feet stumped away. The hinge again, and the clack of a bolt snapping home. Then silence.

It was a long wait and, in that cramped prison, increasingly uncomfortable. The heat had abated somewhat, now that the barrel lay in shade, but his clothes still clung to his body, his eyes burned with sweat, his lips tasted of salt. A seam in his shirt cut his shoulder like a blunt knife. From time to time he heard footsteps, but none came near, nor did he dare call. Now and then voices came, but never clear enough for him to distinguish words.

Then new footsteps approached. The barrel was taken again, rolled for a distance, then abandoned. A heavy door boomed. Silence followed. Then again footsteps came, more softly shod feet this time, feet that whispered on the floor; and a voice that spoke commands.

With a heave the barrel was tipped up on end. Tools attacked it. The topmost band whanged off on the floor. Moments later, as the staves sprang apart, the barrelhead came loose. It would have fallen on him, but he pushed it aside. It clattered on the floor. Mask-cloaked faces looked down on him. He squeezed his eyes against the pain of the stronger light.

"May I come out?"

A thick-fingered hand's gesture gave assent, but his legs had been cramped too long and would not hold him. Several pairs of hands took his arms and he was lifted and borne, dangle-footed, to a stack of plump spice bags in a corner. There, surrounded by the heady redolence of saffron and joss, they set him down.

"So, hatchling."

Though the face was swathed, he knew that voice. He nodded. "You summoned me?"

He choked on the words. His throat was thick, as if full of dust. The same fleshy hand gave a sign. Isak had a glimpse of the ring, a stone the color of sky when only Gamow stood aloft. A mug was thrust into his hand. He drank; wine, cool wine. He fingered his smarting eyes.

The man stood over him. "You've posed a problem for us," he said. "A knotty problem."

"You could merely let me go," Isak said. "I never wanted to make problems."

His Lordship laughed. It was a cold, humorless laugh. "What you may have wanted is not our concern. What interests us . . . your prophecy stands against all reason, yet . . . our scribes are defeated. They can produce no proof it will not happen."

"That is because it will happen," Isak said.

"Our scribes are deeply doubtful," His Lordship said. "They point out that clever argument is not the same as being right, and they are very skeptical of anyone who claims to predict behavior of the gods."

"There is also the error of having too much doubt," Isak said. "Doubt beyond what is justified can be as . . ."

"Hatchling, have a care," His Lordship warned. "We did not

bring you here to resume old arguments. We have decided that it makes no difference; whether your prophecy be false or true, for us it will be useful. And you, hatchling, you will be useful."

"Toward what goal?" Isak asked.

"You do not know?"

"I suspect, but that is not the same as knowing," Isak said.

"Tell me your suspicion," His Lordship instructed.

Isak opened his mouth to speak, but paused to put his thoughts in order. The sack on which he was seated oozed an incense-scented dust. Beside his feet another sack lay as if nudged aside; it leaked a trickle of dry beans. Within range of his sight were a pile of plump grain bags, bundled pepper wands, and a carefully stacked pyramid of pickling crocks sealed with bitumen. There was no skylight overhead; the gods' light came through openings under the eaves.

A factor's wharf shed: one of the hundreds that crowded the river's shore. It could have been any of them. Through the floorboards he could hear the wash of water against foundations, and he knew that somewhere near would be a smuggler's hole, through which a dead man could be unobtrusively fed to the eels. Looking up at those mask-shrouded eyes, he knew this man would not shrink from that.

Still he had to speak truth. "I do not know if you are leader, or if you follow another," he said. "But I believe you seek to overturn the Temple's power. What you would put in its place, or how we would then serve the gods, I do not know."

"Do you think the gods approve how the Temple has abused its power? The greed of priests, the petty use of power to achieve more power till they rule the lives of all of us? Take all, give nothing?"

"I do not know if the gods notice," Isak said.

His Lordship humphed. "Either you are far too wise, or not wise enough," he said. His stance changed. "Very well. You know our purpose. Now, have you thought how the common people will react if, as you have made prophecy, the gods take their light away from us? What they will think if, as you say, our sky turns black?"

"That is why I asked my hierophant to take me to the Brothers," Isak said. "Because it will be a thing they have never known to happen before, and may not have happened in all the time there has ever been. They will be frightened, I think. They will believe they have been abandoned by the gods. But then Blazing Alpher will rise in the east, and the sky will again be blue and again we shall stand in the sight of the gods. And so far as I have been able to calculate, it will never happen again. Certainly not in our lifetimes. If the people are given that foretelling, they will know they do not need to be frightened; that it is only a happenstance of how the gods share our sky."

"You see in that event no portent? No significance?"

"Should I?" The question puzzled Isak. "My studies have shown that the gods change their positions in relation to each other and to our world by orderly, predictable motions; that it is only the complexity of those motions and our lack of reference points, and our failure to carefully measure duration that have prevented us from knowing the pattern. The time of darkness will be merely an accident of that process, and I know of no consequence that will come of it, either among the gods or on our world."

"But if you knew none of that? What then, hatchling?"

"I do not know," Isak said.

His Lordship laughed; a robust, mocking burst. "Hatchling, you may know more about the gods than any other man, or you may not. We have not settled that. But one thing I am sure. You do not know men. You do not know how they think. You do not know what they believe."

"Can anyone?" Isak wondered.

"Individually, perhaps not," His Lordship said. "Considered as a mass, though, I say it can be done. When the darkness comes—*if* it comes—our people will see it as a sign the gods are displeased with those who now sit in the Temple, claiming to serve them but in truth serving only themselves."

"Why should they think that?" Isak wondered. "From the event, no such interpretation can be logically developed. How can you say that thousands . . . ?"

"I say it for three reasons," said His Lordship. "First, they will be frightened; you have said so yourself. Second, very few have failed to notice how corrupt the Temple's priests have become; it touches the affairs of all, from mighty merchant to crippled beggar. And third, already our agents are among them, speaking of your prophecy, and of how the Temple has declared you fugitive—which is true and is known—because they fear you and they fear your prophecy, and that they fear your prophecy for the reason I have told you. So, if it should happen that your prophecy has truth, the people of this city will remember and will have no doubt. We should be able to make use of a situation such as that. On the other hand, if you are wrong and it does not happen, we shall have lost nothing. It will have been a rumor in the marketplace, one of many, for which no man is responsible. And it shall have served to increase our people's displeasure with the priests, a foundation on which we can, later, build."

"But my foretelling—and, I ask, believe when I tell you, it is only a foretelling—it does not presume to claim why the gods would permit such a thing to happen. I have said nothing to suggest . . ."

With a gesture, His Lordship silenced him. "Hatchling, what you believe makes no difference, nor does what I believe. What matters is what our people can be led to believe, and how we can make that useful to us."

"But truth . . ."

"We are not concerned with truth. We are concerned with driving corruption from the Temple. We shall do it by fair means or foul, by whatever opportunity comes our way. You, hatchling, may have brought the opportunity we've watched so long for."

Shocked, Isak looked up into the hard eyes under that man's cowl, then looked away. He massaged his knees, first one, then the other; they still ached deeply from his confinement. He tried to think.

He had to choose: either to join this man's conspiracy or not. Neither choice felt entirely comfortable. To join would mean accepting a violation of truth and alliance with a cause, which, if this man's words and manner were a sign, would only replace one tyranny with another. But not to join . . .

He listened to the water licking stones a few handspans under his feet, and he thought of the ravenous teeth of eels. He thought of the bulge-bellied, old, and arrogant men whom he had told truth and who, not having the wisdom to know it was truth, had ordered his death. He thought of Artaneel in flight down the cobbled Way until the Guard's pike went through him like a roasting spit, and of Kalynn's body made gravid with a priest's child. He thought about Kalynn a long time while he rubbed his knees. Also, there was the small matter of staying alive.

Finally he looked up. His Lordship waited there. He took a breath. "How can I help?" he asked.

His Lordship seemed to grow in height. He set his hands on Isak's shoulders, holding him very still. "You are the prophet, hatchling. When you speak, people will hear. Through walls they will hear you. What you command they will do."

"But it is only a foretelling," Isak protested.

"Is there a difference?"

"It came only from the use of knowledge," Isak said, hoping somehow to explain the distinction to a man not interested in distinctions. "There is no vision, no revelation. It is only the consequence of known facts."

"How it came to you is not important," said His Lordship. "To anyone but yourself it is beyond understanding. To them you will be a prophet. If you want to be useful, you will accept that role."

"What must I do?" Isak asked.

"Much," His Lordship replied.

Any sufficiently advanced technology is indistinguishable from magic.

—*Arthur C. Clarke*

In its time, the cellar where Isak now found himself had been used a hundred ways. Scraps of leather, dusty and stiff with age, had been scuffed into corners for weevils to gnaw. The dark earth floor had the prints and the surrounding stains of wine vats, and a blackened hearth beneath a flue vent—sealed now— and scars marked the wall where fittings had been taken away.

Once a forge had been in that place. Now, though perhaps only briefly, it was a conspiracy's meeting hall.

Cloaked in the hooded robe of a wayfarer, Isak sat in a corner with his knees drawn up. Beside his shoulders what had once been a tapestry extended along one wall, its colors dulled by grit and time. Still full of misgivings, still troubled by doubt that he was doing what the gods would have him do, he waited and watched while—one by one, two by two—His Lordship's agents arrived. (But would the gods permit a man to do a thing of which they did not approve? Could they be gods without that power? Was death the only way they stopped a man, or had they other, more subtle ways?)

How he had come to this place, he knew only in part. From the factor's shed they had taken him, rolled in a bale of undyed cobbler's felt, by boat and then by wagon to a house in the old castle's shadow where, for several passings, he and His Lordship's minions had argued, bargained, and made plans. On his own feet, then, they had taken him through the alleys of the old town to this smoky catacomb of lamps and shadows. There had been only time enough to make sure the two anchorweights had been properly hung before others began to arrive.

Their variety startled him, though when he thought about it he realized it shouldn't have. They were men for the most part, though a few were women. Their garb was as various as the shape of stones. They came from every level of society, high to low; every trade, craft, and calling; they wore everything from a beggar's rags to a priest's embroidered robes.

"Be not affrighted," muttered the one who had guided him hence when the priest was nodded past the guards at the door. "It be the animal inside that matters, not the skin he wears." And chuckled.

The women. Isak hadn't expected them, either, and was surprised when the first appeared. Considering, though, he wondered why he should have been. Kalynn had proved to him that a woman was as capable at many things as a man. He began to hope, then, that she would be among those who would come, that he would see her. He held his breath. He watched for her. Once, when he caught sight of an odd gait and a skirt thrust forward by an abnormal roundness, he almost sprang to his feet; but then the woman turned. He saw the plump cheeks and pinched mouth, the lines around her eyes. Disappointed, he sank back, waited, watched.

Slowly the cellar filled. They sat on the floor. A few knelt. Some leaned on pillars or against the walls. They talked among themselves, a murmur at first, but as their number grew it became a rush of sound as primal as the thrust of sea against the shore. Long after he thought the cellar was full they continued to come, squeezing in between their fellows, older occupants shifting closer together to make room for the ones who came later. He had not thought so many could be brought together so quickly, but then he remembered the conspiracy was not a new thing. He felt their eyes on him, the stranger in their midst. He hugged his knees.

At last Eb—Ebron his whole name was—came to him, picking his way through the crush. Long since in their discussions at the house he had put off his mask; his nose was large, his hair sparse and mostly grey, his cheeks gaunt. Isak had learned his whole name while they argued and bargained. His eyes had the look of a man enduring interminable pain. He crouched next to Isak.

"Keep us here no longer than you must," he said. "If the Guards come on us, I will have your liver."

"I would be the one they want," Isak said. "Should I begin?"

"All of us, they'd want," Ebron said. "I dislike so many of us in one place. Yes, begin."

Isak stood up. Threads of smoke from the lamps filled the high spaces between the roof beams. The place was full of shadows. He pushed the hood back from his shoulders. The sudden hush brought him a momentary fear.

He found his voice. "You have been told of my foretelling," he said. He swallowed and hurried on. "But being told is not the same as knowing truth. You shall be speaking my foretelling to others. Many others. Your master would have you fill the city with it. I would not have you speak a thing you do not know is true. Also, I would prefer you had it from my tongue."

Their faces were turned up to him. He saw skepticism, indifference, and scorn; they would do His Lordship's bidding. Truth meant little to them. Nevertheless . . .

"I will show you a marvel," he said. He went to where the anchorweights were hanging. Standing between them, he looked up to assure himself again that they were suspended the way he had asked. They were; the heavier one's cord fixed to a hasp in the ceiling while the smaller one's was knotted around a rod that spanned the space between two pillars several handspans below the ceiling. At his feet was the urn-stand he'd asked for.

"You will notice," he said, "the ropes that hold these weights are almost exactly the same length, and that if I raise them to the same height above the floor the smaller one would then swing in a wider arc. I will now do that." He bent to pick up the urn stand. "I will need help."

A pepper-bearded man in drayman's clothes rose from among the nearer watchers. "Help ye shall have." He stepped his way through the crowd. His glance went to the weights and a smile itched the corners of his mouth. "Be it thy thews not contain the adequate bone?"

"It is a matter of needing more hands," Isak said. The urn-stand had a very narrow foot; he held it out. "I want both anchors to rest on this. I want all to see they begin from the same elevation."

Pepper Beard cocked an eyebrow, as if thinking such attention to detail was needless. But he did as bade, raising first the small anchor, then the larger, and setting them on the stand's platform. Isak shifted its position a little so that both ropes were taut. When he took his hands away, the stand held steady. He stepped back.

"Would you say the larger one weighs more?" he asked.

Pepper Beard scuffed the earthen floor. "Aye."

"And you have seen it is not hollow?"

"If it be hollow, it be filled with much uncommon stuff." His manner said he thought the question pointless.

"I want it known there has been no deception," Isak said. "I want it known I speak only truth. When I have done, whoever doubts may test the weights and know for themselves."

Pepper Beard bristled. "I be known to these. They know I'd not mislead."

"Nevertheless, they shall have that right," Isak said. "No man's speech is the same as truth. Even mine."

Pepper Beard met his eyes, then grinned. "Aye, lad. Truth be its own."

Already, Isak had turned again to his audience. "I would have you think about this. I would have you notice that the larger anchor, which weighs more, will travel the shorter distance. I would have you wonder which of these will complete its swing more quickly."

"Huh," Pepper Beard muttered as he stalked back to his place. "Obvious."

Isak curbed his impulse to reply. He waited, gave them all time to think the question through. Bending then, he passed a length of cord around the urn stand's base, then backed away with both ends of the cord in one hand, held low. "You will notice also that, by doing it this way, I release both at the same moment." Still holding the cord low, he jerked the stand out from under the weights.

Falling, they moved apart. Gaining speed, they swung through the low points of their arcs and—losing speed now—ascended, paused, and began their return. Downward they came, then level, then upward again to pause together at the same moment, almost touching.

Isak had not moved. Again he let the weights descend, rise, pause, and return. Again they almost touched before once more drawing apart. A murmur of surprise, disbelief, puzzlement rose like the wind of an approaching storm. Only then did he speak.

"I would not deceive you; the similarity is not perfect," he said. "After a few more returns, the difference will become apparent. But you have seen it is not as you expected. And I will tell you also, it is a thing you can test for yourselves; that so long as the cords are the same length it does not matter what the weights may be, nor how wide they swing. So long as they are several times the weight of the cord, they will complete a swing in the same length of time."

He could sense a difference in the way they looked at him now. There was still caution, but he had shattered their certain doubt. They were no longer sure he was a trickster with a supple tongue. Some few of them, even, might wonder if perhaps he was giving them truth. Possibly, though, it was only what he hoped.

"I have shown you not everything in our world is the way you might have thought," he said. "It would not be truth to tell you it is in this mystery that the secrets of the gods were shown to me, though it would be true to say it was in this discovery I found the beginnings of that knowledge. But I have demonstrated it to show you I have knowledge which you do not have."

"Been told that lots of times." The man who spoke leaned lazily against a pillar, rubbed his cheekbone, chuckled. It brought a scatter of laughs.

"And had it proved?" Isak asked.

"Aye. Betimes." He ducked his head, grinned.

"Each time his mouth be open," declared a heavy shouldered man with a scar on his brow. "Give that one no thought, lad. It be y'rself we be come to listen at." He looked at Isak, waiting for his next words.

"I do not have much more to tell," Isak said. "Only that the knowledge I have come to has revealed to me that when Actinic Gamow overtakes the Pale One the second time from now, it will come at a time when only those two stand in our sky, and Gamow shall pass behind her. Darkness shall fall on us. That is the foretelling I give you. That is all I am sure of."

177

The sounds with which they broke the hush of their attention betrayed a mixture of thoughts. Some grunted as if struck, others as if they had expected more. Some made no sound, but frowned or gazed at nothing, wondering. A few stirred uneasily.

Isak went on. "Why the gods should want this thing to happen, I do not pretend to know. It is possible it is just as you have been told: that by this sign the gods shall declare their rage against the men who hold the Temple. But that is not part of my foretelling. I do not know why the gods will do this thing. Only that it will happen."

Behind his shoulder, Ebron spoke, so abrupt it startled him even though he knew it would come. "Do you suggest a better reason?"

Isak made himself turn slowly. "I must speak truth. I do not know why the gods do anything they do. It could be for reasons that have nothing to do with us."

"Such as?" Ebron demanded. And again, triumphantly, "Such as?"

Even though the exchange had been planned, Isak felt the force of Ebron's challenge. He wanted to back away, but knew he must not. He steeled himself to speak the answer they had planned, but instead it was different words that came. "The Temple's priests would have you think they know the gods, and speak for them," he heard himself say. "Either they are deluded or they lie. I do not pretend to knowledge I do not have. I must speak truth."

Far back in the crowd—so far he was only a shape in the bad light—a man stood up. "Destroy the Temple!" he roared.

That also had not been planned, but the response came to Isak's tongue as if born there. "Not the Temple. Those who infest it. We must still serve the gods."

Now there were shouts. Many voices. "Kill the priests!" "The gods be served!" "Cleanse the Temple!" From many lips, in

178

many phrases, the word *prophet* sprang, inflected with reverence, with awe.

Bewildered, Isak turned to Ebron. The question on his face needed no words.

Ebron laughed a savage laugh. "As you sought, hatchling. Before, they would do as our master told. Now . . . you have made believers of them."

"But all I said was . . ."

A powerful voice broke through the tumult. "Brothers! Guards in the street!"

"Kill them!" yelled another throat, and the cellar was alive with bodies struggling toward the narrow door.

A hand clutched Isak's arm. Ebron hissed, "This way," and thrust aside the ancient tapestry. It broke to tatters in his hand. He thrust Isak ahead of him into the opening. "What . . . ?" Isak wondered.

The tunnel was dark as the core of a black stone. The footing was full of pits that trapped and stumbled him. Behind, he heard others following. Ebron's grip urged Isak on. "Did you think we would risk to meet in a place that had but one way out?" his voice rasped. "Ware now! Here's a climb!"

Isak stubbed a toe on the step, but then found footing and started up. He felt a whisper of light; the wall turned and the steps turned with it. They entered a passage full of grey light, slowly brightening as they fled its length toward the glare of the gods' full blaze. A few more upward steps and they emerged from the labyrinth. The street was narrow, the paving stones uneven and wheel-worn, the tenements high on either side. Through the open rift of sky, Isak found Gold Ephron and Embrous Zwicky low to westward. How they stood together told him all the compass points, that the street descended to the southwest, and that they, the Twinned Ones, would soon go under the world. The sky's brightness and shadows against the tenements on the northwest side told him that Bright Dalton was also aloft, midway up the eastern sky while Red Bethe, also eastward, stood lower down. He searched for the Pale One. She would be somewhere in the eastern sky, he thought, but he could not find her. Near her overtaking by Red Bethe, the tenements blocked sight of her.

Ebron thumped his shoulder. "The Guards are down there," he said. "Follow me."

Isak's attention was drawn. From where they stood, still blinking in the light, the street went down toward the river. Still some distance away, a force of Guards was coming up. "I did not summon them," he said. "How could I have?"

Ebron humphed. "You are the reason that brought us here." His grip—it was like a claw—tightened on Isak's arm, and Isak was aware of other men, motley clad and grim of face, surrounding them.

"I have given you only truth," he protested.

At that moment, something broke from a rooftop—leaped out and fell and burst among the Guards. Its watery contents splattered. Another followed, and then other things, smaller, that also shattered. Flames whumped into being.

The Guards scattered. Some dropped their pikes to beat at the flames now clinging to their legs like ravenous parasites. A rabble poured out of the tenements, a hundred doors, yelling battle cries and "Honor to the gods!"—broke upon the Guards with, suddenly, swords in their hands; swords that hacked and struck, hammered and chopped, slashed and stabbed. Men fell. One struggled on the stones in a pool of fire. Twice he lifted his body in an arch, strained, and fell. Flames danced on his back. After the second try he only lay there, feebly writhing.

Ebron let Isak watch until he turned away. "If they be your masters, hatchling, think what your welcome will be when you return to them."

Isak looked over his shoulder, fascinated by the scene. He saw a spatter of blood flung from a sword's tip a moment before it chopped into a shoulder. "In the Prophet's name!" the swordsman shouted. "Truth under the gods!"

"They are not my masters," Isak said, and discovered his throat was too dry for his voice to come out right. "And I am not a prophet."

"For us you shall be a prophet, or die." Ebron nodded to the fight below. "As we thought, they have informers among us. Whether they only took advantage, or whether it was part of a larger plan in which you had a role remains unclear. As you have seen, though, we anticipated them. Now they will be less eager to come to this part of the city. We—" His grip firmed on Isak's arm. "We shall go the other way."

Isak had no choice but to go. Their escort formed a loose group around them and together they set off up the slope. The shouts and clang of battle continued behind them, slowly fading with distance, but time passed long before he stopped thinking of the man in that puddle of fire, and the others who were dying under the bite of swords.

And malt does more than Milton can
To justify God's ways to man.

—A. E. Housman

The dram shop was dark, illuminated only by openings at front and back. The man who picked his way through the maze of benches, stools, and tables toward where Isak and his companions sat, pausing to sip from his overfull mug as he came, wore a wagon-vendor's smock and leathers, a floppy brimmed hat, and a silver ring in the lobe of his left ear.

"One of you be the prophet?" he asked.

Isak's companions looked to him, so obvious they might as well have pointed. He felt the discomfiting touch of their eyes. "Some have called me that," he admitted. "My name is Isak."

The vendor stood there, mug half raised. "Be there doubt?"

"I do not feel like a prophet," Isak said. "Certainly I do not claim it. I have a foretelling, but that is the most I claim for it."

The vendor appeared to consider the information, or perhaps he inspected a scrap of foreign matter in his wine. Snagging a stool with his foot, he brought it over and sat down across from Isak at the table.

"Our host—" He made a nod to where, against the far wall, the shop's proprietor perched on a tall stool behind his serving counter. "Our host be saying no question stands: that a true prophet now does honor to his place. But when that one be speaking thus in one breath, while doing all his tongue be able to bargain down the price of a half-sack of fingernuts in the breath before and the one after, a man be wise to ask more deeply."

"I also doubt," Isak said. He glanced to the men on either side of him, part of his escort. To speak such a thought came close to forbidden things. It was a careful line he trod, between untruth and death. "I say it is only a foretelling."

"Be a foretelling not a prophecy?"

With a nod, uncomfortably, Isak yielded the argument; to a man such as this, the difference would have no real meaning.

He leaned back against the wall and was careful now not to glance again at the men beside him. Their bench was in the shadow between the light from the street and that which came from the small wall-enclosed garden beyond the shop's inner porch and colonnade. Others of his escort lounged in the street, and more were posted in the alley beyond the garden's wall.

The vendor set his mug down. "Our host be saying the gods shall take their light from us, which be a thing not heard of ever, and shall cause the priests to be cast from the Temple, which be also a thing most difficult to believe. Then, argues Hward of the Good Heart, our host, the tithe collectors shall be shorn of their power, and shall disappear like a god's shadow when he leaves our sky, and shall leech on honest men no more. Thus, argues Hward of the Good Heart, a man may ask a smaller price for his goods, and yet have more from the bargain. Be it possible?"

Isak would have spoken, but the man on his right, leaning forward, restrained him with a hand on his knee down out of sight under the table. "If the tithe man takes none of it, a smaller sum would be more than he would have left you with."

After a moment's careful thought and a small sip from his mug, the vendor nodded. "Aye. But that be only if the tithe collectors be taken from our backs. While priests be seated in the Temple, can such happen?"

"When the gods give their sign, the Temple will be cleansed of priests."

Now they were at the heart of the matter. The vendor waggled a finger. "Ah! But shall the gods be giving such a sign?" His eyes watched Isak without a glance to either of the men beside him. "You be the prophet, if any such be sitting here. Speak."

"That is the core of my foretelling," Isak said. Without awareness that he did so, he pushed back the hood from his temples. "There shall be a darkness over all our world. Not the mere darkness of heavy cloud, but the terrible darkness of no god giving us his light. Would you ask a clearer sign?"

A sound made him look up. A circle of listeners had gathered around them. One was another of his escort, drifted over from his table near the serving counter. The one who perched on the corner of an adjacent table was a street man who had listened in before, hoping now, Isak supposed, to hear more than the previous time. All the other faces he had never seen before.

"It be a sign," the vendor said. "But what of?"

"What would you think?" Isak asked. Though he did his best to give no outward sign, inwardly he felt a reluctance; what he would say now would not all be truth, though neither would it not be truth; and while he could have left it for one of his escort to speak, from his tongue it would carry more force. And, he told himself to force his resolve, by speaking it he would do ultimate service to the gods.

"Would you not say that such a sign they would give only to declare their most powerful wrath?" he asked. It got him a wary, grudging nod.

"And what could enrage them more," he went on, "than the conduct of the priests? They who enrich themselves at the expense of other men in the gods' name, who say they speak for the gods and serve them, but truly do nothing but fill their own appetites? Can you suggest some other reason why the gods would send a sign like that?"

The vendor felt the ring in his ear. "Play no games," he said at last. "I ask, be you a prophet? You be saying you be not, but then speak prophecies. Declare thyself."

It was a challenge to again deny his prescience; Isak let it pass. "I can imagine only one other reason," he said. "That their rage is for all men—all men, who have witnessed the priests' corruption and, by doing nothing, let it go on."

That turn of thought was new to the vendor. His head came up, startled. "What can one man do?"

"One man?" Isak echoed. He leaned back, felt the hard, cool bricks against his shoulders. He took a breath. "Very little. Nothing, probably, though I am myself only one. But if many men, acting together . . ."

"Ah!"

"When?" That from the one of his escort who had joined the listeners.

"When the darkness comes," Isak said. "If it does not, believe nothing else I have told you."

"When the darkness comes." Several voices spoke it softly, almost a whisper.

"When the darkness comes," Isak said.

The man on Isak's right stood up. "Hward!" he called, dropping a rattle of coins on the table. "Wine for my friends! The special wine!"

We have come into being in the fresh glory of the dawn, and a day of almost unthinkable length stretches before us with unimaginable opportunities for accomplishment. Our descendants of far-off ages, looking down this long vista of time from the other end, will see our present age as the misty morning of human history. Our contemporaries of today will appear as dim, heroic figures who fought their way through jungles of ignorance, error, and superstition to discover truth.

—James Jeans

The fountain at the foot of the Street of Diligent Stonecutters was one of the few places where the people of Old Town could find untainted water. Flanked by his escort, Isak descended the street, the hood of his wayfarer's robe thrown back, his sandals whispering on the worn, uneven stones. News that he would come had gone ahead; already a crowd was waiting in the square.

"He comes!" He could hear their voices. "The Prophet comes!"

He wished they would not call him that, but there was nothing he could do. On either side of him men strode with naked swords in hand, his escort's captain at his right, that man's lieutenant to his other side. More came behind. The advance party cleared a way for him through the mob—"Way for the Prophet!"—until he stood on the fountain's base. The leader of that squad gestured to a dark red stain on the stones.

"You wondered if a streetwarden would come sniffing," he said. "You see his blood."

There was blood also on the sword he wore scabbardless, thrust through the sash at his waist.

"And . . . ?" Isak asked.

"He feeds the eels," said the squadman with a nod toward one of the narrow streets leading off from the square. "Both parts of him." Though out of sight beyond the kinks and turns, the river would lie in that direction. The squadman gave a savage grin. "Like all good streetwardens! Fear nothing here. Our men hold every way to this place. No Guards will trouble us."

Absently, Isak nodded. But for a turn of fortune, he would himself have been feeding eels. The squadman cocked his head, smiled mirthlessly. "Spare no qualm. He did not serve the gods."

"He must have thought he did," Isak said.

"What he thought matters not a scrap," the squadman said. His voice was impatient now, and hard. "He served the priests. Them only. For that service, he has won his reward." Turning away, he raised a hand to catch the crowd's attention.

It was hardly necessary. They had seen Isak come and knew he was the man. Who else, now, would dare put on a wayfarer's robe? Now the murmur of their voices stilled. Trapped by their expectation, he could only begin.

A waist-high wall of mortared stone slabs enclosed the fountain's pool. Isak climbed up, thinking to stand on the rim, but found that even with one of his escort bracing a shoulder against his knees it was too narrow for him to stay balanced. He slipped back down and found a space where he could seat himself without the narrow stone cutting too hard at the flesh of his thighs. He looked up. Gamow stood high, close to zenith point. The Pale One stood well to his westward, five passings short of their overtaking. He could see no others, though the red tint in the eastern sky told him Alpher was soon to rise. All as it should be. The overtaking would come, and Gamow would appear to overtake the Pale One, and would pass so close to her that a finger would not fit between them.

For a long breath he studied the blend of colors on the Pale One's face: grey and white, a hint of gold, a touch of pinkness on her westward edge. His understanding of the gods—even such small understanding as he had—was a fragile thing; though a thousand bits of observation might confirm it, only one which did not could bury it in doubt. Nothing he saw, though, conflicted with the vision in his mind. Only when he was satisfied of that did he give his attention to the people who had come to hear him.

"I have a foretelling." Until he spoke, he hadn't known he would begin with those words. He surprised himself. He took another breath, began again. Sitting there on the fountain's rim, bareheaded in the solitary light of Actinic Gamow, he told how the foretelling had come, how he had taken it to the Temple—which was the only proper thing a man could do if that man served the gods—and how the Brothers had shown no more understanding than the stones of which the Temple was built. He told them how the Temple's men had sought his death.

"I must wonder," he said—it was a new thought, and the words came even as he thought—"could it be that the gods have protected me? That they would have me live? Would have me no man's captive, and able to tell my foretelling to all who will hear me, as you hear me now? I do not know if it is in the gods' power, or if it is true indeed that I owe my life and freedom to their touch, but I cannot explain by any other cause why I still live, or why I am here with my tongue in one piece, able to speak these words. I must believe they would have the foretelling told."

"Honor to the gods!" The shout was spontaneous. Other throats echoed it. Isak let the outcry rise, expand to a crescendo. When it began to subside he held up his arms to command their attention again. Silence fell.

He told them then what must be done, what the sign of the gods' darkness must certainly command. It brought a few more shouts from the crowd, but from most, for whom it must have been only what they expected, it produced a soft, susurrus, wordless, "Ah!" as if, having heard it now in the Prophet's own words, at last they were satisfied. Now they could believe.

It troubled him a little, that because he spoke it and because he was sure, they accepted it without doubt. It was a thing he did not understand, such docile submission. Before such credulity, how could truth—untested—be known?

Yet he knew his foretelling was truth, and as for the rest of it, who was to say? It could be made to happen, and only if the gods should cause the effort to fail would it not be truth. But for what reason would they do that? It was beyond belief they could know of the priests' corruption without disgust. But—was it possible?—was failure or success beyond their power to control?

A man was struggling to the front of the crowd. A tall man with long russet hair and full beard and a voice as if his throat was full of dust. "I must speak to the Prophet. I must." Three of Isak's escort moved to block him, swords ready. It brought Isak out of his thoughts. He raised his eyes.

"Let him come," he said. It was impulse, but this was not part of His Lordship's contrivance; whatever it was, it came from some other source. Perhaps the gods themselves?

The escort stood back, though still not letting down their

weapons. The stranger wrestled through the last ranks of the crowd. IIis eyes held torment. He mounted the steps of the fountain and Isak slipped down off his perch to receive him. His escort moved to be ready to act if the need came. But when the stranger had taken the last step up he went down on his knees at Isak's feet.

It took Isak by surprise; it was an honor he had not earned and did not seek. He reached down, and with a gesture and tugs at the loose fitting shirt persuaded the man to rise.

Now the man towered over him, which seemed to discomfit the man. He stepped back—back down two steps, until their eyes were level. He pulled off his leather cap and crushed it in his hands. His leggings were work-worn, patched, and thread-bare.

"Yes?" Isak prompted.

"Prophet—" the man began, but Isak stopped him with a gesture.

"My name is Isak," Isak said. "It is only a foretelling."

The man's gaze dropped. He twisted his cap as if to wring the sweat from it. "I come from Rofa. We heard of your . . . your foretelling. I have come. I had to hear it with my own ears. See with my eyes."

Caution made Isak hesitate. Rofa was a nine-passings journey up the river, beyond the mountains and Thunder Gorge, and at least a seven-passings journey back downstream. Was it possible his foretelling had traveled so far that quickly?

"And now you have heard?" he asked.

The man from Rofa nodded. "More than ever. But . . ." He stuttered then, as if words had stuck in his throat. Isak waited. The man from Rofa wrenched his cap another twist. "I must ask . . . It is why I have come . . . if all priests must be thrown from the Temple, I must ask, if that is done, how then shall we—Prophet, I do not know how to ask!—how can we then serve the gods?"

It was something Isak had given no thought to. It was so distant from the hard, true core of his foretelling that no rational thread linked one to the other. Yet, as an ultimate consequence of His Lordship's intrigues it was a reasonable question to ask. How indeed? He took a breath, tried to shape an answer in his mind, took another breath. He looked at the man, who waited.

The men around His Lordship had warned that the Temple might put men in his crowds—men to heckle, and to cast doubt, disrupt, and dispute. Call for his tongue. Kill him if they found the chance. This man could be one such. The two of his escort nearest exchanged a glance and moved closer; perhaps they held the same thought. Isak lifted a hand to forestall them. Having been raised before this crowd, the question needed a reply.

"I do not know," he said. "I have not ever known how we serve the gods. I have known only that, by our lives, by the way we live, we do serve them; and that in return they give us their light, their warmth, their rain, and their wind. Also the pulse of the tides, the ebb and rise of the rivers, the renewal of spring and the bounty of harvest. But now they will take their light from us—though I can tell you it will be for less than one passing—and I must believe they would mean such a thing to be a sign that their benevolence is not without limit, and that for reasons we can only guess we have displeased them. Do you wonder, then, that I would think of the Temple's old men, who would have us believe they speak with the voice of the gods, whose self satisfaction and greed are well known?"

"I?" the man from Rofa wondered, bewildered. "I?"

Isak went on as if the man had not spoken. "And I would ask one other thing: to serve the gods, do we need those men? Is it not possible we might serve them as well—even better?—without the Temple's guidance? What worth does the guidance of such men have?"

It was more questions than his questioner could absorb. The man from Rofa spread his hands, crushed cap in one of them, the other open-palmed. His mouth worked but no words came. Raising the hand that clutched his cap, he touched it to his brow and would have gone again to his knees had not Isak stopped him, raised him again.

"Go back to Rofa," Isak said. "Tell them my words. Tell them the darkness shall come, but it will pass. And if the Temple is cleansed it will not come again in our lives."

The man from Rofa looked up into his eyes, touched his brow again, turned and plunged back into the crowd. Isak watched him go, wondering if he had answered well and whether, through it all, he had spoken only truth. He wished he could be sure. Was not false guidance among the worst of the priests' misdeeds?

His escort's captain touched him on the arm. "Did you hear the trumpet?"

Isak had heard nothing but his own voice. "Trumpet?" He turned, as puzzled as the man from Rofa had been.

"Guards coming," the captain said. "A strong force on—I think—the Netweaver's Way." He nodded toward one of the streets that entered the square. "That quarter, at least. For a while we could hold them, but we would lose men. And they might try coming another way, also. Before they trap us, we should go."

It was no more than common sense, and he had done all he could hope to, here. Isak nodded. The captain made a sign. His men advanced on the crowd.

"Way for the prophet!" they shouted, swords extended as if to carve a path. Those in the forefront of the crowd edged aside.

Isak raised an arm. "Still they seek me," he told the crowd. "They shall not find me. Not here, not anywhere." He started down the steps. "Until the darkness! Wait for the darkness!

Cleanse the Temple!"

The crowd parted for him. The captain and his lieutenant took positions a half step behind him. Not breaking his stride, he scanned the prospect before him. There was hazard in that cleft between two walls of men and women; there could be one in that crush with a blade in his hand, waiting his chance. The Temple would reward such a one. Isak took a breath; it wasn't a risk he could turn from. He who could foretell the gods could not predict his own life; therefore to chance it was his only choice. As he advanced, the people broke apart to let him pass. All but one, a woman who paused, held her place. It was as if the crowd had opened so they could meet. She looked into his eyes. She reached out.

"Please." A desperate voice, a voice beyond hope, yet hopeful still. "Touch me, that I may live to see it happen."

He saw the pinch of pain around her eyes, her withered breasts. A tattered shawl. Her arms were like bones. "I do not have that power," he said.

"Please," she insisted.

It would not be truth, but he had told her that. She did not want truth. He touched her cheek—hard bone under cornhusk skin. "I can promise nothing from this," he said.

Her own hand came up to press his fingertips firmly to the hard bone. The strength in her fingers startled him. Her lips moved, though he heard no words, and the look on her face made him think of Kalynn though he could not have said why. A murmur rose from the people around them, and he realized that they watched. He wondered what they must think and he wanted to shout it was not a thing he could do. His escort captain moved close. "Another trumpet," he muttered. "Best we take to the tunnels."

Isak retrieved his hand. It would be heartless, though, merely to walk away. Nevertheless, he could offer only words. "If it were my power to give, had I the skill, I would give you life and health," he told her. It fclt lamely inadequate. "All I can give you is the wish of it."

"On!" his captain shouted and, gripping his arm, urged him past the woman before he could say more. "Way for the Prophet!"

Behind them Isak heard a sob; whether of gladness or despair he could not guess. Nor could he look back. All the while they picked their way through the god-blinded underground of Old Town, men stumbling, softly cursing, lamps flickering, fetid air, he thought about that sound. Was it possible that out of kindness he had failed to serve truth and the gods? The more he thought, the more it troubled him.

And did he stop and speak to you,
And did you speak to him again?

—*Robert Browning*

Hardly a moment now was his own. Unannounced he passed through a marketplace; his protectors paralleled his path but kept a distance from him so that it would seem he walked alone. By now his wayfarer's robe and the way he wore it, cowl thrown back, were well known. Heads turned. A whisper thrilled through the crowd. A boy ran up and touched his sleeve, then dashed away again as if made fearful by his own daring. Another child watched gravely, wide-eyed, from under a trestle of sweetmeats and shrank back, fingers in her mouth, as he trod past.

"Will it come? Will the darkness really come?" He heard the question asked a thousand ways.

"It shall," he said.

They said he had cured a woman of the wasting sickness, and a lame boy of his limp. When he said he did not have that power, and that he remembered no such boy, they did not believe him, just as they did not believe when he said he was no prophet. It was strange what they would believe and what they would not believe.

"But if we kill the priests, they will give us their light again?"

"The gods? Even if we do nothing, their light will come again," he said.

Now they surrounded him. They reached out to pluck the fabric of his robe. With anxious faces they watched him and spoke questions. Raptly they listened to his words.

"I do not think it wise to believe the gods would punish all for evils done by only a few," he said. "No knowledge I possess would suggest they are cruel. The darkness will be a sign to us, only a sign, not a scourging."

"Aye, but a sign they would have us . . . the priests . . . ?"

One of his escort squeezed through the crush. He edged close to Isak's ear. "Master, a streetwarden. He escaped us."

Isak acknowledged the news with a nod. Similar things had happened several times. The warden would summon Guards, but that would take time. The hazard was not yet large.

"The gods do not tell us what we should do," he told the questioner. "The darkness will show their displeasure, but that is all."

"Aye, but the priests . . ."

"Perhaps it is with us they are displeased," Isak said, "that we permit the priests to lord over us. But it is a thing I do not know. It would not be truth to say I know what the gods would have us do. It is even possible—but in this I speculate, I do not suggest it is so—that they do not care. That is not what I believe, but I know nothing that denies the possibility. I . . ."

The man was looking at him queerly, his puzzled half-smile showing gaps where teeth had been. Not a man, Isak realized, to burden with complicated ideas. Perhaps others in that crowd might understand his thought—the effort was not wasted—but this man . . .

His escort touched his elbow. "Master, we should go."

"The darkness shall come," Isak said. "With the overtaking it shall come. Wait for it, and when it comes . . . when it comes, do as your beliefs lead you to believe the gods would have you do: that we may serve the gods again!"

The escort man advanced, sword out and raised. "Way for the Prophet! Way for the Prophet!"

Fingers brushed his sleeve, his shoulder, his robe as he passed. He wondered—for the thousandth time he wondered—whether he, himself, now served the gods or whether, now, he only served ambitious men. He wondered how he could know, what test or evidence would give him truth, but no new understanding came.

"Way for the Prophet!" his escort cried. Swords glinted in the air. Blazing Alpher watched, standing high.

Try it if Mister Ford's opinions are otherwise.
Try it and see where you land with your back broken . . .
                                        —*Archibald MacLeish*

They dressed him in a tunic and leggings that fitted so loosely he looked like a child. They gave him a hat of woven straw which fitted low across his brow and spanned wide as his shoulders. Men from the far south sometimes dressed that way. In that disguise they took him to a house in Old Town, Ebron and four men with swords. A house with a high wall, a wind tower shuttered to keep out the bats, and bare stones where a garden had been. They did not tell him why. Scraps of a broken pot scattered from his sandals.

Within the house was the earthy scent of dry adobe. Sand scraped underfoot. When he saw the emptiness of the hall he had entered, Isak stopped. Bare floor and naked walls, no furnishings, not even a lamp to give reinforcement to they grey light from under the eaves. No apparent way out but the way he had come in. Ebron prodded from behind.

"Think we would wring the neck of a gekko whose song is so sweet?"

It puzzled Isak. What could he mean? Ebron prodded again. Uneasily, uncomprehending, he took a step. Another. The scuff of his feet made whispering echoes. Across the room, guided by the pressure of Ebron's thumb he found, in what had appeared to be an alcove, a stairway upward; a stairway too narrow for more than one man at a time. He had to remove his hat.

"Yes," Ebron said close behind him. He stumbled in the near darkness. Some of the treads tipped and rattled under his weight, and under Ebron's weight, and under the weight of the men who followed. The stairway turned, doubled back on itself, and brought him up to an alcove very much like the one below, but this one closed off from whatever lay at this level by a heavy curtain through which only a few cracks of yellow lamp-light leaked like narrowed eyes. Again Isak hesitated until he felt Ebron's thumb in the small of his back. As he fended the curtain aside, he discovered it was a supple, dark-green velvet.

That information was so unexpected that his whole attention bent to confirm it, and he was hardly aware of the chamber into which he had stepped. Coming through behind him, Ebron roughly turned him around.

"My lord, we have brought him," Ebron said.

"So, hatchling!" His Lordship rose from a nest of gold-trimmed cushions, set his wine cup on a lampstand, and waited, sternly silent. Here carpets were spread to pave a path; embroidered carpets with borders of iridescent green braid of a kind made only in the southeastern part of the world. Lamp-light glimmered from medallions on the walls. Through a slot window Actinic Gamow cast a band of light diagonally down one wall and partway across the floor. No other gods were aloft, though Blazing Alpher should be rising soon. Ebron prodded him forward and when he did not move at once, prodded again.

Reluctantly Isak took a step, then another. Whatever this man wanted, it was not a wish he shared. Behind him he heard the tramp of his bodyguard. Did they follow to protect him, or to force him forward? Protect him from what? Why press him forward?

Two strides short of where the man waited, His Lordship gestured him to a stop. "Those who serve him touch the knee," Ebron said close to his ear.

"I serve the gods," Isak said, bold enough that His Lordship would have to hear. He saw the man's brow knot with scowl.

"That is what we must discuss," His Lordship said. He stood on a platform raised a stair step higher than the floor; Isak had to look up at him. "My men tell me that you, hatchling, are having the effect we desire. Our people believe in your darkness. Whether or not it comes does not matter; no longer do they accept that those who sit in the Temple hold unquestioned right to rule. No longer are they sure the Temple serves the gods or speaks for them. They are ripe for new . . . shall we say? . . . arrangements. All that remains to be settled is what those arrangements will be."

Had they brought him here only to hear this? Did they want a foretelling? "Who can say?" Isak wondered aloud. "Will not the gods decide?"

"The gods?" His Lordship put thumb to chest. His voice rose in power. "*I* will decide."

Something close to the soul of this man had been touched. "The gods may permit," Isak said as mildly as his tongue was able. At once he saw it did not please.

"Understand this, hatchling, if you can," said His Lordship. He hooked thumbs into his sash, scowled down into Isak's eyes. "You have seen how the crowds respond to you. You have seen how they take your prophecy—"

"It is only a foretelling," Isak said.

"—how they take your prophecy as given truth, how they listen as if the gods spoke from your mouth, how they look to you with the belief you will improve their lives if they will take your guidance. Do not be misled by those signs. I have men in those crowds. You have known that. They are the first to voice that they believe your babblings, first to yell for the heads of they who sit in the Temple. All others follow like herdbeasts. Without my men you would be only a marketplace rattlebrain on whose skull Blazing Alpher has burned too long."

"You have told me nothing I did not know," Isak said. Indeed, he was puzzled. "Why do you tell me now?"

"Out of the suspicion that if I did not, you might believe that when the Temple has fallen you would take its place."

"That is beyond the reach of my foretellings," Isak said. "So strange a thing, why should I think it?"

"If you have never thought it, I suggest you do not think it now." The timbre of his voice made it more than a suggestion. "Now and ever, that is my realm. Mine and my household. Do you bow to that?"

"I serve the gods," Isak said. "If they would have it, then I shall. If not . . ." Where did the courage come from, that he could speak like that? Was truth so strong in him? ". . . then I must not. They give me no choice."

"They? The gods? Not them. I give you no choice."

"I serve the gods," Isak said again, meek and fearful. What did His Lordship want?

"This foretelling of yours—your word for it—it does not reach beyond the darkness?"

"Except for obvious things, it does not touch what men will do." Could that be what he meant? Would knowing it cool the thing that burned in him? "Do you . . . have you given thought to the question? Have you found a pattern that lets you foretell such things? I have noticed nothing like that myself, but I have concerned myself with other parts of the problem. If you tell me what you have learned, it is possible I could help. I . . ."

"One thing I have learned," His Lordship said. "He who waits for the gods to do a thing will wait all his life. Do the task I have given you and put no thought—"

"It is the gods who gave." Was that his voice that spoke?

His Lordship's voice hardened. Thick, black brows crouched over small, dark, burning eyes. Stained teeth glinted in the light of the lamps. "—and put no thought to matters beyond it. It is a realm you know nothing about."

"I know that," Isak said. "I would like to believe, though, I am able to learn."

"Then, hatchling, learn this," said His Lordship. "Fear me. Know that I hold your life in my fist. I can snuff it like . . . like this." With the back of his hand, almost carelessly, he knocked a lamp off its stand. Too well made to break, it spilled its oil on a carpet. Its flame, instead of quenched, began to spread. With a yelp he backed away. "Grishpa! Moltko!"

Two of the bodyguards shouldered past Isak and began to stomp the flames. Already the fire had spread too much. Fresh spouts of flame licked upward under each lifted foot. His Lordship edged farther away. "Ebron! All!"

Isak looked over his shoulder. Ebron and the other men hung

back. He felt the fire's heat on his cheek. Yellow tongues strained toward the pile of cushions, tasting them and turning their gold trim to shriveled brown. Grishpa and Moltko backed from the flowering blaze.

"May I?" Isak asked. Before an answer had time to come, he had moved back a step, bent, and lifted the edge of the carpet he'd been standing on. Stepping forward again, nodding Grishpa and Moltko aside, he thrust the carpet forward. It *thwupped* onto the flames. Instantly most of the chamber's light vanished and the air was full of smoke that stung the eyes. He blinked up at His Lordship.

"What were you saying?" he asked.

"You!" His Lordship screeched. Before he could say more a coughing fit seized him. "Ebron! Out! Away with him! Now!" Still coughing, eyes squeezed against the watering, he turned away.

Ebron's hand clutched Isak's shoulder. They hustled him headlong down the stairs, across the forecourt, out into the street. Under Gamow's strange, sharp-shadowed light the fetid stinks of Old Town had never before smelled so clean. Somewhere he had lost his hat. Blazing Alpher's ruddy forelight stained the eastern sky.

The hard-boned hand gripped his shoulder again. "Do not be misled," Ebron hissed. "Bear in mind it was only a fire, and easily quenched."

He seemed to mean something more than just the fire. Isak tried to understand. "It was I who stopped it," he said. "Why should it mislead me? What did he want?"

Ebron's glare was all fierce eyes. "Do not feign innocence. Even a child is not that stupid."

From somewhere Isak's hat was put back on his head, pushed down almost to his eyes. He searched the gaunt face that glowered down at him as if he could find explanation in the scrunch of brows, ragged teeth, the crimp of an intemperate mouth. "Truly, it is a thing I do not understand. I saw that things do not always happen the way he expects, but that is true of any man."

"That has nothing to do with it," Ebron snapped. "Be warned, hatchling. He is a dangerous man. He will have his way."

"The gods will have theirs." Isak wasn't sure what sparked it from his tongue. He was not even sure it was truth. The heat of the fire still burned on his cheeks. He waited for the rage to break upon his head. Why had he said that? He wished someone would explain. If he could talk to Kalynn again, she would know. Where was she? He had not seen her since they took him from her hiding place. He had not even heard her name; as if she did not exist. He felt very small, and trapped, and terribly alone.

The day of the new Moon in the month of Hiyar was put to shame. The Sun went down [in the daytime] with Rashap in attendance, [This means that] the overlord will be attacked by his vassals.

Author Unknown
[Clay tablet found in the ruins of Ugarit; translation by J.F.A. Sawyer.]

His wanderings through the city went on. He talked with wharf men and boat men, drovers, caravaneers, and troubadours. Husbandmen came to the city with late harvest crops and heard his foretelling, as did masons and pot menders, weavers and herdsmen, sewer cleaners and gentry. Everywhere he went, his robe with the hood thrown back, his face, his words were known.

At each shadow post he paused to read the standing of the gods, assuring himself the tiles were correctly placed, measuring the passage of time. Now and then he scanned the sky. Slowly he saw the parts of the pattern come together, saw the moment of the overtaking and the darkness loom certain like a heavy cloud growing large across the sky. Some time as he went about, though he never could mark the moment, he became something other than the boy he had been. No man can see his words heard with reverence and not be changed.

When only a dozen passings remained, he had been everywhere in the city but the Temple's square and the Preserve of the High Houses, where he went now. On the castle's side of the river, on a broad platform below the heights but above the city's sprawl, a cluster of Old Family households huddled together like survivors on a rock above the wash of the sea. A carriage track zigzagged up the slope, but from its terminus above and below a timeworn stairway of red stone ascended directly. Several times in their ascent, Ebron paused for breath. Though much younger, Isak welcomed the chance to do nothing but sit and watch the view, and think his thoughts. He had seen too much and done too much. Had spoken his message too many times. The ache of fatigue rested deep in his bones. His throat hurt. His mouth was dry.

Below him the city was like a field of tightly crowded pebbles. Across the river, hunched over its brood of lesser buildings, the Temple crouched dark in newly risen Alpher's blaze, while from the west Actinic Gamow's sharper light etched hard lines against its stones. No other gods stood aloft; even the Pale One was somewhere down under the world. Without waxboard or parchment—without even tracing a mark in the thin sift of grime underfoot—he calculated where she would be and when she would come up over the horizon. Lounging on the steps below him, one of his escort offered a bite from his sausage twist, then gnawed off a chaw of his own.

"You must remember, hatchling," Ebron said, "these will be well-tutored folk, and shrewd. Do not think they will be gulled by the same sophistry that persuades more common men." His breath was coming back; his tongue had never lost its sting. "Fortunately, their sympathies are with us already. Their hesitation is only on the question of whether we shall triumph. They are timid and their blood is thin. Our task is to win their support."

"I have no foretelling that would give us that," Isak said.

Ebron made an annoyed sound. Hand firm on a balustrade, he pushed himself again to his feet. "Only a short way more."

They resumed their climb. "Must we have them?" Isak asked. He doubted anything he could say would persuade such men.

Already, Ebron's breath was coming hard. "Hatchling, against the Guards our numbers are a pittance. We must gather . . . all the help we can. From whatever source we are able. These . . . these are men of power and . . . and wealth. We . . ."

"I can only give them truth," Isak said.

Ebron's voice was a snarl. "Your prophecy interests them not. They have heard it . . . heard it and made their judgment. What . . . what interests them is . . . whether we can turn . . . turn it to our purpose."

Isak slowed his pace, pausing between steps, to put less strain on the old man's lungs. Ahead, above them, three sentries moved out from under a canopy to take positions commanding the crest. From their halberds, Blazing Alpher's light flashed so bright the eye was forced to look away; Actinic Gamow's light, though not as strong, gave almost equal pain. Swords hung at their sides. Looking down, they waited.

"In truth, what can I promise?" Isak asked. They were on the last few steps. Ebron shushed him with an angry hand. Isak stopped and turned to him.

"Do you claim . . . ?" Ebron's breath gave out. He breathed deeply twice, glaring at Isak while his chest heaved. "Do you claim, hatchling, you do not know what you have done? What you do with every word you speak?" He smiled savagely at Isak's puzzlement, breathed deeply again, and impatiently gestured him silent. He raised a hand to the sentries waiting above. "We bring the Prophet!"

The men hardly moved. "Aye. We be told he would come," said the one nearest the top of the steps. "Our masters say he be welcome. And thyself. But those . . ." His nod managed to include all their escort.

"Where the Prophet goes, they go," Ebron said.

"Without their tools, then," said the spokesman. "Let them be laid down where they stand."

"Toothless?" Ebron demanded. He turned, went down a step. "Tell your masters the Prophet's regrets," he flung over his shoulder and took another step down.

"Hold," the sentry blurted. Ebron paused. Isak had never moved.

"Protection must our masters have," the sentry said.

"And the Prophet?" Ebron demanded. "The Prophet needs none?"

"In this place, no." The metalled butt of the sentry's halberd rang on the stone by his feet. Isak glanced to Ebron, who stood not moving, fists at sides, stubborn. In a moment, Isak sensed, he would turn and go on down the steps, leaving Isak no choice but to follow. Quickly—it was an impulse—Isak reached out, touched Ebron's arm the lightest touch he could, and started upward. With a startled squawk, Ebron scrambled after.

"It be true! The Prophet knows!" whispered one of the sentries as Isak mounted the last step without a break in his stride. Though he spoke to his fellows, it was loud enough for Isak and Ebron to hear, and possibly also their escort who now were laying their swords on the steps farther down, preparing to follow.

Isak's eyes were level with the sentry's. The face under the studded leather helm was youthful, perhaps hardly older than Isak himself. With a shake of his head, Isak demurred. "I did not know. I have discovered a way of learning. It is not the same thing."

By then Ebron had caught up with him. His chest still heaved from the effort, but he nudged Isak to go on. Only when they had gone well past the sentries and were following the Preserve's central avenue between mosaic patterned facades, green shrubs, a glittering fountain, did he speak.

"You are too trustful, hatchling."

"What did I risk?" Isak asked. Except for their escort they were alone on the street. "Was it likely the Families would give me to the Temple?"

Ebron's reply was a contemptuous snort and a scowl. "Not likely, but a needless risk. As I told you, these are timid men with much to lose should they support us and we fail. It would be possible they would think to gain more by throwing their lot with the Temple."

"Timid men?" Isak wondered. "Would they see no risk in that?"

"I do not claim to know their perceptions," Ebron said. "But the Temple would give much to have you. The fact that they have much already does not mean they are without greed. Nor would it need all of them to make a trap of this. One or two would be enough."

"Then we shall win the support of some, some will take neither side, and others will side with the Temple," Isak said. "But if, as you say, they are timid, I think none will declare their choice. None will do a thing that would show how they have chosen."

"Ha!" Ebron spat. "Hatchling, you assume they are rational men. You assume they act sensibly when their interests are involved. I warn you . . ."

"Do you say they are fools?" Isak asked.

"I say they are ordinary men," Ebron said. "Argue no more. Here is the place."

The gate was not significantly different from any other along the avenue. The hammered metal panels were stained green by corrosion, and the intricate enamel patterns had been chipped by time. Ebron tapped on the smaller door set within and framed by the larger; the postern gate. When nothing happened, he tapped impatiently again. The view slit snicked open. Black browed eyes peered through.

The heavy voice matched the eyes. "Stranger, name thyself."

"We bring the Prophet," Ebron said. He stiffened his back, squared his shoulders.

"That boy?"

"Must a prophet have white hair? No teeth? Wrinkled skin?" Ebron snapped.

"Nay. Nay," the gatekeeper said hastily. "No disrespect be meant, my lord. Be him the one?"

"When our sky turns black, you shall know it."

"Please," Isak said. It was a needless altercation. "I have been called a prophet, but I do not myself make that claim. My name is Isak."

"You be the one our master summoned?" the gatekeeper asked.

"I was told that," Isak said.

"Invited," Ebron said. "Not summoned. Think you the Prophet comes to the beck of any man?"

"I come that I may give my foretelling," Isak said.

There came the scrape and thunk of bolts being drawn, and

the metallic groan of ancient hinges as the postern gate swung outward.

"By our master's command, be welcome." The gateman carried a sword at his side but wore no armor. Iron-grey chest hair showed through gaps in his tunic. His head was bare, bald, and held erect on square, strong shoulders. Past his prime, but for a gatekeeper not yet old, Isak thought as he stepped through the opening. The gatekeeper watched him with wary, fascinated eyes.

Ebron followed, then the escort, one by one. Inside they waited while the gatekeeper shut the gate and dropped the thick brass bars—one, another, and a third—into place and turned to face them again.

With a gesture and a nod, Ebron detailed two of the escort to stay by the gate. They were taller than the gatekeeper, more robust, with longer arms and bigger hands. They took positions on either side of the older man. The heavier one grinned down at him. "We'll get along just fine now, won't we?"

From a bench beside the gate, a page boy advanced. He wore plain smock and leggings, and an emerald blaze on his left sleeve. His eyes were blue, head fair. He raised an arm. "Our master waits."

The flagstone path led around a carriage shed and stable, past a sunken pool where crawdads, water skinks, and skitterbugs darted among the lilies. A bed of big, blossomed flowers gave fragrance to the air. Tall shrubs gave shade. Ahead, beyond the pool, a dense high hedge pinched in on either side of the path. Ebron nodded several of the escort to go through first. To Isak it seemed a needless precaution.

He said as much. "Whatever happens to me, the darkness will come; and it will come as I have told you, with the overtaking. Would these men risk the gods' wrath?"

"Never try to guess what these men would risk," Ebron said.

"But if they are timid . . ."

"Be quiet, hatchling."

They passed through the hedge into view of the mansion's colonnade. A man came down the steps and across the lawn. By his garb—flowing sleeves, silken blouse, and many-colored kilt—this was no servant.

"Welcome! Welcome!" he called as he advanced, arms spread in greeting. "Never has the house of Maggitoro been so honored!" The top of his head was bald as bone, but hair from his temples and the back of his head cascaded smoothly to his shoulders; once dark, it now was thickly threaded with grey. By contrast his beard, even more whitened, was neatly trimmed. Ebron stopped and waited for the man to come to them.

He was still effusive. "You have brought hope! For the first time in many lives, true hope!"

Ebron met his smile with stony eyes. "I am not the Prophet." He jerked a thumb. "He is."

Their host shifted attention with hardly a blink. "Ah! Such a beautiful lad!"

Isak decided he did not like the man. "I am not a prophet, either," he said, "though I am called that. I have a foretelling."

"He does not know his power," Ebron said.

"My name is Isak," Isak said.

"Ah, yes! Well!" Maggitoro turned back toward the mansion. "Our guests await!"

He led them back across the lawn, glancing back constantly as if fearful they would not follow. His tongue never paused. "We have a magnificent feast prepared. Ah, such a feast! Two passings ago in the Skull Dome Hills, my huntsman with a flint-tipped lance had the good fortune to take a full-grown hackabout male complete with dewlaps and crest. All of eight forearms tall at the shoulder it stood! And done with a cast of more than seventeen paces! With only obsidian blades he dressed it and rushed it down the river, that I might have it in time for your coming. My kitchen master has been roasting it on a wood spit since Bright Dalton went down. Never shall metal have touched its flesh!"

At one time in his wandering, Isak had been reduced to snaring scavenger bats for food. It had been that or starve. This man had never in his life felt the ache of an empty gut. The lawn underfoot had no path; he watched where he put his feet and said nothing.

Maggitoro bounced up the mansion's steps with quick, skippy strokes of foot and ankle that belied his bulk, delighted as a boy. "All the Houses are here, Your Lordship, and the Korman of the River People, and the Kellermeister of the Forgemen's Guild. Even Lockstra himself has come, whom I despaired would ever take an invitation from my House. To hear the Prophet! Ah, indeed, it's an exciting time we live in. Exhilarating!"

He conducted them through a hall where iridescent tapestries cloaked the walls and golden carpets paved the floor. Isak did not listen to his noise. Matched wicker benches trimmed with burnished brass and brightly stained leather were spaced along the walls on either side. In a niche two stone figures of indeterminate sex, life-sized, embraced under the stern gaze of a plainly male statue from a niche in the opposite wall. They emerged onto a portico that overlooked a sloping lawn, a garden of shrubs and greens and bedded flowers ending in a parapet, a low wall, and a vista of the city far below. Music came, and the scents of meat and a charcoal fire. At the rail Isak stopped, looked down, and saw the dancer.

She wore only flowers; bands of them around wrists and ankles, and a belt of blossoms at her waist. Her long yellow hair, which made him think of Kalynn's, had been gathered and knotted close to the ends so that it swung as she moved like a skein of satin threads. It was a slow dance, an odd combination of the provocative and innocence that, either by design or accident, did well to display her supple, god-browned body. Oil-rubbed, she glistened in Alpher's warm light as she swayed, turned, raised her arms, strained skyward, then bent under the weight of the god's imperturbable regard. She danced as if not aware of the men who silently watched, there on the lawn; as if knowing only the music that came from the three who crouched to one side of the patch of tiles that was her dancing floor; flute, drums, and lyre. Bobbing from a thong around her neck, a turquoise charm lodged momentarily in the hollow between her young breasts, a moment later swung free.

Maggitoro signed for them to wait on the portico and tripped down the steps to join his guests. Isak watched the dancer, a comely young woman, graceful and poised in her nakedness. He watched, and he found himself thinking of Kalynn. He wondered how she was; her child would come soon if it had not already come. Childbirth was not an easy time for a woman. The drum's thump gained strength, gained speed. The flute and the lyre matched stride. The dancer shifted weight, whirled, flung out her arms and whirled again. In a motion so smooth it could only be part of the dance, she broke the charm from its thong and tossed it high in the air with the whole force of her body; and, continuing the motion, dropped to the tiles with her knees hugged tight against her. In the same instant the music stopped as if the instruments had fallen from the players' hands.

The stone came down among the guests. They scrambled for it on hands and knees, shoulder-butting each other, scrabbling on the ground, gabbling like kakkaburrs over scraps of feed. Leaner than most, craggy-browed, one rose to his feet with the stone between fingers and thumb. Another man made to snatch it, but the first man raised it triumphantly out of reach. The brawl broke up in a cacophony of jeers and raucous congratulations. The winner advanced through a gauntlet of slaps on the shoulder toward the dancer, who stood now to meet him. Isak saw the flash of fear on her face—it was there for only a moment—before she forced a smile and stepped into the winner's embrace. Isak was not sure he understood what he had seen.

Ebron chuckled. "You have never seen a concubine provided before?"

"Provided?" Used that way, the word was new to him.

"The host of this affair wants to make show of his wealth," Ebron said. "So he presents a concubine to a guest. And to assure it is the giving that is noticed rather than whom she is given to, chance is used to decide who shall have her. Among men of this class, it is frequently done."

Kalynn had said, if she went to auction, it would likely be as a concubine. At the time, Isak had not given much thought to it. "What will happen to her?" he asked, even though he knew. At least, he thought he knew.

Ebron sniffed. "What always happens to concubines? If she pleases him, and if she produces healthy young, he will keep her comfortably."

Down below, the dancer's bottom took the print of her new owner's hand. Her body moved against him as if the attention was enjoyed. Isak couldn't see her face.

"And if she does not?" he asked.

"She will bend every effort to make sure that does not happen," Ebron said. "In the class she was born to, this one's achievement is considered good fortune. Many would envy her."

Isak nodded. He knew that well enough; he was still thinking about Kalynn.

The drummer touched his instrument one stroke. It brought attention to Maggitoro who stood now on the tiles where the dancer had been. He raised a hand, that he might be heard.

"If Rikk can delay making deeper acquaintance . . ." he began.

Ribald laughter drowned his voice. One of the musicians tossed a bundle of cloth to her; it was a long, narrow strip, like a banner. She draped it over one shoulder. Though it did little to conceal her body, it gave her the appearance of being clothed.

When the laughter died down, Maggitoro resumed. "My House has promised you uncommon entertainment. So far, while most pleasant—" He nodded and smiled toward the dancer in the curve of her new owner's arm. "—what we have had has been ordinary. Now—" He cocked an eye upward; Isak felt their notice for the first time.

"You have heard, all of you, that a Prophet is abroad in our city. A true Prophet, denied by the Temple and sought by its Guardo. You have heard of his prophecy, though from the tongue of each man I have heard different things. Doubtless your experience is similar. So my House has found him, though the Temple and all its hirelings could not, and brought him here, that you may have it from his own tongue. Whatever its truth, I . . ."

Unease nibbled Isak's mind. "Is he an ally?" he asked over his shoulder.

"He is co-operating," Ebron said, close to his ear. "He would turn in an eyeblink if he saw advantage in it."

"But for now he is with us?"

"Do not be sure of it," Ebron said.

He realized Maggitoro had stopped talking; speaking with Ebron, he hadn't noticed. Now, suddenly, the breathless quiet made him aware they expected his voice. His hand touched the rail. On impulse he swung his legs over and sat there on the verge of the drop, looking down at them.

They were all richly clad in fine cloth and leather and stones and gold. Most were middle-aged or old. Each would be the master of a household. Some, in addition, would command great enterprises, or owned large holdings of land. All had great wealth, wealth that made possible the doing of many things. It was a form of power, possibly even such power that the Temple itself would fall before them if they sought its fall. He wondered what he could say to them that he had not said before—what he could say that would win them to the Temple's overthrow. No ideas came, and he put the thought aside. He could do only what he was able, speak truth and serve the gods.

"My name is Isak," he said. "I have a foretelling."

The words came easily. He had said all of them so many times he hardly had to think. While he spoke he could watch their faces. They listened strangely, not like any others he had spoken to. They seemed indifferent, detached—seemed hardly to hear him at all. A few exchanged momentary glances. Here and there an eye narrowed, a brief, crafty smile worked the corner of a mouth. But for most of them, for all the response he saw, he might have been talking to stones. Even the dancer; he watched her face, but the worries it betrayed had nothing to do with the gods.

Enough. He had expected nothing else. Unlike his other crowds, these were not predisposed to believe, nor even perhaps particularly interested in what was truth or what was not. Only if they saw advantage would they be swayed. Only if convinced beyond doubt the Temple's power would be broken would they join the effort. Speaking truth and only truth, Isak had no thought, no fact, no argument or idea that would make them his. If, as Ebron had told him, the help of these men was vital, he had not only failed, it had been hopeless from the start.

Well, within the limits of honor, he could not do more. Truth was his only blade. "My foretelling does not say the Temple shall be taken," he said. "I do not know if the priests shall be cast out. But the gods must want the effort made, and if it is not it shall fail by default. Nor should we let it fail for lack of commitment. Half-hearted effort can be as fatal as none at all."

He did not speak his other thought; that he knew no way to read with certainty the ultimate goal of the gods; that the gods might want a different thing than men did; that for them to want an effort made did not mean they would want it to succeed. He could not be sure, even, if the darkness would be a portent or sign of anything at all. He wondered if the gods would see him punished for speaking as he had in their name.

Nor did he let his thoughts dwell long on whether a cause that needed the support of such men—men who would make gift of a woman, however willing, as casually as a mug of wine or a sweetmeat—whether such a cause was any better than what it hoped to replace. His thoughts cringed from that question. He wondered how the gods could permit such a confusion of corruption and virtue, or whether it was possible that virtue itself could be corrupted. His glance touched the dancer again, and his voice faltered. She was beautiful. She made him think of Kalynn.

When he was done, he saw his audience smile, nod carelessly, politely applaud. He saw Maggitoro congratulated for his enterprise and ingenuity in arranging such a unique amusement. Maggitoro grinned, laughed affably. His belly jiggled. He mounted the steps to the portico, spry, but by the time he reached the top, slightly winded.

"Marvelous! Marvelous," he burbled. "My House shall be the talk of the district for a hundred rounds!"

For the space of a heartbeat, Isak was tempted to recant; to say his foretelling was false and his sophistry mere sedition. But that would not have been truth. The darkness would come, and all that followed came logically, or could be made to happen.

"I do not know why it is I who must speak for the gods," he said. "It is not an honor I sought, nor is there pleasure in it."

"Yes. Yes. Well . . ." Maggitoro said, still the jovial host. Perhaps he had not heard. "But you must come down now and

214

meet our guests. Some have come all the way from their country estates to . . ."

"No," Ebron said, advancing from his place against the wall. "He is the Prophet. Let them come up. A few at a time."

Taken by surprise, Maggitoro blinked and puffed, stammered wordlessly and gestured incredulously. "But then he will come down, will he not? Join us and partake of the feast I have called in honor of him? Surely . . . ? And yourself also?"

Ebron unbent only a little. "Time may not permit. Would you think you and your friends are all whom his prophecy must be taken to?"

Isak touched his arm. "It is only a foretelling," he protested. "How many times must I say? And I . . ."

"Be quiet, hatchling," Ebron hissed. And to their host, "We shall be pleased to join you, if the Prophet's further appointments allow. You must understand, the gods are a demanding master to the one who truly serves them."

"Ah! Of course! Of course!" Turning to the railing, Maggitoro clapped his hands. "You have heard, my friends!"

So they were brought up, four or five at a time. The steps were too narrow to be used in both directions at once; after the first group it was used alternately by groups coming up or going down. Maggitoro himself presented them. Isak sat on the rail, his feet drawn up against the rail's supporting columns, and nodded as each name was spoken. Some of the names he knew, and they were names to conjure with. No one could have lived long in the city without having learned those names. Some had a familiar ring, as if he might have heard them before, or names much like them. Others were totally new and forgotten as soon as the faces were gone. They bowed to him and—some of them—touched their brows. He nodded and, for just a moment, met their eyes. Then they moved on.

The routine broke only once, when Rikk and his new possession came before him. The cloth over her shoulder left her flanks, her hips, the outside of her thighs exposed, and one breast bare; a very provocative garment. "Rikk, of the House of Aratav," Maggitoro announced. The man bowed, touched his brow. Isak nodded and gestured an acknowledgement. The man started to move on, taking his property with him.

Isak spoke quickly. "And she? What is her name?"

Both Rikk and Maggitoro looked startled. "Your Lordship, she is not important," Maggitoro said.

"I would like to know it," Isak said. Once he himself had been sold, and bought. "Does she not also serve the gods?"

He saw the men exchange a glance, and realized that neither knew her name. To them she was only a female body, something to be used. He looked his question into her eyes.

Fearfully, she touched her brow and bent to him. "I am called Suralyn, Your Eminence," she said in a timid, small voice.

"And I am Isak," Isak said. "I would have you know me by that name. Not any other."

"But you are . . ." The thought vanished from her tongue as a new one came. Impulsively, she took a step toward him. "Can you say how . . . ?" She cast an apprehensive glance back over her shoulder to the man who owned her, who watched their exchange in brooding silence.

Isak slipped down off the railing. He took and held both her hands. He was conscious of her scent—the scent of perfumed oil—and her near nakedness and youth and the fears that burned in her, and sensed that should he demand it she would be given to him as carelessly as a discarded bone. He was the Prophet. Considering his own uncertain prospects, though, to ask would be no kindness.

"I do not know your fate," he said. It hurt, that he had to speak that truth. "I do not even know my own." And to Rikk, who now stepped forward to reclaim his property, "Care for her. Serve the gods."

Rikk's hand clamped her bare shoulder. "With pleasure," he said, smiling fiercely, and took her away.

The procession went on. Isak hardly noticed. He sat and wondered what else he could have done, and nodded to the faces as each name was given to him, and he knew he could have done nothing but what he had done. Which had been nothing. Deep within the swirl of his thoughts a doubt remained; had it been Kalynn, would he have done so little?

It hadn't been her, nor could it have been. Therefore, he told himself, the question was meaningless. Still it troubled him because he did not know. He wished the dancer hadn't made him think of her, even as he thought of her.

And even as he thought of her, another part of his mind was aware that the Twinned Ones, Gold Ephron and Embrous Zwicky, had risen and stood low under Alpher above the serrate profile of the mountains, adding their light and their colors to Alpher's blaze. The Twinned Ones, who never were far from one another. He wished he could go back to their hiding place. His and Kalynn's. It had been pleasant there; the last place he had known quiet and peace, the only place in all his life he could think of as having been his own.

The last group of five was being brought up when a servant came from within the mansion and spoke anxiously to Maggitoro's ear. Maggitoro paused to listen, was still a moment, then resumed the presentation of his guests.

When it was done and the last guest was going back down the steps, Maggitoro went to the rail and looked down. Many of them were crowded around the roasting pit, where sweating servants in breechclouts and mittens cut strips of dripping meat from the carcass with black knives that flashed in Alpher's light. Maggitoro turned to Isak.

"A marvelous thing," he said. "A crowd has gathered at my

gate. Rabble from the city. Servants of the other Houses. They have learned of your presence. The Prophet! They wait for sight of you."

Isak glanced to Ebron, who scowled as he advanced. "How do they know?" he demanded. "It was agreed no one would know but those within your walls."

"And such as must be told to arrange his passage," Maggitoro said with an exaggerated sigh. "What power in all the world can stop a servant's tongue?"

"A well placed knife—" Ebron began, but Isak touched his sleeve.

"I will go to them," he said. "I must, if I would serve the gods."

Ebron gave a sour glance, but said nothing.

"Do not the gods want me to tell all who will hear me?" Isak asked. Without waiting for a reply or to see if anyone followed, he crossed the portico and entered the mansion's hall. Behind him he heard the sound of feet—Ebron and his escort, he supposed—but he did not look back. A true Prophet would have known who followed.

Dick and I knew when we talked how stupid the whole concept was—that a public image was based upon some truths, some half-truths, some innocent rumors, and a few nasty lies. It meant general overexposure and self-consciousness (as opposed to self-awareness) and the constant danger of accepting someone else's evaluation of you in place of your own—your own being practically impossible to make already.

—Mimi Farina

The gate was barred. The gatekeeper stood before it, framed

between the stone-and-mortar pillars that contained it, and also between the two of Isak's escort who had stayed with him. Through the gate came the mumble of massed voices, like the roar of a storm sea on a rocky shore. As Isak approached, the gateman stepped forward.

"Prophet—" he began. "I . . ."

Isak went past him and opened the view slit.

The crowd that waited saw the flicker of the shutter. Excitement blazed, and the rumble of their voices turned to shouts. "Where is the Prophet?" "We must hear the Prophet!" and, beseeching, "Give us the voice of the Prophet!"

It was like all the other crowds he had seen; a chaotic mass of men, women, urchins of either sex, a few babes in arms. Some wore the liveries of important Houses; others were in tradesmen's smocks or aprons. Some wore rags. All had the same anxious faces. Hands reached toward him, clutching air. The gate groaned against the weight of them.

He let the shutter drop and turned. The gatekeeper, Ebron, and all his escort stood waiting. The gatekeeper turned a thumb to a ladder in the cove where the gate's enclosing tower joined the wall. The ladder led up to a walkway on the wall's inner side. Isak ignored the suggestion. "Open it."

"No," Ebron said. He pointed to the ladder.

"A priest would do that," Isak said. "I would have them see I neither fear them nor set myself above them." He rapped his hand on one of the postern gate's brass lockbolts. "Open it."

The gatekeeper looked a question to Ebron. Ebron fumed, scowled, gnashed teeth, but finally—scuffing the dirt—he nodded. "Know that I warned against it," he snapped.

One by one, with much rattle and clash, the gatekeeper lifted the bolts. The voices of the crowd stilled expectantly. The gate swung open with the snarl of a squeaky hinge. "Make way," the gatekeeper shouted. "He comes!"

To Isak's surprise, those nearest the gate moved back to let him come. He felt unease at the mass of people before him but hoped it did not show in his stride or the way he swung his glance from one part of the crowd to another. For the thousandth time he wished he had some new thing to say, but nothing came. He could feel their eyes, their anxious hunger.

At the crowd's edge, close to the avenue's verge, an old, weary drome crouched in the harness of an equally ancient, work-scarred cart. On the seat hunched a white-grizzled man with wet, sagging eyes and much-mended, unclean clothes. The crowd gave way in virtual silence as Isak went to him.

"May I sit with you?" Isak asked.

The old man was startled. "Eh?" Then he understood. "Oh. Aye. But . . ." With an age-twisted hand he gestured behind him.

It was a honey cart. Now that he was close Isak could smell the ripe stink of it, and hear the buzz of coprophagous bugs. Too late, though, to turn aside. "Do not we all serve the gods?" he asked and pulled himself up. Still amazed, the cartman moved to make room for him on the narrow seat.

From that small height he could see all the crowd. There were more than he had thought. Faces turned upward, they pressed close to the honey cart, squeezed together, waited breathless. A ragged woman reached toward him with the stump of an arm.

"I can only give you truth," he said. "If you are sick, if you are crippled, I cannot heal you. Nor can I make a change in your fortunes. My name is Isak. I have a foretelling; nothing else. A foretelling that promises both terror and hope."

He told it to them. The overtaking and the darkness were now only twelve of Alpher's passings off. He had begun to explain the significance of it—the displeasure of the gods and what they would have men do to serve them—when the interruption came.

His escort had emerged from the gate when he began to speak. With half his mind he had seen them mingle into the crowd and had thought little of it. Now, though, two had edged and elbowed their way behind a tall, muscular man in tunic and leggings; the cloth was natural colored, mostly grey and black with random threads of red and blue. Nothing obvious in that. A prosperous man, apparently, and with the part of his mind that watched, Isak wondered why they should be interested in him—they looked so intent—or whether it was only accident that brought them together at his back. All doubt vanished when, suddenly, they seized the man's arms and bore him to the stones. One mounted his back, a knee against his spine.

Surprised oaths burst from the part of the crowd close enough to see. From farther away came wordless questions. Isak stopped talking. "What . . . ?"

The one with his knee in the man's back grabbed a fistful of ear and turned the man's head to expose his face. "Under the helm of a Guard, this face has shown."

For the space of a breath Isak struggled to understand what it meant. The captive tried to wriggle free; the other captor joined his companion, settling his knees on either side of their victim's right elbow. The knife between his fingers pricked the man's throat. "Drink?" he inquired. That ended the fight.

"Wise. Wise," the man with the knife approved.

"Are you sure?" Isak asked.

Captor number one now had his knife out also. With a few quick strokes he slashed the man's tunic from collar to skirt and, spreading the cloth, exposed the band of puckered scars under the shoulder blades.

"Does ye still doubt?"

Too often Isak had seen such scars at the baths to not be

221

convinced. Honor scars resembled nothing else. Not only was this man a Guard, but one of more than common rank. Yet there was still some cause to be uncertain. Had no man ever changed the way in which he served the gods?

"Has he weapons?" Isak asked.

The two captors looked to each other. "We shall inquire," number two said with a flash of teeth. He scuttled back, knife still prepared to stab while his partner took his knee from their victim's back. "Up, offal." His blade nibbled a rib.

Isak winced, as if the knife had touched him, too. It was a needless cruelty. "Don't," he said. "Whatever else, he is a brave man."

"And if he held iron to my throat?"

"Were you to do as you say he would," Isak said, "you would show yourself no better." He put the hardness of command into his voice, and was amazed to hear it ring from his tongue. "Serve the gods."

They stood their captive on his feet and hobbled his wrists behind him with a cord looped from one, up and around his throat, and down again to the other. Against that taut cord the man strained to breathe while, with rough efficiency, his captors sliced the clothes from his body.

"No tools," number one reported, and cast the last piece of cloth aside.

Ebron had squeezed his way through the crowd. "With only bare hands, such a one is dangerous."

Isak gestured him to be silent. He leaned forward to study the captive.

The man stood with feet slightly apart, trying to breathe against the pressure of the cord. A fully mature, hard-fleshed body; dark curly hair on chest and limbs. His face was dark with gorged blood. His lips grimaced with effort and pain. Desperation in his eyes.

"Why are you here?" Isak asked.

It brought renewed effort to breathe, new struggle against his bonds. His captors moved close with their knives. Number two pricked his back where a single stroke could uproot a kidney. His throat uttered a wordless croak; whether an attempt to speak or only proof that he could not, Isak wasn't sure. "Loose him," Isak said. "Let him speak."

"Escape, you mean," number one objected.

"Would they let him?" Isak asked with a glance at the tightly packed crowd. "Does anyone love the Guards?"

Number one followed the direction of his gaze. The crowd glowered back. He looked to Ebron for advice. Ebron looked grim but, before this audience, was restrained from open disagreement. Shrugging, number one cut the hobble cord with one brutal slash of his blade. Both he and his partner backed off a step, knives still at the ready.

After one convulsive half step when his arms came loose, the Guard stood where he was. He breathed deep, as if he had been long underwater. He swung his arms, flexed his shoulders, and rubbed them to work out some of the pain. Slowly, the deep purple color of his face drained away. Only after a long time did he again raise his eyes to Isak.

Isak had been waiting. "Why did you come?" he asked again.

The man tried to speak. His voice came out a strangled rasp. He put a hand to his larynx. Coughs racked his body.

"Let him drink," Isak said, and only then wondered what could be offered. He looked around.

"My pleasure," a voice from above said. Startled, Isak looked up. Maggitoro's guests—even the host himself—watched from the top of the wall. One tall man reached a long arm out and down, a jeweled wine mug in his hand. A boy slipped from the crowd, leaped the ditch and, finding fractional toeholds between the stones, climbed up to take it. Impudent, hanging one-handed, he took a sip before handing it down to a hand that reached up from below.

Over the heads of the crowd from hand to hand it went, into the Guard's shaking grasp. He drank, breathed deep, and drank again. Ebron snatched the empty vessel.

The Guard looked up at the wall, scanned the faces, no longer sure who the donor had been. He raised a hand. "Honor to the gods," he got out hoarsely, and touched his brow. He turned. "And you, Prophet. I am grateful for my life."

It was credit Isak had not earned; the man might still die.

"I gave you nothing you did not have already," Isak said. "You have not said what sent you here."

"Is a Guard so different from other men?"

A growl came from Ebron's throat. "Do you deny you serve the priests? That you live in the Temple's shadow, feeding from its tit, and do its evil work?"

The Guard did not flinch, though Ebron's hand chopped within a fingernail's thickness of his nose. He set his weight evenly on both feet, set his eyes level. "I serve the gods," he said, and though his voice was made a whisper by the harm done him, there was firm strength in it. "All my life I have served them." He breathed deep. "Until now, I had thought that to wear the Temple's leather and its scars, and to obey the priests' commands did service to them, no matter how strange those commands might seem." His feet moved a little. He looked down at the stones.

"And now?" Isak asked.

The Guard looked up again. "Your Lordship, I do not know. I have spoken to my fellows. Many of us now are not sure what we should believe. Some still do not doubt, but others—more of us than not—only know that we cannot believe both what the priests have told us and, at the same time, what we have heard of your prophecy. So I have come, not as a Guard but as a man.

I want to know what is truth. I want to know how we should serve the gods. I do not know if what you say will be either, but I sought to hear what you would say."

Isak considered the man. Ebron would say he spoke a fabrication crafted only to buy his survival. Looking down, though, into that face that looked up, bravely proud, sure even now that he served the gods, Isak sensed truth. Not the truth of demonstrable fact, but the more difficult truth of a scrupulously honest man. For the space of several breaths, through a silence that stretched out until it had to either collapse or burst, Isak felt envy. The simplicity of that man's life.

Only then did he realize their roles had been reversed. The Guard, the prisoner who stood at hazard of his life, had become the questioner and he, Isak, was now the one who must answer. Nor was it only the Guard who waited for his reply. All who watched, all who could hear, waited; all that sea of faces. He took a breath and tried to shape a thought that would be equal in honesty to the honesty of the man before him, but yet would serve the fight against the priests, and even so would serve also the gods.

No glib response, no pre-created argument would do it. He tried to salve the dryness from his tongue—wished he, too, could summon a mug of wine. The words came hard.

"I know of nothing I can say that will prove I speak truth," he said. "I have no special wisdom. Only a foretelling. Nothing I can give you will make its truth evident. You must yourself choose to believe or not believe."

"Then how, Your Lordship . . . ?"

"My name is Isak," Isak said. "I do not claim to be more than myself."

"Aye. Very well. But how . . . ?"

"When the darkness comes, then you will know who has given you truth, and who has given falsehood."

"And if it does not come?"

"Then also you would know," Isak said. "But it will come, and it will come when I have said, twelve passings from now, when Gamow overtakes the Pale One. And . . ." Suddenly the thought was a blaze in him. "And I will say this to you. If, then, knowing you have served false tongues—if then you throw down your pike and your sword, or if you turn them against those who gave you false guidance, you will show how you have truly served. Go back to your fellows. Tell them I said this, and let each take the choice of his own conscience. Go in honor." He nodded to the men of his escort. "Let him go."

The voice of the crowd was a breathed out sigh. Then, "Honor to the gods!" He did not see who shouted it first; then all were shouting It. "Honor to the gods and to their Prophet! To the Prophet! The Prophet!"

Taken by surprise, he could only sit there. It was an acclamation he had not sought, but could neither prevent nor reject. "My name is Isak," he murmured, almost as if in pain, but only the honey cart drover beside him was close enough to hear.

The difficulty lies in learning, that we ourselves encompass forces equally great.

—Gene Wolfe

Ebron declared it unwise to return to the city by the way they had come. Whether the Guard had spoken truth or not, it was too likely Isak's whereabouts were known; and though he might be safe so long as he remained in the Preserve, his descent down the steps or by the road would not escape notice.

"Likely they would be waiting for us down there," he said.

Two of their escort were dispatched with messages to go

down with that part of the crowd which was returning to the city. Another was sent along with two of Maggitoro's servants to retrieve their swords. At a fountain under the cliff's high brow, a stone that the casual eye would have thought part of the living rock rolled easily aside to reveal a cavern's mouth. Uneasy, grim, the escort men traded glances. Torches were lit with mumbled prayers. Ebron nodded them inside, then Isak. He himself followed. The stone thumped heavily into place, sealing them in. But for the nervous flame of the torches, darkness held them. One of the escort groaned as if in mortal pain.

The way ascended. Sometimes it climbed by steep flights of stairs, but more often by long, twisting galleries whose walls gleamed with slime while cold mud squelched underfoot and made the going treacherous. It was a wearisome climb.

"Hatchling, you did well," Ebron said when they paused at the head of a stairway for breath. Gloom lay below them; ahead, the tunnel led off into blackness. Around them, the stone walls oozed a clammy chill.

Praise from Ebron was as unexpected as a feast in the desert—too unlikely to be taken without question. "I did only what I thought the gods would have me do," Isak said.

That brought a skeptical snort from the old man.

"I did not want to see his blood," Isak said.

"Before this is done, you'll see enough," Ebron said. "Hope only that none is your own."

"If the gods would have it, what power of mine could prevent them?"

Ebron hawked his throat clear and spat. "The gods! Have you no grasp of what you've done?"

Puzzled, Isak stared at him. Ebron nodded with satisfaction, his surmise confirmed.

"Whether you schemed to that end or not, hatchling, you won that crowd and the High Houses too. The priests would have you dead and your tongue in parts, but you gave that man his life when our men had it in his throat. They liked that. Do you think the priests would be so generous?"

"I do not want to be like the priests," Isak said, as if no further explanation was needed.

Ebron's laugh was scornful, humorless. "And then you told him—do you claim there was no cleverness in it?—that a Guard who turned his sword against those false tongues would serve the gods. Do you say—and think I will believe?—you do not understand the blow those words struck?"

Isak looked out into the darkness. It was softer to the eyes than the blaze of torches. There was some turn of Ebron's mind he could not grasp. "I only thought if such a man is of the Guards, were they our enemy? And I saw they were not, except they serve the priests. But if they did not serve the priests, but served the gods instead . . . do you know my thought?"

"I see it," Ebron said, "and I see you have not followed it to all its consequences. Consider: by themselves the priests could never hold the Temple. Children with eating knives could drive them out. But while they own the Guards, it will be very hard. Perhaps beyond the effort we could mount, and even should we win it would come at the cost of much blood. But if the Guards—even if only some of them—are persuaded to stand aside or, even better, wet their blades with the blood of priests, our prospects become significantly better. And you, hatchling, blundering and thoughtless, you have given us the tool that will cut them apart. No longer must they stand with the priests out of fear they must share the same fate."

"But if we could not win against them, what had they to fear?" Isak wondered.

"Death as men," Ebron said. "Each man himself. What that one saw eye to eye when the blade pricked his throat." His voice savored the memory of it. "And do you say—speak truth now, hatchling—do you say you had no thought of how the High Houses would see it?"

"I was hardly aware they watched," Isak said. "My attention was all on the man. He wanted to know truth, and how to truly serve the gods. I think . . . I think I felt a kinship to him."

Ebron laughed a harsh, savage bark of a laugh. "Hatchling, you amaze me. I speak truth: you do. In some ways you are unschooled as a babe." He made a sign to their escort for the procession to resume. The tunnel was wide here. Torchlight flickered off slicked walls. Wet, crumbled stone mushed underfoot. Ebron stayed at Isak's side.

"The High Houses, hatchling, have been hesitant to join us for doubt we could win. I told you that. Now you have shown them a device that will make us able to win, and shown them also—yes!—the skill you have of winning men to your cause. Therefore—no, they have said nothing; that is not their way— you have won them also. All but the most boneless. And they, even they, will come, for they will fear even more the consequence for them should we win without their aid. And you, hatchling, you saw none of it!"

He could as easily have seen the spot between his shoulder blades. "I understand the gods," Isak said. "That is, I know one aspect of them. People . . . they do not follow a pattern. Even men who fight each other—both can serve the gods, even as they fight. I think that people . . . I do not think I will ever understand them."

The way led on. It gave no choices. More flights of steps lifted upward. Long galleries probed through stone. Here and there, the walls showed the mark of tools, but more prevalent was the patina of time; slimed walls and chilly darkness. On a stair step the treadstone crumbled under Isak's foot and he sprawled on wetness. "You see?" he cried. "I am not a prophet!"

Once they clambered over a rockfall. Once they waded a

cold, trapped pool. Twice more they stopped for breath and rest before, at last, the passage narrowed and a great dark boulder blocked their way. The walls were dry here, and on one side it was not native rock but fitted, mortar-chinked stones. Three of their escort—as many as could fit in the cramped space—put their shoulders to it. They shoved and groaned. With a grinding protest it moved, gave way and turned aside.

More darkness lay beyond. They filed through the opening, sealed it behind them, and went on. Slowly now, the darkness thinned. Another rockfall blocked them; they picked their way over it, and now the light was perceptibly of greater strength. They turned a corner, and a shaft of Alpher's blaze burned down before them. A crumbling, grime-dusted flight of steps took them upward.

Alpher shone down, with the Twinned Ones close beside, and from the east Bright Dalton sent his rays.

Blinking in that abrupt, cruel light, Isak stopped and looked for bearings, and knew where he stood. All around him, time-battered towers and half-fallen walls, the ruined shell and bones of what had been a fortress. Amid those tumbled stones, Isak pondered the old castle. Great expense and toil had raised it; brave assault had stormed it at the cost of blood and limbs and many lives. He wondered if either the building or the taking of it had been worth the doing, and why those now forgotten men might have thought either was. Underfoot was rubble. Overhead was sky.

Oh yet we trust that somehow good
Will be the final goal of Ill.

—Alfred, Lord Tennyson

The wagon was warped through the narrow gate from the alley into the bakery's yard, and there the sacks of grain were offloaded onto a platform at the back of the building and stacked under an awning. When the wagon had gone, the baker himself cut the cords on Isak's sack and helped him out of it. High buildings all around blocked much of the sky from view, but the doubled edge of a shadow against one eastward wall told Isak the Twinned Ones were halfway down the western sky, while a brighter illumination higher up told him that Alpher, not yet down, stood lower still. Groggy from the suffocating weight of grain bags around him and on top of him, he leaned against one of the tall milling stones and stretched some of the cramp from his limbs.

"Your Lordship . . ." the baker offered timidly.

Isak forced strength into his posture; he still had a role to play. "My name is Isak," he said.

The baker seemed not to hear. "Upstairs . . . if you will accept . . ." He nodded to the door.

"Of course," Isak said, and followed him.

In the family quarters above the shop, the baker's woman gave him a chunk of oven-warm bread, a scrap of meat, and a mug of moderately decent wine. She did not speak, and seemed fearful of him; a fear she communicated to the toddlers, both of them, who peered around pieces of furniture.

Such awe he had not sought. It pained him. When his wine mug was empty, the woman moved quickly to fill it again, and as quickly retreated. "I would prefer to be an ordinary person," he said. He was, after all, nothing else.

"But you are not," she said, as if astonished he would speak to her. Plump she was, with long brown hair in braids and a round, very ordinary face from which watched apprehensive eyes. Made bold by the exchange of words, the smaller of the children came out from behind a settee and stood gravely looking at him.

Wanting to show he was no danger, he held out a hand to her, and she came. At his knee she paused, looked up at him. She tried a timid smile which touched him to respond with one of his own. Encouraged, she grabbed two tiny fistfuls of his robe and tried to pull herself up. He put his mug aside and, conscious of the woman's gasp behind him, lifted the child to his lap. Still she hadn't made a sound. She snuggled down, her head against his breastbone as if to hear the beat of his heart.

"Please," the woman said. "Do not think badly of her."

Isak was startled. That hadn't been his thought. The child's gold hair was silken under his hand. "Did I object?" he asked. "Should I be feared?"

"But you are . . . you are the Prophet."

"I had no choice in the matter," he said. He looked down at the child. "She is the first in a long time to whom I have been only a person. Therefore to be valued."

The woman humphed. "A warm lap," she said with wry scorn. "She is a greedy child. Her father spoils her."

"And you?"

She was still a moment, and he realized he had touched something in her. "I worry about the life she will have," she said. She nodded toward the boy, still lurking behind a couch. "That one also. Each time the tithe man comes . . . Could you . . . ?"

"I can change nothing," Isak said, feeling hurt that he had to speak that truth. "I do not have that power. Nor do I know the fate of anyone. It is possible she will be happy." Even to his own ears it sounded lame. "If the Temple is taken, there would be hope."

"Could it make so much difference who sits in the Temple?"

"I would like to believe it," Isak said. "But I do not know."

232

He stroked the child's hair, that golden wealth. "I have the hope," he said, and tried not to think his doubts. The little girl snuggled deeper into his lap. He wished he could stay there.

O it's broken the lock and splintered the door,
  O it's the gate where they're turning, turning;
Their boots are heavy on the floor
  And their eyes are burning.

                                        —W. H. Auden

Bright Dalton rose and he made ready to go out. When Red Bethe came soon after, he went. Alpher stood low in the west. Already his escort was in the marketplace, dispersed to every corner, aisle, and cul de sac. Their weapons were concealed, their garb was varied, but he knew them. Even from the back he could pick them out, he knew them so well. That one ahead of him, waving his hands as he harangued the man at a shellfish stall . . .

"I say he speaks truth," that one declared. "Why else would the Temple want his tongue?"

The merchant said something too soft for Isak's ears.

"Very well. Doubt if ye must," came the reply. "But when the darkness comes, how then will you serve the gods?"

Hand at throat, the merchant began a response but stopped as the crowd, aswirl around Isak, parted. Isak was careful not to change his stride or shift the direction of his gaze. The merchant pointed an unsteady finger. "Hold! Is that . . . ?"

The escort man turned. "Why yes, I do believe . . ." He caught Isak's sleeve. "Are you . . . ?"

"My name is Isak," Isak said. The two disputants traded glances.

"Tell us. Is it true? There shall be darkness?"

"There shall be darkness, and the Temple shall be shaken," Isak said.

It was a planned exchange; not for a particular moment, but to be used as opportunity permitted. But the question that broke from the merchant's tongue was spontaneous. "How can I know you speak truth?"

"Can a man serve the gods and not speak truth?"

"Ah! But do you serve the gods?"

"If I do not, my life is wasted," Isak said. "How can I know?" Isak stood calm before the merchant's agitation. "I do not ask you to believe," he said. "You know my foretelling, or you would not ask what you have asked. When the overtaking brings darkness you will remember that I told of it. Then you will know, and will know also how the gods should be served."

The escort man let go of his sleeve. He moved on. Even in the short time he had paused a crowd had gathered around him, but a way opened for him to pass and a murmur of words and wordless awe spread from around him across the marketplace. Far off he heard shouts of disbelief, amazement, excitement, hope.

He made his way through the square. Shoppers and merchants interrupted their haggling to watch him pass. Several times he had to pause as questioners pressed around him. It was always the same questions; he had learned how to answer them long before. Only the question he silently asked himself gave him hesitation: the question of where solid truth ended and became the truth that could be made true by men's efforts, and whether one was different from the other in the view of the gods.

A legless, tongueless beggar plucked the edge of his robe in mute appeal. At first when he looked down Isak thought it was a dwarf, but then he saw the stumps, the puckered scars, and saw the crude, short crutches the creature used, and the open, hollow mouth with broken, twisted teeth, and the pleading eyes.

"I do not have the power," Isak said, but the words turned thick in his throat. He touched the man's brow, knowing it would do no benefit even though it was the thing asked, and passed on. Behind him, the rattle of coins falling into the alms bowl took him by surprise, but as the Prophet he could not show it. He could not even turn to see.

He wished he could be himself again. Only himself. Yet how could he, with the gods to serve?

"How do I know?" he echoed a salt merchant's question. He pointed to the eastern sky where Dalton sent his glare past a tenement's cupola. "As I know the Pale One shall rise when he stands highest. The coming of darkness is no more strange to me."

The salt merchant stared at him, amazed. Almost against his will he glanced toward Dalton, then to Isak again. In his eyes Isak saw conviction form, even before the Pale One rose. "Serve the gods," Isak said, level-gazed, and moved on.

The marketplace had been one of the city's first. It clung to a crestline where the slope of the land coming down from the base of the cliffs abruptly steepened. On the side toward the river were tenements. Tightly they crowded wall against wall and step by step descending toward the docks, warehouses, and wagon yards of the floodplain. In the opposite direction, extending to the cliffs and even clawing a little way up those steep ramparts, were homes of the more well-to-do. The people of both districts and of the blended zone between crowded the stalls, haggled the merchants, sampled the wares. Hawkers' cries and the scent of hot sausage filled the air. The grind of pushcart wheels, the mumble of a thousand voices each speaking its own words and the whisper of sandals on stone hushed and thundered. A spice seller opened a bale and sent a pulse of fragrance out into the space around his stall. Bright Dalton burned down.

"Why do I ask such a price for my jellabies? You must ask?" a plump fruit seller protested. Sensing opportunity, Isak paused. Engrossed in their business, neither merchant nor customer noticed.

"First," said the merchant, "you must have heard the crop was poor, this round. I do not know why; the grove keepers are decent folk; but with a disappointing harvest they must now ask a higher price or starve."

"They can eat jellabies can't they?" his customer argued.

The merchant persisted. "And the boatmen. They must bid one against another, or have nothing to fill their boats. An empty boat does not pay for its voyage, and if there are not enough jellabies to fill all the boats, what then?"

"The boatmen can net eels."

"When the water is low?" the merchant asked. "And then, when the boat has come to the dock down there, I must offer a price that is equal to the other fruitmongers, knowing that some will be spoiled and some too green, or I shall have no jellabies for my trade. What can I say to a man such as yourself who asks where my jellabies are? That I have none, though there are some to be found all over the city? He would think I had no skill at my trade. He'd buy nothing. May I ask what trade is yours?"

"I work leather, and I shall eat turnips and yams. Times be hard."

"It is said the yam harvest also was poor. I thought only the tithe collectors had not heard."

"Then turnips," snapped the leather worker. Turning away, he came face to face with Isak. As recognition broke he blinked, stood still, one hand raised as if to speak though no sound came.

Instead it was the fruitmonger who spoke. "Ask him."

It broke whatever stilled the leather worker's tongue. "Your Lordship, what would you do?"

Such questions had come to Isak hundreds of times. In that circumstance he would have been surprised only if it had not been asked. Still it was a question he had to think about. To give full truth would be to say he knew nothing of their prospects, yet that would leave both men dissatisfied, his own commitment abdicated, and the campaign against the Temple not advanced. Would such response be proper service to the gods?

All that he had pondered every time. No new insights came. "The gods have let me see only what they must have wanted me to see," he said. "For greater knowledge I must guess and hope, like any man."

"Your Lordship, that is not what I asked," the leather worker objected.

Isak nodded. "But you must know that I speak only as a man. I believe that when the Temple has been cleansed the gods will send better times, but that is only a belief I hold. It did not come from the gods. First, though, they will send the darkness—that much they have revealed to me—and I believe that then a time of disorder will come. I do not know if it will be brief or long. But to your question: had I the coin, I would buy, for it might be long before I could hope to taste jellabies again. But it is meaningless to say what I would do." He spread his arms, to show that the cord at his waist held no purse. "I do not have a coin."

"You have paid its coin!" the fruitmonger crowed as, in one continuous motion his hand chose a large jellabie from the basket and thrust it into Isak's hand. "My finest! More than its price!" And loudly—no one nearby could fail to hear. "Did you hear? The Prophet has said 'Better times!' "

The leather worker could only yield. "Before such assurance, who be this one to doubt?" He tossed a coin that flashed in Dalton's light and which the fruitmonger snatched from the air as if he had been snatching coins all his life. With a plump jellabie in each hand, the leather worker strolled off into the crowd.

"Better times!" the fruitmonger hailed, dropping the coin into his purse. "Honor to the gods!"

Isak gave the jellabie to a rag-clad crone with a withered arm, a useless leg, and a face that hung slack on one side. With her good hand she thrust it to her mouth, nodding gratitude even as she sucked the juice. When Isak had gone past he heard behind him—again!—the clatter of coins in her alms bowl.

Was it possible he could change their lives by such a momentary touch? He did not dare look back, for fear he would see who followed him.

The shadow posts fronted a shallow forecourt midway along the northern edge of the marketplace. Their location was such that no building's shadow blocked the gods' light on them; and equally no merchant's awning was allowed to put them in shade. It was different from most emplacements, though; instead of the usual solitary pillar there were two, for they dated from an earlier time when it was thought there was significance to where and how the shadows cast by two gods would cross.

Isak stood before them for a time, trying to satisfy himself as well as he could with only his eyes that both stood properly vertical; it was a problem with old posts, but these had been well maintained. While a modest crowd watched from a respectful distance—for the Prophet was conversing with the gods—he paced the stones to confirm that the markers were correctly lodged. Their system of measures was also of an older convention, so it was slow work. Dalton and Bethe cast diverging shadows westward, while the Twinned Ones, low in the west, threw theirs, more narrowly divergent, eastward. Alpher was gone from the sky. Isak stood between the two dark patches that the shadows of the two posts made where they crossed—casting shadows of his own, which also made dark patches where they intersected the others—when Kalynn slipped from the crowd and stood, for a moment hesitant, in the open space between.

He saw her, and in the quick turn of his head she saw that he saw and came toward him. Not knowing what he should say or do, he did not move. In his random course through the city he had seen so many women who, for the space of a caught breath, he had thought was her, that now he did not dare to hope. But as she came to him, instead of differences, he could see only more resemblance. Instead of doubt, he felt a certainty grow in him until no shred of doubt remained.

She walked with a heavy, flat-heeled stride, for she still carried the child. The swelling of her body, gross before, seemed now on the verge of bursting. When she came near and raised her hands to take his hands which he had not known he had raised, the jeweled gold cuff caught a coruscating flash of the Twinned Ones' light, a thousand sparkling, many colored stones, and though he had never seen it before he knew beyond question what it had to be.

She saw the direction of his glance and looked away. "I wanted to see you, Isak." Her voice had strain in it, as if some force compelled her to explain. "A bride of the gods who carries their child should have a right to talk to their Prophet, shouldn't she?"

There were so many false assumptions in those words that he could only stammer. His confusion made her smile. "I know," she said with a glance back at the crowd. "It's not truth—none of it. But no one will wonder about us meeting like this, even if what they believe isn't truth."

"The priests would know," Isak said. "If we fail . . ."

Her chin came up. "We're not going to fail. But even if we do, would they wonder about what a silly girl has done? One they have worked their will upon?" She shook her head. "They'll have worse things to think about."

He had to nod, though doubts still whispered through his thoughts. Wrong assumptions led to false conclusions, and to guess how another mind—a mind equally misguided by assumptions—might judge things was the wildest folly. He said, though, "Have you been well?"

"As well as I could hope," she said with a lift of her shoulders and a downward glance. "Very soon now, and the midwife is encouraging. But I wanted to see you. Before."

The thought came that there might be no after, for either of them, but he did not speak it. "You know there is not much I can do," he said. "I wish it was different, but I am not master even of my own life."

She smiled a small smile at that. "The city is full of talk about you. The miracles you've done. Your prophecies."

"I've done no miracles," he said.

She put a finger to his lips. "I would prefer to believe in miracles," she said firmly.

"It would not be truth," he protested.

"Everyone else believes in them."

"That does not make them truth," he said. "Do the priests? Does your father? His friends? They who have turned me to their purpose?"

A waggle of her hand dismissed such questions. They were irrelevant. "Isak, what I'm trying to say, you're . . . well, important. What you say, what you do. Where you go, they know you. They believe in you. You . . ." She stopped another objection with a quick flutter of fingers. "I don't mean they're all sure the darkness is coming. That's a hard thing to believe.

Even harder than the miracles. But when it does come, they won't be surprised because you said it would, and after that they'll believe anything about you. You'll be the most powerful man in the world."

He wondered how much of that was true foretelling, how much wild exaggeration. And he wondered, too, if saying that was the reason she had wanted to see him and, if so, why. He kept those puzzles to himself. "More powerful than your father's friends?" he asked. It was a danger he had not thought of before. "I do not think His Lordship will allow that."

A frown touched her brow. The thought was new to her, also. "Maybe he won't be the one who decides."

So she hadn't been trying to warn him. Was it something else she wanted to say? "Nevertheless," he said, "it would be convenient for him if I do not live."

"What will you do?"

He had no skill at scheming, and knew it. The other players in the game never moved the way he expected. "I do not know," he said. His tongue felt dry. "Perhaps the gods will help, though that is not a thing I can count on." Even to his own ears it sounded lame.

She looked away; he could see only the pinched tight corner of her eye, the thin-pressed corner of her mouth. Blindly her hand sought his arm. She turned her face to him again. Her eyes glittered with wetness. "How can you stand there and say things like that? You're going to do nothing?"

"What will happen will happen," he said. It was like a cold wind blowing through his bones. "I will have to think. I will do what I can."

She could neither look at him nor look away from him. "Isak, why couldn't we have met somehow differently?"

It was an odd question. Odd and absurd. "It could not have happened," he said.

"It could have happened a thousand ways!"

He shook his head. "You are a prosperous merchant's daughter," he said. "You live in a fine house. You had friends, a whole society that I was not part of. And I . . . I was a scribe, indifferently taught, given only a booth in the Narrow Streets shrine and a wage that left me thin and often bare of foot. We might have passed on the street, though I doubt you would by choice have gone through the districts where I normally was. But if we had, you would not have noticed me, nor would I dare have spoken to you."

As he spoke, she had looked down; perhaps to contemplate the pattern of light and dark shadows on the stones at their feet, the shadows made by the posts on either side of them; perhaps seeing nothing at all. Only when his voice stopped did she look up, her grey eyes for a moment direct and clear.

"Then maybe not everything is as terrible as it could be," she said, almost wistful, as if it was a thing she needed very much to believe.

He had no answer. He could think of no words that would make her see the reality that surrounded them, trapped them, quite possibly doomed them. Still, in pain, he would have spoken and his mouth had opened and his tongue had tensed to shape the words he had not yet found when interruption came.

"Mistress! Guards!"

He whirled. He knew that voice, though it was a moment before he knew its owner's name. By then Hobur was already lurching stiff-limbed across the stones, one arm reaching toward them. "Guards be coming!"

Isak caught her arm. "Go with him. Hide in the crowd. And hide that . . ." In his urgency, he could not adequately speak of the cuff she wore, but his nod and his uncommon lack of words was more eloquent than any words could have been. "It's me they want."

"I know that," she said needlessly. "Isak . . ."

He stood on tiptoe, trying to see over the heads of the crowd. Where a street came into the marketplace, Guards were piling out of a high-sided wagon. Others, already out, were advancing through the crowd which scattered from the tips of their swords. Not one of his escort was in sight, except a long-limbed young man who fled ahead of the crowd.

"With such courage as that shall the Temple be cleansed?" Hobur roared.

Isak looked to another street. A wagon blocked that way, also, and the bobbing helms of advancing Guards, and a crowd in flight before. Another street? The same.

He thrust Kalynn to Hobur. "Care for her," he said in haste, and whirled to run.

"Isak!" Her voice rang clear behind him. The paving stones struck hard at his feet "I wish it was yours!" she cried. "My baby! I wish it was yours!"

He vaulted through a row of vendor's stalls, pelted on through a shambles of tubers, shellfish, and bolts of iridescent cloth. Behind him other shouts now rose; consternation, outrage, urgent commands. He darted through another stall. "Serve the gods!" he gasped to the startled merchant, dodged a pile of green and purple melons, found open space, and ran. From behind he heard nothing now. All he knew was the hardness of stones, and ache and heave of his breath, the beginnings of fatigue in his limbs. He changed direction again, in hope it would confuse pursuit through this warren of potmakers' wares, awnings, and baskets of eels slowly leaking their fetor under Dalton's pallid glare. No thought of destination was in him; only the instinct of a hunter's prey. As he ran, an iron certainty grew in him that no street out from the marketplace would be open. The Guards would hold them all.

Ahead he glimpsed the baker's shop, and he felt the burn of his straining lungs. He made for it, deaf now to any sounds of pursuit, too afraid to look behind. He stumbled against a trestle of warm-scented loaves as he passed, scattering them chaotically and bringing the woman to her feet. One of the children started to scream and the other watched amazed as he plunged into the shop and the shop's dull quiet, the hulking oven radiating heat more shriveling even than Alpher's blaze. He seized a barrel and with all his desperate strength tipped it and sent it wobbling on its rim toward the doorway he'd come through, hoping to block it, and lurched on. The courtyard door opened inward to his grasp, and for an instant he stopped on the threshold, beholding the sight of a Guard in cuirass and helm standing over the baker's body which lay on the turf in a pond of blood, his shoulder joined to his body by only a twisted scrap of flesh. And for an instant more he and the Guard looked at each other dumbly before the Guard began to raise his pike and his throwing stick, and Isak slammed the door and thrust the heavy bar into its chocks and whirled to run, and as he turned felt the tip of the Guard's pike drive through the solid door to nick his arm.

No use to go back out the way he'd come. He looked around. A stairway to his left led down, but a cellar without a way out would be no better than a tomb. Half hidden beyond the ovens, the stairway to the family quarters rose. Isak took it two and three steps at a time.

He burst out into the large room. Here, only so little a time ago, the child had cuddled warm in his lap, but now there was no one, no help, no hiding place. Above, dark with shadow, heavy beams held up a high, blind ceiling; no skylight, no stairway upward, not even a laddered hatchway to the higher lofts. At the front, tall, high-set windows let in the gods' light.

He crossed the distance, climbed on a bench, looked out. It was a long drop to the marketplace below, and it would only put him back in the Guards' grasp. He craned his neck to look upward. If he stood on the sill . . . if his fingers and toes could find a grip . . .

To think was to act. Here and there, scabs of plaster had peeled from the wall, exposing timbers and coarse brick. He tested the plaster, found he could scratch out places for his fingers. He kicked off his sandals and started to climb out. The wayfarer's robe interfered with his movements; he struggled out of it. Back behind him came the scuff of fast feet coming up the stairs. He clawed at the wall; a crust of plaster came away in his hand. Probing anxiously with his foot, he found a notch no deeper than a fingernail. He tried it; so long as his toes had strength it would hold him. He edged away from the window sidewise and upward, prying out new handholds as he went, somehow finding new points of purchase for his toes. Bright Dalton burned uncommonly warm on his nakedness. He hardly knew.

Gritty plaster caked like wedges under his fingernails and turned the tips of his fingers raw. Once he glanced down—those upturned faces far below!—and for a long sick moment he clung unable to move before, taking a breath, he was able to make himself go on. A Guard leaned out the window, yawped an oath, and tried to stab him with his pike, but by then Isak had almost reached the narrow cleft between that building and the next, more than a pike's length away. The Guard straddled the windowsill, drew back his arm to throw, lost his balance. Catching himself, cursing, he dropped his weapon. Isak heard it clatter on the stones below.

Then he was into the cleft, scraping skin from his shoulders and ribs and knees as he squeezed between the walls. There was hardly space to breathe but, a hand's breadth at a time, slowly, he started upward. Hard edges of brick gashed his body, flayed skin from his back, his elbows, chest, and thighs. Horrible masses of filth—bat droppings, grime, wind-wafted trash, and decomposed relics of the bats themselves—came loose in his hands, pelted his face, invaded his mouth and his eyes and all the places on his body where the skin was gone; and everywhere in all those places burning burning burning. Whole lifetimes of filth and the tiny, delicate scatter of bats' bones that crackled under his desperate hands. He gritted teeth and squeezed his eyes to slits and clawed his way upward toward the only hope left him, that narrow band of dazzling sky, mindless of pain and the ache of failing strength and the foulness choking his throat.

It seemed forever. The bricks tore his fingertips. The wall behind him raked his shoulders like an endless succession of fangs and rubbed sulphurous filth in his wounds. His toes and fingers were bloody stubs, all normal feeling gone. All he could feel was pain. Slowly that band of blazing sky came nearer.

Then he reached up, and his hand found nothing. He almost fell, and knew that if he had fallen the bricks would have stripped the flesh from his bones as he went down. He reached again more carefully and found where the rotted rafter stub had been, and—bracing has back against the cruel bricks behind him—edged himself up with his toes. Now he could get his hand up over the capstone at the top of the wall, and after another effort his other hand was beside it.

He hung there, trying to catch his breath through the acrid smut in his breathing passages, trying to gain back the strength he had spent to come this far. His fingers began to slip in their own blood. He dug in his toes. His arms felt like hollow, dry husks; no flesh, and only fire where his hands had been.

He pushed himself up. He flung an arm over the capstone, hung there, heaved another breath, and pushed again. The bricks underfoot gave way and he dropped, wrenching his arm almost out of its socket, but it stopped his fall. Feet scrabbling frantically for purchase, he dangled and heard the rattle of filth cascading down between the walls and the sobs of his own despairing agony. But then, hearing that voice and realizing it was his own, he stopped. A distant, calm part of himself took control.

Ignoring pain, he let his arm carry his weight and carefully probed his toes among the fouled bricks for a crevice that would take his weight, found one, then another, and another higher up than before. With an effort that brought pain like a saw blade to his shoulder he got his other arm over the capstone. Too exhausted and miserable to move ever again, he hunched over the coaming, eyes shut, so wearied in his relief that, if he had still had the strength, he would have cried.

A sound made him look up. He saw the sword first, its tip not a hand's breadth from his throat. Only when the Guard spoke did he notice the hand that held it, or the cuirass, or the twin-crested helm.

"Does you yield?" the Guard demanded.

Isak might have let go, let his arms slip, let himself fall and accept death, but quick rough hands took hold of his shoulders and dragged him up onto the rooftop. They sprawled him on the tiles like a whipcracked eel. A swordpoint pricked his naked belly, down low, in unmistakable threat. A battle-shod foot nudged his ribs.

"How now, Prophet?" A Guard's voice—a different Guard's— sneered, then chuckled. "Some Prophet, eh, lads?"

If he saw anything after that, Isak never remembered. Bright Dalton's glare blinded him.

If the stars should appear one night in a thousand years, how would men believe and adore, and preserve for many genera-tions the remembrance of the city of God!

—*Ralph Waldo Emerson*

The cell was too small for him to lie down. The earth floor was damp, and the rushes had been there so long they were indistinguishably commingled with the dung of vermin. A narrow slot not a hand's length across let in a sliver of light. He slouched with his back against the wall, finding in the cool hard substance of the stones some measure of relief from the burn of his untended sores.

Now and then he could hear the tread of feet in the corridor outside the iron door, and now and then sounds not so identifiable from farther off. Several times a spy hole clacked open and he was thrown a handful of crusts, table scraps, and a bladder of water. Once he heard the crash of another metal door being slammed; the sound of it reverberated. Then there was silence for a time which ended with a scream that stopped as if chopped down. The silence after that dragged long.

He found a slops jar for his needs half concealed in the thick shadows, none too clean. For a while he watched the scrap of sky which was all he could see, but the play of light and shadow on the occasional fluffball clouds told him the slot looked to the north, a part of the sky through which the gods never passed. He could measure their passage by how they tinted the clouds; but most of the time the sky was blue and clear.

It was a time to think, something he had not had since his career as a prophet began. But though there were questions that needed close examination, he could find no shred of fact to give him insight. He could wonder if his capture had been the result of betrayal—some part of His Lordship's scheming he had not expected until Kalynn had (inadvertently?) suggested it. It was possible. At the moment of darkness, a dead Prophet could be as useful to His Lordship as a live one. Perhaps more useful; a living Prophet would need to be dealt with afterward. But equally the Guards could have found him by their own efforts. They had needed no help to capture him; only skill and the turning wheel of chance. Nothing proved one guess more likely than the other.

Hard to believe, though, that Kalynn would have been part of such a scheme. That was a thing he did not want to believe. Nevertheless she could have been as much a gamepiece as himself; a convenient tool to be used and cast aside. He thought back over all she had said, how she had said it—tried to remember every stance, gesture, the look on her face, the tilt of her head. She had never explained why she wanted to talk with him, had not told him what she had wanted to say; nor could he grasp her reason for saying the things that she had. People were not, of course, wholly rational beings, Kalynn no more than anyone else, though he had been well impressed by her calm good sense, her intelligence, her seemingly instinctive grasp of how the world of people functioned. Why had she shouted as he fled that she wished he had fathered her child? It was more than he could understand.

Useless to speculate, though. The Temple had him like a vole in its fist, and he would soon be dead. The only uncertainty that remained was how quickly and the means by which it would be done. He would die not knowing the truth to the questions he pondered. Therefore they did not matter.

He had been in that cell, as near as he could measure, a full passing when footsteps paused outside the door. A massive bolt was drawn with grinding force and the door clanged open. A priest stood there in lamplight. Shadowy behind him, a Guard loomed, lamp held high, sword low.

"So, young Prophet. For yourself, perhaps, darkness indeed." Did he know that voice?

"For all of us," Isak said. It surprised him to hear such words from his own tongue; once he would not have dared speak thus to a priest.

The priest's reply was a curt gesture. "Come."

Isak did not move at once. He had the feeling of having been through it all before. The priest turned away. "Bring him," he told the Guard and strode away.

The Guard advanced to the open doorway. The tip of his sword came up, moved aside as if making ready to chop. By then Isak was slowly getting to his feet. The Guard backed into the corridor and motioned him to come. Isak stepped out. His legs had little strength, and with each step his battered knees blazed as if licked by fire. Far ahead down the corridor, in the light of an acolyte's lamp, the priest strode on. The Guard nodded Isak in the same direction. Behind them a second Guard followed.

Uneven stone lay underfoot, worn smooth by an eternity of footprints. Isak stubbed a toe. It brought new flame to the ember of pain already there. After that he tried to walk with care, but it was no use. The Guard who followed pressed a fist against his back, indifferent to its many sores.

"And when the darkness comes?" Isak murmured, and had the satisfaction of feeling the fist's thrust slacken.

The corridor gave into a larger passageway, and the passageway in its turn to a broad flight of stairs that twisted upward and upward until Isak wondered if the Temple's highest tower could ascend so high. Alpher was standing well aloft, with the Twinned Ones close behind, and at intervals their light came in through narrow high arched windows that laid thin stripes of brightness—white, gold, and red—diagonal down the steps, leaving much else deep in shadow. Scurries of acolytes hurried past with armloads of waxboards and parchment, some downward, some ascending; they gave Isak wide berth, and when he looked at them they seemed to cringe and turned their own eyes away.

Isak's pace slowed. His legs ached and seemed to lack both strength and steadiness. The Guard leading the way, now almost half a turn ahead, stopped and scowled down. The Guard behind Isak took it as a command to prod him. Isak stopped, stoic to the pain, turned, and knocked the sword aside with his wrist.

"I have no eagerness for this," he said, looking down at the man. "I will go where the gods would have me go, but not with haste."

The Guard would not meet his eyes.

"Serve the gods," Isak told him, "so long as you are certain it is the gods you truly serve." He turned and resumed the climb. Cowed, the Guard did nothing to hurry him.

Landings led off the stairway, and through the arches Isak glimpsed halls where scribes and acolytes labored at benches while supervising priests moved serenely among them. Off one landing lay a corridor with richly tapestried walls and large carved doors set with great hinges of hammered bronze.

From one of the nearer doorways a boy slipped out—turned suddenly, slightly crouched as if surprised by a sound. Just at the edge of adolescence he was, with curly hair, dark eyes, supple as an eel. A brief kilt was his only garment, but that of fine linen. A jeweled brooch swung on a neck chain, and on wrists and ankles gold bands set with blood-colored stones gave blend and contrast to his oil-sheened, god-bronzed flesh. For a long, uncertain moment he stared at Isak, mouth open in a speechless O, and his hand came up to finger the jewel at his breastbone. He ventured a tentative smile. Isak met his eyes and the smile went away. The boy turned, flashed a rascal's leer back over his shoulder and swaggered off down the corridor. His gait was odd, somehow mocking, almost like a girl's.

"Ho, Belar," chortled the Guard behind Isak. "Would you believe our Keddie be taking instruction off Old Singlefang?"

The one who led the way spoke over his shoulder. "I'd not have thought he be able."

"Still has a finger, do he not?"

"Nah. All they be limp as noodles also. And with those fingernails?"

"Ah well, perhaps he does but help him to remember."

Isak took advantage of the ribaldry to pause and rub his left knee, which felt as if grit had worked between the bones. The Guard who had been following moved up beside him. With a glance and a nod he showed he had noticed, and Isak saw that under his helm he was not much older than himself. "We be commanded to deliver ye," the young Guard said, "and it go rough for us if we be slow. Ye still be able?"

He sounded honestly anxious. Nevertheless, he wore the Temple's leather. "It goes hard because you serve them," Isak said, and with a hard glance forced the Guard to look away. He tried a step; it was like kneeling on a knife blade but, if he must, it could be endured.

"We be commanded also, if ye do not walk, ye shall be dragged." It was almost an apology.

Belar, the senior Guard, had paused on a step farther up. "Be you waiting till the gods have died?"

Isak took another step. His other knee was almost as bad. "They will not die," he said. "They will let a darkness happen, but then they will come again with their light. It is only that they must give us a sign. They are not cruel." But he resumed his climb.

"Serve them; no others," he said through pain, and saw the look of guilt on Belar's face as he turned to also resume his upward course.

It was only a little way more; another turn of the spiral, one more level to the topmost landing. Belar paused long enough to glance back; satisfied that Isak still followed, he strode off along the gallery. Isak paused too when he reached the top, got his breath, and let some of the pain go out of his legs. Then, as the young Guard came up beside him, he went on.

To his left the gallery was open to the wind. It breathed cool on his back and his wearied limbs. Above a parapet that came not quite to waist high, the high-arched openings were separated only by narrow pillars. Isak could see a reach of the river, the tight-packed tenements and warehouses on the far shore's floodplain; the High Houses of the Preserve, white amid their green gardens, and the villas of the lesser houses clinging to the slope under the bluffs; the dark bulk of Citadel Lagash on its promontory and—ragged faint blue shadows in the haze of distance—the mountains beyond. The young Guard was close behind, but even so the thought was in him that he could be over the parapet, falling and falling, before the Guard could interfere. That would be death, of course, and it would be a final thing. Pain still was preferable; that and the hope—though they owed him nothing, had promised him nothing—the gods might give him back his life. Had he not served them?

How could he know?

Trudging the length of that gallery, he turned his eyes away from that temptation, watched instead the carved stone mural that was the inner wall. From it the gods glared outward, personified as radiant men; stern, lordly, all-powerful, and holding in their hands the fruits of river, sea, and forest; field and grove; wind, cloud, and sky. As he passed each one he raised a hand to his brow, gave them honor; for they were the source of all fortune and he had need of them now. If they noticed, they delivered no sign.

By then he was a hairsbreadth from knowing for sure where he was being brought. At the gallery's end, where the personified Actinic Gamow peered with small eyes over a bleak, wind-scarred land where tiny men addressed their pleas toward Red Bethe's warm regard, two Guards with butted halberds stood at the arched entranceway into the hall beyond. In that chamber two more, similarly armed, held station in front of a portal whose high, darkwood doors bore in silver and gold the symbols of the six gods and the Pale One, great hammered hinges of black iron and, embedded into the panels, geometric designs of emerald, ruby, and sapphire.

At a gesture from Belar, the first pair of Guards passed them through with a nod. In front of the second pair they stopped.

"We bring the Prophet—he who claims the gods will send darkness," Belar said, speaking as if the words were filth on his tongue. "By command of the Brothers."

"Stand," replied the nearer of the pair, "and wait their pleasure."

"My name is Isak," Isak said. "I have no other."

"Wait their pleasure, clutterwit," the Guard repeated. The hand that gripped his halberd moved just enough to be noticed.

The other Guard turned to the door, tapped its metal. It opened a crack. He made a series of odd finger signs. The door thudded shut again. Still unspeaking, the Guard turned from the door, resumed his station. Under his helm, his eyes watched like hard, small stones.

"I never said I was a prophet," Isak said. "It is only a foretelling."

Belar drew his sword. Its tip pricked Isak's navel. "Silence, speaker of lies."

It did not frighten. Death could be slow or quick; for all of hope, no other choice waited. "Is it my voice you fear?" Isak asked. "Or what I say?"

For the space of a breath, two breaths, their eyes met. A crafty smile worked the side of Belar's mouth as he looked away. "We be commanded to deliver ye whole." He sheathed his blade. "Hazard not the gods' wrath."

"And you?" Isak asked.

Belar's only reply was a hateful grimace. His sword stayed in its scabbard. So it would be the slower death, unless the gods turned kind. Nor did that seem likely; ultimately, it was the gods who had brought him to this place and moment.

Whatever more might have been said was struck from their tongues as the door boomed full open. The priest stood there— the same priest, the one who had come to his dungeon. Now, in this better light, Isak knew him: Balchin, Legate Priest to the Council of Brothers. He should have known it could be no other. Those brows, that stance, were unmistakable. The thick-lidded eyes flicked from one Guard to the other, then settled on Isak. Isak stood unflinching, met those eyes with a firm, steady gaze of his own, for all that his body felt a chill like mountain water pouring over stone. Peripherally he noticed the Guards take stance as the confrontation stretched out. Abruptly, Balchin's hand chopped air, then jerked a thumb into the doorway behind him. Turning, he led the way inside as if in no doubt but that he would be followed.

Nor could Isak refuse. Belar's hand at the small of his back thrust him forward, stumbling, and when he got his feet under him the hand was there to propel him once more. He was allowed no time to protest or resist or even catch his breath; and the third time an expertly placed foot hooked his ankles and sent him sprawling on the hard stones. He was down before he knew what had happened.

"Stand, wretch."

For a moment he did not know where he was. Then it came back. He got up slowly. One of his knees was bleeding again and all his other hurts had been wakened. He was deeply aware of his nakedness and the filth that covered him, and that—in that condition—he was in the presence of the Council of Brothers. The Guards were gone and the doors were shut, manned only by two stolid, deaf-mute doorkeepers.

"Approach and be judged." It was the Legate Priest's voice, who stood a step below the highest level of the dais where old Sedmon slouched in a high-backed chair carved from a giant stonemelon husk inlaid with polished jade, obsidian, and gold. On either side of him, in smaller chairs on wings of the dais not quite so high sat the Brothers. Isak could feel their eyes inspecting his nakedness.

"I do not concede your right to judge me," he said. But he advanced; what would happen would happen. He hoped they would think him brave. Had he not served the gods? He wished he could know what fate they held for him.

The floor was tight-laid stone polished to glistening smoothness. The walls were stone rising to a high vaulted ceiling. Tall windows on three sides let in the gods' light. On the fourth, behind Sedmon, six sunbursts of silver and gold and electrum, each randomly placed and each a different size, spread rays to either side. Down to the floor. Up to the ceiling's high arch. And, rayless, one perfect disk of pure white stone. Before that splendor, Sedmon and his Brothers in their silken vestments were ugly old men.

Isak advanced. Though wary of being tripped again he kept his eyes not on the floor but level with old Sedmon's, declaring without a word that though he might die he would not abandon truth nor dishonor the gods. When he was still several strides from the dais, Balchin moved a half step toward him, one step down from his previous place, and raised a hand commanding him to halt.

Afterward, thinking about it, he saw he should have chosen his own place and moment to stop rather than let them direct him. But he had been blown by the winds of authority and circumstance most of his life. The habit died hard. Obedient, he stopped.

For a moment there was stillness. Isak gave no glance to Balchin or to the Brothers. It was Sedmon's hand that held his life. The moment lengthened, turned brittle, broke. "Kneel, creature." Sedmon's voice was husky, dry; an oddly whispery voice. Isak hesitated.

"Creature—!" Sedmon commanded, raising himself. One of the doorkeepers scuttled forward and struck the back of Isak's knees with a brass rod. Isak went down with a startled cry. The stones were hard and cold under his ruined knees. He steeled himself to endure.

Sedmon turned to his Legate. "What is this specimen?"

Balchin fingered his torque. "Eminence, he claims a prophecy."

"A foretelling." Isak found his voice. "A mere foretelling."

"I did not hear that," Sedmon said. Moreover, his tone declared, he would not. "Say more," he told Balchin, and let a hand rest on his globular belly.

"A doomsayer, Eminence," the Legate Priest said. "And typical of the lot. His claim is that, when next Actinic Gamow shall overtake the Pale One—which is imminent, I would add; not this passing, but perhaps the next or between that one and the one that follows, while they are under the world—"

"No," Isak said. He glanced at how the gods' light fell through the windows onto the floor, how the pools of light were wedged with shadow. It was hard to measure their divergence by eyesight alone, there was not a great difference between one passing and the next, but Dalton was newly risen, and if what the Legate Priest had said was a guide . . . "It will not be until the one that follows. They will stand half up the sky when it happens—" That much he was sure of. "—and there will be no others in the sky when . . ."

He broke off. Sedmon's gaze seemed to go past him to the wall far behind him, an impression so strong Isak felt a need to turn and see what Sedmon saw. But he did not. A stillness grew as slowly as a spider vine.

"He does not hear you," Balchin said. Then he addressed himself to Sedmon again. "He has said that with the overtaking will come darkness, which is not within belief, but . . ."

Some of the Brothers had begun to stir in their chairs. Sedmon's almost lipless mouth moved. "That we have known and judged. Proceed."

The Legate Priest stiffened. His mouth clamped shut, but his temper held. "He has said also—and this is his blasphemy, Eminence—that the darkness shall be a portent, though as you know there is no reason why it should be."

"None?" Isak asked. Even as he thought, the word came from his tongue.

"We do not hear you, wretch," Balchin said.

"Do you say you know the gods?—can say their thoughts? Their purposes? Their goals? When you cannot even say how they will share our sky?"

"We do not hear you," the Legate Priest repeated, his voice edged with temper. He turned again to Sedmon. "Eminence, you have seen and heard. It remains only to settle what should be done with him." His glance shifted momentarily to include all the Brothers. "Be there dissent?"

He waited. None responded. "Eminence?" he asked.

Sedmon tipped his head, traced the line of his jaw with the tip of a finger that was little more than bone. "You would propose . . . ?"

One of the Brothers roused himself. "Make an example of him." White-haired, scrawny-necked, both his front teeth missing. "Can't let every little bit of scum say what he wants about our Temple. Or our gods."

The Brothers stirred. "Aye! Split his tongue."

"Cold knife!"

"Let him drink blood! His!"

"No! The hot knife! Ah, they do not die as quick!"

The Legate Priest waited them out. When the last had subsided, he spoke again. "Eminence, he and his followers have spoken to much of the public. The city is full of his forebodings. The streets whisper his words . . ."

"Like gavials," one of the Brothers muttered. "Believing the first thing they hear."

"And anything else," growled another.

"So long as it soils the Temple." A third.

"Therefore his . . . ah, reward," Balchin went on, "should, be equally put before the public's eyes. Having listened to his falsehoods, they should hear his screams. His tongue should be split its full length—I think we are agreed on that. Myself, I would urge the cold blade. It is true a slower death might be more satisfying, but in this creature we have not the usual charlatan. Rather a most clever one, and with some part of a scribe's skills. Take speech from him but let him live and he would put his heresies on parchment. Carve them on stones! Let such stuff be put abroad and we, with all our powers, could not scratch it out. I say, let his tongue bleed. Let the flow of blood strangle him and be done."

"While those who fawned on his absurdities watch him writhe!" A fist like a melon cluster came down on a knee as fat and round as a sausage. "A spectacle for god and man!"

"Aye!" A gleeful finger jabbed at Isak. "For his offense, a bleeding tongue! The perfect cure!"

"Ha! Let him contemplate the honor of the gods while his blood bubbles!"

Once Isak had thought them the wisest men in the world. Now the need to tell them their stupidity was unbearable.

Hardly knowing that he spoke, he told them that when the overtaking came, the truth of his foretelling would stand beyond argument—beyond even their power to deny. Would they dare, then, do harm to the one who foretold it? His words were drowned in the rattle of voices. Even he could barely hear. Was it possible he only thought he had spoken?

The Legate Priest waited until silence came again. "Eminence?" he inquired.

"May I not speak?" Isak asked. "If no one else will speak in my behalf . . ."

For a moment, Balchin looked blank. "Eminence, he asks to speak." He turned to Isak. "Be warned, wretch. You are friendless here, nor are these men disposed to credulously hear your heresies."

"Even so, I would ask to speak," Isak said.

Balchin looked to Sedmon. "Eminence?"

The old man's smile had nothing of kindness in it. A man who enjoyed watching the torment of lesser creatures would smile like that. Isak felt ice touch his bones. The hollow-set eyes examined him. A claw-thin finger came up to nick the smile. "We shall be pleased to let it speak," the whispery voice said. "It shall have so little opportunity when we have done with it."

Balchin turned to Isak. "Speak at your hazard, wretch."

The pain in Isak's knees had grown until it was as if he knelt on mangled stubs. "May I stand?" he asked.

Old Sedmon's brow arched. What effrontery was this?

"Now he asks to stand," Balchin said with fastidious scorn.

"Next he will ask to live," said one of the Brothers. It brought a flutter of chuckles.

Sedmon waited through it. "Objections?" he asked.

"Only equals stand before us," a Brother said, his jowls aquiver. There was a mumble of assent. Heads nodded.

"Speak as you are," Sedmon said.

Well, he had endured this long. "As you choose," Isak said. "I have not much to say. Only that I have tried at all times to speak truth. I was puzzled when you failed to consider my foretelling seriously, and when you sent the Guards to make me captive I could not believe it was happening. Ever since, I have tried to understand your thoughts. I find it very difficult."

"Do you question us, wretch?"

"I have tried to understand," Isak said. It was a distinction. "In that, I must admit I have failed." He swallowed. This wasn't what he had started to say. "I have told you a time of darkness will come, and you have chosen to disbelieve. You have decided I will die, and I admit you have the power to make that happen. But my death will not change how the gods share our sky. When my foretelling is shown true, and your judgment of it has been shown not true, will that not prove who better understands the gods? Who serves them, and who does not? And would that not suggest . . . ?"

They let him say no more. "Heresy," one blurted.

"His tongue condemns itself," growled another.

One voice cut through the babble. "If!" it declared.

In Isak fierce anger, stoked by the agony of his knees and body, blazed high. "If I have spoken false, if the overtaking shall prove me false, I will consent to die," he said. "But if . . ."

Sedmon's upraised hand commanded him to silence. He gave it no heed.

". . . if it shall prove I spoke truth while you have spoken what is not . . ."

The Legate Priest came down from the dais, advanced, and with a sweep of his arm dealt Isak a clout to his head that flung him sprawling. Standing over him, both fists clenched with the need to strike again, face gorged with hot blood, the man thundered, "Honor the gods, wretch, and they who serve them." His heel stomped Isak's ribs, driving out breath. For a long time he lay there, knowing nothing but red pain and the chill stones.

When he came to himself, he was on his knees again, his burning knees. Two doorkeepers crouched beside him, propping him upright. Balchin had gone back to his place at Sedmon's elbow.

"Eminence," he was saying, "his argument does suggest a refinement to our disposition of him." He touched the fire opal on his torque. "What better than to slice his tongue while he sees his prophecy proved the lie that it is?"

"And if it is not?" Isak asked. For a moment he glimpsed a hope of living, after all.

Balchin's chuckle dashed it. "He forgets, Eminence, in addition to making claims upon our gods, he has put slanders on those who serve them. Such brash behavior should not go without its proper reward."

He had known there was no hope when they took him, but still he had dared to hope. Now that last shred withered. All the power of his reasoning, all his arguments, had been useless as a reed against the tide. He looked from one face to another—all those old, plump, small-eyed grey men—and felt in those eyes the final judgment of the gods. He might as well have looked for mercy in the stones of the wall behind them. In the end, he came back to Sedmon and the Legate Priest.

"Eminence?" Balchin asked in the silence.

"At the time of the lesser overtaking," Sedmon pronounced. "An icy blade."

Beaming with delight, Balchin made a sign to the doorkeepers, who lifted Isak by his arms, turned him from that implacable tribunal. For a breath, Isak tried to resist, but he had no strength. Without their help he could not stand. "It is my single hope," he said. "That is when the darkness shall come." He hoped they would think him brave.

"He does not hear you, wretch," Balchin's voice boomed triumphant to his back. "Nor do our gods!"

The doorkeepers took him away. He could not walk. Thrust into the hands of the Guards who had brought him, he could only lean against them, his knees giving way. In the end, the young Guard carried him, cradled in his arms like a child. All the dreamlike way down to his cell, one thought droned through his thoughts: that when the darkness came, it would be like the closing of an eye. For the first time since there had been men, the gods would not watch. He wondered what it would mean. He wondered what could happen while they did not watch.

Ah, love, let us be true
To one another! for the world, which seems
To lie before us like a land of dreams,
So various, so beautiful, so new,
Hath really neither joy, nor love, nor light,
Nor certitude, nor peace, nor help for pain;
And we are here as on a darkling plain
Swept with confused alarms of struggle and flight,
Where ignorant armies clash by night.

—Matthew Arnold

Through the narrow high window he watched the slow change of light and shadow on the clouds. From that he knew the passage of time. So he knew, when the Guards came again, the moment had come. He got to his feet as they entered his cell. As wary as if he held a sword, they approached him. Suddenly one caught his arm and flung him down. Before he knew what was happening a thong bound his wrists behind him and shackles joined together by a chain were being screwed tight around his ankles. While that proceeded another Guard stood in the doorway, blocking it with his body and his drawn sword.

They ignored his protests and his questions. They crammed a rag into his mouth and secured it with another rag knotted behind his ear. They jerked him to his feet and noosed a rope of braided thongs around his neck. They pulled it tight until his breath was squeezed and he could feel his pulse against it. They led him forth, a Guard holding each end of the rope, one ahead and the other behind. The chain between his ankles was too short to allow a normal stride. To avoid stumbling he had to take short steps while the Guards with the rope walked at a normal pace. The Guard with the sword fell in beside him and encouraged him with the flat of his blade when he lagged.

The stairway, the same as before, took them upward. As they climbed, the dim light filtering down from above grew stronger. Walking was easier on the steps; the chain's length permitted him to go from one step to the next without hindrance while the Guards had to limit their strides to what the steps allowed. Being taken toward death, he could still feel grateful that a smaller torment had stopped.

The Guard beside him, matching him step for step up the stairs, gave him a sidewise glance and a peculiar smile. Abruptly, with no warning but the smile, he barked, "Choogh!" and, crouching, darted his sword between Isak's ankles. Hobbled and bound, dragged on by his leash, Isak could not avoid being tripped. The Guard ahead of him, warned by the shout, leaned against the increased weight on the rope. For a long moment—it seemed forever—Isak hung suspended while the Guards plodded stolidly upward, dragging him while the rope cinched more tightly around his throat and he struggled to get his feet back under him. The Guard laughed a soundless laugh and, reaching out again, sliced the edge of his sword across Isak's belly. Blood welled from the cut.

They left the stairway at the second landing and emerged into a broad passageway. Narrow windows laid strips of light across their path. All else was gloom. A squad of Guards fell in step around them. Ahead, in golden vestments, walked Balchin; no lesser priest would claim the privilege of seeing the Prophet quashed. Following that stately presence marched two acolytes in scarlet with a huge bronze gong suspended from a yoke between them. The passageway turned. They passed under an arch, mounted another short flight of steps, and emerged into the light of the gods on the steps in front of the Temple. The brightness stung Isak's eyes. One of the acolytes stroked the gong.

They started down the steps. Isak had never seen such a human mass as packed the square. They filled it. At the gong's sound, heads turned, looked up; thousands and thousands of eyes. They made him conscious of his nakedness. They had come to see him die. The stones were warm under his feet. His chain rattled. The air felt cold.

He looked skyward. In the west, orange brightness stained the sky where Red Bethe and Bright Dalton had lately gone down. Halfway up the eastern sky, the Pale One and Actinic Gamow stood together, so close they seemed almost to kiss. He tried to see if there was still a space between them, but Gamow's brightness stabbed his eyes no matter how tightly he narrowed them. He had to look away.

By then they had come down off the steps. The Guards advanced to open a way through the crowd. Far off through the throng, Isak could see the waiting scaffold with red and gold pennants fluttering from its cornerposts. The Obelisk's shadow darkened its nearer flank. An incense pot vented green vapors into the air.

Something tickled his foot; he looked down. Blood from a

gash on his shin—when had that happened?—dribbled down the side of his heel. From the slit across his abdomen blood also came; more than a hand's count of rivulets streamed down his thighs. He looked up again to Gamow and the Pale One. They seemed not to have moved at all, though he knew they must have. He wondered if they would save him and how they could do it if they did. He wondered if anything could save him.

Acolytes, arms linked and chanting in Old Tongue, held open the way the Guards had cleared. As the wedge advanced, more acolytes materialized from the crowd to hold the lines and more had joined the escort around him, creating with clapperboards, ratchets, and thunderdrums a compulsive, rhythmic roar. The rope dragged Isak on. His feet stubbed uneven stones. Shouts from the crowd made mock of him.

"Better times!"

"Darkness for the Prophet!"

"Wag your tongue two ways, lad!"

Isak wanted to answer them, wanted to shout he had spoken truth, that the darkness was almost upon them, that the gods must be served. But the gag sealed his mouth and his hands were tied behind him so he could not point skyward, could not make them see how close now the two stood to each other. He caught an acolyte's wandering gaze, made the man look at him, meet his eyes. He felt a tiny triumph when he saw the man falter in his chant and, embarrassed, look away.

A melon husk struck his shoulder, breaking the spell. Something squishy glanced off his knee. Other objects, most of them wet and soft, landed on the stones near his feet. The Guard beside him stopped, helm knocked askew; he raised his sword high, shouted a command. The bombardment faltered. A yellow-green something splattered Isak's side. A bit of it stained the Guard's cheek; he yelled a curse. Some of the other Guards were trying to dodge, not always with success. They drew their swords and menaced the crowd. The barrage ceased. The procession moved on.

"Feed him to the eels!" the crowd jeered. "Honor to the gods!" One of the acolytes struck the gong, and struck again. The drums sent forth shudders of sound.

A steep stairway, lightly built, came down from the platform. It sagged and quivered under Balchin's weight, forced him to lean well forward and grip the rails to keep his balance. The acolytes with the gong did not try, but turned aside. Isak, when his turn came, realized he would need his hands, but they were still tied behind him. No one came to loose them. He stopped. The Guard ahead of him, already climbing with the rope lugged over his shoulder, paused midway up and looked back. A dark growl shaped his face. With a motion of his shoulders, Isak pantomimed helplessness.

For a moment, then, the impasse held its shape. Isak stole a look upward; Gamow and the Pale One stood virtually together, close beside the Obelisk's dark towering column. No different from before. If they would save him, he needed them now.

Nothing happened. The Guard who had followed with the other end of the rope moved past and started up the steps. The Guard who had walked beside him nudged him to the foot of the steps and, sheathing his sword, boosted him onto the first step. Following close behind then, his shoulder rammed into Isak's back, he supported Isak and forced him to climb while the Guards with the rope pulled on him from above. It was as if the gods had pondered and settled his fate; he should have remembered he was not the first trussed man to go up steps like these, that his escort would know how to make him climb.

The steps creaked and trembled under the weight. Isak felt the wind. The rope rasped his throat. His breath came hard. His sense of balance thinned and died and all he knew was the squeeze at his throat and the thrusting rough force behind him.

He reached the platform in a half-blind daze. He staggered and would have fallen, but they caught his shoulder, steadied him. Mercifully, they loosened the rope. After a while his sense of balance came back and he could see again.

Here above the heads of the crowd, the wind breathed cold on his nakedness. It ruffled the Legate Priest's robe and fluttered the pennants on the cornerposts. The wicker of which the platform was woven creaked and gave under the leather that covered it. A troop of musics on the stones below flared their brasses. The Guards marched Isak forward to stand before Balchin.

The Legate Priest's head was freshly shaved; not even eyebrows sprouted from that sleek skin. Gamow's brightness glinted on his glossy pate, struck sparks from his torque's jewels. "Wretch, kneel," he said. Before Isak could move, a sword's flat to the back of his knees set him down regardless what he willed. He had forgotten the condition of his knees, still barely started to heal. It was like kneeling on embers.

The crowd cheered as, sick, he swayed.

Pointing the head of his staff at Isak, Balchin spoke first in Old Tongue to signify that he spoke with the approval of the gods. Then he shifted to ordinary speech.

"You have declared prophecies that are not true," he said. The staff's crest trembled less than a handbreadth from Isak's eyes. "See for yourself! Actinic Gamow burns as ever, bright against our firmament. As ever, we receive the bounty of our gods. As ever they cast their shadows across our land. How say you now, false prophet?"

The question expected no answer. Against the wad in his mouth, Isak could not even clench his teeth. Neither could he see Actinic Gamow, who shone warm on his shoulder blades and laid his shadow at Balchin's feet. Neither could he see the Pale One, though the two had to be close, and narrowing the gap between them every moment. The Obelisk's shadow lay beside his own, but to his eyes its sidewise movement was too slow to measure. The platform had no marker tiles, but surely it could not be much longer. Desperately he wanted it, all this, to end; he no longer cared how.

Balchin's staff struck him a sweeping blow. He fell on his side. "Enough of insolence," the Legate Priest boomed. "False prophet, kneel." The staff's crest raked Isak's brow.

Urged and, to a degree, helped by the Guards who still held the rope, Isak struggled again to his knees. Without the use of his arms it was hard. His vision could not focus, nor could he hold himself steady. Now though, he turned eyes skyward. There he saw through bleariness that now he faced the Obelisk, that he knelt in its shadow, and that it blocked Gamow and most of the Pale One from his sight. He felt blood trickle down his cheek.

He wanted to see Gamow, could not endure not knowing how the god and the Pale One (was she also a god?) stood now. By leaning to his left, so far he almost fell again, he caught a glimpse, and for a chilled instant he thought his foretelling had been wrong, after all. The Pale One's cool white edge came into view beside the Obelisk before Gamow, which meant the overtaking had begun; yet there was no darkness. Then, narrowing eyes, he saw that Gamow stood above the Pale One's trailing edge but well below her northernmost extreme. As the overtaking advanced the god would pass behind her, just as he had always known. Then the Guards grabbed his shoulders and forced him to turn on fire-touched knees to face the Legate Priest again.

Again Balchin pointed with his staff. "Hear now a prophecy that is true, false prophet!" His voice roared; he spoke not for Isak's ears but for the crowd. "Your tongue, which has articulated lies, shall henceforth be in two parts. Your blood shall bubble in your gullet. You shall die in the sight of the god whom you said would forsake us."

He swung his staff in a wide arc. Its crest caught glints of Gamow's light. The Guards jerked the rope. Isak fell. They dragged him helpless across the platform to where the lattice of rod and withe waited, the tongue cutter's frame. They lifted him onto it, thrust his shoulders back against the crosspiece that would hold him half-erect while the work was done, and trussed him onto the frame by the rope at his neck, then by thongs at his waist and—making his protesting knees bend double—his ankles. The hobble-chain they cast aside. They fitted a basket-work cowl about his head, laced it iron-tight across his temples. It took from him even the small freedom of being able to turn his head.

Still they had him in the Obelisk's shadow, but his back was to it. Neither Gamow nor the Pale One stood in his sight, nor was he in theirs. Had they forsaken him?

Balchin advanced, a shiny black blade in his grip. "Now shall you taste truth, false prophet!" The Guard with the sword sawed through the cloth that gagged Isak's mouth. He would have spat it out, but saw the shadow of another Guard coming up from behind with an object in one hand that could only be the tongs to catch hold of his tongue. He clenched teeth on the rag as hard as he could.

The one with the sword set its point to his throat. The other waited, tongs poised. It was hard to watch both at once and also the Legate Priest; and there was at least one other Guard somewhere that he couldn't see. He tried to read the shadows. Surely if he could delay a little longer the darkness would come. The sword's tip probed his throat.

"No! Touch him not!"

It was a different voice, a woman's voice from somewhere below. Other voices came then. Men's. From many throats.

"Hear her! Through her speak the gods!"

Isak couldn't turn his head and likely couldn't have seen if he could. But Balchin was looking that way, his brow wrought by a puzzled scowl. The sword eased its pressure.

The voice came again, urgent. "I must speak, must tell you . . ." It sounded nearer. And the other voices: "Hear the gods speak!"

With the voice of a woman? How could that be?

The platform shuddered with the tread of new feet on the steps. The Guards looked to the Legate Priest. Balchin watched, his scowl turning more and more to thunderous rage. Isak took advantage of the distraction to spit the wad from his mouth; the Guard with the tongs saw, but wasn't quick enough to catch his tongue. Snarling, the Guard struck a blow on the side of his head, hard enough that flares of yellow light blazed in his eyes, and for a moment whose duration he never knew he was aware of nothing but the shock.

When it passed, the Guard had got his mouth open. The iron tongs intruded roughly against his teeth, seeking. He tried to clench his jaws again, but something had been wedged in to block that. The tongs found his tongue. He could not draw it back far enough, couldn't evade the searching, snapping bite that tasted of metal and pain, pain that watered his eyes, pain that . . .

"Don't!" The woman's voice, anxious, very close now. "Let him go! Please! You must hear me. I carry the gods' child. I . . ."

Kalynn? In spite of his bonds, the stabbing pain in his tongue, Isak tried to wrench himself around. He wanted to see, wanted to know. It was not possible.

"He speaks to me. I hear him," she cried. "He commands. I must tell you the Prophet speaks truth. There shall be darkness. That the Temple and all who are in it . . ."

She came into view. Two Guards followed a half step behind

her, short swords naked in their hands. The wrap she wore left her right arm and shoulder bare. On her wrist, gold and crusted with jewels, was the cuff of a bride of the gods. She held it high. Its jewels flashed in Gamow's light. That she carried a child none could doubt. No garment, no matter how artful or loose fitting could have concealed the swelling of a baby close to term. Her awkward stride was the gait of a woman soon to give birth.

". . . Do them dishonor by the way they serve in the gods' name. That . . ."

"You are deluded, woman!" Balchin roared. He gestured, but it was the hand that held the blade, not his staff. Isak heard the crowd gasp. "Our gods are mysterious. They speak to no one; even their signs are not understood except by the most gifted. As for your . . ." He feigned a laugh. ". . . your condition, you would not be the first silly girl to have suffered an accident at the baths. So long as the gods hold our sky there shall be no darkness. Our gods shall not abandon us. Now, stand aside that I may ensure this charlatan shall speak no further slander on our gods and those who serve our gods."

"No." She did not move. "The gods' child tells me the darkness shall come, tells me . . ."

Impatiently, Balchin moved to fend her aside. One of her escort advanced to block him with a sword. "What . . . ?" A silent startled moment. Then: "Guards! To me!"

Swords out and poised, the Guards on either side of Isak moved to the command. Kalynn's other escort turned to meet them, his sword already out. Its point stood poised against whichever one came first. Under the brow of his helm, Isak saw Hobur's pale blue eyes, his grim and thin-drawn smile. The Guard who had dropped the tongs began to circle wide. Hobur backed a step closer to Kalynn. Slowly the Guards advanced, blades searching for their chance.

None of them had eyes for anything but the shifting, darting points of blades, so it was Isak who noticed first the change in the sky. Most of it was the same white-tinted blue it had always been, as full of light as a lamp's globe. But there to the west, though still blue, it had become a darker blue such as he had glimpsed once through clouds while crossing a high mountain pass. As he watched, the darkness deepened.

He watched it grow until he was sure, and when he was sure he shouted it with all the force his body could summon. "The darkness!" His voice was a croak. "The darkness! It comes!"

For a moment, the tableau before him did not change. Each stood frozen, intent on those who menaced him. The light was very strange now, as if Gamow shone through tinted glass, all shadows sharp but his brightness muted. Perhaps Balchin sensed that, for he looked skyward, suddenly aghast. At that instant, the darkness came.

Cries of fright and dismay broke from the crowd below.

Eastward, the sky was still blue, and light still came from it, but rapidly the light was fading. In the west, the firmament was black, black as obsidian or death, but for a few faint scattered sparks—sparks too faint, too tiny to be gods; but what else could they be? Gods never known before? Was that possible?

Balchin uttered a hoarse, anguished cry. The blade fell from his hand. Slowly, as if he did not know what he did, he raised his staff, held it up first with one hand, then with both, its crest offered toward the place in the sky where Gamow had been— still was, behind the Pale One.

"Return," he cried. "Forgive!"

The Guards who faced Hobur began to retreat while Hobur, wary for a trap, cautiously advanced.

Now Kalynn slipped a hand inside her garment, brought it out again with the slim, curved length of the tokku like a whip extending from her fist. Continuing the motion with which she produced it, she whisked it through the air before the Legate Priest. His staff fell to the platform; with it, still clutching its haft, went his hands. In disbelief Balchin stared at the stumps and the blood that jetted out of them. A terrible sob of despair burst from his throat. Slowly, he went to his knees, bending forward as he sank. Again her blade whicked air. His head struck the platform, rolled, bumped to a stop. Headless, shorn of hands and contorted by spasms, his body slowly folded down on the platform. It lay, still jerking, in the smear of its own blood.

By then Hobur and Kalynn's other escort were driving the two Guards—what had happened to the third?—back and back toward the platform's edge. Though well helmed and armored and equipped, they had no will to fight. Not now, abandoned by the gods. Hobur made a sudden feint; his target dodged, tried to set foot on empty air, yelped, and fell. His companion shot a glance, looked back too late as a sword tip touched his cuirass, forced him back, off balance, and abruptly gone.

Kalynn's blade, sticky with blood, sliced Isak's bonds. "They hurt you!" she cried. Wild. As if she felt the wounds herself. "They hurt you. They hurt you."

"What's happening?" Isak asked. He really didn't know. She was cutting the rope at his neck; he was very conscious of the long, deadly blade close to his ear.

"The gods sent their darkness," Kalynn said as he felt the rope come free. It was still knotted around his neck, but no longer bound to the lattice. She knelt and sawed the thongs that closed the basketwork around his head. "Are you all right?"

"I don't mean that," Isak said. "I mean . . ." It was too much.

"You are the Prophet," Kalynn said. Her face was close to his as she worked, but she watched her hands. "You said the darkness would come, and it came. The priests said it wouldn't, and they are discredited. Now the Temple . . . Oh, you're bleeding. Don't you feel it?"

He could feel a thousand aches and a need to know more things than his tongue could touch. "How did you . . . ?"

"Don't talk," she said. "It's . . . The Temple is . . ." She pulled the basketwork off his head, tossed it aside, and started on the thongs at his waist. Her wrap was splattered with blood and the cloth was slashed where she'd drawn the sword, exposing one breast. Still bewildered, he looked again at the sky. Though it was dark, it still gave light, enough that he could see—not well, but neither was it the darkness he had known beneath the house of Palovar. Tiny, bright bits of—Of crystal? Of gods' light?—spattered the firmament like seeds in a fresh-sown field. And from behind the Obelisk came a strange, wan light. Was it possible that Gamow shone through the Pale One, after all? He did not understand.

The thongs at his waist went slack. Kalynn moved to his ankles. "The streetwardens said they would cut your tongue. My father—his friends already were planning, if the darkness happened—I don't think they really believed—they were planning to seize the Temple, kill the priests, all the Guards. And when they said they would cut your tongue, I . . . I didn't want it to happen. And Duke Lagash—"

"Is that who he is?" Isak asked. One foot was free now. She went to work on the other.

"Didn't you know? He said it would be better than he hoped, and he would put his men in the crowd, and if the darkness came . . . and it did come, Isak. It did come."

"But it is not such a darkness as I had thought," Isak said. "We can see. I am trying to understand."

"The Pale One is giving light," she said. "There!"

Suddenly his other leg was free. He tried to rise, but with his hands still tied behind he couldn't get his feet under him. She bent over him, lifting his shoulders, and for a moment as her face was close to his he saw her features suddenly tighten, as if with pain. "Are you hurt?" he asked; he couldn't remember seeing either Balchin or the Guards land a blow on her. He frowned, trying to recall those moments such a short time ago, but already they were gone in the confusion.

She didn't answer. She made sure he was steady on his feet, then moved behind him. He could feel her working at the thongs around his wrists. The tip of her blade touched his thigh.

He could look around him now. It was a colorless light that came from the sky, strong enough to cast shadows but not so strong that he could see things clearly. He could see shapes— the Temple with its towers, the Obelisk that was said to be the Center of the world, the three—three?—in Guards' clothes who now stood guard at the head of the platform's steps. Had he not known already what they were, his eyes could not have told him.

He tried to edge out of the Obelisk's shadow. He had to see for himself if it was true, that now it was the Pale One who gave light. It was hard to believe. She had never given light before. Kalynn tugged his arm. "Hold still. I don't want to hurt you."

"Nothing you do will hurt me," Isak said. He wasn't sure what he meant, saying that—knew only that he spoke a truth. But he held still while she worked on his bonds. He watched the fighting below them in the square.

Fighting? Momentarily he thought it was simple disorder. Then he saw the pattern of it. Many, trying to escape from the square, formed a jostling crush where the Great Way entered. A smaller mob pushed against a cordon of Guards who blocked the West Road where it led off past the Brothers' residency. Out in the broad expanse of the square, sprawled shapes like castoff rags lay—wounded? Dead?—on the stones while more than a few figures—acolytes and unhelmed Guards among them— knelt or stood motionless, some looking skyward at the marvels there revealed while others, more practical, warily watched those who fought.

There must have been hundreds doing battle, sending up a din of battle shouts combined with cries of pain, of metal clashing metal and the duller sounds of blades on wood and leather, cloth, and human flesh. Close formed in squares and circles, Guards fought a rabble armed with blades of every type from longswords to butchers' knives, indifferently armored in mail and studded leather and rust-scarred plate, and helmets made of almost anything from a cooking pot with holes punched for eyes to a turban with a flower stuck in its folds. Others, less well equipped, stood behind their kin holding torches high and tossing, now and again, strawballs and knotted rags soaked in oil and set aflame. Against blades the Guards' skill served them well, but they could not stand against those gobs of fire. They ducked and dodged and backed from the thrust of a long-handled torch at the eyes. As they tried to avoid the touch of fire, blades found them. One by one they fell.

"Better times!" a man yelled, swinging his blade. Others echoed him. "Better times!" Isak wondered if times would truly be better for those who died.

The thongs that bound his wrists came loose. He turned to her, unwinding the leather strips as he spoke. "I am still your prisoner." He had meant to say that he owed her his life, but it didn't come out that way.

She looked up, straight into his eyes. "We couldn't let them hurt you. You're our Prophet." He saw again that sudden pinch of pain touch her face.

"Are you all right?" he asked again. There was blood all over her; he thought it was the Legate Priest's, all of it. He hoped it was.

She forced a smile. "You wanted to see the Pale One. Now, go and see." She touched his shoulder, urging him to turn again.

He was torn. He didn't want to turn from her, but also he wanted to see the source of this strange light. With her urging, he turned and stepped out of the Obelisk's shadow, and beheld a wonder.

It was as she had said: the Pale One shone—shone with a bright, cold light that was different from any light Isak had ever seen before. There was a whiteness to it, unlike the metallic blaze of the gods. It neither burned nor hurt the eyes. Shining out of a black sky, the Pale One gave a light uniquely her own.

At last he turned to Kalynn again. "I do not understand. She has never given light before."

"Does it matter?" she asked. "Does it make a difference?"

He spread his hands. "I do not know. And those . . ." He gestured to the sprawl of tiny lights across the sky. "Are they all gods? There must be millions!"

"Could they be something else?" Kalynn asked. "Have they always been there, and we did not see them because the gods are so bright? Or did they only come now? What do the gods do, that makes them gods?"

"I am wondering the same things," Isak said. "There is so much I do not know."

"Might begin with wondering if we'll keep our lives," growled a voice at his shoulder. He knew the voice. From under a Guard's helm, Palovar's dark brows scowled. "So far we've had the advantage of them, but . . ." His nod directed Isak's glance across the square to where the Great Way entered. The Pale one's light gave silvery touches to the helms of Guards streaming toward the square. "Thousands of them in the city. If all of them come . . ."

"They'd lose the city if they do," Kalynn said. "They wouldn't dare."

"They'd let us take it before they'd allow their Temple to fall. Here's where our strength is. If they defeat us here, they can take back the city whenever they want."

"But they won't," Kalynn said. "The gods favor us. See?"

They looked where she pointed. There, on the Great Way, the first of the fleeing mob had almost reached the leading Guards. As they watched, the Guards halted, took battle stance; some knelt, pikes nocked against the cobbles and slanted forward while between them, feet set wide, their fellows stood with hefted swords. The first of the crowd, faced by that threat, tried to stop, but the press of those behind forced them on. Pikes spitted them. Blades rose and hacked them down. But then, protected now by a buffer of dead and dying, the mob pressed on, breached the Guards' line and trampled them into the stones along with their own fallen. The Guards who had been behind the line backed off, formed a new battle line, stood ready. By then some of the mob had collected pikes and swords, and others had discovered that cobbles could be prized from the pavement underfoot and, with effort, thrown. And, appearing at the avenue's far end, the leading few of another mob—more coming into sight with each heartbeat. They carried swords and torches, pikes and billhooks and maces. One held aloft on the point of a sword a knobby object topped with something that looked like a priest's tricorn. Too far, and the light was too dim, for Isak to be sure. At sight of the Guards the mob yelled and quickened its pace. The Guards turned to meet this new attack.

"Those will be all we see from the city," Kalynn said.

"Let us hope," her father said.

Isak saw the look of pain come again to her face. He touched her shoulder. "Kalynn . . ."

"I'm all right," she said, too quickly. "I'm fine. I . . . it's just—" But then as if with terrible effort she clenched her teeth and fists and could say no more.

For a dumb moment Isak stared at her. Then he understood. He stepped to the edge of the platform.

"A midwife!" he shouted, loudly as his throat could call. "We need a midwife for a child of the gods!"

He scanned the scene below. There were fewer Guards than before. He saw one back away from the battle, throw down his sword, throw off his helm, and yield. "Honor to the gods!"

Another joined him.

Isak searched for a sign that his call had been heard, but saw none. "A midwife for a child of the gods!" he called again.

She touched his arm. "You know it isn't," she said, but softly; only he could hear. "Please. I'll be all right."

"I know what you have told me," Isak said. "I would rather believe the gods gave it, no matter how it was done. And . . ." He glanced out over the square. "Would a midwife come now for just an ordinary child?"

"But—" A twist of pain stopped her words.

"Do you say you want no help? You need none?"

Still in the grip of her pain, she gave no answer. He turned outward again and repeated his cry. "A midwife is needed! For a child of the gods!"

The woman who appeared as if from nowhere at the foot of the platform's steps was middle-aged, lank, and gray of hair. She paused with one foot on the lowermost step, looking up. "I be needed?"

Hobur, guarding the top of the steps, hefted his sword but glanced to Kalynn. "Let her come," Palovar said.

The woman stumped up the steps with an awkward, arthritic gait. Hobur reached down to help her the last few. She strode to Kalynn without a glance to anyone else and looked her up and down. "Child of the gods?"

"It was given in their name," Isak said. "We claim no more than that."

"Humph. Neither the first nor the last." Her glance swung to Isak. "You be the Prophet?"

"I have been called that," Isak admitted. "Both false and true. Will you help?"

The woman put a crooked finger's tip to a point above her left eyebrow. "If the gods' Prophet asks, it be an honor." She returned her attention to Kalynn. "You, child. Not enough sense to not let yourself get all excited? How old be you?"

"Almost eighteen 'takings, grandmother," Kalynn said. The woman watched her face, even while putting out a hand to touch her swollen body.

"Your first, I'd presume." She didn't wait for Kalynn's answer. "Aye. Well, little enough to fear. A child of the gods, perhaps, but no different from any other, for all that. And it now be coming soon enough. You be able to take the steps? Walk?"

"I think so," Kalynn said. "I could a little while ago. But—" Again the pain came. Her teeth clenched shut. Her eyes squeezed shut.

"You'll come, then," the woman said. "No sense to make a public spectacle. Hard enough without all the men in the world looking over each other's shoulder." Her claw took Kalynn's arm, steered her toward the steps.

Palovar moved to interfere. "Hold. You can't . . ."

"My help be asked," the woman said.

"But where . . . ?"

The woman pointed toward the Temple's looming mass. "Where else for a child of the gods?"

Isak took Kalynn's other arm, fearful that she might stumble. Palovar stayed them with a hand. "We do not know who holds it."

The midwife gave him a scornful eye. "Did you not see? When the darkness be on us, some of those that had torches killed the portal Guards and went inside. A great number of them. I saw the flicker of their lights through every window of the tower, all the way to the top. Look, they be still up there. And I saw the bodies come out of those windows. Did you not hear them yell as they came down? Have no fear. It be your friends that hold the Temple, not . . ." She nodded to the headless body at their feet.

Palovar grimaced, nodded, and strode to the top of the steps. "Ho! An escort we must have."

Down on the stones, a man looked up. "How many?"

There was less fighting now. Busy figures were stripping armor and weapons from fallen Guards, dispatching those who, still alive, resisted. Scattered randomly were still knots of conflict where swords hacked and blood still spurted on the stones, but the way to the Temple was open. "Five . . . six," Palovar said uncertainly, then reconsidered. "Ten."

The man below moved off. "And find clothes for the Prophet," Palovar called after him.

Isak looked down at himself with true surprise. He had forgotten his nakedness, just as he had lost awareness of his wounds. Kalynn broke into laughter. "You didn't know?"

"I was thinking other things," Isak said. Even as he spoke he realized how foolish it sounded; he didn't want to be foolish in her sight. He gestured to his injuries, the crusts of blood, his half-healed knees. "So much has happened."

"So much you made possible," she said. "So much you've caused to happen."

She'd done so much more than he. He'd been helpless through so much of it. "And you," he said. "You also. More than I."

"Could I have done anything less? Isak—don't you realize? Without you we'd still be wondering how we could win against the Temple. You're our Prophet. A true Prophet, Isak. Now—" She broke off, and again the pain was on her face.

He touched her arm. "Now," he said. "Come." The midwife

took her other arm. They helped her toward the top of the steps.

"I can walk all right," she protested. "Really, I—"

Her foot struck Balchin's head and she would have fallen but for the hands that held her. She looked down. "That is the face I remember," she said. A thrust of her foot sent it rolling, two bumps and gone off the platform's edge. Bending, she plucked the torque from its puddle of blood and hurled it away into the darkness. "And that!" Then she looked from Isak to the midwife and back again. "Now we can go," she said.

Except for one moment on the steps, when the pain came again, she was sure-footed enough. When it came she stopped and they waited until it passed; then they helped her the rest of the way. "Is it supposed to hurt like this?" she asked.

Their escort was waiting with swords and high-held torches, a rabble with white kerchiefs at their throats and blood on their torn clothes. Some of it was their own. They cheered her, touched bloody swords to brow.

One of them passed Isak an acolyte's cloak which, if bloodstains were a sign, was no longer needed by its previous wearer; and a white kerchief which he realized only then must be a device to self-identify the rebel force. It, too, was stained. He put them on. Until that moment he had not known how cold he had been. The escort closed around him.

Surrounded thus, Kalynn, Isak, and the midwife set off across the stones. Ahead the Temple towered, but Isak felt more awe, now, at the treasure that walked beside him, close enough to touch, and the thought of a child about to be born. A fitting place indeed.

Softly, one of their escort dared begin a hymn, a solemn hymn of honor to the gods. At first only a chanted tune, a scattering of Old Tongue words, it quickly gathered strength. The others of the escort took it up, then Hobur, Palovar, the midwife, Kalynn; finally even Isak. As they neared the Temple's steps, the song came loud and brave and strong. Their torches blazed.

So, let's say you've brought the world to cusp. Fine. Excellent.
Now, toward what star, and how, would you set our course?
Bear in mind, there will be no turning back.

—*Benjamin Dana*

Duke Lagash—His Lordship and now, presumably, new master of the world—came to Isak as he waited on the steps of the Temple. Except for the dead and those who scavenged from the dead, the square was empty; but the sky—the sky was strewn with brilliant, tiny gods. Millions.

Definitely they were gods, Isak had decided, even though all of them together did not give as much light as Embrous Zwicky, for he had watched them. They were fixed to the firmament. They moved across the sky, as did the gods, at the pace of the turning world. What could they be, then, if not gods?

And while Isak watched the gods, Palovar stumped up and down across the steps, impatient and restless and, like Isak, forced to wait. When they had come to the room where Kalynn would lie, when—careless of their vandalism—they had torn leather storm curtains from the windows and hangings from the walls to make a couch for her and had seen her comfortable, the midwife had ordered them out. Palovar had objected and Isak had been reluctant, but the midwife vowed to go herself if they did not. This thing was women's business.

Before such fierce authority they'd had no choice but to withdraw. Hobur, pressed into duty as keeper at the door, promised to bring news when there was news to bring; but unless there was trouble there would be no news until the child had come. Isak wanted to believe that nothing would go wrong, but knew how possible it was. He sat on the steps, his shoulder against a prominence, and watched the gods.

"So, hatchling," said the Duke. Behind him hovered a cluster of lieutenants, not so close as to seem to be with him, but close enough to quickly answer his call. Isak let a long pause pass before responding. The Pale One stood now near the highest point of her arc across the sky; he still did not understand how she had become a giver of light like the other gods. Was it possible she had always given that light, but it had not been noticed against the more powerful brightness of the other gods?

He brought his gaze down from the sky. Slowly, wincing at the pain it brought to his wounds, he got to his feet. "Your . . ." He struggled for a word that would give this man nothing. "Your Ascendancy," and met the Duke's eyes with stony calm.

"We have the Temple and the city," the Duke said. "Three Guards captains have already declared for us, and two other troops have brought me the heads of theirs. The rest will come, one way or the other. Those who still live. In time we shall have the land, but that will take longer. Your role in that was not small. We are grateful."

Isak kept his reserve. "I am grateful for my life, Your Ascendancy."

The Duke dismissed the matter with a gesture. "I would have you know it was not our plan they should capture you. That was an accident of chance. The girl has been—shall we say?—rather hysterical over the question. I would hope you are more willing to believe."

"I wish that I could," Isak said, still giving nothing.

"Had it been our plan, you would not have survived."

He still might not, Isak thought. But he said nothing. When time had passed enough that the point was made, the Duke cast the matter aside with a chop of his hand. "Whatever, when they made known their plans for you, we saw the opportunity it gave. The rest you have seen."

Isak looked out over the square. Scavengers were stripping bodies and loading them into a wagon. The eels would get fat. The platform where he would have died looked very small at the foot of the Obelisk that was—so men had believed—the Center of the World. They had been wrong about that, also.

He nodded. "I have seen," he said. It no longer mattered. It was all in the past and, for the moment, he still lived.

Now all he wished was to be left alone. He wanted to contemplate the Pale One, wanted to learn the secret of her transformation. He wanted Kalynn's child to be safely born.

But the Duke was not about to go away. "The Temple is empty. It cannot be left that way."

To Isak it was hardly a matter of concern. He said so.

"Left to itself, it would fill itself," the Duke said. "That must not be permitted. In the end, it would mean a return to the condition we have only now corrected."

True enough, Isak supposed, but still it didn't involve him. He wanted to learn about the Pale One, the firmament, and all those tiny gods. He wanted Kalynn's child to be born without harm to itself or to her. Only those things mattered.

"You shall hold the Temple," said the Duke.

Isak's thought had not been on what the Duke was saying. He wasn't sure, at first, what he had heard. He looked at the Duke, who repeated his words.

"But I am not a priest," Isak protested. "I am only a scribe, and not even properly schooled. I do not even know what the gods truly are."

"Nevertheless," said the Duke, "you know them more than any other man."

Palovar had paused a few strides away. Now he approached. "You will accept," he told Isak. "You are the Prophet, and therefore hold the strongest claim. You—"

"No," Isak said. The prospect frightened him. "I am not a prophet. Nor have I been, ever. I do not know how many times I have told you that. It was only a foretelling. But no one believes. Only Kalynn—"

"Hatchling, what is true is not important," said the Duke. "What matters is what people believe. To them you are the Prophet. What you believe about yourself changes nothing."

"But still—"

Palovar stopped him with a curt gesture. "You are the Prophet, and because of that you hold power." He gave a nod to the Duke. "He would have you where you can be seen. Watched. The Temple's tower would be such a place. The other choice would be for you to not be seen again, ever, by any man."

"I think I would prefer that," Isak said. "I never wanted—"

"I think you would not," Palovar said. "We could not risk that later you might reappear. Too many men will think you might be useful to them. And their ambitions. No. We would have to take measures that ensured you would not return. We would prefer to have rewarded you."

So that was it: he could accept the Temple and all the privilege and honor that came with it, earned or not, or he could feed the eels. It wasn't much choice.

"Would I be permitted to continue my research?" Isak asked.

"You could devote the Temple's whole resources to it," said the Duke. "Better in that direction than some others. Understand you would not be our tool. Within the Temple, you would speak with your own voice. We would not dictate word or deed to you. But know this also, hatchling: you shall know how you came to that place, and that, if we should deem it necessary, we could remove you. Yes, and the tongue from your mouth. Do not challenge our power, and we shall not challenge yours."

As the Duke spoke, Hobur appeared in the portal. He

stopped on the uppermost step and beckoned. Palovar glanced a question to the Duke; the Duke nodded dismissal. Palovar mounted the steps. He stood, head bent intently to hear Hobur's news. Isak ached to know what he heard.

"Do you understand, hatchling?"

Isak met his eyes. He could not hope to oppose this man; it would accomplish nothing and lose him much, nor did he know if there was reason why he should be opposed. "I shall want to serve the gods," he said, unsure what that might entail.

"So shall we all," the Duke said. "Do you accept?"

Once, to achieve such station would have been more than Isak had ever dared to dream. Now, with it thrust into startled, unready hands, it seemed far less the incomparable prize, rather, it was like a garden of pebbles and bare ground. Yet what other choice did he have?

"I would require some conditions of you," Isak said.

At once the Duke turned careful. "Name them."

"You shall give honor to the gods, and serve them," Isak said. "Serve them before yourself."

It was hardly the sort of thing a new master of the world could refuse, however reluctant. Duke Lagash looked grim but spoke no objection. "And . . . ?"

"You shall cause no man hurt for serving the gods in different fashion from yourself, so long as he serves the gods."

"We might have arguments on that," the Duke warned.

"Then we would argue," Isak said with a firmness he had not expected of himself. "Do not be sure men would do your bidding if I bade them not."

His own words startled him. Was it, he wondered, possible? Until he spoke he had not imagined such a thing. Could the gods, unseen, unfelt, have spoken with his tongue? How could he know? Dared he believe it?

"Credit me, hatchling, with more wisdom than the ones we

have deposed," the Duke said. "What other bargains do you want?"

"One other thing, Your Ascendancy," Isak said. He held himself steady, took tight control of his tongue, his tone, the shape of his words. "My name is Isak. I would have men know me by that name. No other. But you, Your Ascendancy—" He did not shy from those dark eyes. "—you shall call me Eminence."

The Duke flinched as if slapped. He blinked. But then he threw back his head and laughed. "Well struck!" A hearty bellow. "Well struck!"

He made a fist. His teeth gleamed with pleasure. Nevertheless, he sobered almost at once, so instantly that Isak wondered if it had been feigned.

"You learn swiftly . . . Eminence," said the Duke.

"I have been told that," Isak said, not sure he had made a wise bargain, but not knowing either how he could have made it better.

"It is settled then?"

Isak's glance had gone again to where Hobur and Palovar conferred. Not even a murmur of their voices came to him. "There is still much to settle between us," Isak said. "We must decide how much is yours and what still remains to the gods. But I would leave that for another time. For now, one small last matter . . ."

The Duke was caught by surprise. "Oh?"

"You must know, Your Ascendancy, it is the custom that a scribe shall have a fee for service he has done."

"So?"

"So I must ask my wage." He wondered where such boldness had come from. He had not been born with it. "Have I not done service for you?"

"Indeed you have," the Duke admitted; indulgent, amused,

wary. "Provided the opportunity to restore my House to its rightful status, which is not to say that it came to me without cost. But I am giving you the Temple and its treasures—all the privilege it commands. Do you expect a fee additional to that?"

Isak demurred. "I did not know the Temple was yours to give. I thought it was the gods', who are greater than you or I. They might yet turn me out of it, as they have turned out those who held it before."

"Hah!" The Duke spoke with scorn, suddenly humorless. "*I* turned them out. My men stormed it—hacked their Guards to bleeding meat and cast the Brothers from their tower like slops from a tenement. The gods did nothing."

"They gave this darkness," Isak said. "And caused the Pale One—if she is not herself a god—to give such light as we have, which she has never done before, to give assurance that their displeasure with men is not absolute. Without those, could you justify what you have done? Could you persuade that, acting against those who held the Temple, you did not also act against the gods?"

"Had you not brought this opportunity, I would have found another," snapped the Duke.

Isak nodded. Perhaps he would have. "Nevertheless, I ask a fee. Scribe's wage for service done."

Nettled now, careful, the Duke cocked his head. He scowled. "Name it," he said at last. "But know if I judge it excessive you will have it not."

"I would be grateful, Your Ascendancy," Isak said, and touched his brow, "if, for my service, such as it was, you would pay one farthing. But I must have it now."

Though the heart be still as loving,
And the moon be still as bright.

         —George Gordon, Lord Byron

The tower's steps were smooth as glaze, cold underfoot, and though the Pale One's light shone through the windows, much of the stairwell was deep in gloom. Isak had to feel his way. He should have asked for a torch, but eagerness had burned such practical thoughts from his mind. The little slug of base metal, rough on one side where the mint's bondsman had stamped it, was a satisfying kernel of hardness between his fingers. Something real in an uncertain world. Somewhere above, a lamp's glow touched a dark wall with unsteady light. It beckoned.

It had taken some persuasion to convince the Duke he was not being made the butt of some lugubrious jest. It had taken longer still to secure the coin; the Duke's own purse yielded nothing smaller than a dinar, and few of his lieutenants had brought money; not when there was likelihood of battle. Death they might have risked, but not the risk of being robbed while they lay dying. In the end, a common citizen was found who, with puzzlement, willingly exchanged a farthing for a gold piece and wandered off, mystified, to tell his tale and start a legend.

By then Hobur and Kalynn's father had vanished. Isak entered the Temple—his Temple. It was a strange thought; it would be long before he could begin to think of it that way. No, never: it was the gods'. He could not be more than their servant in it. He tried to think how he could serve them, and by what signs he could know what service he should give. He groped his way through the chancel's gloom, found the stairway, and began to climb.

At the door to Kalynn's chamber, guarding it, was a man whose face Isak did not know: gray beard, blue eyes, and shaggy brows. He wore an ill-fitting buckler of age-cracked leather with verdigris damaged brass rings, a white scarf, and around his head a bandage that oozed wet blood. His slouch straightened as Isak came up the steps into the lamp's fitful light, but after a moment's measuring glance his hand let go the hilt of his sword.

Still, when he reached the landing, Isak paused. "May I go in?" he asked.

The man's head gave a glance toward the door. Scars marked it where the silver and jeweled decorations had been pried from it. A crack of lamplight showed from within. "Could this person refuse the Prophet anything he asks?" he said, and stood aside.

"But I am not a prophet," Isak said. He had never been that, no matter what others might believe. "Only a—" He tried to think how it should be said. "A servant of the gods," he said at last.

The man bowed his head. "Some serve more fully than others," he mumbled, as if shamed.

Isak was terribly conscious of the bloody rag on the man's head. "Of some the gods expect more than from others," he said. "It is not an honor to be envied."

It brought a shrug. "The gods do what they will. I . . ." He touched his brow and nodded to the door. "I can only stand from your path."

Such deference troubled Isak. It hadn't been earned; neither, it seemed, could he refuse it. Oddly humbled, almost furtive, he opened the door far enough to slip inside.

It was still the Chamber of Judgment, still the hall where the Council of Brothers had condemned him. Now, though, it had a far different look. Darkness filled it, scantly leavened by a flickering lamp in a corner. Its rich furnishings had been tumbled aside. On the dais where Sedmon's throne had been, under the pattern of sunbursts on the wall, Kalynn lay on her improvised couch. Halfway down the steps, overturned, the throne sprawled aslant. Some of its jewels and gold were gone, thieved. Shadow was everywhere.

Before he had obeyed the midwife's command to leave, he had stolen a moment to hunch down at Kalynn's side. "Will you teach me about the gods?" she asked. Before he could speak her look of anxious hope became a hard-clenched grimace of effort and pain.

He had given her a strip of thick leather he had cut from the throne for her to bite on. "Everything I know," he promised. He could almost feel her pain himself and his thoughts were full of the terrible things that could happen in childbirth. "I want to," he said. "When you are done with this, if the gods will allow."

She tried to smile, but then the pain came again and she could neither smile nor speak. Aimless, wild, her hand caught his wrist and squeezed until he thought the bones would crack. For the space of a heartbeat it was as if they shared one mind, knew only a common fear, hope, and pain. Then the midwife had clamped a hand on his shoulder and curtly ordered him away.

Now he was coming back, and with a farthing in his hand. An acolyte's cape had been spread over her, but that was the only change. The lamp in the corner, lodged behind a fallen chair, cast leaping splashes of light on the walls. The Pale One poured her softer, more restful pools of light on the floor. One of them included part of Kalynn's couch, part of the cape that covered her, and one pale hand.

The midwife intercepted Isak before he was two paces inside. She blocked his way. Even in the poor light, he could see her fierce eye.

"I would speak to her," he said.

The woman shook her head. "Better you be letting her rest. Hard work it be, getting a child out. Later, when she be hurting less—"

"Isak?" Kalynn asked. "Is it you?"

"Kalynn—"

"Please. Let him come. It won't hurt as much."

Thwarted, the midwife shot an angry glance around, but she stood out of Isak's way. "Remember, I spoke against it," she cawed, but Isak scarcely heard. He knelt close by Kalynn's shoulder, and hardly felt the blaze of pain from his knees. He hadn't thought about his knees. She smiled up at him; her face was in shadow, but he could see the smile.

"You're all right?" he asked.

"Going to be." She sounded very sure. She folded back the edge of the cape to show the child. "A girl," she said. "I'm glad."

Every child safely born was a cause to be glad. This one was incredibly small, so small his hands could have gone around it. It lay cuddled against Kalynn's side, one tiny paw pressed into her breast's softness. Suddenly exposed, it tried to burrow into her. Kalynn laughed. "I don't think she likes it out here."

There was something both mysterious and miraculous about a new life. He wanted to touch it, to be sure of its reality, but fear of doing harm held him back. It looked so terribly delicate. "She's probably cold," he said. He lifted the cape's edge to cover her again.

"It's a cold world," Kalynn said. She shifted slightly, as if to move the child closer to her than it already was. It complained, then went quiet again.

"Not always," Isak said. For a time he had lived in a land where the oceans froze. "Not for everyone." Suddenly the lump of metal was in his hand; it had been there all along, but now he knew its presence again. It was warm and slightly moist from the sweat of his grasp. "Look." He held it out between thumb-tip and finger.

At first she didn't know what it was, though he held it in the

Pale One's light. With her free hand she reached up and touched a finger to it. "I don't . . ." she began. Then she knew. "A farthing? What . . . ?"

She didn't understand. It was a hollow moment. He hadn't planned to offer it that way, and the words he'd intended to use were gone like a broken bubble. Clumsy and artless, he'd blundered ahead and now, though he wanted to call it back and start over, it was too late. He could only hunch there, foolish and miserable, with the farthing in his hand.

"You asked me once—" he began, and knew how lame it sounded, and stopped. And waited.

"I know I did," she said in a quiet voice. "I said a lot of silly things." She wasn't looking at him; her head was turned away, as if something in the deeper shadows next to the wall had to be watched. "Is it what you want?"

"Can you doubt?" he wondered. "But for you, I would not even have my life." That didn't sound right either. It hadn't anything to do with his reasons, but his reasons didn't fit into ordinary words.

Now she looked up at him again. "Isak, I have a child now." She moved her arms under the cape. "She isn't your child. And you . . ." Her voice held strain. ". . . You are a Prophet who has spoken for the gods, and for whom the gods have shown their favor. You could claim any woman you wanted, for the asking. You wouldn't need a farthing, or any coin at all."

It was a new thought, and strange; but it made no difference. "You have told me no reason I should go in search of something I have found already. And . . . and you know it was only a foretelling, and the rest of it was contrived."

"I would know it. Other women would not," Kalynn said.

"And what better consort for a Prophet than the mother of a child of the gods?" he asked.

"Isak, you know it didn't happen that way."

"I know what you have told me," he said. "So we would know each other's truth. Would it matter so much what others believe?"

"It wouldn't be true!" she protested.

He nodded. She was right. But it changed nothing. "I have learned people believe what they want to believe, no matter what they are told," he said. "No matter what truth is, I think I will need a person close to me who knows my truth. I may need to be reminded of it."

He saw no response in her, no sign even that she heard. "And I think I will need someone who understands people better than I," he said. "I . . ." He plunged. "I want you to be that person," he said, and waited, but still she did not speak.

"Would you have me claim a woman by deception?" he asked.

At first he thought the sound she made was laughter. But why would she laugh? Her face was turned away from him. The mystery of her thoughts was more inscrutable than the gods. Wanting her to look at him, wanting her to know his want and his need, he touched her cheek, felt wetness.

Confused, he drew back. Marvelously more impossible to know than the gods. He waited, wondering helplessly what he could say. Finally, her voice came again.

"Isak, please. Give me time to think. I . . . I . . . I'm tired, and I hurt, and you're so clever with words, and ideas, and things. I can't . . ."

He didn't feel clever at all. "Do you fear I might persuade you to a thing you do not want?" he asked.

"I don't know," she confessed. "I think I'm just as afraid that you won't. I want . . ." She stopped.

"Yes?" he prompted.

"I don't know what I want," she said. "I want to be happy. I want you to be happy. And I'm afraid . . ."

She had gone into danger with only a sword. She had come

out victorious. And she had borne a child, all in less than half a passing. Now she spoke of being afraid.

"Fear nothing," he said. "I cannot promise happiness. Only the gods can give that, if they will. But happiness is what I want for you. I would try to help you find it." He sought her hand under the cape, to press his coin between her fingers.

The ache in his throat was a fear she would thrust it away, but as their fingertips touched she caught his hand and held it fiercely. The coin was caught between their palms, hard and hurtful. She turned her head to look at him. He saw her hesitant smile.

Hoping, he thought, and dared to hope. Her fingers tightened, pressing the coin ever deeper into the flesh of his palm until it was the only thing of which he had awareness. Without words, it was answer enough.

Kneeling there, for once needing no words, he lost all sense of time. Afterward, he knew only that time had passed when he became aware of a difference in the light. He looked up. The shadows were less deep. The colors had changed. The Pale One's light was not as strong, nor the lamp's. From the square below came a murmur of sound, shouts, fragments of a hymn. For a moment, as if dazed, he did not understand.

He got to his feet, hardly aware of the stiff pain in his knees. He hobbled to the eastern windows, dragged a chair from where it had been thrown and climbed up on it. He leaned against the sill.

He beheld a strangeness in the sky. He had thought no further marvel it might show could possibly surprise him; he was wrong. None of the wonders already seen had prepared him for this.

The blackness was gone, and with it all those tiny, inexplicable, myriad gods. High overhead it was blue gray and dark—the kind of sky sometimes seen when clouds lay heavy. Downward to the horizon it became lighter and lighter, gradu-

ally blending toward brightness until to the east above the serrate shadow of the mountains, it blazed with a lustrous light
more powerful than the Pale One's—almost as bright as a true
god's. Had it been brighter, he would have had to look away.
And floating above the horizon a scatter of cloud tufts, but
cloud tufts that blazed like flame and incandescent gold. As he
watched, a higher cloud took fire and blazed with a steady,
slowly expanding radiance—a red that reached higher and
higher into the fabric of the cloud and, as the red crept upward,
the regions where it had been became gradually orange, then
amber, brightening all the while. Isak watched until his chest
ached for lack of breath.

It was when he realized he hadn't breathed for a long time
that he knew what he saw. Or thought he knew. To make sure
took only a moment. Dropping down from the sill, he crossed
the chamber, found a chair he could climb on, and mounted to
one of the windows on that side.

The Pale One stood high. He'd expected that. The light she
gave was faded now, though not yet dimmed to the chalky whiteness of her familiar self. The sky around her still was dark,
though not as dark as when those tiny gods had sprinkled it. A
few bright sparks still glittered in the west, where blackness had
not yet given way, but even as he looked one turned faint, then
vanished. As the sky inexorably brightened, another went, and
then one more. He looked again up at the Pale One. Without
reference points or measuring tools it was hard to estimate accurately, and now she no longer cast shadows. Nevertheless, it
was clear that she had moved a little past her zenith point and
had begun her descent toward the western horizon.

To know that was to know enough. He slipped down again to
the floor, returned to Kalynn's couch. He knelt beside her.
"Can you stand?"

"Can't I just lie here?" she asked. "I'm awfully tired. I might even sleep for a while."

Isak could remember having slept only three times in his life. He thought how exhausted he had felt each of those times; did giving birth tire a woman that greatly? As if to answer him, the midwife shuffled across the floor. "Near enough half my ladies sleep when they be done," she said. "This one be strong and healthy as a team of drome, but best to be leaving her be."

Isak nodded, accepting it, but . . .

He spoke to Kalynn. "I think you would want to have seen this." And, looking up at the midwife. "If you would see a wonder . . ." He tilted his head toward the eastern windows.

The midwife snorted. "What's be in her arms be wonder enough."

Kalynn's chin lifted. "Help me up."

She let him take the child. The tiny body struggled feebly and protested loudly until he maneuvered it inside his robe and held its nakedness warm against his ribs. Supporting it in the crook of one arm—he found he could do that—he helped Kalynn rise with the other. He helped her walk to the windows. She was indeed weary. She leaned against him. He helped her up on the chair.

"Isak," she breathed. "It's beautiful."

He climbed up beside her. Now the whole eastern sky was ablaze. Rich ruby hues, and amethyst, and shiny gold against a tapestry of flawless blue. "That is Blazing Alpher," he said, "coming up to the edge of our world. Already we see his light. Any moment now he will show himself."

As he spoke, a blood-red spot, brighter than the sky, so bright it burned, appeared in a notch between two peaks at the edge of the world. Not yet so bright they had to look away, but almost. Slowly the spot enlarged, became an arc above the ridgelines, and lifted slowly like a leviathan lifting its brow from the water, and became a full half-circle, bloody red and incredibly huge, and burning and sending its flames across the sky in streamers and plumes, bathing every scrap of cloud and all the land in its blaze, and lifting at last completely free of the horizon, red and round and hot—so hot that now they had to turn their eyes away, and for a long time after, in the lesser light inside the Chamber of Judgment green glowing lights floated in the air wherever Isak turned his gaze.

"I knew he would come," he said at last. "The darkness will go now."

His arm was around Kalynn and she leaned her weight against his side. Against his other side the infant stirred. A small hand searched blindly, clutched a fold of skin, tried to pluck it away. Already the child was trying to learn what kind of strange world she found herself in.

"Telling us we have another chance," Kalynn said. "That we can . . ." She ran out of words.

"Perhaps," Isak said. He didn't know what the gods were saying. Perhaps they were saying nothing at all. He would have to think. And he would have to tell her about the Temple; but that could wait.

"Did you talk to Father?" she asked, moving only a little in the curve of his arm. Alpher's light shone on her cheek and her hair, a token of his favor. Her face seemed to glow.

"Had I offered him a farthing, would he have thought me serious?" Isak asked. "Or honorable? No, it was for you to accept or refuse."

She trembled with sudden quiet laughter. He saw the delight on her face. He tightened his arm around her. Her head leaned under his chin. Her hand felt the child under his robe.

"I should let you rest," he said. "Here, I'll help you down."

But she did not move. "I'll talk to Father," she said against his throat. "What would you say if you were him? A Prophet's farthing. It should be worth something."

He let her talk. Her voice woke music in him, and her body was warm against his, promising mysteries. Her child . . . it seemed suddenly proper to think of it as his own, that it belonged in the cradle of his arm. And the gods . . . ?

He looked. The red and yellow and orange and gold were all gone from the sky. Only blue remained, and white tufts and wisps of cloud, quickly thinning, and Alpher's blaze now as bright as he had ever been, as if nothing had happened, nothing had changed.

"A whole world," he said, speaking into the scent of her hair. He looked again toward Alpher, now too bright to look at more than an eyeblink, ascending his sky, remote, all-watching, silent, giving his light to all the world.

So much he still did not understand, so much he ached to know. Those tiny gods; the Pale One's unexpected light; how the gods caused rain to fall or not fall, clear skies and cloud, cold winds and warm. He wondered if he would ever know the secrets of those things. Would mystery cloak the gods forever? What knowledge might they yield?

He took a breath. So many questions! Dared he hope he would ever find an end to them? Every discovery he had ever made had contained, like a kernel within its pod, new mysteries.

He felt a vision. God-sent? Simple memory? A mountain path, and in sight ahead mountains beyond mountains beyond the mountain already climbed; but that was not a reason to abandon the path. Rather, it was reason to press on. Nothing behind was worth returning to. The journey ahead would be interesting. There would be adventures.

Kalynn's lips moved against his throat. Not words; only a soft, contented murmuring. Her weight rested against him. Asleep? Dreaming? There were stories told about dreams.

"A universe," he said. Full of marvels, he thought. "A universe."

AFTERWORD

If the stars should appear one night in a thousand years, how would men believe and adore, and preserve for many generations the remembrance of the city of God!

—*Ralph Waldo Emerson*

Isaac Asimov's "Nightfall" stands almost unchallenged as the greatest exemplar of Big Idea science fiction. Mankind abruptly confronted with a strange, never-imagined universe. Cosmic terror. When I realized that no one had taken a second look at the proposition, and that perhaps some other story could be developed from that theme, I felt obliged to read it again after a lapse of some twenty-five years.

Several aspects startled me. Most notably, I had forgotten that, though apparently human in every other respect, Asimov's people were instinctively fearful of darkness. It was wired into their brains. That they would respond with madness, therefore, became a foregone conclusion. The question posed by Emerson was not truly addressed.

Emerson, of course, believed the response should be awe. Uh huh. Sure. If, that is, you begin with Emerson's religion-based mind-set. However, working from another point of view, it becomes a whole new ball game. Asimov had done this, but left plenty of room for a thousand other tales.

No one had tried.

I also had trouble accepting Asimov's astronomical construction. For the purpose of his story he postulated a moment when the sky above one hemisphere of his imaginary world contained only one of its several suns, and that this single star would be eclipsed by an utterly black astronomical object just barely detectable by indirect means, whose existence was unsuspected by all but a few abstruse researchers. Those few, of course, had neglected to publish.

Further, he assumed that this eclipse would black out the entire inhabited world. For that to happen, the eclipse would have to include nearly all of the globe and persist for at least half of one rotation.

This, when thought about, is hard to swallow. On our own world, whose moon appears very nearly the same diameter as our sun, a solar eclipse traces only a narrow path—never more than 166 miles wide according to the textbook on my lap as I write—and lasts less than eight minutes at any one place. For Asimov's event to happen, an extremely huge, dark, slow-moving body would have to pass in front of a much smaller (as viewed, that is) sun. For comparison, in one twenty-four hour day our moon moves against the fixed stars something like 25 times its diameter, and would therefore occult a fixed point of light—say, a distant star—for a little less than an hour at most.

Consider also that our moon is among the darkest objects in the solar system, reflecting only about twelve percent of the light it receives from the sun, yet that is enough for it to be clearly seen, white, in the daytime sky. Thinking of this, I found it difficult to believe any normal body, moon or planet, could be so dark and unblemished as to reflect no light whatsoever. Now, with Asimov's huge, imaginary object blocking light from the single sun standing aloft, but with all the other suns casting light on the face it holds turned toward his world, how deep a darkness could such a world have?

With these considerations and others in mind, I began work on the story that became **Dawn.** The eclipse became a somewhat less preposterous event and somewhat more easily foreseen. My people, I hope, behaved more as people would behave in the face of abnormal conditions. By the time I was done, the title seemed imperative.

Please understand this nitpicking should not detract in any way from Asimov's achievement. For his objectives, astronomical details were a distraction to be dealt with briefly and set aside, and for creatures who have always known at least one source of daylight a catastrophic reaction to darkness might not be unreasonable. Change the game's rules, however, and you have a different game. He, not I, broke the ground and planted the seeds. Without "Nightfall," there would not have been *Dawn.* I am in his debt.

Note further: my people are not one hundred percent human either. Except in exhaustion they do not sleep. While it might be interesting to explore how this would make them different, I made no attempt.

As for astronomical aspects, while I took care to make consistent how the "gods" share the sky at any given moment, I did not calculate orbits or masses for the seven gravitationally significant bodies, nor did I address such difficult questions as the precise climate effects which the collective radiation from six of those bodies at various—and varying!—distances would have on a rotating world possessing an atmosphere. When I began I did not know how. I still don't (and if we're talking about the weather, nobody else does, either). As I planned it, my multiple-star solar system scheme might not work, might be unstable, or might not be possible to have formed to begin with. Someone more technically competent would likely have no trouble finding fault.

Just for starters, modern astrophysics puts severe limits on both diameter and mass of a non-luminous astronomical body composed of matter such as we are familiar with. Whether the eclipsing body I describe could be fitted within those limits I'm afraid to ask. Years before I began work on *Dawn*, I'd encountered this as a theoretical conclusion, but had completely forgot. This in spite of the fact that twice while I was still in high school my father brought home as a dinner guest the man who made this peculiar discovery. Only later did I make the connections. Some ways I'm slow.

—DMcL, 2004

ABOUT THE AUTHOR

Dean McLaughlin was born in 1931 and exposed to science at an early age by his astronomer father. Science fiction he discovered on his own. He sold his first story to *Astounding* (now *Analog*) in 1950, and has been writing ever since. Realizing early that a full-time career would be an easy way to starve, however, he spent 35 years in the retail book trade, retiring in 1988. Previous books under his byline include *Dome World, The Fury from Earth, The Man Who Wanted Stars,* and *Hawk Among the Sparrows.* His work has been translated into German, Italian, Spanish, and Polish. He lives, still writing, in Ann Arbor, Michigan.